MEN WHO FLY

WAYNE N. ALLISON

Wayne N. Allison, Publisher
Gunnison, Colorado

Cover design by Michael Donahue

Wayne N. Allison, Publisher
P.O. Box 12
Gunnison, CO 81230

Library of Congress Cataloging-in-Publication
Allison, Wayne, 1911-
     Men who fly / Wayne Allison.
          p.   cm.
     ISBN 0-941599-17-5
     I. Title.
PS3551.L458M46   1991
813' .54--dc20   91-27708

Acknowledgement

To Doctor Sharon Ziegler, my step-daughter, I give full credit for the completion of this book. Without her constant encouragement, advice and assistance, I do not believe I would have been able to complete this work.

She was my critic, my adviser, and my guide. She was like a lightning bug, glowing, glowing and lighting my way. She had an unerring instinct for good writing and a ready red pencil for that not so good.

She constantly asked for the best. I apologize if I have failed, but hope you will enjoy my effort.

Dedication

I dedicate this true story to the memory of David L. Behncke, President of the Air Line Pilots' Association, Int., who, for over eighteen years, preached and nourished the themes of safety in flight and security of employment.

It grieves me greatly, even in the twilight of my life, to look back at the many accomplishments he achieved for the airline pilots and realize how little they appreciated the big, rough diamond that had always been theirs—until they threw it away.

Preface

This is a story, a true story, about the management of a large and dishonest airline in its treatment of pilots and their safety in flight along with their security of employment in spite of Federal Air Regulations and contractual obligations with the Air Line Pilots' Association. Names have been changed including that of the president of that airline who alternately served as president and chairman of the board.

The names of the other company officials, employees, pilots, stewardesses, union officials and attorneys have not been changed when quoted herein. The certified testimonies of those witnesses and the hearings enumerated herein, as well as that of the attorney arguments, are a matter of record, along with the falsification of reports over pilot signatures, as submitted by the company to the CAA.

To: Chuck Wilcox — 6-16-93
Old friends are like old
bull friends or elk — they
get more scarce with
each passing year.
Wayne J. Allison

Table of Contents

Chapter 1

Memory Lane

Veteran airline pilot John Pricer died at fifty-three, just ten minutes before he was due to lift the big four engine commercial airliner, from New York's busiest air terminal, into the murky rain soaked clouds. Slumped in the cockpit of his three hundred mile per hour air giant, and by a strange coincidence, with fifty-three passengers patiently waiting for the departure, he completed the takeoff into the last twilight—alone.

I knew him well. At one time, in the middle thirties, I had been his copilot. In forty-three, when we were both flying military cargo and personnel across the Atlantic, I helped him out of a rough surf in Brazil. And many times during the war years when our vapor trails frequently crossed, from points north of the Arctic circle to points far south of the Equator, I sat across the poker table and watched his gray head gradually turn white.

In South America, Africa, Europe, Iceland, Greenland, the Azores, the East Indies and in the States our trails frequently blended during those hectic war torn years. How many fronts, how many thunderstorms, how many low approaches, how many engine failures and forced landings his heart had surged through in over twenty years of airline flying plus several years of military and barnstorming work, no one could guess. But each had left its indelible mark.

I can hear his booming voice now, as I heard it in 1936, above the surging roar of the engines and the sharp clatter of ice against the fuselage as the old DC-2 pitched, shuddered, and fingered its way through the inky blackness of a midnight frontal storm.

"Give us a little more carburetor heat, son," he had roared, "and pour a little more alcohol on the windmills—thar's a few more ridges 'tween us and Washington."

I stood in the San Francisco operations office of Amalgamated Airlines with the light reflecting on the four gold braids on my sleeves and studied the teletype message that told about Johnny. It had happened that evening while we were sleeping in preparation for the return trip that night. Lost in thought, I studied the message while operations' clerks, my copilot, engineer and two stewardesses noted my quiet manner. They had already seen the message.

I saw him across the poker table, peeping at his cards. I saw him raise those clear blue eyes under that white bushy head and grin: "Little Abner, I'm going to raise you five!"

Little Abner. He had always called me that after an episode in the Brazilian surf. Why I had never known and he had never said. Perhaps my build, perhaps my dark bushy hair, perhaps my strong arm, or again, maybe he considered me a little slow mentally. But it didn't matter now.

"Will you look like that, El Capitan, when I kick the gong?" questioned Jimmie, a shapely bright eyed brunette.

She had big dark brown eyes that seemed to probe the depth of my feelings while they shifted from one of my eyes to the other at half second intervals as though checking to see if both were telling the same story. It was a very unusual characteristic.

I noted the look of deep concern in her eyes which were surrounded by perfectly shaped features and almost black hair that indicated Indian Blood. In fact, we had both come from northeastern Oklahoma near the little town of Nowata where I had known her father and mother.

"Oh, I knew Johnny," declared Jackie, a black headed girl of French descent sitting precariously on an operations table and swinging a shapely leg as she applied fiery red nail polish to some rather long nails. "I flew some with him out of Memphis. Not a single wolfish gleam in his eyes."

"Gad!" she exclaimed, flashing her black eyes and stretching a wide, red mouth into a big smile, "but he made me feel ancient!" Then she added as an after-thought, "Swell guy."

"More than that!" I murmured softly, scarcely recognizing my own voice as I laid the teletype message aside to scan the weather. But my mind's eye lingered upon the sordid picture of cargo handlers having to wrestle Johnny's chunky body out of the control-filled cockpit.

Thunderstorms and a frontal condition lay between Albuquerque and Oklahoma City, the same old stagnant stuff we had plowed through coming out. Mentally I compared the present day weather with what Johnny and I had encountered in the thirties. It was the same, only it was different. Johnny was gone, and there was a trace of gray at my temples where all had been dark brown. But the night was the same; yet it would not be the same, it could not be the same. Yesterday, today, and tomorrow would never be the same on an airline. The difference is in the horses we ride.

I glanced out the window at the giant four-engine airliner leaning forward with its tail high in the air, eager to lunge through the ozone at three hundred miles per hour with a trace of wildness in its attitude. I sighed. Why did it have to look so restless, so eager to grapple with the elements? I wasn't.

Someplace in the last million miles I had lost that eagerness, that wild touch. How many million? The first one had slipped under my wing in '39. Then they had come with increasing frequency. And they would continue to arrive with greater frequency.

I thought of that ancient 1933 fact-finding board's report, later incorporated into the Civil Aeronautics Act relative to a limitation on an airline pilot's flying. It had established eighty-five flying hours as a monthly maximum, yet had dodged the mileage question simply by stating that the industry was too young for a mileage limitation. However, it did foresee the need, even in 1933.

Suddenly the giant four engine conqueror of distance was not there. In its place was a two engine Curtis bi-plane. It was the first airplane I had flown with Amalgamated. In eighty-five hours each month with it, I had flown fourteen passengers nearly nine thousand miles.

Then it was gone and the Douglas DC-2 was perched on its three wheels like a sitting puppy. I felt a wave of eagerness to fly it into those mid-western thunderstorms. It would feel good, I decided, because the plane would slow down to a mere hundred miles per hour. At that speed the hail did not strike so hard. It would roll and toss and wallow and finger its way on through. Almost fun, and in it I would fly fourteen passengers only eleven thousand miles during eighty-five hours. The DC-2 was suddenly a little fatter, more sleek, its wings a little longer and more pointed, its engines a little larger.

Again I felt a freshness, a desire to carry twenty-one passengers nearly thirteen thousand miles in eighty-five hours flying with that work horse of the airlines, the DC-3.

It looked like the Douglas DC-6 but it wasn't. The windows were round, the engines smaller, the fuselage shorter, and it did not carry its tail so high. It didn't exactly appear to enjoy resting, but it did sit peacefully on its tricycle gear.

The Douglas DC-4 had been the first to make me feel the increasing speed. At two hundred miles per hour during the war on long over-water jumps at reduced power to conserve fuel, it was not too bad flying in it eighty-five hours each month.

I thought briefly of those one hundred and sixty transatlantic crossings that had trickled under my wing, to say nothing of the trips into the Arctic, down south into South America, across Africa, and shuttle runs from Marrekech and Casa Blanca to England and Scotland while dodging marauding Germans like a wild pigeon.

In a way it had been fun. There was a war to win and the airline pilots had turned in long impossible days and nights of flying, weeks and months of the same. And I had done three long years plus a few months.

How many plane loads of healthy boys I had taken across and traded for litter loads to bring back, I did not know. It had not seemed to matter. There was a war to win!

I recalled the two times I had flown twenty-four hours at one sitting, without rest, and only one stopover for fuel, in addition to the innumerable seventeen and eighteen hours at one sitting. At times I had been so tired that I didn't give a damn whether or not it rolled on the landing.

Later, many of us were shocked to learn that Amalgamated had received government pay at cost plus ten percent, even on our salaries, while at the same time exerting political pressure to prevent many of us, with reserve commissions, from going back into the service. It had burned.

Back on the commercial airlines after the war, the DC-4 was cruised at two hundred and forty miles per hour. This caused problems. The fronts were closer, the bad thunderstorms were more frequent, and we had to hit them at a faster speed.

The tail was tall again, the windows square, the four engines larger, the wings thinner and more pointed. It leaned forward restlessly, eagerly. In eighty-five hours with the DC-6, I was hauling fifty-seven passengers over twenty-five thousand miles.

I stared at it. It was growing larger, longer, and more sleek. The tail tilted to the rear. The wings were smaller thinner and had shifted back to the middle of the fuselage with a wild sweep to the rear like those of a sailing prairie chicken. Racing wings!

Then I noticed the pods—two, without props, on each wing peeking out with alligator faces. I recognized it as the new jetliner Amalgamated had been considering ordering for tomorrow. Hush, hush to everyone, I had nevertheless obtained its specs. As a representative of the pilots on the two year-old stalled contract labor negotiations, I had made a point of obtaining all the data on tomorrow's airplane.

Six hundred miles per hour was guaranteed. And it would land at one hundred and thirty. That meant we would have to hit those midwest storms at or above two hundred and fifty. A cold chill ran up my spine at the thought. In that jet I would be flying over fifty thousand miles each month. Small wonder, I thought, that the pilots had to have a monthly mileage limitation in place of that obsolete monthly hour limit of eighty-five hours.

It wasn't the hours, weeks, or years on duty that made a pilot age early. It was the miles. The speed, the worry, and strain of trying to give the passengers a good ride seemed to produce a nerve fatigue. Often I had likened it to battle fatigue. And, in a way it was, a constant battle with the elements.

I turned from the window and studied the teletype weather reports my copilot had been eyeing thoughtfully.

"Set the flight plan up at twenty-one thousand, Len," I directed, "and figure the gas pretty close, we may try to run over that stuff tonight."

"Is it going to be rough again tonight?" Jimmie asked with concern in her big brown eyes while she studied first one of my eyes and then the other at half second intervals.

"Gad!" Jackie exclaimed from her perch on the table as she concentrated with the red paint on the wolf neutralizers. "Those storms almost threw us coming out last night. Think I'll wear spurs tonight."

"It may get pretty rough," I answered Jimmie. "But I am hoping that we'll be able to short gas enough so we can top all the weather at around twenty-five thousand, most of it, anyway."

I continued, "That bright flight dispatcher on duty last night insisted on our taking so much gas out of Oklahoma City that we had to plough through the weather. That extra five hundred gallons that we didn't need gave us an extra three thousand pounds of load and cut our maximum altitude by three thousand feet. It was just enough to make the difference between a rough trip and a smooth one. We actually landed here with over one thousand gallons of gasoline."

"Why did he do it?" Jimmie stood close and asked thoughtfully, while she wrinkled a pretty forehead in a frown. I was conscious of her sleek fitting uniform and the sweetness of her breath.

I shrugged. "It's the same old problem of dual authority but not dual responsibility. The flight dispatchers are supervisors and they imagine they are keeping us out of trouble by giving us lots of gas. Actually it is their own jobs they worry about. If they load us down with gas and we tear an airplane up trying to plough through a thunderstorm because we are too heavy to go over the top, well, they feel awfully sorry for that poor crew and passengers. But no one calls them on the carpet about increasing our load unnecessarily. Not a word, not a worry about their jobs. Criticism is only directed at the poor, dumb pilot for not having enough sense to keep his nose out of that particular storm.

"Then too," I added thoughtfully, "the flight dispatchers seldom feel the responsibility to the traveling public for a smooth, safe ride that a flight crew member feels. Their idea of safety is all the gas possible for each flight. It's a screwed up business on Amalgamated. Heavier than necessary loads on takeoffs when an engine loss is most critical, heavier then necessary loads for climbing cuts the speed, cuts the maximum cruising altitude, and cuts the structural safety margin when turbulence is encountered.

"So," I smiled, "we end up trying to duck, dodge, and jump over thunderstorms like a broken field football runner with his pants padded with lead."

Jackie giggled. "Just call us 'schooner,' —don't they have leaded bottoms?"

"It'll be rough, Jim," she decided. "Whoopee," then she wiggled uncertainly on the table edge while she swung a fiery tipped hand in circles over her head. "Rope 'em young and ride 'em wild!" She laughed and added as an afterthought, "And come and get your own damned coffee. My Tulsa boyfriend wants to take me away from all this," she confided and then gagged. "Each time he gives me that line I see a sink full of dirty dishes getting closer and closer."

"Not at home, you don't." Jimmie declared, giving her roommate a sweet and knowing little smile.

"Now, now, baby," Jackie cautioned, "shall I tell how you snore?"

"Jackie!" Jimmie cried, her eyes flashing, "don't resort to lies."

"Twenty-six hundred and fifty gallons," Len, my copilot exclaimed as he gave his computer a last whirl and slipped it into his shirt pocket. He pushed the flight plan toward me for signature.

I studied it thoughtfully. Five hours to Oklahoma City, two thousand gallons, one hundred and fifty gallons to Tulsa as an alternate, one hundred for a possible instrument approach, and four hundred for the required reserve. It was as required by the Civil Aeronautics Authority in the government regulations covering scheduled air carriers. It was ample.

I signed it and nodded. "That's all we want too."

"How many passengers?" I asked an agent busy with the load computations.

"Full load of fifty-seven tonight, captain," he responded, "and five standing by for possible openings."

"Ye Gads!" Jackie exclaimed. "If this keeps up they'll be installing rollaway chairs on the wings." She assumed a blank look. "What'd I say? Don't ever repeat me!" She giggled and laid a hand on Jimmie's arm. "Imagine Jim, delivering a cup of coffee to a wing-tip passenger."

"Oh well," she philosophized, "I guess working conditions could be worse—it gets awful dark out there."

Working conditions! Working conditions! My brain reeled at the subject. Months and months of serving on the negotiating committee for the Amalgamated pilots in an effort to conclude a new labor agreement had resulted in a complete and hopeless deadlock on all issues. All came under that broad term. Hours on duty—hours of flight—test flying—trip selections—system adjustment board neutral—and that bone crusher—mileage limitation! I groaned to myself. Working conditions on an airline meant everything.

The agent computing the load suddenly looked up at me. "Here's a telegram for you, captain, I almost forgot it," he apologized.

I took the envelope and opened it while my crew watched. It read:

"Contract negotiations to be resumed ten a.m. Tuesday. See me Monday night." It was from David L. Behncke, president Air Line Pilots' Association.

"Damnation!" I exclaimed and passed the wire to my copilot. "More contract negotiations! I thought things folded up the last meeting. Now we have a System Board of Adjustment hearing scheduled for Wednesday. I'm likely to have two meetings at the same time. But, I guess the company has the same problem.

"Let's have a last look at the weather map" I suggested to Len. "See you on board." Jimmie sang out and flashed us an ivory smile as she and Jackie picked up their overnight bags and headed for the DC-6.

Chapter 2

The High Road

Together, Len and I walked down the long passenger ramp into the terminal enroute to the U.S. weather bureau. Len's long face was somber. I was thinking about the System Board hearing and contract negotiations coming up in the same week.

"I thought the negotiations were finished, had broken down," Len began, "the committee returned the matter to the Master Executive Council and the Master Council voted to strike, and the field backed it up."

"That's right," I mused while my mind raced on. I wondered how much I could tell him at this time.

"Then why don't we strike to settle the unsolved issues?"

"We should," I agreed, "either strike or give up the issues."

"Give up mileage limitation?" He almost glared at me in sudden irritation. "If we give that up, what future is there in this business? A handful of pilots will fly the nation's airlines tomorrow—the jetliners."

"Not for long," I insisted grimly. "The eighty-five hours in jets each month will wreck their nerves in a few short years, especially as the jets get larger and faster. Soon they will be building planes that will carry one to two hundred passengers and go faster and faster. Then the nerve fatigue factor will begin to show up. Of course, they will call it something else, like pilot error. I have had several discussions with Dave Behncke on this. He is a very far-sighted individual and is always thinking ahead for the pilots."

"Without mileage limitation this business sure has a nice future to look forward to, doesn't it?" He laughed sarcastically. "No promotions, constant cut-backs in pilot personnel with each new airplane on a given route, more and more miles for the same old eighty-five flying hours, and as a consequence, we have to work more and more days each month."

"I know, Len," I cautioned gently. "Remember that I've been arguing the facts across the negotiating table with the company for two years now."

"But what's the pitch?"

"Something may have developed that we don't know about, the company may have made a real proposition," I did not believe my own words.

"Not Amalgamated." Len scoffed at the idea as we mounted the stairway to the weather bureau. "It'll take a first class strike for C.R. to lay anything substantial on the table. You have said that yourself," he reminded me.

I smiled at his memory, then added, "Either something of importance has developed, or we are too weak to strike."

"But the overwhelming vote for a strike has been in for over a month," he argued. "The ALPA (Air Line Pilots' Association) convention voted unanimously to permit the Amalgamated pilots to strike for a mileage limitation and we're all set for it. What do you mean by too weak?"

"Save it until later," I admonished tersely as we entered the weather bureau. But I continued to think of the ol'man, David L. Behncke, president of the Air Line Pilots' Association from the beginning of the Association, now going on eighteen years. Could it be that he was afraid to call the strike, I asked myself. Or had something else developed, some major concession on the part of the company, to warrant another try at direct negotiations?

The weather map made the United States look quite small and insignificant, no mountains, no rivers, nothing to indicate the long miles to New York. It was just a flat outline with the weather code marking for each station printed at the station location. The meteorologist on duty inserted the weather symbols and then drew the map. It was usually re-drawn every four hours.

The isobars, lines of barometric pressure, were quite close and thick between Albuquerque and Amarillo. In between was a heavily shaded front, extending from the southwest, in a northeast direction toward Chicago. It looked as though some child had tried to draw a Christmas tree, became uncertain, and ended it all with a confused mass of erratic lines and circling pencil marks. Though Greek to the public, it was the airline pilots' most frequently viewed map.

I studied it thoughtfully while the slight, bespectacled meterologist stood silently to one side. It was the same old weather, I reflected, that Johnny and I had seen in 1936. But it was different. The difference was in the horses we rode!

Yesterday's weather, today's and tomorrow's would have a repeat frequency. After a number of years of map study I had found conditions did duplicate themselves. But they were made different— oh, so different—by the variations attached firmly to my seat belt.

Each variation had started as some unknown aeronautical engineer's or crackpot's wild dream. From that dream it sneaked across the drawing board, through the factory and eventually attached itself to my seat belt. Again I thought briefly of the variations that had surged under me and carried me through the ozone at an ever increasing gait. I could clearly feel the flat rumble of the jets.

I recoiled slightly from the map. It suddenly seemed to contain a coiled rattlesnake in the isobar lines. A warning buzz seemed to electrify the back of my head. It was the same map I had seen before. Long ago, Johnny had shown it to me.

"Thar's one for you, kid," he had boomed. "When they get a hump in their back like that one, don't try to ride through it for it'll scatter your guts all over the cockpit." I smiled at the way Johnny had always expressed it.

"Here's last night's map," I pointed to a sheet and spoke to Len. "We know what was in that." I had a fleeting thought of Jackie's wing-tip passengers.

"And, here's tonight's." I frowned as I smoothed out the last sheet. "We're going to find out what's in it, unless we can run over it."

"There won't be much difference," the meteorologist spoke up, anxious to make his vast knowledge available to the poor airline jockey.

"Are you sure?" I questioned seriously while still feeling the buzzing refrain in the back of my head.

"Well, yes," he countered, "the front has deepened a little but it should not affect you."

"Why not?"

"It merely makes the tops a little higher," he answered easily.

"Well," I smiled, "it was rough last night, rough as a cob. How high will those tops be tonight?"

He shrugged. "Twenty-five or thirty thousand."

"Where?"

"Probably east of Albuquerque and west of Amarillo." He waved a finger across the map between the two cities.

Enroute back to the operations office I explained the map to Len. Carefully I listed the few little things an airline pilot should watch on weather maps. I listed the closeness of the isobars near the front the thunderstorm activity along the front; the general line of the front; the bottom of the overcast; the tops of the overcast, when known; the radar reports on thermal activity along the front, when available; surface winds; upper winds; other pilots' reports together with a few other little things such as the terrain along the front and whether or not the front is cradled on a side of a mountain range. Last, but not least to consider, is the season of the year. Each item adds a different shade to the picture, never complete but nevertheless a picture.

"And," I concluded, "someone is going to have a ride tonight, for all hell is going to break loose in the vicinity of that front. That meteorologist is unaware of what's developing. He works eight hours, draws his weather maps, makes his forecasts, and then goes home. Whether or not he hits or misses and how much he misses is not impressed upon him so he doesn't recognize and remember repeat performances in the weather. They are too far apart for him."

"Now take us," I explained, "we look the map over, figure what we think we'll encounter, then go out and encounter what is actually there. And we're impressed! Believe me, you remember too.

"In this airline piloting business you only get to make one mistake, if your name is Allison," I added significantly, "or if you have done a lot of union work, as I have, they'll fire you if they can catch you looking crossways at the regulations."

Len chuckled. "The officials really do seem to be watching you," he agreed. "Anderson especially." He was referring to the chief pilot at the Tulsa base.

I thought of Anderson's bare year and a half as an airline captain before being selected for the chief pilot's job. It is true he had been a chief for several years, but desk flying never seemed to improve airplane flying technique. I laughed at the thought.

"He takes his orders," I stated quietly. "That's why he is a chief pilot, recently renamed an assistant superintendent of flight. But regardless of the title, he's been like a bloodhound on my trail for nearly three years.

"The more I represent the pilots union, the harder he seems to work on my trail. It sure keeps me walking a tight rope," I complained a little bitterly.

"But think of the distinction," Len kidded me, "being a big Air Line Pilots' Association wheel-horse, Behncke's trouble shooter."

"Yes, it's like having your picture on a post office poster. That Phoenix manager of operations wasn't kidding the other night when he told me there was a price on my head," I reminded him.

"How come he would tell you that?" Len questioned.

"Several years ago, before WW II, I was flying out of the Boston base and he was the station manager there," I recalled. "His wife was very sick, needed an operation, and Ed did not have the thousand dollars necessary. He appealed to the company and they referred him to the company officials. The credit union was happy to loan him the money at twelve percent, providing, of course, he would get another older employee to go on his note."

"Did you go on his note?" Len was curious.

"No," I answered shortly. "I gave him the money."

Len's eyes studied my face as we passed the TWA constellation unloading at gate four.

"Did you get it back?" he questioned.

"Fifty dollars each month until it was all paid back. I didn't ask for a note or a co-signer."

"How about the interest?" he questioned with a smile.

"That was paid in Phoenix the other night." I smiled back.

In the operations office I signed the flight clearance and scanned the very latest company weather reports. The flight dispatcher had set the gas figure at 3320. That would gross us near the maximum.

Under my breath I cursed his ignorance while I called Los Angeles to talk to him personally. The thought occured to me that the passengers should be treated to a look at some of the desk-pilots who, through lack of knowledge, fear of their jobs, and an exercise of misplaced authority, frequently jeopardized their safety.

But that government agency known as the Civil Aeronautics Authority had approved the division of authority, principally due to the politics exercised by the major companies, and the passengers along with the flight crews had to endure it.

Tandy, a former meteorologist, was the dispatcher on duty at Los Angeles, and, after considerable argument on the phone, agreed to cut the gas to 2800 gallons. I tried to pull him down to twenty-six fifty but was unable to. Actually, as a dispatcher, he was a pretty good guy. He understood my reasoning.

"How could I explain it, Wayne," he asked, "if you ran short and something happened?"

The same old flight dispatcher jitter-bug disease, I reflected. What he was saying was that if we met with an accident, later attributed to a shortage of fuel, the higher company officials would have him on the carpet. But if he could show that he gave me all the possible fuel, then he would be cleared automatically.

"Tell them the same thing I'll be telling Saint Peter," I growled, "and that way they can't get our stories crossed."

Casually I thought, as I hung the phone back on the wall, of a fifteen page letter I had written to the president of Amalgamated, when Ralph Damon was president several years ago, in which I had pointed out the dangers and inefficiencies that were accumulating due to permitting the flight dispatchers to slip into the position of controlling flights rather than coordinating them. That letter had been approved by all of Amalgamated's one thousand pilots. But it didn't turn the tide, just slowed it a little.

Picking up my flight kit I stalked out the operations door to the flood lighted DC-6 where all was bustle and hurry. Passengers were trickling through a gate and up the long steps into the airplane. I caught a glimpse of Jimmie's dark uniform and ivory smile as she stood in the doorway and checked the passengers tickets before permitting them to find seats. It was funny how often a passenger with a Los Angeles, Seattle, or Honolulu ticket would try to board a New York bound airplane.

Cargo dollies stood under the airplane while two cargo men stuffed mail and baggage into the belly compartments under the supervision of an agent. An endless loading belt was carrying other cargo into the front compartments from the opposite side. A gas truck stood under the right wing while a mechanic, flashlight in hand, crouched far out on the wing tip and watched the fuel pour into a wing tip tank. Occasionally he stuck a long stick into the wing to measure the fuel. Twenty-eight hundred gallons of fuel meant just that, no more or no less. In this modern time it still had to be measured by stick. The gauges in the airplane were not accurate enough to rely on for close readings, all because a certain company official has a brother-in-law representing a company selling airplane instruments. Better and more accurate gauges were available, but we didn't get them. The Civil Aeronautics Authority never seemed to make an issue of it—so we stick measured.

I stopped near the passenger ramp as Tom, my full chested and husky flight engineer, hurried up.

"They're putting in twenty-eight hundred," he remarked as he looked up at the man crouching on the wing tip.

"I know," I smiled, "but that's better then thirty-three hundred."

"You know," he drawled with a humorous gleam in his eye, "if those desk pilots increase the gas load much more, I am going to draw a bonus with a pet suggestion of mine."

"Yes?" I questioned.

"Simple, real simple," he confided. "I'm going to design gas trucks shaped like an airplane wing and show how much easier it would be to shift the wings rather than pump the gas."

I laughed and eyed the nearest tandam tires, one new, one old. It was Amalgamated's way of getting all possible use out of an old piece of equipment even if it compromised safety.

"That outside tire looks pretty thin," I suggested. "It won't stand much rough treatment."

"It meets the minimum in regulations." Tom grinned. "I checked the latest regulations with the maintenance foreman. He thought it should be changed too, but neither of us could figure how we could justify pulling it."

"Anyway," he chuckled, "the way you ease them onto the runway—we could run the inner tubes bare."

"Are you apple polishing for a raise?" I asked smiling.

But my landings were good. They had to be good! I had to be better than good. That was necessary in representing the pilots, that is, unless I eased up a little in the critical spots. Otherwise, the company would soon have me out on some pretext.

Of course my union work would have nothing to do with it. Not at all! It would just happen, that's all. By federal law under the Railway Labor Act, the Airlines were forbidden to discriminate. So Amalgamated wouldn't discriminate, it would just happen.

The newspaper stories of how the various companies tried to work with the union to promote safety was stuff for birds, on Amalgamated anyway. The Railway Labor Act providing against discrimination would be adhered to with strictly verbal utterances only. Of course, according to the officials, it was just accidental whenever a strong union pilot was selected for disciplinary action. By easing up a little in the critical points when representing the union, a pilot in my position did not have to walk a tight rope. He could make a few mistakes, bust a tire now and then, over-shoot occasionally and indulge in a frequent drink without suffering any dire consequences.

In so doing he had to secretly take company orders. He could put up a good front for the pilots, win many small issues, but give in on the critical points, such as mileage limitation. My lip curled at the thought, and as I eased up the ramp with my flight kit, I thought of how I had twice been approached by a company purchasing agent. He wanted to buy my cooperation.

Lost in thought I passed Jimmie's quick and lovely smile, paused while a mother hustled identical twins into seats, and waited in the aisle while Jackie located another mother with her infant in a front seat where she could have a bassinet at her feet.

"But what'll I do when it gets rough?" questioned the anxious young mother.

"Relax," Jackie gave her a reassuring smile, "our captain has promised us a nice smooth ride." To me, behind her back she held up two crossed fingers.

Up forward I passed the huge cargo bins and squeezed by the cargo handler as he loaded a bin from the endless belt conveyer. Huge as each new airplane appeared to be, it never seemed to hold enough.

The cockpit appeared spotless and the seat felt cool and soft as I settled into it, adjusted my seat belt, head set, rudder pedals, arm rest, and nose-wheel steering and then began a systematic cockpit checklist. Len read aloud the long list while I checked each item. How monotonous it sometimes seemed!

In a few bustling minutes the cargo handler was gone, the side door closed with a bang, cargo dollies scattered like ants, and a lone agent, standing well ahead of the left wing and in sight out the side window, signalled the engine starting order. Behind me the inverters gave off a high pitch whine as the headset came alive with the control tower giving an airways clearance to a United plane at the end of the runway, destination Honolulu.

Tom dropped into his seat between Len and me. Number three engine caught instantly and drowned out the inverters, then four, then one. Number two hesitated and rotated several times before coughing up an overcharge, then joined the throaty roar of the pack. A vast array of instruments jumped to attention for instant reading.

Carefully I set the RPM of all engines at the prescribed one thousand and from the headset heard Len, across the cockpit, asking the tower for a taxi clearance. The agent signalled us away with a smart salute as I released the toe brakes. The big plane tilted forward ever so slightly and began to crawl forward at the same time the tower cleared us to taxi to the designated runway. I swung the nose wheel steering to the right and watched the left wing clear a Western Convair wing by a few feet. Flight forty-eight was enroute, the captain's responsibility.

I permitted the plane to nose slowly and smoothly down the rolling taxi strip. Mentally I could see Jimmie and Jackie hustling up and down the fuselage to get everyone settled and strapped in for the takeoff. I had to be careful that I didn't throw them by too quick a turn or by heavy application of the brakes. I took pride in being a smooth captain with an airplane, both in the air and on the ground.

As my left hand controlled the nose wheel steering, my right hand the throttles, my feet the rudder pedals and brakes, my left ear listened to the tower giving Len our airways clearance direct to Fresno, direct to Las Vegas, direct to Albuquerque, then via green four airway to Oklahoma City, point of next landing, to cruise at twenty-one thousand feet, while at the same time my right ear listened to Tom read off the load sheet giving the total passengers as fifty-seven, cargo load, gas load, total weight, V-1 and V-2 speeds. It was tricky work and all had to be done at about the same time. I dared not miss anything.

At the end of the runway I stopped the plane gently and set the brakes so that it was almost impossible to feel the plane stop.

We took a few minutes to warm the engines, run them up, complete the takeoff check list, and set the flaps at the takeoff setting. Len's clear and crisp voice crackled in the left earphone as he asked the tower to open the gate. I smiled faintly at his humorous way, and a little thrill, as always, surged up my spine as I turned the plane down the runway between the two long rows of flush type lights that marked the runway boundaries.

I thought of the long years it took to reach that position of command as I eased the throttles forward and listened to the throaty roars turn into howling banshees. My body felt the long forward and sustained surge of the airplane. The rolling vibrations of the tandems grew less and less as I turned loose of the nose steering and steadied the course down the runway with rudder. Easing the control wheel back, I lifted the weight off the nose wheel and permitted it to float inches off the runway.

"Ninety—ninety-five—one hundred!" Len chanted out the air speeds.

Tom adjusted the throttle evenly at the full power as I shifted my eyes back and forth from the runway to the four manifold pressure gauges. We all watched those gauges, for the seconds between ninety miles per hour and one hundred and twenty were the most critical, the most dangerous of the many hours we flew each month. Loaded to maximum for most takeoffs, it was essential that not one engine missed a beat between those critical speeds. If one did, our hearts usually surged a bit also.

The nose wheel floated a little higher and for a space the ever lightening tandems impressed the plane with the runway swells. Then their vibrations faded, I signalled gear up by turning my right hand palm upward and felt Tom snap the gear retract lever from the locked down position. We were floating in space with two long rows of lights ending abruptly ahead of us at the bay shore. Flight forty-eight, bound for New York, was off the San Francisco airport at twelve ten.

Tom slowly raised the flaps from the takeoff position by degrees to the full retract position. Len retarded the throttles to climbing power while I pulled the master prop control to climbing RPM and watched the nose climb up to blot out the lights outlining the south end of Oakland.

The engine settled down to that full throaty roar as my eyes flashed across the sky ahead, back across the engine instruments, then back to the sky ahead. I rubbed the palm of my right hand down my pant leg to remove the moisture, took a deep breath as I adjusted the stabilizer to climbing attitude, and felt the plane settle into the long climb to twenty-one thousand feet. My eyes roved across the flight instruments making sure of the speed, direction, and artificial horizon readings but not failing to frequently sweep the star studded sky for other traffic. There was none reported, but the cockpit vigil has to be constant.

Len checked out with the San Francisco tower with a cheerful good morning, switched to company frequency and reported off San Francisco to the Los Angeles flight dispatcher.

Tom set the cabin pressurization and we all leaned back in our seats to relax a little while our eyes continued the vigil in the darkened sky ahead. I snapped off the "No Smoking, Seat Belts" sign and we were ready for coffee.

Leveling out at twenty-one thousand, I watched Tom set the power to cruising and listened to the motors roar that long distant song. It almost seemed that they settled into a groove like four horses in a steady swinging pull.

The cockpit door flashed open for a few seconds, and Jimmie's light complexion glowed in back of us in the reflection of the instrument lights.

Tom moved off his seat and offered it to her while taking his coffee. Len and I accepted our coffee without glancing back while our restless eyes clung to the horizon ahead.

"Wayne," Jimmie leaned close and her voice was barely audible even with her red lips a bare three inches away. "I am terribly sorry to hear of your troubles."

I removed my eyes from the distant lights of Fresno, motioned for Len to take the plane and turned to look into her eyes, noting the width between them, the smooth sweet line of her face, the full throat and perfectly moulded figure beneath the blue blouse. Again I was intrigued by the way her eyes shifted so automatically at half second intervals.

"Meaning what?" I studied the instrument panel again and made a pretense of resetting the throttles.

"Your divorce, Wayne. I read about it a few days ago in the Tulsa paper. It was just a tiny article saying that it had been granted. Why didn't you ever tell me?"

"It didn't concern you, Jimmie, and I saw no reason to talk about it. Anyway," I continued, "it has been coming for over a year. I did everything I could to keep it hushed up. Did you expect me to conspire with you?"

"No," she smiled, "but I almost wish you had. I know it must have been pretty rough."

"Yes," I replied, "but it was all cut and dried." Then I sat silently studying the horizon ahead.

"Did Betty want much?" Jimmie was suddenly more inquisitive than I thought she should be. But I didn't mind.

"Everything," I answered simply. "And the children too." Then that which I had kept locked so closely inside me seemed to erupt into words.

"I gave her the home and most of my assets if she would agree to a joint custody of the children. That she hated to do but finally signed on the dotted line when her attorney told her I was giving more than she could win in court. No alimony was involved."

"But the farm, Wayne, you gave that too?" I knew she was thinking about me for I had frequently discussed it with Len and Tom where she and Jackie could hear. I had made it evident how much I enjoyed it.

Jim was a farm girl, I knew. She had been raised on a combination farm and ranch in the area of Oologah, Oklahoma, a short ten miles from Claremore where I had been raised. I had known her folks long before I met her. In fact, my Dad had drilled a well on their farm when I was in high school.

Slowly I nodded my head, not trusting to look at her. "I gave that too," I answered simply. "As a matter of fact, she has already sold it. Then she went back into court with her attorney, claiming that the joint custody deal on the children wasn't working, and the judge gave her full custody. I think they had planned that all along."

"I'll get you some more coffee." She squeezed my arm a little as she left.

Fresno faded to our right. The Sierras reared up under us. They held scattered clouds clinging to their tops. I studied the east and caught the distant glow of lightning. The company radio operator gave us the latest Albuquerque, Tucumari, Amarillo, and Oklahoma City weather. Len had to ask for a repeat on Amarillo.

The same picture, I reflected, except that the frontal trough was deepening. But it was the same picture, just a little different hue, a darker shade.

I took the second cup of coffee from Jackie who promptly accepted Tom's seat, fired up a cigarette and kicked off her shoes. "Almost everyone is asleep," she reported. "Even the babies have given up."

"How many do we have?" I questioned.

"Three, five, and one," she replied.

I looked at her quizzically.

"Three babies in arms," she explained, "five brats, and one angel."

"Who's the angel?" I asked smiling.

She slapped my shoulder and laughed. "That's me, boy, that's me!"

The glow of the lightning ahead was brighter now, more constant and moving to the north and south as far as we could see. Underneath us the scattered clouds had turned into a solid overcast and it was beginning to crowd us at twenty-one thousand.

"Ask Las Vegas for twenty-three thousand," I directed Len.

In a couple of minutes airways had cleared us to twenty-three thousand. I shifted the props to climb and pointed the nose toward the stars that had begun to grow hazy. At twenty-three thousand they were clear again and we continued to drone on eastward.

I thought of my ten year old boy and four year old girl, and felt my heart grow a little tighter. It was tough, tough on the children, because they could not understand. It did no good, I knew, to hash and re-hash something that was already done. The divorce was final.

With an effort I tore the thoughts from my mind.

"I'll take it, Len." I spoke and took the controls. Ahead, below, and on either side now the clouds were constantly illuminated by lightning. It wasn't the clear, crisp type as seen from the ground with no intervening clouds, but was the glowing, puffing kind shielded by capping cumulus. It would glow and glow in one spot, then another, then split out to other cloud tiers. It ran up, down, and extended itself to the east, north, and south in long flowing sheets, as though to warn me that this was one frontal storm there would be no going around.

The plane sliced through some choppy air and I took it up another five hundred feet.

Len called Albuquerque, and checked in with the army radar screen giving them our identity, position, altitude, and approximate time of entrance into the Air Defense Identification Zone. It was extremely important that the "bug-eyed boys" know our whereabouts, otherwise the jet fighters would look us over, give us a good buzz and keep us writing letters for six months trying to explain why we had failed to comply with regulations in entering an Air Defense Zone.

Len leaned over toward me. "Think I had better get a five hundred on top clearance?"

I nodded, then listened to the way El Paso answered back, clear and crisp, in spite of the thunderstorm static. It was marvelous, I thought, at the facilities the airline pilot had at his finger tips.

In a relaxed state I sat there smoothly flying the plane. My eyes kept my arms and legs coordinating to the flight instruments without mental concentration. It had taken years to learn that trick, that I could free my mind to think, to wrestle with any problem I chose, and continue to fly the plane smoothly.

Somehow, it was easy to think clearly up there so high with placid stars for a roof and swelling flashes of lightning in towering cumulus clouds crashing underneath. I was a part of the world but detached from it. I was a part of the sky, yet I did not belong. I was a poacher in God's Heaven.

Abruptly Len leaned over toward me and asked, "How much higher are we going?" He grinned. "The company regulations limit us to twenty-three thousand, you know."

Consciously I glanced at one of the altimeters and noted that we were at twenty-five thousand with a true airspeed of two hundred and seventy miles per hour. Ahead I scanned the dark towering flashes and thought of the ominous map I had studied a short time back.

"Yes," I smiled, "unless an emergency exists. And if we get into that stuff, it'll exist real sudden."

I thought of the violent turbulence that I knew lay just a thousand or so feet below. Here it was still fairly smooth, but ahead—that was the problem.

"How's the gas, Tom?" I questioned.

"Still under the flight plan," he reported after checking his chart.

Abruptly the Automatic Direction Finders rotated to the rear. "Over Albuquerque," Len remarked. "Shall I report our altitude?"

"No," I decided, "not unless we have to. Report five hundred feet on top and ask for twenty-seven thousand in case we are unable to stay in the clear, and let's try to top that stuff ahead."

Len was dutifully working both the company at El Paso and the Civil Aeronautics Authority at Albuquerque when the cabin door opened and Jimmie's face gleamed behind Tom's left shoulder.

"How high are we, Wayne?"

Tom answered her with the airplane altitude.

"More coffee?" she asked. "I thought I felt a little dizzy."

I turned and looked at her smooth red lips. "The cabin is at eleven thousand five hundred feet now, Jim, and we're going to be pretty busy for a while. And," I added significantly, "it may get a little rough, Maybe you had better get the passengers in the seat belts, just in case."

She nodded and laid a hand briefly on my right arm.

"Treat us gently," she requested with a smile.

Len hung up the microphone as Jimmie faded to the rear.

"Air Traffic Control cleared us for twenty seven thousand and anything above, says the whole upstairs is ours, nothing above twenty thousand," Len explained.

The headset on my temples suddenly cracked with flight forty-nine reporting off Oklahoma City to cruise at twenty thousand. I sat upright and looked at Len. His questioning eyes studied my face in the glow of the constant lightning.

"Who was that?" I asked.

"It sounded like Max Stocking," he offered.

"He flies with Ellis," I recalled. "Oh, brother!" I breathed, "again I repeat, somebody is going to get a ride tonight!"

I pointed the nose upward toward twenty-seven thousand and called for more power, the last that remained. The plane was beginning to feel sluggish now and I wished I could have Tandy with us to get a first hand picture of the frequent wisdom of leaving available fuel behind.

"It looks like we travel the high road, tonight," Tom laconically remarked.

I leaned forward and studied the vivid fire above and ahead. Glancing at the outside air temperature guage, I noted that we had an outside temperature of a minus five degrees Fahrenheit. That looked good. Usually frontal conditions were not too bad if hit at or below zero.

I wondered idly if that was the reason the company officials had placed an arbitrary ceiling of twenty three thousand on enroute flying, except when an emergency existed, to make sure the pilots caught it rough. But of course, they did not know about that zero temperature angle. I had only discovered it a few months before and had failed to get any company official to place any credulence in the report. It was damned hard for a 'line pilot' to tell a desk pilot anything, especially if the 'line pilot' was a strong union man.

"Seat belt and no smoking sign on," I ordered. Taking the phone in one hand, I caught Jackie on the other end. "Tie everything down," I ordered, "and make sure you girls are down too, within five minutes."

"Is it going to be bad?" she asked; I could feel the tenseness in her voice. Often I had thought that the stewardesses had it tougher than the pilots in bad weather. With fear clutching at their hearts, they had to smile, cheer the passengers, juggle babies, hold hands with suddenly scared wolves, and pray that the 'knot-heads' up front knew what they are doing.

"Not bad," I answered easily, "I just don't want to take any chance with my private harem. Anyway," I continued, "remember what you told the woman with the bassinet."

"Oh, that little bastard!" She laughed. "I wouldn't object if you shook him up a little. Already I have had to give him a diaper change three times. Honest to God, Wayne," she continued, "I think he's overdoing himself just to be onery—like all males." She hung up hurriedly.

I wondered what induced a girl to take a job as stewardess and willingly do the dirty work of waiting on people and babies in flight, work they would not do on the ground. It was a puzzle.

"The cabin's near twelve thousand!" Tom warned. I glanced at the cabin altimeter, cabin pressure, and cabin rate of climb instruments.

"Shift it to manual and see if the manual control will give us more pressurization," I ordered.

Tom complied and suddenly the cabin rate of climb indicator showed a healthy descent with the airplane still climbing. The cabin pressurization needle began to move above 4.2, the maximum for normal operations.

"Well, I'll be damned!" Tom exclaimed. "Do you think it is safe?"

"The book says so," I smiled at him. "But be careful and don't blow a gasket. I'd hate like hell to have to dive down through this stuff under us."

"You can think of the most pleasant things," Len exclaimed.

On a fleeting thought I took the microphone. "Forty-eight to forty-nine," I called.

"Forty-nine to forty-eight. Go ahead," boomed back into our earphones. Ellis was on the line.

"How does it look from your lowly perch?" I questioned.

"Fine," he replied. "Lots of fire, but smooth and silky. We've been in it about ten minutes now. Where are you?"

"Climbing." I hedged, "with lots of fire under us. Will let you know where the tops are in a few minutes."

Ellis was pro-company in his leanings and had once spent a couple of years as a flight dispatcher. Also, he was reputed to be a little weak in his flying, which frequently went with a pilot willing to play the company side, and willing to vary the comb of his hair to please any company official, but a nice enough guy, if you liked the wishy-washy kind.

"Not interested," he replied. "We've got it too good here!"

I shook my head to Len. "Maybe I'm nuts," I muttered. "But it seems to me that he's asking for it."

Then a big black sheet enveloped us and we were suddenly rolling and pitching with frequent jabs from all directions. It wasn't bad, but rough. I rode the controls as softly as possible and tried to make the corrections as gently as I could. Pulling the nose higher I cut the speed to a minimum of one hundred and twenty, and with the flaps down a little to give a little more lift, the bumps softened. We were like an old water-soaked log in a rough current, floating, but barely. Our motion was like a rocking chair as we edged along.

The plane wouldn't climb much now, but the small degree of flaps helped at the slower speed and we kept edging upwards. I wished we were two or three thousand pounds lighter with less gas. How I wished I could trade that gas for altitude. Jackie was suddenly there with coffee.

"It's pretty good back there." She was being careful with the coffee.

"The cabin's down to ten thousand," Tom called out. "We have a pressure of four point six, airplane altitude, twenty-nine thousand."

I sipped the coffee and rode the controls like a teenager kissing a girl for the first time. Jackie leaned over Tom's shoulder to tell me that she had even changed the little bastard's diaper in the choppy air, then returned to the cabin.

Suddenly there was an unintelligible scream on the radio. It was followed by a few broken words. "Forty-nine—heavy turbulence—heavy hail—emergency descent—damage—." The voice rose and fell as though the sender was having trouble keeping the mike within a foot of his face, and simultaneously having trouble keeping from swallowing it.

Len and I locked eyes for a few seconds, then listened to El Paso call for a repeat with our headsets clamped tightly to our ears. The air seemed charged with suspense as we strained to hear.

Mutely I reflected that only once before I had heard a pilot's voice reflect stark fear on the radio. That was when I had been a new copilot flying with Johnny and we had tangled with a tornado near Texarkana. It had snatched us up at fourteen thousand and taken us up to twenty-two thousand and a few hundred with both engines idling and us fighting to keep the airplane from getting on its back.

That old DC-2 was tough, tougher than I was at that time. I had tried to tell on the radio what was happening to us. Scared as I was, I had noticed the fear in my own voice. The memory was not pleasant.

"Shut up!" Johnny had ordered with that booming voice. "We either sound like men or let them figure it out from the debris."

Slowly the cool El Paso operator worked that sobbing voice, with intervals of interruption during which we could mentally picture two pilots fighting frantically for control over a wild, crazily pitching and crippled airplane. Piece by piece we gathered the story of smooth air and then suddenly wild turbulence, a stone wall of hail, severe damage to the airplane, one engine inoperative, and an emergency descent being made. I felt a cigarette burn my fingers and put it out.

Then we caught a belt from beneath, not severe, but a long sustained swell. I pulled the nose up and we rode the wave up, higher where the air was cleaner and clearer. If we had some way of harnessing the power in that stuff, I reflected, we could forget about atomic power. The DC-6 shuddered and shook and I could feel the wings flex, even at that slow speed, from the variable forces pushing us upward.

Pulling back a little more, I nosed the plane up a few more hundred feet and we were in smooth air again, on instruments of course, but in glassy smooth air. I knew we had it made, like a canoe leaving rough water and gliding into a calm pool.

The fire continued to be intense, so much so in fact, that it made the instruments difficult to read. Len rang the girls on the phone and Jimmie brought us up some magazines which we promptly squeezed into the "V" of the windshield while we floated smoothly along in a semi-stall position.

Forty-nine came on the air a few minutes later, with a voice more under control, and requested all available ambulance, doctor, and first air service at Amarillo where they were making an emergency landing.

"My God!" I exclaimed. "Do you reckon he has the seat belts off?"

"Could be." Len shrugged. "He sounded pretty confident when he talked to you."

The flight dispatcher, desk pilot, suddenly went to work on us. He wanted to know our altitude. He suggested that we avoid twenty thousand between Amarillo and Albuquerque. He also suggested a circuitous route to avoid the thunderstorms. He wanted to know our fuel on board. In fact, he had his desk squeezed so tightly into our cockpit that we could scarcely breathe.

Len read my expression and calmly announced into the mike: "The static is severe, unable to read you. Will call you back later."

We settled back to enjoy another cup of coffee and the air, so glassy and smooth.

Len was flying, Tom was back fixing a leaking coffee container, and Jackie was perched, like a kitten, a sweet scented purring hundred and fifteen pound kitten on Tom's seat and leaning her back against my shoulder with her feet on the back of Len's chair arm, when she suddenly straightened up.

"Listen," she announced, "Jim just told me the news. We have decided to grant you diplomatic immunity this week only. After that it's open season!"

I laughed. "Are you threatening me?"

She pulled her feet to the floor and turned to face me squarely. With a big smile she squeezed my arm. "I like the idea," She admitted. "But right now, at this time, I have a Tulsa boyfriend problem."

We both laughed together as she swung the seat around and slipped her shoes back on her feet.

"I'll send Jim up with more coffee," she promised.

The sky seemed to stay alive with fire, keeping the cockpit almost as bright as daylight with an eerie illumination that reminded me of the Arctic northern lights when on instrument near the Arctic Circle. Of course we were still on air that was glassy smooth, but the sharp flashes of lightning that seemed to get in the cockpit with us had abated. So we removed the magazines and papers from the windshield, marveling at how slick the air felt. It seemed to absorb the engine vibration normally felt in an airplane.

Tom and Jimmie came back up front about the same time with Jimmie carrying coffee. Tom took his coffee and Jimmie took his seat between Len and me with her coffee cup in hand.

"This is pretty nice," Jimmie remarked looking out at the unnatural glow of light on the props and settling in Tom's seat. I've never seen anything like it."

"Neither have I," Len added, "but we're sure playing anti-over ball on this storm."

Then the Civil Aeronautics Authority (CAA) called us on their frequency and advised that the army wanted to know our altitude. I cussed fervently for fifteen seconds while looking at Len, shaking my head and ignoring Jimmie's look of amazement.

"Now I'll have to write a report about exercising emergency authority and all that crap," I complained.

"Let's give them twenty-three thousand," Len suggested.

"Nothing doing." I vetoed the suggestion. "Not with the 'bug-eyed' boys looking at us through their periscopes. They know our altitude better than we do and they are checking to see if we will tell a lie." Then I added after thinking about it a little: "It may be that we are so high that they are doubting the accuracy of their instruments."

Reluctantly I took the mike and announced that we were at thirty-one thousand feet.

Chapter 3

The Booby-trapped Road

Amarillo slipped by with the usual radio signals. I wished I had an opportunity to see Ellis's damaged airplane. No doubt the publicity would get a good hush job. Ellis had been classified as 'a loyal company employee' or 'desk pilot.'

Midway between Amarillo and Oklahoma City we broke out in front of the weather into clear air. It was such a clean line of demarcation between good weather and bad that it was like leaping from a hugh cliff and plunging outward instead of downward.

"How'd we get up here?" Len laughingly inquired while rubbing his eyes. "Anyway," he claimed, "altitude never affects me, affect-affects me." He trailed off like a cracked record and acted as if he fainted. I had to agree with him, it was a hell of a ways down.

I jerked my thumb for him to take the controls and fly while I looked out the side window into the gray dawn that was very bright to the east. Everything was so miniature from up there.

"Better start it down, Len," I suggested. "Otherwise we are going to be circling Oklahoma City for thirty minutes."

Far below, out the side window, I saw scattered lights of an oil field. Picking out a single cluster I thought of that derrick floor far below, the heavy work that was routine and the crew that was working the graveyard shift.

My mind's eye pictured the scene most vividly as I recalled the years of my youth, depression years, during which I had worked for my father, dressing tools on a drilling machine in northeastern Oklahoma. It was a cable tooled machine, requiring only two men in the crew. Starting at fifteen I had spent summer after summer and many weekends on that work. It helped cinch me a starting position for three years on the high school football squad. That wasn't work; coming out of the oil field, it was fun.

My back ached, not at the thought of the football, but at the thought of the heavy wrenches, the red hot bits, the sledge hammers, the hot steam boilers, and the coal shovel, with which I had fed the boilers. In fact that was the reason I was up here tonight, looking down and back at a youth of heavy labor, nearly twenty-five years back.

I squirmed in my seat and thought of the last well on which I had worked before joining the army for a crack at the army flying school. It had been a wonderful well in a way. We had laid a half mile of pipeline to an old gas well and fired the boiler with gas—not coal. The twelve hour shifts had been much easier.

I laughed aloud at the memory of that well, the one that had decided my career in aviation, and recalled the one morning when Dad and I, loaded with wrenches, connections and pipe cutters, had decided to walk the gas line to locate a leak that was causing a low gas pressure.

We had followed the pipeline into a small wooded creek and surprised a bootlegger cooking off six barrels of mash in a large copper still which was being heated from a connection tapped into our gas line. It seemed like yesterday, and again I saw the startled look on the bootlegger's round moon-shaped face as he leaped to his feet. A look of relief followed as soon as he recognized us.

"Damn it, Joe," my father had greeted the young depression dressed farmer. "Don't waste so much gas. Put a small jet on your line and you'll get twice as much heat and burn about one tenth as much gas."

"I ain't got one," Joe Browder had grinned while fumbling for his tobacco pouch. "Wood smokes too much, and they're out looking for me," he added significantly.

"Do you have to run that stuff?" Dad had asked seriously while offering Joe a cigarette and eyeing the sizzling still. Bug-eyed I had stood and surveyed my first still in action.

"Damned right, Allison." Joe had grinned, his white teeth flashing in contrast to his sun-browned face. "The river got most of my corn, but I still got four kids to feed." He paused and pulled hungrily on the tailor made cigarette.

Dad had stood there for several minutes watching the still and the hungry way Joe had dragged on the cigarette. Then he spoke to me.

"Son," he had directed, "run back to the machine and get a small one inch jet. I'll tighten Joe's leaky connections and we'll show him how a gas jet will make that still climb a tree."

Hours later we were on the derrick floor drilling deeper in Mother Earth when a rickety wagon pulled up in the timber near the derrick floor. A pair of nondescript mules powered it and stood patiently switching their tails at the flies while Joe Browder set a wooden keg down on the corner of that derrick floor. It looked as though it held about seven gallons full, with a cute little wooden spigot for a bung.

"It's new and hot, Allison," he had grinned, "but it'll be good with a little time in that wooden keg."

Vividly I recalled how Dad, after eyeing the keg for an hour, while we drilled, had instructed me to anchor the keg on the end of the walking beam with soft rope and nails into the wooden walking beam. The walking beam rotated up and down over a three foot stroke and did about forty-five strokes per minute, the keg would receive constant agitation riding that beam. Somehow, Dad had calculated that a day's drilling would age the whiskey a good six months.

That evening when we shut down, which was at sundown, Dad had me climb out on the walking beam and draw out about one finger of whiskey in our one-half pint drinking cup that we kept with the ice-water can. It wasn't much different than clear water in looks when I handed it to him.

While I gathered the hand tools, oil, and greases to lock up in the dog-house, Dad had seated himself on the bottom step of the derrick stool and tasted the contents of that tin cup. I noticed that he poured out a little just as we started for home.

The next night when we shut down at the end of the day's work, I thought I could see a little color in the whiskey, and Dad didn't pour out any before we started home. On the third day of drilling with the keg mounted on the walking beam, the whiskey had a definite color to it. Also, Dad asked for a second little helping. So I climbed up on that walking beam twice that evening.

The next night, when we shut down, the whiskey had a nice amber color and I drew out one and one-half fingers in the tin water cup. Dad didn't object and disposed of it quite well, for there was a little leftover ice in the water can to dilute it a little.

On the fifth day the whiskey had a beautiful amber color, a deeper color than the day before. Also, Dad asked for two fingers in the water cup with a little leftover ice. He climbed in his oil field Buick and said, "You drive home, son. This is damned fine whiskey." And he didn't criticize my driving!

In the afternoon of the sixth day we suddenly drilled into a big gas well. That was good, for we were looking for gas. Oil was worth little during those years, in fact it was difficult to sell for over seventy-five cents per barrel while gas was bringing fair money, something like eight or nine cents per thousand cubic feet.

Then, while the well was blowing in and piling rocks and gravel on the derrick floor, and with the fire out in the boiler, the well had caught fire by lightning from a little thunderstorm. It had immediately turned the well into a hugh benzene burner with the base of the flame some twenty feet in the air and with the top some eighty or a hundred feet, nearly fifty feet above the top of the wooden derrick.

It didn't take long for the wooden derrick, floor and machine, all of which were oil soaked, to become a blazing mass of burning timber. It soon swallowed the derrick, the walking beam and the keg, as well as lighting the countryside for miles around during most of the night while we struggled, with help from two nearby machines, to quench it.

By daylight we had snuffed the gas fire and wooden remnants with steam and water from two boilers. Then we moved a little pulling unit and started running tubing to stop the flow of gas. That gas well kept a vapor of oil and a little water, coming from an upper formation, spraying in the air. It had turned the ground around the well into muck that was half knee deep and kept us well saturated while we were setting up the pulling unit.

Drenched, filthy, and with the smell of the burned derrick and machine—mixed with the odor of the salt water, oil and gas—constantly in our nostrils, we had paused to look up at a real low flying airplane. It was silvery in the early morning sunlight, with three engines and was flying so low we could see the pilots.

Evidently they had seen the fire the night before and, on their return trip from Tulsa, had decided to have a good look.

Their faces looked so white and clean and the silver plane looked spotless. I had looked up through an oil film and remarked: "That looks like real clean work. I think I'll change jobs!"

"And here I am," I mused, taking my eyes from those oil field flares and rubbing the soft seat arm while looking at the neat and clean cockpit. "Here I am, looking down at the derrick floors." I glanced at my clean uniform and smiled at the memory of that muck and the pulling unit.

We had to circle the Oklahoma City airport in a wide swing to give the cabin time to depressurize at an even and acceptable rate. But, it didn't matter, for we were twenty minutes ahead of schedule.

Mentally I was relieved at having won again. The knowledge that I had accurately gauged the enroute weather as highly dangerous, in spite of the forecasts to the contrary, gave me an inward glow of pleasure. I had flown it safely and given my passengers a good smooth ride on a route where another pilot had failed.

Truly, I felt sorry for Ellis. He was a nice guy and would have some explaining to do. But overloads, faulty equipment, irresponsible handling of flights by needless cancellations and misinformation to the public would continue to be ignored by Ellis and a number of his kind. Too large a number, I reflected gloomily, perferred to do that for a sense of job security, rather than give the public and themselves real safety by active support of a union where the number one objective was safety in flight. I shook my head with the thought.

The tandems kissed the Oklahoma City airport with a light and feathery touch as I permitted the nose to float high for a few seconds to taste that giddy sensation which came as our weight returned to earth.

Pulling the throttles rearward I reversed the props and with the brakes brought the plane to a slow roll. Propeller braking, truly a wonderful feature, I mused as I steered the nose wheel down a taxiway and swung the long fuselage gently and smoothly into a gate so as not to throw those passengers who, in spite of the warning signs and stewardesses, would be scrambling to deplane.

"Four and one-half hours," Len exclaimed, totalling the log book on his knee while I leaned out my side window and watched the woman with identical twins herd them down the ramp. An army captain met her at the bottom step with a long kiss and an arm for each twin. For her a long and much planned trip was speedily terminated. Twelve hundred miles in a few short hours of napping.

And another front lay behind me.

I utilized the extra time due to the early arrival to make out a couple of F-27 forms, interrupted flight reports, to the CAA, explaining the use of emergency authority in the high altitude flight and the emergency pressurization. They might be needed, I realized, but shook my head at the required red tape.

Len made the takeoff while I guarded the throttles, watched the engine gauges and handled the radio. Tom took care of the flaps and gear. It was a short flight of thirty minutes to Tulsa, during which we talked about flight forty nine.

The Oklahoma City agents had informed us that Ellis had hospitalized fifteen people at Amarillo in various stages of shock and injury. Terry, a cute little blond and semi-red headed stewardess with Ellis, had apparently broken her back, or rather, Ellis had broken it for her. The other stewardess had escaped with only minor injuries. In addition, an indeterminate amount of damage to the equipment in the heavy hail had been sustained. It was reported as being extensive.

Poor Terry! I recalled her sweet smile that always came with a cup of coffee. And I thought of the dangers, the suffering, and long convalescence period she might have to endure. The possibility of paralysis, a stiff back, a weak back and future trouble in later life passed through my mind. It was a tough break, and all because one pilot has made one little mistake! Or had the 'desk pilot' made it for him by insisting that he considered twenty thousand to be the best altitude to fly. Probably a cause of the blind leading the blind, I thought.

I handed Len a little folding money and asked him to wire Terry some flowers for me as I would be going on to New York and wouldn't have an opportunity until much later.

"Only if you'll do something for me." He grinned across the cockpit.

"Of course," I smiled.

"Then tell Mr. Behncke," he emphasized his point with a finger, "that there is only one way in which AA will ever give a mileage limitation, and that is to stop a pilots' strike."

"And Wayne," he pleaded, "will you do everything in your power to put that point over with him?"

I studied his lean and serious face and nodded slowly. Then I smiled. "You kids are always begging me to help you. When are you going to help me?"

"Wayne," he was dead serious, "you know there isn't a copilot on

Amalgamated who wouldn't swear that black was white for you. Name it and we'll do it!"

"I know," I laughed, "I was just joshing you. We all have to work together."

But that was probably true, I realized. And, in serving the copilots I had worked for the captains. There was no doubt but that I had done as much for the captains as for the copilots.

I thought of the many years I had served on various master executive councils and committees, as chairman, even as pilot representative on the System Board, as well as on three different contract negotiating committees. Oh yes, and there had been a couple of airline accident investigating committees.

Long years of pilot representative work flashed back to my mind. A union watch-dog, I was, constantly watching to bay at a company encroachment, or nipping at the heels of an official poaching on pilots' rights. Why had I done it? Why had I become involved with a labor union and made myself a target for company officials? I really did not know, and turned the question over once again in my mind. I carefully sought an answer.

Was it because I enjoyed conflict? No, I decided. That could not be the reason. I recalled the many times I had gone on pilot representative tasks with distaste. Just another dirty job to be done. And I was a "wheel-horse" as Len called me.

Was it because I wanted to help the pilots? Possibly that was a portion of the reason. A desire to promote fair play was, no doubt, a factor.

Was it because I wanted and believed in the principles of the union? Yes, I decided, that, too, might be a part of the reason. I thought of the pilots' union, the way Mr. Behncke had organized it, and, for months, ran it from the cockpit until a minor accident had made the pilots fearful of losing him. That was in 1932 and now it was composed of almost one hundred per cent membership on Amalgamated and other airlines within the United States, and had grown into an international organization.

Strictly a volunteer membership deal, it had drawn the strong and weak alike. Of course, a few of the weak were also "stool pigeons," but they were members and entitled to union protection as provided in the agreement between the company and the pilots' union. We could not exclude them.

Yes, the principles of the union were probably the real reason I had done so much union work, the main one, no doubt. In truth, it was like wading into a cold river. The first touch of the water was a shock, a real shock, as I had sustained the first time I uncovered a company dirty deal and realized that it was an intentional act on the part of the company official involved. Then as I worked deeper into the river, the colder it became, the dirtier the deals became until I met the company purchasing agent.

The thought of that meeting gave my mouth a green persimmon taste, even though it had occurred four years back. It was on the screening deal in 1947. The purchasing agent had been a brother pilot. He wanted to persuade me with the promise of company favors to permit the company to get rid of certain undesirable pilots. Of course this came after the company became aware of the fact that we had the company in violation of the Railway Labor Act and were going to push the issue.

The principles of the union! What were they? I thought of the first one, Schedule with Safety. It was a real jaw breaker. The company encroachments on that one were many, constant and devious in routings. I thought of the one old and one new tire on the left side. I thought of the constant stream of company petitions to the Civil Aeronautics Authority for greater loads for takeoff, more airplane and engine time between overhauls, lower landing and takeoff minimums. I stopped my thoughts at that point. Hell, there must be another side to the river, if I just kept wading!

An interesting thought—the other side of the cold river. When and where would it come? That I rolled around in my mind and decided it would come when Amalgamated met the pilots in the middle of the table on all issues. When the officials desired to administer fair play as much as the pilots desired to obtain fair play, and both groups sincerely desired to promote a company policy of scheduling with safety. Then I would be across the river. The thought provoked a thin smile.

Len's landing at Tulsa, just before the sun peeped over the eastern horizon, was very good and as we floated giddily down the runway with the nose wheel high in the air and the airplane settling gently on the tandems, Tom emitted a loud moan: "Oh Lord, please deliver me from Hot Pilot Heaven!"

Leaning out the left side window I carefully turned the plane into gate four at the terminal which was directly in front of the company's operation office. My gaze roved over the thirty or forty spectators. I noted the two out-going stewardesses standing neat and trim near the passenger gate.

Red headed Mary Schissler and a tall striking black haired girl, who was vaguely familiar, were the two. Both smiled at me and Mary gave me a little wave. I wondered where and when I had met the black haired one. Some place, I was sure. Mary had flown with me many times in the past two years.

Then I noticed George Schustman, the out-going pilot, standing outside the door to the Amalgamated operations office with his luggage. That was unusual. Normally he would wait inside, talk with the incoming crew, and then rush out to the plane a few minutes before departure time, secure in the knowledge that his efficient crew would have everything in order for departure. Something was wrong.

We unloaded down the front ramp, leaving my personal bag on the plane and hurried through the passenger gate. At Amalgamated's door I stopped at the corner of the building beside George with a smile and a nod of greeting.

He was a slim tow-headed man of medium height and age, near forty, with bright twinkling blue eyes, a quick smile, a quick nervous way of speaking and ready wit, combined with a Pennsylvania Dutch accent. The flight crews thought he was wonderful to fly with, especially the stewardesses. The company officials thought he was a nice guy, but badly misled by Allison. One had told him so!

"I checked you in," he greeted me with a quick smile, "here's your ticket, but I'll give you ten to stay home." His bright blue eyes left me and followed Mary Shissler and the black head as they went up the passenger ramp to the plane.

"Who is she?" I asked.

"My date tonight," he replied with a wistful smile.

"George," I gave him a serious look, "she's too tall for you."

"I brung my high heeled boots," he replied without a moment's hesitation, "and spurs too!"

I laughed. "Who's flying your trip back?"

"Jim Jewell, he's going as my copilot. New York is to furnish him a copilot for the return trip. Is the System Board meeting date still firm?"

I nodded and thought of Jim Jewell. He had filed a grievance several months back against Anderson for promoting a pilot junior to him at the Tulsa base. The case had come before the System Board and we had reached a decision more than a month back. It was a clear violation of seniority as provided in the contractual agreement between the company and the pilots' union. Dave Little, a company representative, had conceded it. Jim Jewell was to be paid for all the flying done by his junior. It amounted to over eight hundred dollars.

George Schustman and I were close friends and had been from the time we first met in the Army Air Corps flying school, eighteen years back. Drifting apart in Army Air Corps assignment, we had joined AA within a few months of each other. We had been based in New York and then Fort Worth as copilots, then back in New York and Boston as junior captains.

After that, and until its termination, WW II had kept us crisscrossing around the world. Now we were both based at Tulsa and had been since the close of the war. He resided in the city of Tulsa and I moved back to my home town of Claremore some twenty-five miles from the Tulsa airport.

Before the war, and during, there had been no pilot grievances. Right after the close of the war George and I were surprised to find that we were the two pilot representatives on the AA System Board of Adjustment with grievances coming in from the field. Now, several times a year we met with two company representatives to hear and decide the pilot grievances brought before the Board.

It was dirty work done for the pilots. In addition, I was on the contract negotiating committee. It was more dirty work, the dirtiest of the dirty!

Briefly I told George of the wire from Behncke and the conflicting dates. He listened closely and we both decided we would have to iron it out in New York.

"C.R.'s inside," he suddenly remembered and laughed. "He's surrounded by all the Tulsa officials, including Anderson. I'll bet they haven't been up this early in months."

He laughed again. "They're taking turns kissing his arse. It's so bad I had to get out of there for some fresh air."

"Oh brother!" I breathed deeply at the thought of the company president, C.R. Brown, being inside. "Think I'd better show my face inside?"

"Why not?" He countered. "Maybe they'll kiss that too. It don't look much different!"

We laughed together while our eyes spoke our contempt for the 'brown ringers' as the pilots called the type.

"Tom Boyson is inside too," he added. "He's traveling with C.R."

"Did you talk with him?"

"Of course!" He grinned. "Remember I was his copilot for almost a year in Stinson A's. He still thinks of me in that light. He says I'm a nice guy in bad company." He lit a cigarette.

"Well, well!" George exclaimed as Jimmie and Jackie passed with tired smiles and entered the operations door. "Now I'm not worried about you stealing my date. With them in 'Frisco, you can't have any boost left for New York!"

"We slept," I stated emphatically.

"I'd like to sleep with them too." He smiled.

I laughed at him. "Jackie says Jimmie snores."

"Does she?" George asked with a serious face.

"Not with me." I assured him.

Nonchalantly I entered the large operations office and dropped my flight kit in a corner. A long counter, similar to that found in stores, was located on the left of the door I entered. On my right the windows overlooked the ramp and a part of the public parking area. The space between the windows was used for company mail boxes for the individual flight crew members.

Past the windows, several chairs, a large table with a miscellaneous collection of books, manuals and briefing folders, together with a bulletin board, occupied one corner. It was all conveniently arranged in a crew lounge. Beyond that, doors led to the various offices, ticket counter, and lobby. It was in the vicinity of the table and lounging chairs that C.R. and his 'yes-men' had congregated into a small informal group. I was conscious of their close scrutiny as I dropped my flight kit and turned toward them.

C.R. was a tall, dark, heavily built man with heavy jowls and a bulging waistline. A rather large, protruding hooked nose that narrowed considerably at the bridge seemed to accent the closeness of his piercing black eyes. Behind, a very sharp and piercing mind raced with apparently effortless speed.

He was a protege of E.L. Cord who had lost in a conflict with the pilots of Century Airline in 1931 and 1932. The pilots of Century, represented by the Air Line Pilots' Association, had, with David L. Behncke as president, put the airline out of business and forced Cord to sell the remnants. That loss had not been lost on C.R. Brown.

Elected president of Amalgamated in 1934, C.R. had lost no time in merging several small companies, with E.L. Cord's backing, into a sizable airline. He successfully imbued each pilot and each employee with the idea that Amalgamated was "their company" and that they must build it. He harped on the theme that no rule and no regulation could or should supersede the use of good common horse sense. And that line worked! The pilots especially liked it. They hated restrictive regulations. It was enough having to put up with some of the CAA's asinine regulations.

C.R. was quick to enter any controversy, large or small, and was equally quick in dispensing justice. A pat on the back here, a quiet rebuke there, and a constant reminder that we were building an airline and that "we gotta take them where they wanta go to collect the dough," did wonders with the employee morale. It was his theme song and it fired the imagination of all.

The pilots were particularly responsive. They began rolling them. Rain, hail, ice, snow and storms of any proportion soon became well acquainted with the Amalgamated pilots. It was their airline, their future, and they were building it.

Once in Nashville, in very bad weather, an incoming pilot was asked what the ceiling was when he came in. "Hell," he had snorted, "I had four passengers for Nashville and I wasn't measuring the ceiling, I was landing."

They flew for over five years without a single passenger fatality.

About the time I came with Amalgamated in the early part of 1936, the airline was just beginning to throb. I could feel it the first day. It was a fascinating feeling.

The engineer behind the scenes, lining up the deals, making the shrewd calculations, figuring where C.R. should step in, coaching him where he should pound a little, when he should buy new equipment and where, was Ralph Damon, the vice-president.

He set the stage for C.R. He rigged the deals. He was the dynamotor behind the light.

C.R. signed the first labor contract of any airline with the pilots of Amalgamated. That was in 1938 and it was a good labor contract. But it meant very little, at the time there were no grievances and few gripes. Anything could be settled quickly, by walking into the official's office who had jurisdiction over the problem, putting your feet on his desk, along with his, and talking it out. Horse sense was all that was discussed on the issue.

Then the war, WW II, came on, and AA went to war. C.R. was one of the first to go. He went in on the ground floor, as a full colonel, compliments of the Army Air Corps. They wanted him to organize a transport system.

C.R. organized the Air Transport Command. Of course AA obtained ample transport contracts to all parts of the world. By a strange coincidence, only a small percent of airline pilots were ordered back to active duty, and those without commissions did not have a chance for military duty as pilots. But all could fly in the Air Transport command as civilians, and the companies they represented would make ten percent profit on their salaries. It was a cozy deal, and it worked.

It worked because the airline pilots made it work. They delivered the goods. To all parts of the world, in and out of war zones, in all kinds of weather, they pushed the Air Transport Command airplanes to the remote corners of the earth. They flew as civilians, clay pigeons for any trigger-happy gunner, imbued with only one thought—there was a war to win!

Their work made C.R. a general.

And it gave him another star.

All this flashed through my mind as I stepped forward and extended my hand.

"Well," I exclaimed, "how are you, Mr. C.R.?"

He took my hand in a grudging sort of way. I wondered if my hand felt as cold and clammy to him as his did to me.

"Going to New York, sir?" I inquired courteously.

"South!" he grunted.

"Oh, heck!" I complained. "I was in hopes you were going east to sign the contract tomorrow with Mr. Behncke. Just a few minor points to be ironed out, you know."

He gave me a thin smile. We both knew quite well that not one major point had been settled. And he seemed to appreciate the humor of my remark for he followed the smile with a little snort.

"It would already be signed," he grumbled, "if you hardheads didn't want so much money."

It was my turn to smile in appreciation of his humor. We both knew that working conditions, rules, an automatic neutral for the System Adjustment Board, and the mileage limitation were the big points at issue. For once, the dollar was crowded to one side at the bargaining table.

My eyes dropped to Tom Boyson standing beside C.R. He was much smaller than either of us, about five feet eight inches in height, dark-haired with light blue eyes, a crooked nose, leathery skin, and ears that appeared to have a cowlick characteristic.

A big pipe was gripped in one side of his mouth. He had the odd habit of chewing on the pipe, starting to speak in a slow and reluctant manner, removing the pipe from his mouth, and then launching into rapid fire speech. I had often wondered why he didn't toss the damned smelly thing away. It was quite apparent to me that he had not learned to talk with it in his mouth.

With a rather strange feeling I extended my hand to Tom Boyson, assistant to the president. We had first met in 1936 at Newark when I started flying out of Boston as a copilot for Amalgamated Airlines. He had also gone through the army flying school, a couple of years ahead of me, and it gave us something to talk about after the introduction. Yet, I had had a strange feeling about him from the very start.

Perhaps it was his light blue eyes in contrast to his dark hair, frosted eyes, that never appeared to meet a friend. Perhaps it was the fact that he had just been promoted to first pilot and was already looking at the chief pilot's desk. Anyway, I tried hard to like him and only succeeded in neutralizing any feeling of dislike that I may have had. So, I had started off neither liking or disliking Tom Boyson, an attitude that remained for a number of years, until the termination of World War II.

It didn't take the other pilots long to see Tom's ambitions. He had been a fawning, boot-licking, ass-kissing, but highly efficient copilot. Naturally, most of them had disliked him. Then, when after being promoted, he began cultivating the chief pilot and other officials by constantly offering to do extra work, such as checking copilots, fixing maps, running errands, and making himself useful by doing any dirty work that would curry a little favor with an official, the pilots started talking. They began making dirty cracks in Tom's vicinity. Maybe that was why I tried to like him for I could see nothing wrong with a pilot being ambitious. For me, I wanted to fly!

Within a month after our introduction, I found that we were dating the same company secretary. To put it more truthfully, I began to date the cute little blond secretary he had been going around with periodically and semi-seriously for nearly two years. That spurred him to action and he doubled his attention to Betty Kelton, the secretary.

At the same time, my flying out of the Boston base doubled. I stopped getting any of the nice day trips to Newark from my base in Boston, trips with long layovers in Newark and opportunities to invite a secretary out to lunch. Soon I became acquainted with the dirty night trips that only paused briefly in Newark and never during the office hours. It slowed me down.

Then it happened. Maybe it was my change of pace that did it for I can still remember my grandfather cautioning me that a fast dog always ran over a lot of quail. Maybe it was the fact that Betty got wind of the deal and decided to torture him a little, for she learned that he was fixing my schedule through his friend, the chief pilot.

So she suddenly took her vacation and visited an aunt, who lived most conveniently in Boston. Naturally that made her most convenient to me, too.

After a week, Tom could stand it no longer, and, on a day off, purchased a ticket to Boston. Of course he had arranged me a day schedule that day through his friend, Walt, the chief pilot. All I could do was loan Betty my car to drive Tom around on a scenic tour of Boston.

This I did quite willingly, cautioned Betty that Tom was likely coming to propose, wished her the best of luck, and went out in a carefree manner on my arranged schedule. It hadn't occurred to me that she wasn't looking for Tom's proposal. After all, Tom was a first pilot.

That night I learned that I had been correct about the purpose of Tom's trip to Boston. It jolted me considerably when Betty told how he had proposed, how she had gently refused and that was that. I was number one!

Two weeks later I was transferred to Fort Worth, Texas, and I married Betty Kelton enroute. She had resigned her job that morning, packed her bags, and was ready by noon. It was a real surprise to everyone, including me, for only a few knew that I was in the running, including me.

Then for months thereafter the pilots coming in contact with Tom would start singing "somebody stole my gal—and took her away." They made it pretty rough on him because his popularity hadn't improved any, and, apparently they thought I was okay. It really hurt him, according to Schustman who was flying with him at the time.

"It hurt his pride mostly," he insisted. "Tom loves only Tom."

In a short time Tom was offered an assistant chief pilot's job with Walt Braznell. According to the pilots' version he ran over two passengers and a baby carriage getting upstairs to accept the position. Anyway, he beat everyone else to the position, regardless of his lack of experience as a first pilot. And the pilots began paying for their promiscuous singing.

Tom later married a United stewardess and then went into the war as a captain and C.R.'s right hand man. That role he rode to a full colonel and back to Amalgamated as "assistant to the president."

Then, in 1946, after years of casual, friendly greetings, chance meetings at military bases, overseas and in the states, we were both back flying for Amalgamated, or rather, I was back flying and Tom was "assisting the president." But in a short while we had locked horns, on the Pilots' System Board of Adjustment. He was representing the company and I was representing the pilots.

Up until that time there had been no grievances on Amalgamated, nothing that could not be talked out with an official. Suddenly Amalgamated fired twelve pilots who had been sent to a company school at Ardmore, Oklahoma, supposedly for equipment familiarization. But when they returned home after completing the course they received letters of discharge.

Seven of the twelve pilots whose services were abruptly terminated, filed grievances that took several months to reach the System Board. Tom and another company official represented the company. Schustman and I represented the pilots. The battle started in early 1947 and went through the entire year.

Tom's pale blue eyes snapped my mind from the past and I could not help but marvel at the way he shook my hand with a warmness that was almost genuine. Yet I knew that he hated me with an intensity that was only betrayed by the way he bit at that pipe stem. And, from the pages of his guide book, he had every right to hate me. Of that I was certain, and I could not keep from admiring the way he covered his real feelings. He was a much better actor then C.R. who had just finished shaking my hand with difficulty.

"How's the family, Tom?" I met his frosted blue eyes and shook his hand warmly. His family had long been a laughing matter to the company employees. Tom and his wife had finally given up having any children of their own and had adopted two little boys. Then his wife, a few months later, had presented him with twins, both boys!

"How's Betty?" Tom chewed his pipe and asked in return. I felt an inward sense of guilt when I replied that she was fine and both our children were well. At the same time I wondered if Tom knew of the divorce and was gently shafting me.

I had learned that Tom had what I termed as an "automatic angle computing brain." Each time his jaw clamped his pipe, his mind circled the entire horizon about three times. A deadly foe I well knew.

My eyes drifted to the six men flanking the 'big wheels.' Three were important maintenance men from the modification center across the field, so named because of its wartime activity, which had been taken over by Amalgamated and made into an overhaul base. I nodded to big, fat, bald and apple-polishing Andy Williams, the Tulsa station manager.

Beside him was a tall, grey-headed, lantern-jawed Don Ogden, a one time darling of Louisiana State University's football squad. He was chief pilot over the Dallas-Fort Worth division and was Anderson's immediate superior. As copilots we had flown out of Fort Worth on the same runs, with the same captains, in the same weather. Although we had never been friends, we had respected each other as copilots. As captains my reputation had rapidly surpassed his in regard to weather flying. Then he sought the haven of a comfortable desk job about the start of WW II where he remained throughout the war. Rumors from copilots credited him with fearing to be alone at night in God's Heavens, among thunderstorms that few pilots really understood.

Our eyes met, our hands met, our lips exchanged courteous greetings while two old football players sized up each other's physique. At the same time I wondered if he knew that his hips were spreading, his stomach beginning to bulge from under his belt, and his shoulders beginning to droop. It was funny I reflected, how quickly 'aerodynamic drag' built itself into a 'desk-pilot.'

"Hi, Joe," I spoke easily to Anderson, the short, swarthy, black curly haired man of near my age. His temples were gray with a distinguished look which was spoiled by the surly expression he habitually wore. His smile, if and when it came, was tight, thin-lipped and brief, which gave me the feeling that I had watched him shift the knife into his right hand.

Mentally I braced myself for the thrust as his smile was only a shadow under his heavy scowl. Three years back, when he first came to Tulsa as a supervisory pilot under Odgen, I had learned that he hated me with a real passion. Why, I did not know.

"How's the weather?" Joe questioned.

"So-so," I shrugged. "The weather never bothers me—it's the women that trouble me," I laughed, wondering if any knew of my divorce.

"Did you hear about Ellis?" he questioned.

"I heard him," I corrected. With tight lips I added significantly. "I heard about Terry and a plane full of injured passengers."

"How was the weather?" He repeated.

He's parrying for the thrust. I told myself with the knowledge that the group was paying very close attention to his question. But, that didn't surprise me considering that I had just come over Amarillo.

"All instruments from Fresno to Oklahoma City," I replied. Long ago I had learned to tell him as little as possible.

"Was it bad?" A slow coloring darkened his features.

"We didn't have any trouble," I added.

A quick thought occurred to me that he might be after Ellis and, if so, I could hang or save Ellis by my answer. If I said the weather was not very bad, as the condition of my airplane, passengers, and an on schedule arrival would indicate, then the company was in excellent position to severely discipline Ellis, even discharge him. And then I, as a 'wheel-horse' for the pilots union, would justify the company's action to the union.

It was a beautiful play, I grudgingly admitted to myself, and one I knew Joe had not thought out. Then C.R. or Tom must be the real adversary.

But why was the knife pointed at Ellis? He was harmless to the company and quite helpful when they wanted to use him. All they had to do was give his string a little pull.

Then the knife was really pointed at me. They were just making it appear that it was aimed at Ellis. C.R. didn't dagger 'loyal company employees' as he had once referred to two pilots out on the contract negotiation.

It had taken me months to expose the deal to the pilots of AA. Then C.R. had made them both assistant chief pilots, blood brother to Anderson, and Ogden's assistants. Thereafter the pilots had laughingly referred to them as Judas one and two. However, they had tolerated them as officials, even treated them decently. It had been hard for me to understand.

"Was it bad?" Anderson repeated. I sensed that this was a key question and felt a little buzzer warning in the back of my head. Anderson frequently, in past years, had set it off.

"I'll back up Ellis," I smiled and shrugged. "If he says it was bad, I'll buy that. If he says it was not too bad, I'll buy that too." I knew that Ellis could do nothing but claim bad weather, very bad weather.

"He had an emergency." Joe admitted. "Did you?"

"Of course!" I replied, smiling as I side-stepped the flashing blade that I could feel rather than see. Then for good measure I added, "I had two of them!" Their plan, I could now see was to get me to claim a normal trip and then torpedo me with my reported altitude to the CAA.

"Two?" Joe was puzzled as well as disappointed with my reply. I thought I could hear the knife clatter on the floor. He was not a good poker player.

"Oh sure!" I blandly replied. "I had two men in the cockpit with me and I had two girls in the cabin. It seemed fitting that I should have two emergencies at the same time."

I made the crack knowing that Jackie, Jimmie, Len, and Tom were collected around the mail boxes, appearing to be busy with their mail, but in reality listening to every word spoken. I could feel their mental support. Even Ogden managed a thin smile. I had the feeling that he didn't care too much for Joe.

"Maybe you'd better explain it." Joe tried to sound very officious.

"It's all contained herein." I pulled a letter airily from my inside coat pocket and handed it to him. "We had to go a little over twenty-three thousand feet. If you'll have your secretary type it up I'll sign it for the CAA."

"How high did you go?" He never looked at the letter and I knew that he knew the answer as well as I did.

"Thirty-one thousand!" I replied easily.

"Thirty-one thousand!" He tried to sound shocked. "Then what was your cabin altitude?" The second question came so quickly that I knew it had been prepared ahead.

"Under twelve thousand." I waved a hand nonchalantly and side-stepped the knife again. CAA regulations firmly forbade taking passenger above twelve thousand, cabin altitude.

"Impossible!" Joe exclaimed angrily. He turned to a maintenance official for verification. "At thirty-one thousand, Sam, what would the cabin altitude be?"

Sam frowned and appeared to think carefully, "Seventeen or eighteen thousand," he replied.

"Mine was under twelve," I insisted.

"Impossible," Joe snapped.

"Look, Mr. C.R.," I smiled at Mr. Brown, "if you'll cancel this flight or trade airplanes here at the ramp I'll show these too well-informed company officials that this airplane will climb to thirty-one thousand feet with a cabin altitude of only twelve thousand. If I fail, I will reimburse the company for double the amount of the revenue lost. And," I added significantly, "if these two officials are equally sure of their knowledge, then they should not object to reimbursing the company for double the revenue lost should I succeed. How about it. Joe?"

Joe hesitated.

"That's out of the question!" C.R. cut in hurriedly. It was clear that this conversation wasn't going as expected.

"How do you explain it?" C.R. asked.

"It's all contained in the letter." I waved my hands and shrugged. "That was the second emergency. I shifted the cabin pressurization to manual, operated the cabin superchargers at maximum output and utilized the emergency authorized pressurization for four point six instead of the normal four point two."

Joe looked stunned.

"But that might rupture the cabin and cause explosive decompression." He hung on like a bulldog.

"The Douglas manual of operation, accepted and approved by AA, says the airplane has been tested at four point six and is safe to use at that pressurization in an emergency. It is all contained in my letter of declaration of an emergency to the CAA," I smiled at Joe.

"Why didn't you turn around and back out of that kind of weather?" Joe still hung grimly to his purpose.

"You gotta take them where they want to go if you expect to collect the dough," I quoted C.R.'s most famous expression, and at the same time winked at Mr. Brown.

Inside I was suddenly laughing. They had been so sure I would proclaim the trip to be a normal one to give the company grounds to criticize Ellis, a pro-company pilot. In so doing, they expected me to trap myself. It was a neat trick and it had taken more than Joe to think of it. They were such a nice bunch of bastards!

"Thanks for the waltz, Joe." I smiled, knowing that everyone there, including my crew who seemed to be having trouble getting their mail from their boxes, knew what I was saying.

Chapter 4

The Low Road

Picking up another traveling bag, which I had previously left in the corner of operations for the occasion, I rushed out the door toward flight forty-eight going to New York. Sending my bag up the front loading belt, on the tail end of the other luggage and mail, I then crossed under the airplane to climb the passenger ramp like a normal passenger. Jimmie met me at the bottom of the ramp. On some pretext she had hurried back out and boarded the plane for one brief minute and then descended casually to meet me as I started up the ramp.

"Wayne," her dark eyes were starry bright and shifting at the usual half second intervals. She was breathing a little deeply from the exertion, "It was wonderful!"

"What happened after I left?" I questioned rapidly.

"Nothing. Mr. Brown just looked hard at Mr. Boyson, then at Mr. Ogden, then at Mr. Anderson and then turned and walked into the breakfast dining room. He didn't say a word—just acted real disgusted with them."

I whistled softly, and whispered, "Thanks, Jimmie, you have told me a lot."

"Will you be back for our next trip?"

"I doubt it." I shook my head regretfully.

"Then I'll trade a trip and come to New York" She gave me a glimpse of those ivory white teeth as she moved away.

Thoughtfully I climbed the passenger ramp and stooped a little to enter the cabin door. Mary stood at the door with her clipboard listing of passengers held close to her breast.

Her soft brown eyes surveyed me carefully while a slight breeze touched the light red hair blossoming from under the pert airline cap.

"My name's Goldberg." I informed her in broken English. "Did Mr. Brown tell you to save a special seat for me?"

I saw the freckles on her nose draw slightly from the smile. "Yes, Mr. Goldbrick," she laughed. "Take the double opposite the buffet."

It was my favorite seat for dead-heading and most of the Tulsa girls knew it. I wondered if Mary liked for me to sit where I could watch her shapely figure while she worked. Anyway, turn about seemed like fair play. Several times she had been up front and watched me nurse a DC-6 out of a bad spot.

"Did Mr. Brown tell you to give me special attention? I practically own Amalgamated, you know," I continued in my broken English.

"Sit down!" She ordered. "You look just like a wolf to me." She laughed that little subdued laugh of hers.

I was asleep by the time we started the takeoff run. Yet as the plane gained speed I awoke, listened intently to the beat of the engines, felt the plane skip lightly on its tandems, then float. George had a light load that morning, no moaning and groaning on the takeoff. I glanced out the window and saw the modification center flash by, knew the end of the runway was behind and listened to the engines settle down to climb power as he pulled the reins on the four hard running horses. I sighed and dropped back into slumber. The plush cushions felt awfully good right then.

Mary was sitting beside me knitting when I awakened. I surveyed her through half-closed lids for several minutes. Her nimble fingers were moving so fast I could not follow and I raised my head to get a better look at the knitting.

She gave me an appraising look. "Well, Mr. Goldbrick," she smiled, "are you ready for your breakfast? You have been sleeping soundly for over an hour. All the passengers have been fed and we are still keeping yours warm."

Yawning, I decided that I'd better eat.

"George wants to see you," she added.

"Then would you serve me up front?"

She nodded, arose, and moved to the buffet.

Standing up, I brushed my uniform coat and proceeded up the long fuselage, catching a little of the idle chatter of passengers leisurely enjoying a smooth flight. Some, I could see, had been on the plane all night, and, unknown to them, had been with us at thirty-one thousand feet. I smiled at what they might say if told that during the night they had ridden through the top of a tornado nearly six miles above the earth.

Stopping in the men's lounge, I combed my unruly hair and washed the sleep from my face. I reflected on the many problems involved in the installation and operation of those washbasins with hot and cold running water on an airplane that wandered from sea level and a temperature of over a hundred degrees to nearly six miles high and low temperature of sixty degrees below zero. I spoke courteously to the one man using an electric razor before the large mirror and wondered if he had any knowledge of the razor's source of power. Probably never gave it a thought, I reflected.

Spinning the combination lock to the door of the pilot's compartment, I stepped into the eight foot hallway between the cargo and baggage bins. It was a lot of airplane to be tied to your seat belt, to lift gently into the air, to wheel through a violent thunderstorm, and to ease back upon Mother Earth with the same care one would handle an infant. Truly a multimillion dollar corporation on the move. And entrusted to the care of one man!

Marty, George's engineer, quickly offered me his seat and I sat down a foot to the rear and midway between the two pilots. It was a favorite with the stewardesses when they could spare a little time to sightsee.

Marty moved back onto a straight backed chair that latched in the hallway about two feet behind the engineer's seat. George motioned for Jim Jewell, the copilot, to take the controls, turned slightly in his seat and lit cigarettes for himself and me while my eyes naturally roved the instrument panels. Suddenly I stared at the panel. "How long has that cabin supercharger been out?" I questioned.

"It was out when we started the engine." George grinned. "I just thought that you burned it up fanning your arse above that Amarillo tornado."

"Oh, brother—!" I laughed.

Then I told them about the episode in the Tulsa operations office and the proposed wager. We all laughed over how red my face would have been had my offer been accepted, and I had found myself attempting to supercharge the cabin to four point six pounds at extremely high altitude with only one cabin supercharger. It would have been an impossibility.

Jim Jewell was a tall, sturdy built blond with a fullback's physique, a square jaw, and piercing blue eyes. He spread a big hand across the four throttles and gave them a minor adjustment, then turned his head fleetingly from the instrument panels to look me full in the face.

"I never had a chance to thank you and George for that decision on my case." He spoke slowly, then swung his eyes back to the instruments.

"Forget it." We both laughed. "Thank the company official who agreed with us."

Jim had been with Amalgamated for over eight years, during the last two he had been a reserve pilot subject to call as either a captain or copilot, depending on the company's need. A regular captain flew only as a captain.

The reserve pilot was the in-between man, drawing his pay for each flight in conformity with the seat he occupied in the cockpit: captain's pay when in the left seat, copilot's pay when in the right seat. System seniority was the determining factor on the flights a captain or a reserve pilot flew. It was a right guaranteed by the labor agreement between the company and the pilots, as represented by the Air Line Pilots' Association.

In Jim's case, the company had moved another reserve pilot into Tulsa who was junior to Jim, yet Anderson had assigned the captain reserve flying out of Tulsa to him. It was an out and out violation of the seniority provisions of the agreement. Quite plainly to the pilots, it was a 'fair-haired' deal!

Jim had endured the financial penalty imposed by Anderson for several months. Finally he filed his grievance, but it took over three months to be heard because company officials employed their usual dilatory tactics. When the grievance reached the System Board, George and I forced a prompt hearing.

A minor and obscure company official appointed to the Adjustment Board by Amalgamated, had voted with George and me. After the two opposing attorneys had argued for half a day, that official had stated quite simply that being on the pilots' seniority list was a privileged right that guaranteed 'fair play' rather than 'fair-haired' treatment.

When we signed the decision, it was binding on both the company and the pilots. Mr. C.R. couldn't change it, Mr. Behncke couldn't change it, and no court in the land would change it. It very effectively nailed down system seniority on Amalgamated.

The System Board of Adjustment decision was all powerful because in 1938 both the president of Amalgamated and the president of the Air Line Pilots' Association had signed contractual obligations covering the pilots System Board of Adjustment. It was continuous and had remained unchanged to date, in spite of numerous company attempts to modify it.

The decision had meant nearly a thousand dollars to Jim Jewell. To Amalgamated it meant paying two captains for the same flight, a loss of nearly a thousand dollars, and a discouragement to future abusive practices. To the pilot group it meant a far-reaching precedent that would likely guarantee future decisions on like cases, should they arise. To George and me it meant another victory for the pilots.

Mary brought everyone coffee, together with my breakfast. She leaned against my chair and smoked a cigarette while I ate. Suddenly George turned to Mary. "Have you fixed me up with the new girl back there?"

"Oh, sure!" Mary smiled. "I explained that you are the bashful type, that you want to take her out to dinner tonight, and that you just cannot get up enough courage to ask her yourself."

"That's right, that's right!" George nodded his approval.

"Also," Mary continued. "I told her that you are only married in Oklahoma, that your wife doesn't understand you, and in a very short while you will likely be available in all forty-eight states."

"Yup, yup, yup!" George chortled and rubbed his hands together in anticipation. "And don't forget to tell her that Allison is up for bigamy!"

"You will be too," Mary cautioned, laughing, "if you ever find a girl that takes you seriously."

George took the controls and started the big plane downward toward a Nashville landing. I chatted with Jewell a few minutes and then followed Mary back in to the cabin. There I relaxed with a second cup of coffee while I watched Mary and the new girl, June Tabler, clean up the buffet, answer passenger calls, and prepare the deplaning passengers for the Nashville arrival.

Finally Mary settled in the seat beside me with her knitting. I talked with her about Terry, the injured stewardess now in an Amarillo hospital. Terry and Mary were roommates, close friends, and they usually flew together. Mary had traded for this New York trip simply to accommodate another girl who had a boyfriend in San Francisco, the stewardess with Ellis who was unhurt.

Mary's nimble fingers hesitated in her knitting and she glanced shyly at me. "Wayne," she spoke very low, "I read of your divorce."

I shrugged. "Actually," I explained, "I moved out over a year ago and quietly settled everything as quickly as possible. That notice in the paper listed it as a divorce, but actually, it was the finalization of that divorce which started a year ago. I am free to remarry should I desire."

The fingers were nimble again on the knitting as she silently kept her eyes on her work. I knew she sensed my pain.

"Dinner with me tonight, as usual?" I asked airily.

She gave me a sweet little smile and a nod of acceptance.

Deplaning at Nashville I found Wylie Drummond and a couple of the Nashville-based Amalgamated pilots waiting for me at the gate. They knew I was on George's plane and wanted to see us both. George had seen them from the cockpit and joined us.

Wylie Drummond was the Nashville chairman. Near thirty, tall and slender, he had proven himself to be very articulate and a shrewd leader. "What about the flight allocation grievances," he wanted to know, "has the resumption of the contract negotiations delayed that?"

George and I both shook our heads at the same time.

"We'll have them as scheduled starting Wednesday and probably going through Thursday," I explained. "There are too many pilots wanting a showdown with the company on those flight allocations problems, and they are coming to New York to sit in on those hearings."

Wylie and Wes Kingsbury, another pilot, nodded with instant approval. They stressed the necessity of having those hearings as soon as possible.

They insisted that pilots all over the system were upset at the way the company had been jumping the flight time from one base to another. Their thought was that the company was just doing it to harass the pilots. They were pretty hot about it.

Back on the airplane I was sleepy and promptly dropped off into another nap. This time, the takeoff did not awaken me, and for another hour, I slumbered.

The lurching of the airplane finally caused me to rise and take a look around. Outside the window all was fog and rain. The seat belt sign was on and I noted that the girls were having difficulty moving around. Mary dropped into the seat beside me.

"George says it is going to get pretty darned rough, says that he cannot get above it with only one cabin supercharger." She smiled a little tightly, "and we have four men in the lounge who are all first riders. They're scared to death. Would you give them the treatment?"

"For a cup of coffee," I bargained.

"That's part of your equipment along with the uniform you are wearing," she reminded me.

Balancing a cup of coffee in my hand, I made may way slowly and carefully to the rear lounge where four men were huddled in their seats, their belts at tight as the saddle girdle on a bucking horse. It was quite evident from their tense faces that the turbulence had them spooked; the big plane was tossing rather roughly. I knew that George was having to do a little wrestling on the controls.

I seated myself in the one vacant seat in the circular group, nodded pleasantly to all, balanced my coffee precariously, and in between the bumps, I sipped it. Years of experience had taught me how to balance that cup of coffee, and the four men couldn't keep their eyes off it. I wasn't spilling a drop and was actually drinking the coffee.

With my other hand I picked up a magazine, spread it on my lap, and studied it intently. Finally, in a preoccupied manner, I latched my seat belt with one hand and continued reading, balancing the coffee and sipping it occasionally. I felt their eyes studying me, my uniform, and my coffee. They couldn't understand my carefree manner.

I would liked to have talked with them, reassured them with words, but that was not in the 'treatment.' Words would not impress the way careless actions do.

"It's getting kinda rough, isn't it, Captain?" one of them ventured.

I glanced up from the magazine, smiled, turned a page, and answered in a preoccupied manner: "A little—not bad." It was obvious that I was intently viewing the picture of a pretty girl.

Finishing my coffee, I stuck the cup in a magazine holder. It was so rough by this time that the "no smoking" sign had been turned on by the flight crew. That was the signal for the stewardesses to get into their seats belts. So I turned a few more pages before beginning to nod off to sleep.

Increasingly I found it hard to hold my head up. Each rough bump would snap my head around, and I would sleepily look at the magazine for another minute or so before dropping off again. After each rough bump I would frown slightly and try to find a little more comfortable position in the seat. It was quite evident that I was only irritated with the turbulence because it was keeping me from a nap.

Finally I gave up completely, pushed the magazine to one side, and appeared to drop off to sleep with my head cradled on my shoulder. With my body relaxed, I allowed it to roll and swing with the motion of the plane. To all who could observe me, I was sound asleep.

"It don't seem to be bothering him," one of the four men cautiously observed. "He's sound asleep."

"Hell," another remarked, "I thought the airplane was about to come apart about the time he went to sleep. How does he do it?"

"I guess he knows what he's doing," another ventured. "Look at those stripes on his sleeve. He should know when to get scared."

"Then what are we worried about?" One of the four laughed nervously. "If it doesn't keep him from going to sleep, then surely it can't be very bad. Do you think we can go on with the card game?"

So for thirty minutes I appeared to be sound asleep, and actually did nap some. Occasionally I stirred slightly to seek a more comfortable position while the plane tossed and wallowed along. Now and then I peeped a little at the four men who had decided to continue their card game.

They began to have fun holding their cards down, watching the bumps and cautioning each other about losing their false teeth. Others in the seats ahead soon noticed that they were playing cards, heard an occasional laugh from the rear, and they too, decided that it could not be so bad.

Chapter 5

The Converging Roads

George made an on schedule mid-afternoon arrival in New York. I walked down the passenger ramp with him thinking about what the airplane had gone through in one transcontinental flight. I had flown half of it, dead-headed the other half, and here I was in New York feeling pretty good.

In the company operations department we met Shipley and his wife Nat, his second to be exact. The first one had given him twins, then wanted her freedom back. So he gave her that freedom and kept the twins. He even gave her some operating capital.

Shipley was a screwball in every a sense of the word. He was quite different from the ordinary run of pilots. His brain never seemed to tire, and he loved problems, especially two legged ones. Once fired over a minor infraction of a no smoking rule, he had been subsequently reinstated by ALPA pressure from Mr. Behncke.

Before his discharge Shipley had worked full time at developing a mystic-psychology on the stewardesses. In other words, he was a skirt-chaser. But he took good care of that pair of twin girls. From the age of two he fed them, clothed them, and made tomboys of them until they were nine when he met Nat.

After his reinstatement he only devoted half of his time to the stewardesses. The other half he devoted to ALPA problems. Not satisfied with an ALPA council that had become weak and ineffective, Shipley threw his hat in the ring for council chairman of Amalgamated's large New York council. Since not many pilots were interested in the job he was elected.

Thereafter he announced to small groups of pilots and individuals as he found them, that about half the pilot council was going to lose its union cards unless certain individuals did not immediately stop ass-kissing and stool-pigeoning to company officials. He named no names but indicated that he would have a complete list of them at the next council meeting.

Needless to say, he had a good turnout at the next meeting. Also, he had a list, a substantial number of pilots names were on the sheet which he kept waving around while making a real good speech. He did not permit anyone to see the list, but by the time he had finished speaking, half of those in attendance were pretty certain that they were on that list. They really did not want it read.

Shipley, in his speech, insisted that he was going to be a chairman of a strong airline pilots union or a strong company union. He wanted no half and half outfits. Then he insisted on a vote in writing, with signatures. And he had printed forms available. Of course, all were members of the Air Line Pilots' Association which had a charter from the AF of L but he made them vote on it again, in writing.

Within two weeks he had turned the New York council around into a strong prounion council. In a short time, an increasing number of pilots were wearing their ALPA lapel buttons on their uniform coats. Shipley was suddenly the undisputed chairman of a council that had developed a passion for union loyalty and a thirst for hunting 'stool-pigeons.'

I thought of all this as I stood beside Schustman in the New York operations office and watched Shipley striding toward us with a firm and purposeful stride, while his tall and long-legged wife, Natalie, broke into a trot to keep up. With one hand she held a hat firmly on her head and with the other she clung determinedly to Shipley's arm, at the same time exclaiming in a laughing voice: "Throttle back, Des, before I soar out of my girdle." Des was a short version of Desmond, his first name.

Natalie was almost as tall as Shipley, who was five feet ten inches tall, with large feet attached to her long legs. Her blue eyes, so bright and friendly, girlish grin, ready wit, and sharp, fast-thinking brain soon convinced any new acquaintance that here was a woman whom no man could fool for long.

Nat had first met Shipley in her father's law office in New York City where he was a prominent attorney specializing in labor cases. She had practically grown up there, and after college, had settled into doing legal research for her father. Evidently Shipley realized that here was quite a woman, for he promptly invited her to lunch. From that luncheon, he never left the trail. In three months they were married. Although there were twenty years' difference in their ages, and a good hundred in experience, he promptly started including her in all his thinking, and in everything he did.

I shook hands warmly with Shipley, noting his tanned boyish face, his firm grip, impish grin, youthful figure in spite of his forty-five years, and probed his clear eyes to catch a glimpse of that spinning gyroscopic brain.

"Hi, Georgie," Shipley slapped his former copilot fondly on the shoulder. "Grab your bags," he ordered. "You're both coming out to the house for the night."

"No can do, Ship." I spoke firmly. "The ol'man, Behncke, has called a special meeting of the negotiating committee for tonight, and he asked me to have George attend." It was always difficult to keep from visiting the Shipleys. They both were so very hospitable.

Finally he was content to shoot a few rapid fire questions about the new contract meeting, the probable reason, and the schedule of the system board hearing. We could tell him only the schedule of the hearing. I didn't have the faintest idea what had reactivated the negotiations.

Ship wanted as much information as possible so he could issue a memorandum to all his members and make certain that we had a healthy attendance at the system board hearings. Long ago when George and I had sat through weeks of hearings at various bases, relative to C.R.'s famous 'captain's elimination boards,' later renamed the 'screening board,' we had learned that a good turnout of pilots for each hearing convinced company officials of the pilot interest and discouraged any fast deals at the hearing. The pilot interest in the flight allocation grievances was tremendous.

He wanted to be sure all knew of the hearing dates and the schedule of the hearings. He was representing his council in a grievance he had filed for his entire council. So he and Nat walked with us, together with George's crew, down to the limousine, and agreed to come into the city for dinner with us the following evening.

Nat warned us that she was coming too, so there would be no need for us to get Shipley a date. It brought grins of appreciation from all around, especially from George's crew. They had met Natalie before and appreciated her wit.

George and I unloaded with his crew at the Hotel Belmont Plaza and then walked around the corner to the Lexington where we had reservations. Long ago, we had learned to live apart from the company's favored hotel when on union business. That made it more difficult for the company to follow our activities. And that made it much easier when it came to walking a couple of stewardesses up to our room for a drink. The company had a tough regulation, subjecting any pilot and stewardess caught fraternizing to dismissal. But somehow, no one seemed to take it seriously, no doubt due to the many definitions of the word 'fraternizing.' The pilots had given it some choice definitions.

The room was a large corner room, bright, pleasant, several floors up, and well away from the street noises. We promptly prepared for a before dinner nap and I called the ol'man, Dave Behncke, at the Plymouth Hotel, where he always stayed when in New York, to let him know of our arrival. His secretary, Miss Forrest, explained that he was out but that she would give him the message, then she advised me the meeting time was set for nine that night. We were both pleased.

At six Mary and June walked around to our hotel, as prearranged. We took them to a little French restaurant over on East Fifty-third Street. It was a cozy place where we could have a couple of drinks and dinners without wrecking more than one fifty dollar bill.

June Tabler, as I had told George, was too tall for him, so he walked in with Mary and I escorted June. The minute I caught her arm she gave my hand a little squeeze. I glanced again at her sleek chassis, glowing cheeks, bright eyes and tried again to remember when and where I had met her. She appeared to be several years older then most new stewardesses, about twenty-seven to twenty-nine, with a more mature look.

The restaurant hostess remembered George and me. She eyed our girls and gave us both approving smiles, then led us to a secluded corner table where George took immediate charge of June.

Two hours flew by on racing wings.

Around eight-thirty we dropped the girls by at their hotel and taxied over to the Plymouth with George vowing that he was going to have that June if he had to chase her for a year and a day. I laughed, for I had never seen George, to whom the girls came easily and quickly—

probably due to his Shipley schooling—quite so worked up about one girl as he was over June.

I wrinkled my brow in thought about June, her little arm squeeze, and her apparent lack of any fear of being caught out with pilots. That was quite different from most new girls, fresh from stewardess school and endless lectures about pilots, wolves, pilots, wolves and so on until the two were synonymous in their minds. Probably due to her age, I thought, and tried to dismiss it from my mind. But it lingered, like a faintly nagging tooth.

The meeting room in the Plymouth Hotel was a large well furnished one. The hallway door was open and George and I walked in to find the five other members of the negotiating committee together with the headquarters representative, Walter Ohlrich, who had been assigned to negotiate the Amalgamated contract, engaged in idle chatter. Including myself, the negotiating committee consisted of three first pilots, three copilots, and the headquarter representative. George and I shook hands all around. It was quite evident to us that they were glad to see us and promptly began to ply us with questions about the flight allocation grievances which were the result of so much pilot unrest. We pleaded ignorance, reminding all that we had not heard the cases and knew little about them.

That drew a laugh all around, for all knew that George and I had quietly encouraged various chairmen to file grievances in behalf of the members of their councils. It was an intolerable situation that had to be resolved. The only solution available to the pilots had to come through the grievance sections of our labor agreement. All knew that the outcome would be far reaching.

"What's this meeting all about?" I asked.

Bill Cary, the chairman, a red-headed, quiet, slow talking, pipe smoking southerner of about my age, but considerably junior in seniority, chuckled. He was serving on his first negotiating committee and was chairman because Howard Woodall, the senior member of the committee, a man with whom I had flown copilot some in 1937, would not consider the job.

I had refused the position due to being chairman of the Pilots System Board. I had explained to the group that I did not believe that anyone could do justice to two major chairmanships at the same time. They understood my reasoning and promptly settled on Bill.

"I don't know, exactly," Bill Cary answered me slowly, "I do know that the company asked for the meeting and that it had something to do with the Korean War."

I arched my brows at that. "Then the company hasn't made any concessions?"

Bill grinned, knocked the ashes from his large pipe bowl, and looked at Walter Ohlrich. "No such luck, Wayne." He made a wry face. "You know Amalgamated!"

"The boss hasn't told me, either," Ohlrich, a heavy set man of middle age, injected. "But both he and Sayen decided that they would attend the meeting. I am being excused to go to Washington tomorrow morning on another matter."

"Is Sayen here?" I asked quickly and then stated: "You know, I have never met the man."

My mind spun back to the Air Line Pilots Convention in 1947-48 when the convention had mandated the president, Mr. Behncke, to hire a fulltime vice-president. The convention membership had approved twelve nominees, all active airline pilots, from which Mr. Behncke could select a vice-president.

The nomination was a flattering gesture by the convention, everyone agreed. But who would give up an airline captaincy for a twenty four hour daily desk job and at the same time, take a four thousand dollar per year pay cut?

Sayen, however, had wanted the job. He was still a copilot and the ol'man, Behncke, had finally appointed him to the job after twice calling for more nominees to apply. I really don't think anyone else wanted it.

It seemed natural to me that Sayen would want the job. It would give him a substantial pay increase. Also, his wife seemed to like the idea of living in Chicago. I was elated at the chance to meet Sayen after missing him in several trips to the Chicago headquarters.

Chapter 6

David L. Behncke

David L. Behncke, president of the Air Line Pilots' Association, suddenly appeared in the doorway with his gray hair combed back and, as usual, slipping a little to one side. His sloping forehead, Roman nose, iron gray mustache which he habitually stroked, and square protruding jaw gave him a little of a bulldog's appearance. Perhaps the slightly hunched shoulders, a result of years of fourteen hour workdays for the airline pilots, accentuated that appearance.

And a bulldog he was! In 1931, while flying the line as a captain for United Airlines, he had organized the Air Line Pilots' Association, or union, primarily to promote safety in flight and to prevent irresponsible firings of pilots by nonflying company officials—issues of grave concern to the pilots.

In 1933, David Behncke gave up flying at the insistence of the pilot membership of the association and became the association's president, a job he continued to hold, without opposition, throughout many turbulent years until 1947 when a sizeable revolt rose in the ranks.

It started at Amalgamated, a revolt against his dictatorial handling of the association business, and his long-winded letters to the membership on how hard he was working. Actually, the first was an excuse for the revolt; the last was the real reason.

It is true that Dave was working as hard as he said and few members doubted it, but it was a simple fact that they did not want to keep hearing about it. A slave they wanted and had, but they did not want the slave to keep reminding them that he was slaving for them.

A dictator they also needed, for few airline pilots would hesitate to value their own opinions, regardless of their limited knowledge on the subject, more highly than the opinion of a learned man who had placed much thought, time, and study on the question. Therefore they needed a smart dictator to study their problems, figure out the answers, and then crack the whip for action.

In Dave, they had such a man, and the advancement of their profession from obscurity to a position recognized as on a par with that of a doctor, a lawyer, or a highly skilled technician was proof of his wise leadership. The emergence of the organization from a one company union into an international organization was further proof of his deep commitment and wisdom.

But the pilots did not like his long-winded letters. Egotistical, self-centered and weak, as many were, and much given to profound respect for their own opinions, they nevertheless were quick to place a minor weakness of their president under a magnifying glass. The pro-company men were the loudest in their clamor that something be done.

So, in 1947, Proctor, an old Amalgamated pilot and association master chairman, and pro-company in his leanings, threw his hat in the ring for the presidency. He was immediately given much support by Amalgamated and several other airlines. Pro-company pilots, men who thought their company had the best interests of the pilots at heart if only they would send a gentleman in to deal for them, quickly flocked to his banners.

Others looked at some old long-winded letters from Behncke and were uncertain. It was amazing how the pilots, grown men, the most advanced in their profession, suddenly began to think that if they replaced Behncke with someone more acceptable to their companies, then all their pilot problems, lengthy contract negotiations, and points of friction would vanish.

I fought for Behncke with all my ability. Bart Cox, Shipley, Schustman and a dozen others on Amalgamated joined me to stamp out the company union drive that Proctor was heading. We recognized it for what it was, called it by name, and began to drive the facts home.

I filed charges against Proctor under the association bylaws to expel him from the union. The hearing, held just prior to the presidential election in Chicago, resulted in him remaining in the union, yet I had exposed the fact that he had dealt 'through the side door' with the company in a former contract negotiation, which had resulted in the Amalgamated pilots being hurt financially. That turned the tide, for most airline pilots worship their pay checks; their god is the dollar and, in their thinking, they are the first cousins to Superman!

Behncke was reelected. But not until I had stood on the rostrum at the convention, before that two hundred and twenty pilots from all parts of the world, representing over five thousand airline pilots, and talked. I talked about airline pilots, their strength of character, their rugged individualism, their bravery in the face of nature's worst elements, and potential dangers of flying at ever increasing speeds.

I talked about aging pilots, for an airline pilot is more sensitive of his age than a chorus girl. I talked about the companies, their companies, that were trying to get rid of their aging pilots to escape the financial burden of having to retire them a few years later.

Then I talked about a work horse, a good old horse, that had pulled the plow for many years for the airline pilots. I conceded that during the last few years, war years, when most of us were in foreign lands, he had wandered a little aimlessly in his plowing, but insisted that it was due to the fact that the war had robbed his reins of the experienced pilots' guiding hands.

I pictured the old work horse as being healthy and still able to pull the plow for many more years if only the pilots did not do to him what their companies were trying to do to all the pilots who were beginning to show white at the temples.

Slowly I talked at first, and fairly low, yet loud enough a quiet audience could hear me on the back row. And they were very quiet, listening, looking and measuring the tall Amalgamated pilot on the rostrum, the one who had exposed the facts about Proctor, who had, with some other pilot, broken up the firing board on Amalgamated and succeeded in reinstating all of the fired pilots who had filed grievances, with full back pay, in addition to eliminating any possibility that they, too, might have to go to Ardmore for the process of elimination.

Security of a pilot's job is an all important consideration and one which Dave Behncke had preached and worked for in so many years. The pilots weighed me, and listened while I talked about their companies, what had been planned for them at Ardmore, with Amalgamated getting paid for castrating them.

My voice rose as I talked about the old work horse and I recalled some of the dirty furrows he had plowed for the airlines pilots during the war, with little help. I told of his part in the Ardmore fiasco, how many times he had called me late at night, from his office, to keep close watch on the Ardmore deal because he was aware of how vicious that deal would be to the airline pilots if it were permitted to exist. I concluded my talk with a plea that firmer hands be placed on the reins and the pilots accept their responsibility for directing the course of the plowing, rather than think they could cure all their plowing problems simply by replacing the horse.

When I walked off the rostrum, for a split second, I had the impression that the roof was falling in. The applause was thunderous, it roared through the auditorium. I looked back to see pilots standing, yelling, and waving their arms. That was in early 1948. After the voting, I was the ol'man's fair-haired boy, his trouble shooter, his in-fighter.

All this slipped through my mind as I watched the ol'man cross the room with his slow measured step to shake my hand, then Schustman's, then the others. His faded blue eyes met mine with a warmth that had always been there, since the day I walked off that rostrum.

"Well, well," the ol'man rumbled, "with Allison and Schustman here it looks like we are ready for the heavy fighting." He laughed that loud, hearty bellow, which, in past years, had made so many company officials squirm. And he had a way of using it to advantage whenever a contract negotiation reached what he termed as the 'nut cutting time.'

He gave my shoulder a heavy and affectionate slap.

"Look out, boys," he cautioned the others, "old Chief-Bring-Home-The-Bacon has a hungry look in his eye."

For years he had poked fun at my Indian ancestry, dim and distant though it was. Then he laughed again, shook his head as though remembering some special deal, and took a seat in a chair behind a small table to one side of the room.

He started to speak again, but Sayen entered with Dave's personal secretary, Miss Forrest, a tall broad shouldered, deep chested woman of about thirty-five or forty. She carried such a broad span of bosom that the pilots had long nicknamed her Acres.

Sayen himself was a short dark-complected and black-headed man of medium build. His features were very regular and his smile was that of a well-groomed politician. His white teeth and inscrutable black eyes flashed well together. I found myself shaking a hand that was minus the forefinger and it was difficult for me to keep my eyes from inspecting the amputated joint. However, I managed to gaze deep into his eyes and smile, shaking his hand at the same time.

"It feels like you've already been mouse-trapped by a stewardess," I allowed slowly.

The howl of laughter was almost immediate. Miss Forrest did not understand and watched with amazement at the way the ol'man choked, laughed, and slapped the table. Sayen gave me a wide and appreciative smile and, after all the introductions, seated himself at Dave's right with Miss Forrest and her notebook on Dave's left. It was indeed a friendly atmosphere as Dave looked around the room at the three captain representatives, three copilot representatives, Schustman, together with the headquarters personnel, while he fumbled with the wrapping on a cigar. Shaking his head to Sayen, he rumbled:

"Old Chief-Bring-Home-The-Bacon has no respect for a vice-president. Why," he gave me an appreciative look, "let me tell you of one he pulled on the president—mind you—the president of your association." He looked around and paused to let his words sink in, then continued. Expectant grins followed. The ol'man was a good story teller.

"A few weeks ago our legal department came to me about a certain grievance that had been filed by a member of the Tulsa council. It related to the system seniority promotion provisions. Our legal department was much concerned with the grave consequences that would follow if such a grievance was lost. Well, I listened to their tale of woe and finally decided to write the chairman of the System Board, since he resided in Tulsa, and see what could be done about having the grievance withdrawn. So I gave him the song and dance routine as given to me by our legal department." The ol'man then paused to relight his cigar and let everyone digest his words.

"Well," he continued, "I was just about to wind off my dictation of that letter asking to hear from him on the matter, when my office was interrupted by Mr. Walter Braznell, Director of Flight for Amalgamated, calling personally to see me. Now that is a most unusual happening at our offices, to have an Amalgamated official call personally to see me about some matter as my health and good disposition. Usually they stay in New York and relay messages that I should drop dead." He paused and joined in the laughter.

"So," the ol'man continued, "we roll out the red carpet for him, the same way Amalgamated does for its passengers so they'll look at the carpet and not notice the oily and smoked up engines that haven't been overhauled in five years."

The group smiled their appreciation of the scene as he described it.

"Well," he drew on his cigar again, "Mr. Braznell spent some time passing the time of day and getting me to talk about our new headquarters building. We had a nice talk, with me even showing him some of the blueprints of the building and so on. Finally he got around to talking about his reason for being there.

"It seems that a certain pilot at Tulsa had filed a grievance related to the system seniority promotion provisions. Mr. Braznell is quite upset over this grievance because he insisted he was doing all possible to adhere to system seniority. However, with four classes of equipment in operation for the company, there unquestionably has to be some little inequalities due to the impossibility of keeping all pilots checked out on all types of equipment."

Dave leaned back and surveyed the ceiling before continuing. "So," he rumbled on, "I listen to him going into the many problems of trying to please over twelve hundred pilots scattered throughout fourteen bases. His request that we give him a little consideration, in the application of strict system seniority, didn't appear to be too far off base. So I promised to look into the matter of that little grievance filed by that inconsiderate Tulsa pilot by the name of Jewell."

He paused to blow a little smoke at the ceiling and stroke his mustache a couple of times before continuing very solemnly. "So, I promptly called my secretary and asked her to take a letter to the chairman of the System Board who happened to reside at Tulsa. And, I gave him the same routine that Mr. Braznell had just given me and wound it up by asking to hear from him on the matter."

Then the ol'man fumbled in his breast pocket and pulled out some papers. "Here's the reply." He glumly opened the papers. "Here's just what he said."

"Dear Mr. Behncke: In reply to the letter of so-and-so date in which you expressed a grave fear of the association losing the Jewell case, and further, in reply to the latter part of the same letter in which you expressed a grave fear of winning the Jewell case, I am attaching the System Board Decision on the Jewell case for your perusal. All I can say, Dave, is that you have won it. Now—what the hell are you going to do with it?"

Everyone laughed. The ol'man looked so solemn. I laughed too, wondering if they were laughing at the ol'man or at me. Then we settled down to the business at hand. Dave pulled on his cigar and studied the end of it thoughtfully.

"Ohlrich has kept me well-informed on the progress of your negotiations," he began seriously, "or rather, the lack of progress. We have a good strike vote from the Amalgamated pilots and at your last meeting you broke off contract negotiations, is that right?"

We all nodded and the ol'man continued, "Shortly after the termination of negotiations I received a telephone call from the chairman of the Mediation Board in Washington in which he proffered arbitration. As you all know, that is a deal in which both sides sign up to accept the decision of a government appointed neutral. He would settle the points in dispute."

A couple of the copilot members of the negotiating committee chuckled. I too, smiled.

"Dave," I offered, "the whole darned contract is in dispute, everything. We have been unable to settle anything. The company will not even accept any paragraphs of last year's agreement, which now has run well over an additional year."

Dave nodded slowly, "yes." He acknowledged, "and that's the reason we cannot arbitrate at this point. To go into arbitration with the entire agreement—well—," he rolled his faded blue eyes toward the ceiling and shook his head.

"Now," he continued, "the company has asked for a meeting with the negotiating committee relative to the Korean War. We are to meet with them tomorrow morning at ten. At that time they might try to reopen the negotiations by some direct across the table talking, or we might do so. What do you boys think?"

Around the room it went and after a time the general opinion of the negotiating committee seemed to be that it would be a waste of time and a show of weakness if we reopened the negotiations. Sayen was quick to pick up that point and disagree.

"Do you boys think it would be a show of weakness for Mr. Behncke to reopen a discussion on the contract?" he asked with a smile.

No one answered. He studied the group thoughtfully.

"Yes, I do," I finally replied. "It doesn't matter who reopens the discussion on such a flimsy pretense. It still shows weakness." I met his black eyes fully.

"And further," I continued, "since you haven't had the hours, days and weeks run into months at the negotiating table like we have, trying to deal with Amalgamated Airlines, you can't possibly comprehend what we are bucking." Several members nodded and I continued: "They have told us point blank across the table that until we drop that mileage limitation section of the proposed agreement, nothing will be settled."

"That's a good point," he rolled easily with the punch and smiled in a wise sort of way. "I am glad that you have brought up that point, that mileage limitation. If that point was settled with them, do you think that we would be able to make progress on the rest of the agreement?"

"Of course!" Several answered together.

"How?" Someone asked.

"Salesmanship!" He smiled broadly and let that soak for a good ten seconds. It was quite obvious that Sayen was enjoying being the center of the stage. I studied the ol'man's face. He was apparently trying to study mine. A sly wink from the pair of blue eyes did not help my poker face. Then I saw the play.

A cocky vice-president had been trying to tell the ol'man how to get these negotiations moving and the ol'man was tired of it. So he had brought the vice-president over for the negotiating committee to knock some of his corners off and let him get a taste of Amalgamated. That had to be it!

Sayen was speaking as I tied things together in my mind.

"Let's sell them on mileage limitation, but let's not call it that." Sayen explained like a college professor, beginning to lecture a class. "Let's call it an increased mileage increment—the IMI formula—and sell them on that idea."

Chapter 7

Salesmanship

I glanced at Bill Cary. He was fumbling with his tobacco pouch. Howard Woodall, the short heavy-set captain and senior member of our committee snorted and then chuckled.

"Go ahead," Howard urged Sayen. He looked at me with a sly smile.

The three copilots looked at each other. Schwartz, a dark, curly-headed and good looking youth of about twenty-eight, laughed aloud. He was truly a handsome man and knew it. Starting a premedical course in college, he had ended up with a degree in psychology. Although he talked a great deal, he was quite entertaining and frequently came out with the bare truth and used it as a club without any attempt to salve the feelings of the opposition. I had frequently called him the little Prussian of our group.

Schwartz laughed again, louder. "Let's paint a brick yellow and sell it to them for gold at the same time," he suggested.

Sayen didn't like that and it showed. But he smiled broadly at Schwartz. "Let's sell them one brick at a time," he suggested.

Spencer, a slim, sallow-complected youth of near thirty with a crooked nose and a mild-mannered way of speaking, raised his hand to signal for the floor. He didn't look like a professor, but he had more degrees than the entire committee. So we called him "Doctor."

Why he had taken up flying, no one knew, but here he was on the negotiating committee for the second time, as were the other two copilots, and he had already made himself famous as the statistician of the group. No one on the committee could mention anything regarding figures without first checking with "Doctor" Spencer.

But there Doctor Spencer's ability ceased. He could not talk forcefully, he could not drive any point across to anyone. With his mild-mannered way of speaking, he could easily lull anyone to sleep with a prolonged talk on a subject. That is, anyone except a stewardess. With them, he was a total washout. They had his number and it had become increasingly difficult for him to secure a date with one.

Spencer's status with the stewardesses had become a standing joke with the committee and a good subject for discussion when light entertainment was desired. It seemed that he disliked very much to spend any money on a girl, and besides, when he did secure a date, he seemed to take it for granted that everything was arranged for her to spend the night in his room, and, the quicker he got her there, the happier she would be—that was his attitude.

Bill Cary pronounced him all wolf, from the top of his ears to the bottom of his feet. In fact, Bill insisted, Spencer didn't look at any girl, he glared. And the girls could read his glare like newspaper headlines.

"I would like to observe," Spencer spoke mildly, "that we have been trying to negotiate a contract with a tough company; if it is a simple matter of salesmanship, then, perhaps you had better demonstrate your meaning."

It was what Sayen had been wanting someone to say. Again he smiled. Again he spoke.

"Well, if the committee has no objections, I'll have a little try at it tomorrow when the opportunity presents itself."

"I don't like it," I objected. "Then we are back in negotiations. Right now we are in a position to arbitrate or strike. Nothing will be gained by going back into direct negotiations."

"Wayne has a point," the ol'man observed reluctantly. "However, I think I can preface my remarks to the company in such a way that Sayen can have an opportunity to make his play." He looked around at the group, saw that his suggestion was satisfactory, and moved the meeting along.

"Do we arbitrate or strike?" he asked quietly.

No one answered immediately. Bill Gary lighted his pipe again and observed, "Dave, we are pretty much in accord as a committee. We think the company is daring us to strike, and, in fact, making it impossible for us to get anywhere until we do."

The ol'man digested that. "What would they gain by provoking a strike?" he inquired.

Bill shrugged and glanced at me. I know he wanted me to do the talking on that point.

"Dave," I took the cue, "we have about come to the conclusion that they don't think they are provoking a strike; they think they are about to put us in our place. You see," I explained, "they have the attitude that we are at the table to demand or beg. So far, in their estimation, we are demanding. If they can force us to abandon that position, then there is only one left. Dropping the mileage limitation is the signal they are looking for, and when we do that, they will start tossing us a few scraps." I smiled grimly.

"We'll see them in the bread line first!" The old man growled. Then he brushed his mustache slowly and gazed again at the ceiling with those faded blue eyes. I felt a sense of pleasure from the way he said it.

"Then let's set a date for the strike." Schwartz was eager, his face glowed for the conflict.

"The trouble with that," the ol'man mused thoughtfully, "is that the entire contract is wide open. Nothing has been settled, but let's wait and see what happens tomorrow. Then we can plan our strategy after that."

Dave soon brought the meeting to a close and requested to see Schustman and me after the meeting. We told the others good night and watched them drift out. Dave excused Miss Forrest and we four huddled around the little table.

"This new negotiation has clashed with the hearings on the flight allocation cases." I began talking more to Dave. "We are supposed to start the hearings day after tomorrow. George and I had planned to spend tomorrow getting things in line."

"Sayen and I discussed that." Dave leaned across the table and spoke earnestly to me, "and I called the company's Director of Labor Relations, Di Pasquale, about it. He said that he was in the same position of having to attend both meetings and that this meeting tomorrow wouldn't take more than half a day. So we should be finished by tomorrow night."

"Good," I replied. "Then I'll wire the chairmen that the hearing dates are firm."

"And," Dave added as an after-thought, "let George here line things up for the hearings, I want you at the negotiating table tomorrow."

"Where do we stand on these flight allocation cases?" Sayen asked as I nodded to the ol'man.

Briefly I explained that the grievances were a result of the company starting an indiscriminate program of shifting the flight time from one base to another. By shifting the flying time around, the company had been able to change the pilots' working conditions by forcing several pilots at a given base, with curtailed flying time, to move to another base to avoid demotion.

Since the agreement had no provisions requiring the company to pay moving expenses for first pilots, and since there were no provisions in the agreement to prevent the company from floating the time from one base to another at the slightest whim of a company official, there appeared to be nothing to prevent the company from exacting a financial penalty from the pilot group at will.

"For example," I explained, "a round trip to Chicago from New York that had previously been flown by New York crews for some time, might suddenly be changed so that Chicago based crews flew the round trip, even though there was no change in the departure or arrival times of the trips involved. The surplus pilots at New York could then accept demotion to copilot status, and the surplus copilots moved at company expense, or they could bid the vacancies advertised in Chicago. If successful they could then, at their own expense, move to Chicago with no guarantee that the time would not be moved back to New York at the next change in schedules, which frequently came at two week periods.

"It is a vicious attack," I continued, " a real 'labor baiting technique' and many pilots recognize it."

"Has this been discussed with the management of Amalgamated Airlines?" Sayen wanted to know.

"Hell, yes!" I replied and caught George's faint smile at Sayen's question.

"Our Master Chairman, Gene Burns, and I, together with an association attorney, Bennett, went in to see Mr. Braznell right after the first shift of a large block of flying time, a round trip from the Tulsa base to the San Francisco base. It caused the demotion of the four junior captains at Tulsa. Gene Burns was one of them."

"Walt Braznell claimed that the needs of the service were such that the company opined it necessary to fly that round trip from San

Francisco. Then he followed it up with wholesale shifting of flight time."

Dave stroked his gray mustache with the tips of the fingers of his right hand and gazed at the ceiling in deep and quiet thought.

"Is there any pattern to this promiscuous floating of flight time around Amalgamated's system?" he finally asked.

I nodded into the faded blue eyes. "Sure, look at the whole picture. Amalgamated's Master Chairman has been demoted because he refused to chase the flight time to San Francisco. No doubt if he is a good boy as an association Master Chairman and doesn't give the company any trouble about overloads or poor maintenance, they will shift the time back again in a month or so."

"And," I continued, "the wholesale shifting of time has resulted in pilot bases where we have pro-company chairmen getting the most flying time. It has caused many promotions at the weak councils and many demotions in the strong councils. New York has lost much time and Chicago has gained most of it. Los Angeles has lost and Fort Worth has gained. Tulsa has lost and San Francisco has gained. Nashville has lost and Cleveland has gained.

"Your weakest chairmen are those in Chicago, Cleveland, San Francisco and Fort Worth. Their pilots are laughing and giving their chairmen credit for their prosperity. It may help their reelection."

"Actually," I explained further, talking directly at Dave, "George and I are of the belief that the company intended to get the different councils fighting each other over the flight time. Of course that destroys the effectiveness of the association because the conditions then deteriorate to the point that the chairman or council who does the best 'brownring' job with Braznell gets the best flights and the most flying time."

"The proper answer to that," Sayen suggested with his smooth forehead wrinkled in thought, "is to write moving expenses for all pilots in the contract."

"Sure," George beat me to the punch, "that sounds like a nice little point to sell. I'll bet the company will buy that in a hurry!"

Sayen flushed slightly and I caught the shadow of a smile on the ol'man's face.

"So," I gave George an appreciative glance, "when the chairman of several councils asked George and me for a suggestion as to how to meet this situation, we encouraged them to file grievances and let the System Board find a solution. We cautioned them to do everything possible to discourage friction between councils and suggested that they preach unity. That approach appears to be working," I finished dryly, "for we have six council grievances, a dozen personal grievances and system-wide interest on how the problem is going to be solved by the System Board."

"Wayne," the ol'man spoke heavily, obviously apologizing for Sayen's suggestion, "you have kept me pretty well informed of the conditions on Amalgamated while I have kept Sayen busy working with a couple of the smaller and more ethical airlines. Tell him about that 'screening deal' on Amalgamated. And, George," he waved toward a phone, "order us some coffee."

I smiled at Sayen's smooth regular features and met his black eyes in a very direct look. I wanted to like him, wanted to see him succeed on the job he had taken. Working for the ol'man would be no easy task, I well knew, and I also knew that the ol'man needed some good, fulltime pilot assistance. It was impossible to hire anyone who could go into the association's headquarters and lift the load on the ol'man's shoulders unless he had been a line pilot.

I found myself hoping that Sayen's line experience had been enough to give him a good footing, his judgment mature enough to cope with the daily problems, and his loyalty strong enough to resist any desire to undermine the ol'man and take his job. Gazing into his black eyes, I found myself hoping sincerely that the ol'man had secured the best man out of the group nominated by the convention. At least, I thought, he has the appearance of being a smooth article.

"In 1946, at the end of World War II," I began, "Amalgamated leased the airport at Ardmore, Oklahoma from the government. The purpose given was to set up a pilots' training school for Amalgamated pilots from all AA bases. It was to be a unified school. A staff of young, budding chief pilots was selected to give yearly qualifying check rides to the Amalgamated line pilots, train new copilots, and teach the line pilots how to fly the new equipment on order. A director of flight assumed command and, in addition, a school was set up there for new stewardesses. It had the appearance of being a general training operation.

"Everything went along fine for a few months while Amalgamated set up the training school. Then suddenly the company ordered about sixty copilots and junior captains to Ardmore for 'screening.' When they arrived there, they were told that they were being tested for a few days, that their jobs depended on their performance while they were there, and that various chief pilots, in addition to the ones at Ardmore, would ride with them to determine their fitness to remain as pilots for Amalgamated."

"In complete violation," Dave interrupted, "mind you, *complete* violation of the section of the Railway Labor Act which prohibits air carriers from changing the rates of pay, rules, and working conditions as incorporated in the agreement. Our agreement specifically says that a pilot will not be on probation for a period greater than one year. That gives Amalgamated a year to look any seedling over and decide whether or not they want to keep him."

Dave's voice was so serious and the depth of his feelings so intense that I smiled a little, lighted a cigarette, and sat mute with the others listening to the ol'man.

"The first I knew about it," Dave continued, "was when I started getting phone calls, telegrams and letters from the pilots sent to Ardmore. Before I could investigate, the pilots were all ordered back to their bases, and Ardmore was again a routine training school.

"Then the calls started coming from all over Amalgamated by those pilots who had been sent to Ardmore. They told me that they had been advised by their company to resign, and that if they resigned, they would be given a letter of recommendation that would help them to secure another job.

"But if they did not resign they would be discharged with no recommendation of any kind. Of course," Dave added, "I advised them not to resign but to immediately file grievances upon receipt of the letters of discharge. I had an attorney draft a short grievance letter, sent a copy to all who called, and tried to get in touch with the others. There were twelve all together. Twelve out of sixty being tested.

"However, " he lamented, "only seven filed grievances. The other five bought the letter of recommendation with their signed resignations.

"Can you imagine that?" He looked at George, Sayen and me in horror. "An airline fires pilots it considers unsafe, yet is quite willing to recommend them for other flying jobs if they will give no trouble and resign."

He leaned back in his chair and closed his eyes in thought.

"The first I knew about it," I smiled at Sayen, knowing the ol'man wanted me to continue, "was when Bob Parrish called me from Tulsa and told me he had been given the works at Ardmore.

"Bob had been my copilot for about a year during the war when I was flying transatlantic and I knew him to be a good careful and conscientious pilot," I explained.

"I drove over to the Tulsa airport, picked him up and kept him overnight. He gave me the full story together with the names of all those who had been in his group at Ardmore."

"The seven cases," I recalled, "came before the System Board approximately four months later, after going through the first two hearings in front of two company officials. These officials rubber stamped the firings of those who refused to resign."

"Where were the System Board hearings held?" Sayen questioned. "I recall hearing something about that on Braniff."

"We held them at each pilot's base in order to make it easy for the pilot to have home based witnesses. The company flew in their chief pilots who had flown with the discharged pilots," I replied.

"During the hearings," I continued, "it developed that the company had subjected the twelve discharged pilots to an impossible situation. Giving each a southeast takeoff out of Ardmore they cut the right engine right after breaking ground. If the pilot being tested circled to the left and kept his good engine under him, he was criticized for poor headwork and going around the field on one engine where the terrain was the higher. If the pilot circled the field to the right where the terrain was lower, they criticized him for violating the basic law of engine-out flying with multi-engine equipment by banking to the right and getting his good engine above the airplane.

"On all the other pilots they tested and passed, they cut the left engine on takeoffs. It was developed at the hearings that the company had two lists of pilots to be tested, those who were passed, and those who were to be fired. In short, the victims had been selected prior to the testing."

I discarded my cigarette and continued: "When the chief pilots were questioned, they admitted that they had performed the tests in accordance with a directive issued from the company headquarters. No one had a copy of the directive, and the company refused to produce it for the System Board.

"When Walt Braznell, the director of flight for AA was called to the stand, he freely admitted the directive was written in four parts, two signed by himself and two signed by Tom Boyson who was sitting on the Board as a judge. That put Tom Boyson in the light of a proud father judging his own baby at a baby show!"

I laughed at the recollection and enjoyed Sayen's big grin of appreciation.

"At Memphis," I related, "where the last two hearings were held, and where Dave had sent the entire Master Executive Council of Amalgamated to hear and get a taste of the last two cases, I met the company's purchasing agent."

"The what?" Sayen asked, his eyes wide in astonishment.

"The price wasn't quite high enough—almost, but not quite!" George interjected. "If they had offered to make me an official instead of Wayne, I think we could have made a deal." He grinned. "But they wanted to make me an assistant to Wayne."

I continued, ignoring George's ever present humor. "Boyson sent one of my brother pilots, a good friend of his who wanted badly to be a chief pilot, to buy us off. By that time they knew that we had the company in violation of the Railway Labor Act."

At that moment the coffee came and created a brief recess before I continued the story.

"We met in executive sessions with the company members of the Board, day after day after day," I recalled. "They couldn't refuse to meet with us without being in violation of the Railway Labor Act together with the provisions of the System Board of Adjustment provisions as contained in the labor agreement." I stopped and stirred my coffee.

"Finally we held a meeting in New York where Dave ordered the entire Master Executive Council on Amalgamated, twenty-eight men representing over twelve hundred pilots, to New York to act in an advisory capacity to Schustman and me. The purpose was to put pressure on the company."

"While they were there," I explained, "Dave had the Master Chairman, Captain Jimmie Burns, call the president of Amalgamated Airlines, Mr. Ralph Damon, who had been made president of Amalgamated a few months before the Ardmore fiasco, while Mr. C.R. had moved on up to the position of Chairman of the Board of Directors, and asked for a meeting with him and the System Board.

"At the appointed hour, the twenty-eight members of the Master Council of AA, together with Schustman and me, entered Mr. Ralph Damon's office to find Mr. C.R. there also. No one had invited him. But there he was, big as life, sitting in a corner of the front of the spacious office of the president of AA, making himself at home by chewing tobacco and spitting at a spittoon in careless disregard for accuracy. The company members of the system Adjustment Board, Tom Boyson, and an assistant were sitting nearby.

"Mr. Damon, from behind his large desk, surveyed the pilots assembled, the company members of the System Adjustment Board, as well as Schustman and me, and with a side glance at C.R. gave the floor to the Master Chairman, Jimmie Burns.

"Captain Burns, in turn, gave the floor to me with a brief statement that he had asked for the meeting in order to have me, the chairman of the System Adjustment Board, brief the president of AA on the screening cases, as the pilots saw them," I paused to let Sayen visualize the picture.

"Wayne did the talking," George interposed. "His oil field delivery is most impressive!"

"I talked for about twelve minutes," I recalled. "I gave a brief history of the cases, quoted from the screening directive which bore the original title of Captain's Elimination Board, and pointed out three absolute violations of the Railway Labor Act, together with numerous contract violations."

George laughed and took up the story. "When Wayne finished talking and sat down, both Mr. Damon and Mr. C.R. asked several questions. It was quite obvious that Mr. Damon didn't know what had been going on at Ardmore, and it was also quite obvious that Mr. C.R. did, even though he tried to make it appear otherwise.

"So then, when neither of them asked any further questions, Mr. Damon just sat there for several minutes looking out the window and brushing his curly gray hair, with its middle part, down with the flat of either hand. The room was very quiet while Mr. Damon said nothing and kept looking out the window. Finally he jumped to his feet and walked hurriedly out of the room mumbling that he'd be back in a couple of minutes.

"We sat there," George continued, "for several minutes, and watched Mr. Damon pound a typewriter through the open door to the adjacent office. When he returned he pressed a desk buzzer to call an assistant, gave him the typewritten sheet which he signed first, right in front of us, and ordered the assistant to put it into effect immediately. The assistant glanced at the paper, gave Mr. Damon a surprised look, nodded, and disappeared with the typewritten order. I guess we all looked like we were trying to read Greek."

George laughed again and kept on: "Mr. Damon then gave Mr. C.R. a wolfish smile and turned to us. He spoke to the entire pilot group as he permitted his eyes to rove over us.

"'Gentlemen!' Mr. Damon addressed everyone and even swung his eyes toward Mr. C.R. who was just taking another shot at the spittoon. 'This may be my last official act as president of Amalgamated Airlines, but I have signed it and ordered it placed into effect immediately. It is an order on the company treasury to pay full retroactive pay on four engine equipment, to all pilots, for all such flights flown since the war.'

"The applause from the pilot group was immediate and loud. All the chairmen followed the Master Chairman, Captain Jimmie Burns, to shake Mr. Damon's hand and personally express their appreciation over having that nagging problem cleared up.

"It was something the pilots had about given up as lost, for the company had paid us DC-3, or two engine scale, because we did not have a contract that defined pay for four engine aircraft until about two years after the time we had started flying four engine equipment commercially. The company had repeatedly referred to that question-able pay as a negotiable item."

Dave and I laughed as George exclaimed: "C.R. nearly dropped his teeth spitting at that spittoon. Mr. Damon gave away a half million bucks of C.R.'s money just like that!" He snapped his fingers to emphasize the point.

"That's what he did to C.R. for leaving him holding the bag as president on those Railway Labor Act violations that C.R. had engi-neered." George shook his head with a little smile and stirred his coffee.

Dave leaned forward and continued the story: "And a couple of weeks later Ralph Damon called me and suggested that we quietly arrange a way by which those boys who had grievances pending could go back to work with full back pay."

"That was easy," he chuckled. "We simply agreed on three line pilots to reexamine those seven fired pilots. They all passed!"

"Then shortly after that Ralph Damon left Amalgamated and went with TWA as president. We've gotten along fine ever since," Dave concluded the story.

Sayen shook his head and smiled a little. I could see the story was hard for him to believe.

"But the screening directive," he questioned, "where did you get it? All Dave has told me is that it is a deep and dark secret."

George laughed. "We didn't! After the last hearing at Memphis, it just happened that Wayne and I were on the same airplane that the company attorney was on. I rode back in the rear and talked fishing with him while Wayne rode up front on the extra cockpit chair and memorized the directive that was in the attorney's brief case."

"You rifled his brief case?" Sayen was shocked.

"Oh, certainly not—!" I smiled. "His brief case fell out of a baggage compartment where it had been stacked high on other baggage. A streak of rough air shook it out into the passageway and spilled papers all over the floor. In gathering them up," I finished lamely, "I happened to read the directive that set up the Captain's Elimination Board."

"We just made them think that we had the hidden ace," George explained further to Sayen. "Wayne kept quoting from the screening directive at our System Adjustment Board meetings where we were trying to reach a decision on the cases. Each day he would come up with something new and ask the company members to explain it. But it took the briefing to Mr. Damon, in which Wayne pointed out the absolute Railway Labor Act violations, to cinch the case."

It was late in a cool summer night when George and I walked out of the Plymouth Hotel and headed across town to the Lexington. Neither of us realized how late it was until we saw the crew from Flight Two unloading from the limousine at the Belmont Plaza Hotel as we walked by. The limousine usually arrived near midnight.

The pilot, fat, company-minded Dan Landall, was no friend of ours, but we were not interested in him. It was the stewardesses that caught our eyes, or rather George's. He knew them both.

From the way he maneuvered the tall, shapely and dark-headed

Jinnie to one side of the crew, I knew George had something lined up. She had been in Tulsa for some time and was one of the older girls there and had flown with me several times in the last few months. I considered her to be smart, competent, good-looking and very entertaining with both crew members and passengers. The other girl, Jean Thurson, I did not know for she had only flown a couple of trips, both with George. So I introduced myself and politely walked her to one side to give George and Jinnie a little privacy.

Jean was not as tall as Jinnie; neither could you call her short, for she had a nice range look. I found myself bending over her and looking into a pair of gray-blue eyes that were sparkling as though she was just starting to work rather than finishing a tiring trip.

Blond hair, with a reddish tint boiled from under her stewardess cap and her nose turned up slightly. When she smiled at me I glimpsed beautiful white teeth. I don't know why, but her smile made me think of Eric the Red. Maybe it was the reddish hair.

"Thur-son," I rolled her last name on my tongue and asked: "are you by any chance from Min-ne-so-ta?"

"Of course!" She flashed an even wider smile. "But how did you know?"

I laughed. It was fun to watch her smile, for it came as a fresh breeze and seemed to flow all over me.

"George has been telling me all about you." I lied like any other wolf with a line.

"What did he tell you?" She studied me thoughtfully.

"As much as he knew," I parried, "about your being from Minnesota and the reason you left and took a job as a stewardess."

"Why did I leave?" She studied me intently.

"Wasn't it to meet me?" I smiled. "George said that was what you told him!"

She laughed and her laughter had a nice musical note. "Now I know where the big timber wolves of Minnesota went years ago. My father often told me that they followed the game into Canada and never returned. But now I know that they really went south to Indian Territory. George has told me that you are part Indian," she added with another smile.

"They're coming over for drinks," George informed me, and gave Jinnie our room number. I watched Jean give Jinnie a questioning look and sensed that she was about to refuse.

"Please do," I urged. "That migration occurred several decades back and all the offspring are now heavily diluted with coyote blood."

"I'll judge that by the howl." She shot me another smile. "It's too dangerous to wait for the bite."

"Hurry, change your clothes and come on over," George insisted and gave the two girls a push. We wandered away as though we had told them good night. We couldn't let Dan Landall get any ideas. He might drop a hint to Anderson.

Naturally that was one of the main reasons George and I always stayed away from a company-favored hotel when on association business. We were too easy to track in a company-favored hotel. And stewardesses would have a drink with us in our hotel room much more willingly than in a company-favored hotel room. Basic psychology, George called it.

Fifteen minutes later I was pouring four drinks and he was keeping a watchful eye on the hallway. Suddenly he called softly.

"Business is approaching—double. Now remember," he admonished me, "you are dead tired and have to have some sleep tonight. You have an early meeting tomorrow."

I laughed at George, while at the same time realizing he was right on both counts. "Are you trying to push me off to bed?" I inquired reluctantly.

"I gotta plan," he informed me.

"Explain it." I was curious.

"I gotta plan," He repeated. Then squaring himself in front of me, taking Sayen's stance and confident smile he swept the room confidently with his eyes while mimicking Sayen's deeper voice in declaring: "Salesmanship!"

I laughed as a light knock sounded on the door.

Jinnie, clad in a sleek and tight-fitting dress, pranced into the room and permitted George to give her a quick hug and a peck on the cheek. With two drinks they settled together in a large over-stuffed chair. I could not help but wonder who was 'wolfing' who.

Jean was clad in a well-tailored blue suit that fit her figure very nicely, yet did not prominently display its wares. I complimented her on the suit and admired her trim legs at the same time. To cover my lowly appraisal, I also complimented her on the way her shoes matched her suit.   Stewardesses   I had noticed frequently failed to dress themselves with taste and a conservative touch which makes a far more lasting impression than the 'whistle producing' and 'figure advertising' clothes that so many were prone to wear. It was quite evident to me that Jean knew how to dress.

"To our first," I touched glasses with her, met the clear blue eyes steadily, and added to myself, "and many more."

She smiled and I felt that she had read the thought in my mind after skipping lightly over the one on my tongue. I was greatly intrigued.

Then Jinnie monopolized the conversation and began giving us all the latest gossip on the line. The first thing we learned was that Landall had made a terrible landing at New York. She described in detail how hard they had hit the ground and how all the trays had fallen out of the racks and on the floor, littering the cabin aisle with silverware. George and I both laughed, but it was nothing new to us.

Landall was a poor pilot; we both were well aware of that. Numerous copilots had told us of similar incidents. Once he had sprung the gear on a DC-4 so bad that it had required extensive repairs. Another time he had blown out all four tires on a rough landing.

Landall, however, was a company man, so nothing much was said or done about the incidents. He bowed and groveled to Anderson, and was most difficult for copilots and engineers to fly with because of his ugly disposition, but if an official happened by, his mouth was filled with honey.   In addition, I suspected him of 'stool-pigeoning' to company officials concerning our union business.

Jinnie moved from the Landall landing to the Ellis accident to tell us that just before leaving Tulsa they had received word from Amarillo that further tests had proven that Terry's back was not broken, just badly sprained. I felt a genuine sense of relief over that news, for Terry had flown frequently with me and served me many cups of coffee. I hoped that Len had sent the flowers I had asked him to send. But, knowing Len, I felt sure those flowers were in Terry's room and had been there since early morning.

They also reported that six passengers had suffered serious injury. Others were in shock.

A preliminary estimate had fixed the damage to the airplane at slightly over a hundred thousand dollars, and the Civil Aeronautics Inspector in charge of the investigation had told Amalgamated that he wanted to talk with the captain of flight forty-eight of the same date.

I laughed. "That's probably right and I'll bet Anderson will want to go in with me to edit what I say." George joined me in laughing over the idea.

"And," Jinnie gasped, reaching hungrily for the second drink which I was mixing while she chattered, "I have saved the choice morsel for last." She paused dramatically and caught her breath.

"Give—give," George urged.

"Wayne Allison is divorced!" Then she laughed as I felt a deep flinch inside.

"Tell us about it, Wayne." Jinnie insisted.

It was an awkward moment. Both George and Jean sensed the knot she had suddenly tied inside me.

"Do you like to go fishing?" Jean asked me, calmly ignoring Jinnie and quietly guiding the conversation into a private one. George quickly pulled Jinnie, who had risen after the second drink, back down on his lap and covered her gabbing lips.

I felt grateful to Jean and we enjoyed talking of fishing for a while. During the second drink I began to feel sleepy and, in spite of myself, could not keep interest in Jinnie's story telling even though she was quite entertaining. My eyelids began to droop, and Jean, sitting beside me on a sofa, was quick to notice it.

"Poor Wayne," she sympathized, "he's so sleepy. We should leave and let him go to bed."

"That's just a come-on he's giving you," George informed her and at the same time winked at me and gave me the 'keep going' signal. I wondered what his plan could be, but didn't much care.

Jean didn't believe George and said so. "I think you should go to bed," she told me seriously, after hearing George announce that I had been up all the night before.

"Don't rush me," I chided her gently and knew from the smile and faint blush that she caught the double meaning.

"I've had a long day and do have to get up much earlier than George," I acknowledged, "but I don't want to spoil a good party."

"Oh, don't let that bother you," George hastened to tell me. "They're going to stay for another drink or so before I walk them back to the Belmont Plaza, and it'll be okay if you go to bed." He glanced at his watch, which was reading near two in the morning. "I'll entertain them both!"

Both girls laughed at him. Jean rose to go, but George pushed her back into the chair.

"Just face the windows," he directed the two girls, "and I'll see that junior gets into his flannel nightgown."

I kicked off my boots, turned the cover back on the corner bed and, as soon as the girls had turned their backs, I slipped out of my clothes and climbed into bed. George hung my clothes while I called for an eight o'clock ring.

Jean rose to go again, but George insisted that she remain. He exclaimed, "I wouldn't think of letting you go home this late at night with all the wolves roaming the street. Why, I'll bet there are at least a half a dozen in the lobby of the Belmont Plaza, just waiting for you."

His eyes grew big and round as he stared at her. "Big timber wolves!" He insisted. "Minnesota wolves!"

I chuckled at the way George never missed a stray remark and snuggled deeper into the bed. It felt so good.

"Well, I know where there is one," Jinnie decided, "and he's just around the corner from the Belmont Plaza."

"Yeah, yeah, yeah." George chortled. "Can you hear my teeth clicking?"

It was dimly daylight through the drawn blinds when the phone awakened me. I thanked the operator and began shaving while making as little noise as possible. George, I know, would sleep until about eleven, have lunch with the girls in the Belmont Plaza dining room, and leisurely check on all the arrangements for the System Board hearings. That was really my job as chairman, but George had agreed to take care of it and leave me free for the negotiating table.

I cursed softly to myself as I shaved, while I thought of George having lunch with Jean. Somehow, I had a feeling that I should do that.

I wondered how she would look in the light of day, how she would look if I seated her in the dining room so that the sunlight would strike her hair.

"I'll bet she would be beautiful," I murmured to myself.

I stopped my shaving and looked myself in the eye.

"What's eating on you?" I asked softly.

"You'd better get your mind off her," I murmured, "Start figuring the company plays for today."

"What do you think of Sayen?" I asked softly aloud.

"A real nice appearance," I answered myself, "but I didn't get much impression of anything else."

I shook my head. "Sure hope he turns out to have the stuff," I murmured. "The ol'man needs help badly. And he needs a good thinking head to sort of set up the pins for him, the same way Damon once did for C.R." I repeated that aloud to emphasize the point.

I finished shaving in the bathroom, showered, and then slipped out into the darkened room for my clothes. Quietly dressing in the semidarkness, I paid little attention to George. Many times in the past I had done this same stunt, that is, dress and slip out without awakening George. He was a notoriously late sleeper while I enjoyed getting out early. So, as usual, I left the room in darkness except for the light from the bathroom and the dim outside light coming through the drawn shades.

It is difficult for me to say exactly what caused me to take a good look at George. Maybe it was the shape of his figure, maybe he wasn't rolled up in a knot the way George usually slept, and again maybe it was a sixth sense. Anyway, I paused while pulling on my boots and took a close look at the well-covered figure with only the exposed top of the night cap which George always wore to bed. It was his trademark, probably a habit acquired from his Dutch parents. Anyway, it didn't look right.

I leaned over and pulled George's covers back slightly. There was a giggle that ended in a peal of girlish laughter. I hastily snapped on a light and found myself gazing into Jean's laughing blue eyes. George's night cap only half way covered her mass of reddish blond hair and for a second she looked like something out of the Arabian Nights.

"Have you been here all night?" I asked and sat down on the side of her bed.

She pulled the covers more tightly under her chin and laughed again.

"Sure." She stretched slightly and exposed a bare arm and shoulder.

"Where is George?"

"He traded beds with me."

"He what?" I asked in amazement.

She repeated, smiling.

I smiled too, thinking of George. No one ever knew what he would pull next. "Tell me about it."

"There's really nothing to tell." Her sparkling blue eyes gazed steadily into mine. George and Jinnie conspired against me last night after you went to sleep. They insisted on my sleeping here and George simply confiscated my bed and my roommate. Of course he made it sound so easy, saying that you would never notice, and then he told me about how you sometimes talk to yourself. I love to listen in on people talking to themselves. My father did it quite regularly when I was a girl." She laughed again.

I laughed too and then caught my breath.

"Oh, baby!" I breathed. "And George spent the night in a stewardess' room."

"Don't worry." She urged. "Jinnie promised to take good care of him."

"No doubt," I chuckled and studied her more closely. I looked down into her bright blue eyes, her clean face clear of any make-up and marvelled at her smooth girlish complexion. For the first time I noted the sweet contours of her lips under that little upturned nose. On an impulse, I leaned forward and kissed her.

I paused, then folded her gently in my arms and kissed her again, long and earnestly. My left arm slipped around her shoulders and I realized that she had gone to bed without benefit of night clothes. I pulled her closer. The covers slipped down a trifle and her arms slipped around my neck. For a long moment I floated in the sweetness of her kiss while realization dawned upon me that her business suit had certainly deemphasized the fullness of her warm breasts.

I paused again, brushed her hair back carefully with my right hand and slipped that arm around her body. She kissed me again, then gently pushed me away while struggling to pull the covers back up over her shoulders.

"Wayne," she whispered, "I didn't come here for this." Her eyes were big and blue with the knowledge that she was on some very thin ice.

"No?" I smiled in reassurance. "Then why are you here?"

She studied my face intently for a few moments, then replied.

"I stayed here because it was obvious that Jinnie and George wanted to 'shack' and if I stayed here I knew that they would feel better about the whole deal. And too," she giggled, "I wanted to hear you talk to your-self."

"And what else—?" I questioned.

"Nothing—." She paused and searched my eyes again. "George has talked so much of you. He says you are a gentleman and the most honest man he has ever known. And the other pilots have mentioned your name so much and shown so much respect for you that I was just dying to see more of you."

"Then you didn't stay here to 'shack' with me?"

"No," she whispered, her eyes wide again.

"My mistake," I apologized and lit a cigarette after offering her one and getting a quick shake of the head.

"Don't apologize," she urged. "It's just that—well, I—I never have!" The truth shone in her clear blue eyes.

I studied her thoughtfully for a long minute while I pulled on the cigarette.

"And this isn't the time, place, or the right man?" I murmured.

"It isn't the time, it isn't the place, and the man—I don't know." Her eyes had a troubled look.

"Of course." I smiled with complete composure, patted her cheek, and told her to sleep as long as she liked, have breakfast in bed, and sign my name to the chit.

"And," I added significantly, picking up my coat and briefcase, "I'll be looking for you up and down the line, sweetness."

Her smile was tender, half pleased relief and—I wondered—could it have been half regret as I closed the door behind me.

Chapter 8

Negotiations

I met the other members of the negotiating committee in the downstairs lobby of the company's swank office building on Park Avenue. It was the same building Schustman and I had entered with the Master Executive Council of Amalgamated over three years before, when we had met with Ralph Damon and C.R. on the screening cases, first named the Captain's Elimination Board. But for some reason the first name was quite unpopular with the captains of Amalgamated.

Everyone seemed quite cheerful while we waited for Dave and Sayen to appear. Schwartz, with his wavy brown hair in immaculate tiers from a center part, was in especially good humor. Displaying newspapers with big headlines concerning the outbreak of hostilities in Korea he laughed, showing even rows of perfect teeth.

"I'll bet the company had us come here to tell us there is a war on in Korea," he declared. "You know how much smarter the company officials are than the pilots on the line. It's so amazing!"

"What?" Red Cary pulled on his pipe and eyed Schwartz casually.

"The super-intelligence of the officials," Schwartz chuckled. "In their opinion there is such a gulf of intelligence separating the two groups that only one of two plausible conditions exist; that is, super-intelligence on their part or single-celled creatures operating their extremely complicated machinery. That's us, you know."

Red chuckled. "Why don't you ask Di Pasquale for the solution? He knows all the answers. He'll tell you."

"He'll tell us without asking," Woodall declared in that quiet manner that seemed to go with the older captains.

Everyone laughed for Woodall rarely wise-cracked. Dave and Sayen appeared about that time and we all took the elevator together.

The conference room was a large elaborate room with a long oak table in the center of the room and sturdy chairs on either side of the table, behind the chairs. The room was air-conditioned, quiet, and well equipped with ash trays, pencils, scratch pads, a telephone, and a call buzzer for a company stenographer.

I did not like to use company conference rooms. My dislike stemmed from one occasion, right after the close of WW II, when we were attempting to negotiate a four engine pay scale. We had utilized such a room at the airport adjacent to the company's airport offices. It was convenient is all I can say for it. That was before the negotiations were taken over by a federal mediator and moved to Park Avenue, where the big wheels reigned. That time it had taken three years to conclude a one year contract.

At the initial airport meetings one conference had run until late at night, or rather, early in the morning, with each side taking frequent recesses for little private huddles. The Air Transport Association had a hired negotiator working to make all airline contracts read the same, and he was trying to do all the negotiating for the members of the Air Transport Association. It was a real fiasco!

When one side or the other asked for a huddle, the company officials assisting the Air Transport Negotiator always politely withdrew and left the pilots to huddle in the company conference room. It was very considerate of them and it gave us a good taste of what was in store in negotiating with the Air Transport Association and Amalgamated Airlines.

These withdrawal and return meetings continued for some time, with the company side always seeming to be prepared with a good rebuttal for each pilot attack. Finally I took a couple of minutes during one huddle to look for a hidden microphone. It was cleverly concealed in the light fixture hanging over the table.

Leaning over it I remarked: "Dave, don't you think the Amalgamated officials are really honest officials to deal with?" Then I cut the cord with my pen knife. After that, the officials were not nearly so well prepared and brilliant in their rebuttals. So, to begin with, I was prejudiced against company conference rooms.

We seated ourselves along one side of the table in the sturdy oak chairs and relaxed for a few minutes smoking. Dave had always insisted on being early at any negotiations. As he said: "It gives you a chance to look the other birds over while they're squatting!"

Di Pasquale led the parade to the company side of the table. He was the company 'yakety-yak' man, the Director of Labor Relations. It didn't matter which side of a controversy the pilots took, Di Pasquale would quickly take the other side.

Once, on a pilot grievance filed for the simple purpose of securing a System Board ruling on a pilot's right to a prior run, a ruling that was designed to stop the company from interpreting the clause two different ways, depending on whether or not the pilot involved was a 'fair-haired' boy with some company official, the association attorney had simply stated the case. Then he had stepped back and asked:

"Mr. Di Pasquale, which side do you want?"

That approach had so surprised Mr. Di Pasquale that he had been unable to state his preference. Finally the association attorney had taken a position on the issue and Di Pasquale then arrayed the company in opposition. To those who witnessed the incident, and there were a dozen pilots there, it had given a lasting impression of the purpose of the Director of Labor Relations.

Mr. Di Pasquale was of slender build and dark of complexion with gray at his temple. A lawyer by profession, he was one of the war recruits who had floated to Amalgamated on C.R.'s coattails. A persistent rumor about him had filtered down through official ranks and to the pilots. According to that story, C.R. had hired Di Pasquale for the job during the war at a small foreign post where his airplane had stopped for repairs. Two fifths of scotch, both owned by Mr. Di Pasquale where no other was available, had convinced Mr. C.R. that he had found the right man.

Ed Hamilton, the Assistant Director of Labor Relations, followed Di Pasquale. He was a big, burly, slow thinking lawyer who had started as a clerk in ALPA's Washington office. In fact, Dave had helped him through law school with association funds while he worked in the office. Then, about the time he had come to be of some real help to the association, he had suddenly accepted a position with Amalgamated.

That unexpected switch had made Dave pretty mad at the time. It was considered unethical for an association employee, an attorney, to suddenly switch sides and take his knowledge of the association, Dave, and unresolved cases to the other side.

Walter Braznell was the third and last member of the company group. He was an old pilot, near fifty, but youthful and dapper in appearance with wavy gray hair, a dark gray mustache which he kept well tailored, a square chin with a big dimple, and an athletic figure. He had become a chief pilot about the time of my employment as a copilot, in early 1936.

Throughout the years he had moved upward to the position of Director of Flight. In turn, his assistant as chief pilot, Tom Boyson, had leaped over him and forged upward to the position of assistant to the President and Vice-President of operations, which had made him Braznell's boss. It had been a bitter pill to Braznell.

I thought of all this as the three entered, and I recalled how much Braznell had enjoyed coming to Fort Worth from either Chicago or New York, at every opportunity, to bird hunt with me during my copilot and junior captain days. We had become friendly hunters behind my bird dogs.

Then after the war, my persistent pressure in representing the pilots for fair deals instead of 'fair-haired deals' had gradually chilled that friendship. No doubt that was a result of my frequently placing him in a difficult position because of his poor administration of the pilot group and his frequent indulgence in favoritism.

As a System Board member I seemed to be constantly righting grievances attributed to his inefficient administration of the pilots. As a pilot negotiator on the last three labor contracts, and in working closely with David Behncke, I had been instrumental in the proposal of new contract provisions that would seriously curtail his practices of 'fair-haired' treatment of individual pilots. He just could not resist giving a choice charter trip to Bermuda to some friend, especially if it rightfully belonged to some pilot who had differed with him over some issue.

We shook hands all around the table as though we had not spent weeks and months in fruitless effort at negotiating the long overdue contract. Dave introduced Sayen to the company members, and I watched Sayen and Braznell as they were introduced. Perhaps it was an accident, perhaps it was an optical illusion, but I was startled to see Sayen, with a big friendly smile on his face, shake Braznell's hand and slyly wink at him. I caught the wink in the wall mirror behind Braznell.

Everyone settled in his chair with Dave in the middle of the table and directly across from Di Pasquale, who sat between Braznell and Hamilton. As usual, I sat on Dave's left side with Sayen on Dave's right. The others lined both sides of us three. I resolved to watch Sayen and Braznell closely.

Di Pasquale, the company yackety-yak man, led off.

"Gentlemen," he began, "we asked for this meeting more as a briefing meeting than anything else."

I glanced at Dave, with his pale blue eyes boring into Di Pasquale's nervous ones. So it was a briefing, I thought, they are merely telling us. Okay, I thought, they are going to brief us while Sayen sells them a mileage limitation. I nudged Red Cary and our eyes met while he hid a smile with his pipe stem.

"As you all know," Di Pasquale continued, "our country is beginning a major offensive in Korea. The sudden demand for men, material, and munitions on the other side of the Pacific has resulted in our government calling on the airlines to assume a major roll in the transportation of key men and materials. Therefore we have agreed to do our part."

He paused to allow his words to settle. Then he continued: "Pan-American, because of its wide operations and bases across the Pacific, has been designated by the War Department as a primary carrier. We have decided to subcontract a number of DC-4 Douglas airplanes and the necessary pilots to Pan-American to become an intricate part of their operations. In fact, we have already signed such a contract with Pan-American."

Dave continued to watch Di Pasquale's eyes. I knew that Di Pasquale expected him to ask a multitude of questions. Yet Dave just sat there and slowly stroked his mustache, his eyes never wavering from boring into those nervous brown ones across the table. The rest of us took our cue from Dave and remained silent, barely moving enough to disturb the slow rise of smoke from individual cigarettes.

Di Pasquale cleared his throat nervously and glanced up and down our side of the table as though inviting comment and questions. Yet the silence remained unbroken. Finally Walt Braznell broke the silence. He cleared his throat twice then began: "I have wired each pilot base for volunteers to participate in the Pacific operation. The crews selected will be from those volunteering for that assignment, with our taking into consideration the seniority of those volunteering, their equipment qualifications, their previous experience in transatlantic flying and the recommendations of the various chief pilots on our system."

"For example." Braznell continued, giving me a friendly glance, "Wayne here will be pretty sure of securing the assignment with his three years of over-water flying, his seniority, and his flying record."

I smiled wryly. "You mean, Walt, that I am being drafted?"

"Oh, no!" Walt hastened to assure me amid the laughter. "You will have to volunteer!"

"Then scratch one Okie." I told him flatly.

"Why?" he questioned, obviously puzzled. "It is going to be a good deal."

"So was the last one." I looked at him steadily and spoke softly with my eyes never wavering from his dark ones. "It seems that I recall the company talking a rush-rush deal with a war as an excuse. Pilots were needed badly to haul cargo and passengers across the Atlantic. And the company called for volunteers."

I laughed while grinding out a cigarette. "Your pilots were very patriotic and almost all volunteered. In a little while you had a hundred pilots in Presque Isle, Maine, ready to haul cargo and passengers across the North Atlantic. At the same time you had another hundred in Natal, Brazil, ready to haul passengers and cargo across the South Atlantic. So they waited, and waited for two months because someone forgot to figure out where the airplanes were coming from that were to be used. And while they waited they didn't know their status, their pay, or whether or not they would get expenses while away.

"The company made ten percent profit on that last deal, even on the pilots' salaries." I smiled slowly without mirth and again looked at him directly as I asked. "What percentage is the company making this time?"

Walt hesitated and looked at Dave who merely returned his gaze in silence. Then he leaned over and said something to Di Pasquale. Clearing his throat he replied. "We don't have that kind of a deal, Wayne," He spoke slowly and earnestly. "The subcontract from Pan-American, the prime contractor, calls for so much pay per airplane mile flown. There is no guarantee of a profit. We furnish our own airplanes, four crews to each airplane, and we do the major overhaul work. Everything else is taken care of by Pan-American."

"It does sound a little different," I conceded. "Would you tell us a little something about the pay, insurance, prisoner-of-war status, and the pilot protective features?"

"It is all covered in a policy letter I am issuing to explain the details to the pilots," he replied. Then he launched into a rough summary of the different features as contained in his policy letter. But he didn't have a copy of the letter for our perusal.

The others asked numerous questions and the ball went around the table several times. Dave, alone, sat quietly and let the company talk and talk and talk. Di Pasquale was especially eloquent about having the pilots show their patriotism to their company and country.

Braznell talked about the necessity of securing experienced pilots with previous over-water navigational experience. It was quite evident that he wanted to place a group of senior pilots on a job that would draw pay on an airplane-mile basis. Otherwise, the company was in a position to lose a considerable sum, especially if a few of their four-engined airplanes failed to return, providing, of course, that Braznell was telling the truth when he said that there was no guarantee of a profit. But that didn't sound like Amalgamated—to jump into a deal for the government without a guaranteed profit.

I thought of the last war, WW II, and how Amalgamated had made ten percent over and above the cost, including the salaries of the personnel utilized. And the ten percent was paid on Amalgamated's bookkeeping. I personally knew that the company had charged a large figure for pilot training when actually little was expended.

Once, shortly after the end of the war, Ralph Damon had come to Tulsa to explain Amalgamated's bookkeeping system as utilized at Amalgamated's big aircraft modification center working on a government contract. Apparently he wanted to make sure that the cream was heavy on all government jobs and explained the bookkeeping system used. It was one in which Amalgamated kept two sets of books, one for the government's inspection and one for the Amalgamated officials. He didn't say that they were different; he didn't have to say that. He just kept repeating that the company wanted to make sure that all the supervisors understood the necessity of keeping a close account of all work done for the government and were making sure that a suitable amount was charged as government work.

Schustman and I were there, listening enthralled, due to having been invited by mistake to a supervisors' meeting. Damon was well along in his explanation when he suddenly spied us, changed color considerably, and declared an abrupt recess. In the intervening recess the Tulsa station manager, fat Andy Williams, had approached us and politely inquired if we realized that we were attending a supervisors' meeting.

We shook our heads and in turn asked him if he realized that one of his assistants had invited us to attend. We explained that we just thought that he, Andy Williams, wanted to have a good turnout for Mr. Damon's speech. He was stupid enough to believe us, but it was the truth.

George and I faded out before the end of the recess, which was a pretty long one. We laughed all the way to George's home over the way Mr. Damon's face had changed color at recognition of us. As George explained it, he looked like a big tom cat that had suddenly realized that two little rat-terrier dogs were watching him steal the canary.

That had caused George and I to make a mutual vow. We solemnly agreed to do everything in our power, as System Board members, to make the company deal honestly with the pilots. Damon's lecture had shaken from us any remaining shreds of belief that Amalgamated meant to deal honestly. Neither of us spoke it openly at that time, but we both realized that we were working for a crooked company—one whose officials were practicing and encouraging dishonest dealings.

It had given both our mouths a green persimmon taste.

"Dave," Braznell appealed directly to the ol'man, "we are asking you to confer with us on this problem in order that no obstacle will delay the performance of this very important work for our government. It is for our national defense that we are asking the pilots to volunteer for this and we want you to see it in that light."

"Suppose not enough pilots volunteer?" Red Cary surprised us all with the question.

Braznell turned his eyes to him.

"That is a situation we sincerely hope will never happen to Amalgamated when the company is trying its utmost to cooperate with the War Department. However," he hesitated, "if that should happen, it would be necessary to assign junior captains and junior copilots in the reverse order of seniority."

"In other words," Red persisted, "the Amalgamated pilots are going to fly this assignment one way or another?" I was amazed that Red, who usually sat back and puffed on his pipe, and allowed others to push the needling questions, was so quick to nail the situation down.

Walt Braznell nodded slowly. "That's about right, Red."

There was a silence, with each side studying the other. The ol'man took his eyes from Braznell and looked up and down the table. It was an open invitation for further comment.

"Would we get to Honolulu?" Spencer asked with a wolfish look and smile.

"That will be a main stopover point," Walt quickly answered. "Each crew will go through to Japan with stopovers for rest and return the same way. Some routings will be via Alaska and others will take different routings. Pan-American will set up the trip assignments and work our crews in with theirs. It will amount to considerable flying for a week or ten days and then two or three weeks off."

"It sounds like a lark," Sayen decided with a big grin. "Could you use an outsider?"

Walt laughed with pleasure. "Maybe so, if Dave will give you a leave of absence."

Dave brushed the hair on his head back with his left hand, which was a signal that he did not want the conversation to continue in that vein. All other times he used his right hand.

"Walt," I questioned quickly, "has the company a definite contract proposal to cover this operation?" Dave turned his head to look at me, and it was a signal for the others to give me the floor until he interrupted. I was a little surprised at this, for that made it quite obvious that he did not want Sayen to continue.

"We don't consider a contract necessary," Walt replied. "My policy letter covers the situation completely and it will be strictly adhered to by the company."

"Walt," I questioned again, "didn't you say that Amalgamated had signed a contract with Pan-American covering the operation?"

"That's right. We are subcontracting a certain amount of flying from Pan-American. That company has the primary contract with our government."

"How long did it take Amalgamated to work out the contract with

Pan-American?"

Braznell shrugged. "I think it was a couple of days."

"Then don't you think Amalgamated should take a couple of days and sign a contract with the pilots before you request volunteers?" I locked eyes with him again.

"My boss, the vice-president of operations, has informed me that a contract with the pilots is not necessary at this time. After the operation is working and we have concluded our present contract negotiations by signing a domestic contract, we will consider a supplemental contract covering the Pacific operation, should one be desired and necessary at that time."

"In other words," I pursued him, "you will not conclude a supplemental contract covering the Pacific operation before the operation goes into effect?"

"Wayne," it was easy to see that he was growing irritated, "in the interest of national defense we must place this operation into effect immediately. We cannot take the time to dicker on a pilots' supplemental working agreement when our government wants the program expedited with all possible speed."

"But you took two days to sign one with Pan-American."

Braznell ground a cigarette into an ash tray. He was clearly about to lose his temper.

Dave suddenly interrupted. "Let's consider that point for a little time," he spoke softly and easily as he looked straight into Braznell's eyes. "We'll discuss it further with you after lunch."

"Now," Dave continued, "we would like to have you take one more look at the main stumbling block in our present contract negotiations. Sayen here has a new approach to the subject which we believe will place it in a new light for you to study."

The company members looked with renewed interest at Sayen. They were obviously curious.

Sayen rose and pulled the blackboard to the head of the table with a big smile on his face.

"Gentlemen," he began, eyeing both sides of the table from his position. "Mr. Behncke and I have followed closely the contract negotiations with Amalgamated Airlines. We have carefully studied the position the company has taken on each major issue under consideration at this negotiations. And, after a very thorough and comprehensive evaluation of the positions taken by both the company and the pilots," he paused and studied the attentive faces of the company representatives as well as those of Mr. Behncke and the pilot group, "we have come to the conclusion that a new approach toward the major stumbling block might be agreeable to both sides."

"Heretofore," he smile broadly at the company representatives, "the mere mention of a mileage limitation has been like waving a red flag in front of a bull. And," he added soberly, "in consideration of a yearly contract, I can see some justification of the company's position.

"Mr. Behncke and I have discussed it numerous times and finally came up with a completely different approach to the problem." He paused and studied the interest the company representatives were giving him.

"In the first place," he continued, "the term of mileage limitation was a poorly chosen phrase. In the second place, it is inappropriate because it only deals with Douglas DC-6 equipment. It doesn't consider the DC-7's, the DC-8's, etc.

"Now today," he smiled broadly, "we would like to have you forget about a mileage limitation and think in terms of an increased mileage increment, to be known as the IMI formula."

"Is this a formula?" Braznell asked as Sayen paused.

Sayen nodded.

"For all equipment?"

"For all equipment." Sayen smiled again.

"Now you're talking," Braznell could hardly restrain himself.

"Then it's not a mileage limitation on a pilot's flying?" Hamilton questioned bluntly with his bull-like voice.

Sayen hesitated and I smiled to myself. He was giving the company an approach I had worked up a couple of months back and submitted to Dave for his consideration. It dealt with all equipment and was most far-reaching in its effect on airline flying for the future. Dave had written me that it should be held up for a time and not mentioned so that it would come as a complete surprise to the company.

I felt flattered that Sayen had so much confidence in an idea which I had submitted privately to Dave. I wondered if Sayen knew the idea had come from me. At least he had not presented it in that light, not that it mattered, but it was quite evident that he was cutting himself in for a share of the credit.

"Yes, and no," Sayen answered Hamilton. "I'll lay out the IMI formula, which is designed to be applicable to all types of equipment flown today and tomorrow by Amalgamated." He turned and wrote the letter "X" on the blackboard.

"Let's say "X" equals the number of miles any one pilot should fly any one airplane in any one month of any year," he began.

The company members as well as a number of the pilots pulled pencil and paper close. All were intensely interested. Dave sat low in his chair, relaxing against the back, his eyelids almost closed as though he was about to catch a little nap. It was one of his favorite tricks. And sometimes, I often thought, he actually did catch a little nap, especially when some company official was giving a long and tiring dissertation.

"Is this formula a proposal?" Di Pasquale wanted to know.

"If you care to consider it as such," Sayen beamed at him. "I am quite confident that you are going to like it."

"Will it apply—," Di Pasquale hesitated and considered again before adding, "to possible jet transports?"

Again I smiled to myself and thought of the jet transport with a speed of six hundred miles per hour which we had learned C.R. was considering buying. Di Pasquale was giving away the company's thinking. It was the first time the company had mentioned a jet transport across the table to the pilots' negotiating committee.

"This is an all inclusive formula." Sayen smiled a wise little smile.

"Now," he continued, "the DC-3 cruises at 180 miles per hour. By multiplying that against eighty-five hours we have the total monthly mileage a pilot can fly a DC-3 in one month. That amounts to 15,300 miles."

Pencils followed his board calculations. Then turning from the blackboard, he spoke quietly and earnestly.

"Your pilots have never objected to flying the DC-3 a full eighty-five hours each month. With the advent of the DC-4, a four engine aircraft, there were rumblings of discontent.

"The pilots' unit of production is the mile flown and they objected to more units of production being demanded of them when their principal pay was calculated on the hours flown; at the time their company continued to collect from the passengers on the basis of the miles flown."

Sayen continued seriously and in a very earnest voice. "The coming of the DC-6 and the company's continued policy of paying the pilots for the hours flown and collecting on the basis of miles flown has created a condition which the pilots do not think fair. They have been called upon to produce more and more units of production by flying more miles, encountering more weather, at faster speeds, and at the same time, operating more complex equipment that requires more knowledge and presents more hazards in eighty-five hours of flying.

"On the other hand," he waved a hand at Di Pasquale who was beginning to squirm in his seat and starting to interrupt, "the company is entitled to more units of production and greater productivity of revenue for each hour of flight for providing new and faster equipment, and thereby improving the public service." He flashed another smile at the company officials.

"Therefore," he paused dramatically, "if we take the monthly mileage a pilot can fly the DC-3 in eighty-five hours, and combine it with the monthly mileage a pilot can fly in any other type of equipment purchased by the airline, and divide that figure by two, we have a fair solution of the figure X. That figure is the Increased Mileage Increment or IMI for short."

Sayen paused and lighted a cigarette while pencils worked on paper and whispered consultations occurred on both sides.

Red Cary leaned over and whispered to me. "It seems to me that he took the words right out of your mouth. I recall you giving me that same kind of approach over two months ago and then asking that I forget it."

"He's selling it," I smiled. "If he can get the company to buy and brand that calf, we'll never say anything about its real mammy!"

Red took a long pull on his pipe and smiled knowingly.

Hamilton figured furiously for a few minutes, then looked at Sayen with a wolfish smile.

"That's actually a mileage limitation," he announced.

Somehow he reminded me of a big sheep dog that had gone renegade and joined the wolf pack. That made him doubly dangerous in my estimation, for he knew too much of the ways of the sheep.

"No," Sayen smiled back. "It is an increased mileage increment for both the company and the pilots."

Hamilton started to say more, then flashed a glance at Di Pasquale, his boss, and subsided. I knew that under the table a foot had nudged a foot.

Walt Braznell looked up at Sayen from the figures he had computed on a piece of paper.

"Have you the calculations for the monthly pilot hours your proposal would permit a pilot to fly on each type of equipment we have discussed?" he asked, looking at the piece of paper.

Sayen smiled broadly and shook his head. "I have the miles only. The hour is not a unit of production."

Referring to a sheet of paper, Braznell read: "Where a pilot flew a DC-3 15,300 miles in a month, this formula would permit him to fly a DC-6 a total of 20,400 miles, a DC-7 a total of 24,650 miles, a jet transport a total of 30,150 miles, based on an assumed speed of six hundred miles per hour.

"The way I have figured it," Braznell smiled a tight thin lipped smile and continued reading, "under this formula our pilots would only fly a DC-6 a total of sixty-eight hours each month, a DC-7 a total of sixty-one hours, a jet transport only fifty-two hours."

"But look at the miles they would fly!" Sayen grinned broadly while we all laughed.

Then Dave took command of the meeting. He began talking slowly about the time when pilots flew hundred mile per hour airplanes without aid of instruments and solely by the seat of their pants and drew their pay based solely on the miles flown. He didn't forget to remind us all that Walt Braznell was one of those hearty pioneers.

Dave told about how the pioneer airlines had suddenly changed the method of paying pilots, from mileage pay to hourly pay. Curiously, he brought out, that was done just before several of the companies had purchased airplanes that cruised at one hundred and thirty mile per hour. It had meant a terrific pay cut for the pilots.

"That," Dave rapped the table firmly with his knuckles, "coupled with the unsafe flying characteristics of the new one hundred and thirty mile airplanes, was the real cause for the organization of the Air Line Pilots' Association."

He paused to allow that point to sink in and then continued. "And today," he struck the table with his fist, "your pilots are not paid as much for flying the most modern and complex equipment as they were paid for flying those old hundred mile per hour airplanes. Sad but true!"

He paused and fixed his pale blue eyes on first one official and then another before continuing. "Yet, curiously, our major point of difference at this negotiations is not over pilot pay, but over the desire of the pilots to persuade the company to desist from attempting to multiply that monthly mileage figure by another four."

Dave looked directly into Braznell's eyes. "Surely," he concluded, "surely, Amalgamated Airlines must realize the fairness and necessity of a formula that will permit both the company and the pilots to share in the greater speed and productivity of the higher speed airliners of today and tomorrow."

Dave's short talk was so forceful and appealing in its sincerity that even Di Pasquale had to clear his throat before he could thank Sayen and Dave for their able presentation of a new and interesting formula. It was quite evident that the company members wanted to go upstairs with the idea. They suggested lunch, with another meeting at two in the afternoon. That would give them over two hours for lunch and a conference with a higher official, I mentally calculated.

As we rose from the table, Sayen looked directly at Braznell and asked him if he wouldn't join him for lunch. Walt hesitated for a couple of seconds and then accepted. It was an unusual invitation and it took us all by surprise. I caught a surprised look on even Dave's poker face.

In the past we had refrained from crossing the table for lunch or coffee unless everyone was invited to attend. I recalled the impression I had obtained at the start of the session, that Braznell and Sayen had met before.

Shortly after lunch the entire negotiating committee met with Dave in a meeting room at his hotel. Sayen was absent and the ol'man finally called the meeting to order without him.

"The first question for us to take up," he decided, "is the question of a contract to cover the Pacific operation that Mr. Braznell is in such a hurry to get under way. Could I have the feeling of the committee?"

It didn't take long for Dave to find out what he wanted to know. The group members were close in their thinking, and as Red Cary expressed it: "Policy letters written by Braznell are notorious for their ambiguity."

Schwartz also brought out the fact that a policy letter can be changed overnight, rescinded and ignored without any consideration of the pilots. A contractual obligation could not be so easily circumvented. It would be far more protection to the pilots.

"Then it's all settled," Dave decided. "We'll give them two days of our time to conclude a contract with the pilots."

Everyone laughed, for we all knew that the company would haggle forever if they could just get the pilots out flying the Pacific before concluding a contract.

Suddenly Sayen appeared, his face slightly flushed and a cat-eating-cream grin on his handsome features. I could not help but note his elation. Dave evidently noticed it also, for he leaned back in his chair and fumbled for a cigar. I handed him one, for as usual, he was out. With Dave I always tried to have a few extra on hand.

"Well," he rumbled, "did you get everything settled with Amalgamated?" I took that as a sly dig, but Sayen just grinned broadly and gave us all a most confident look.

"I think I have things moving along," he claimed pulling a chair up near the ol'man and trying to assume a modest look.

Dave said nothing, just sat fingering the cigar and eyeing Sayen.

"Well, give us the dirt!" Spencer urged Sayen. "Did Braznell buy the IMI formula?"

Sayen lit a cigarette slowly, offering the ol'man a light at the same time.

"We had a most enlightening talk."

"Enlightening for whom?" Red Cary chuckled through his pipe smoke. I knew he viewed Sayen as sort of a junior copilot in contract negotiations.

Sayen ignored him.

"Walt told me some of the problems facing the company, and in general we discussed ways and means the company and the pilots can work together."

"Did you discuss the formula?" Spencer was impatient.

Sayen nodded. "We talked about it for some length. He is quite understanding of our problem. In fact, he chose to describe it as a burr under the pilots' saddle. Then he told me of one or two that are bothering him."

"Burrs or saddles?" Schwartz laughed.

"For one thing," Sayen continued, ignoring Schwartz, "he is quite upset about these flight allocations cases coming up before the System

Board tomorrow."

"He has a right to be," I commented dryly, growing wary.

I wondered how the ol'man was taking this line of talk and glanced at him. His features were impassive, his eyes expressionless and fixed on Sayen with a childlike intentness. I could read nothing of his thinking.

"What did you work out with Braznell?" I knew there was a tinge of frost in my voice even though I tried to keep it out.

"Nothing." Sayen gave me a big smile. "We merely discussed an exchange of favors between the pilots and the company."

"Like what?"

He shrugged and then looked directly at me.

"They suggested that if we dropped the flight allocation cases and do a good job for the company on the Pacific, they were certain that the company would look favorably on the IMI formula."

The room was suddenly very quiet. No one stirred. Nothing moved except a thin trace of smoke oozing from around Red Cary's pipe stem. Only Dave's faded blue eyes shifted from Sayen to me.

"'They'—who?" I asked very softly.

"Oh—." Sayen exclaimed realizing his slip, "Di Pasquale dropped by just as we were finishing lunch and joined in the conversation for a few minutes."

I was furious at the Association's new vice-president. To me I suddenly saw him as a former copilot, with little seasoning, projected into a position of importance, and he was ready to wheel and deal.

"I thought you were here to sell them the IMI formula rather than give away our nuts in a 'side-door' deal." There was icy sarcasm in my voice.

"Just a minute," Dave rumbled. To Sayen he asked. "What did you tell them?"

"Nothing—nothing at all. I merely said that I would take it up with the negotiating committee. I didn't promise them anything. I made no deal with them—side or otherwise." He shot me a sharp glance.

"Hell!" I snorted to Dave in disgust. "He told them he would take up the matter of trading off the flight allocation cases—individual pilot grievances—for a favorable glance from the company at a contract proposal."

I arose, pushed my chair aside, glanced around the room, and faced

Dave. In a flash I decided to use the same line of talk I had heard Dave make in a speech to a pilot group. It had greatly impressed me.

Pacing the floor in front of Sayen and Dave I began: "The most sacred section of our working agreement with Amalgamated is the grievance section. Originally it was written very broadly to permit a pilot or a group of pilots to grieve and be granted a hearing about anything one or more pilots might desire to file a grievance over. We have kept it that way throughout the years, since the first working agreement was signed with Amalgamated back in 1938.

"Under its provisions the company is forced to grant a hearing on any grievance, regardless of how small or large. Under those same provisions, one or more pilots can carry a grievance—regardless of how small or large, and regardless of how many may oppose the issue—all the way through the Pilots System Board of Adjustment. No one can stop it, neither the company nor the association. The right of the grieving pilot, or pilots, to bring a disputed point to a final settlement is almost sacred."

I stood to my full height and swept the entire room with hard and angry eyes as I moved a little nearer the doorway. They were accustomed to seeing me smiling and laughing, joking one minute and dead serious the next, but always in a good natured manner with my temper well under control. The room was deadly quiet.

"Several years ago," I addressed them all, "I was appointed to the Pilots System Board of Adjustment for a period of one year or until relieved. Each year Mr. Behncke has refused to relieve me. During that time I have heard many disputes and learned that the most cherished portion of our working agreement is the 'right to grieve.' It is a pilot's only defense against unfair treatment. The System Board of Adjustment is the pilots' Supreme Court.

"Recently the company officials saw fit to start a system-wide juggling of flight time, regardless of its effect on the pilot group. Blocks of flying time were moved from one base to another with reckless abandon and many pilots were placed in the position of either moving to follow the flying time, with no assurance that it would stay at the new base, or revert to copilot status, even though their system seniority did not warrant such a reduction in status.

"In defense against this unfair treatment, the pilots literally flooded the company with grievances. My briefcase is full of appeals to the

System Board. Tomorrow the Pilots System Board of Adjustment, of which I am chairman, will hear those cases. The individual rights of the pilots must be maintained.

"And today," I paused, "the new vice-president of the Air Line Pilots' Association has the audacity to discuss, with a couple of company officials, a plan by which those pilots' individual rights would be discarded for some nebulous glance at a contract proposal. And he calls it salesmanship!"

I took a couple of long strides toward the door and turned. "I'll have no part of any meeting in which such a proposal is even discussed," I exclaimed.

"Just a moment, Wayne." Dave growled from deep in his throat. He chewed at the end of his cigar thoughtfully, eyeing both Sayen and me at the same time. "Let's see what the rest of the committee thinks of the idea."

The room was extremely quiet again. No one stirred for a long minute. Then Red Cary slowly knocked the ashes from his big pipe. Meticulously he blew through it to make sure it was clear, then slipped it into his shirt pocket.

"Well, Dave," he commented, "I have attended several council meetings here in New York in which the flight allocation cases came up for discussion before over a hundred pilots. As you know, I am vice-chairman of the New York council, which is the largest on Amalgamated Airlines, and I took particular pains to note the feelings of the various members."

Slowly Red rose to his feet. "Next to mileage limitation, or," he glanced at Sayen, "the increased mileage increment, which ever you want to call it, the pilots of New York consider the flight allocation cases as the most important issue confronting the Amalgamated pilots today. I am certain that they would take a very dim view toward trading them off, especially when it involves trading individual rights for some very questionable group benefits. This pilot council has much at stake in those cases, and the pilots are well aware of it.

"So," he glanced around at the group, "excuse me while I walk with Wayne."

We didn't get far down the hallway before Schwartz joined us. His immaculate tiers of curly hair seemed even more curly. His face glowed with excitement, while his even rows of white teeth flashed as he talked.

"I pointed out that seniority, rights to a pilot run, and rights to promotion from copilot status meant nothing if we traded off the flight allocation cases. Then I walked," he explained.

Close behind him was Howard Woodall, senior member of the committee, and Dick Lyons, junior member, both laughing as they joined us.

"We just got up and walked out without saying anything," they confided, still chuckling.

In the hotel lobby Spencer joined us with his Adam's apple working overtime. He made the sixth and last member of the negotiating committee. We had walked out on Sayen's suggestion, and, indirectly, the ol'man's meeting.

It had never happened before. Never had an entire negotiating committee walked out on Dave. We stood around in a circle at a loss for words until Cary allowed as how he could stand a good scotch and soda. That sounded good to all and we were soon lined up on stools in the adjacent bar, like vultures on a fence.

There we were, sipping scotch with a little soda in outward contentment, when Dave found us some twenty minutes later. At first he looked in the doorway, for Dave was a teetotaler and did not know how to nonchalantly stroll into a bar.

Not one of us appeared to notice him as he eased himself onto a stool at one end of the group. But when he told the bartender that he would have the same, I felt Cary nudge my arm and noticed Schwartz hump up a little more on his stool, while Woodall had to drag out a handkerchief for a good blow.

There we sat for several minutes, silently sipping our drinks, apparently oblivious to the ol'man's presence. Hesitating for a minute, he finally sipped his drink. A little later he tried it again, and then seemed to be tasting it more thoroughly.

"H-a-r-u-m-m!" Dave cleared his throat and took a good sip of the drink. Leaning over the bar he looked past two of the group and spoke to me.

"We've just had something come up back at headquarters," he lied lamely, "and I had to send Sayen back to take care of it."

For a moment I thought a couple of the boys were going to laugh out loud, especially Schwartz, who suddenly shook as though he was having to absorb a six-inch sliver from the barstool in silence.

"Too bad." I commented and toyed with my glass without a change in expression. Then I took another sip from my glass. Dave and the others did likewise.

"Then what do you propose for this afternoon?" I questioned.

He leaned toward me and spoke to the entire committee.

"We'll go back in there this afternoon, give them an answer on the Pacific operation and then just let nature take its course. But," he added significantly, "we won't trade anything."

"Suits me." I nodded. The others also nodded in silent approval.

We had to hurry to be back at the negotiating table a few minutes early. I only had time to make a few notes and reflect on the wisdom of the ol'man's policy of being early in order to watch the other birds squat.

We didn't have long to wait until Di Pasquale came breezing into the meeting room closely followed by Walt Braznell and Ed Hamilton. I couldn't help but notice the difference in their mannerisms as compared to that morning.

Now they were almost jovial and had a cheery greeting for everyone. No doubt they sensed a fast deal on the pilots. Di Pasquale was quite friendly, even to me.

I could only smile inwardly and marvel over how much some company officials seemed to prefer a deal that was considered unethical rather than a straight across-the-table negotiation with the entire committee. In this case, they expected to finger the deal through Sayen and have him do the fixing with the members of the committee. In turn, they would make him a lot of promises about what the company would do on the 'increased mileage increment'—promises that would fade like smoke—but they would receive a pat on the back by a higher official for screwing the pilots. I had seen it happen in the past.

Sitting there, trying to watch the company officials without appearing to do so, I marvelled at what caused men to deal as they were trying to deal. I knew all three too well to believe anything they would promise. Too many times in the past I had seen all three promise and lie, agree to something and go back on their agreement, and then take the position that a higher official had countermanded their order or refused to honor their promise. Most of the time, they just brazenly fail to remember the wording of the agreement.

Then I recalled a problem my father had given me as a boy on the farm. The barnyard and grain bins were frequented by rats and I had occasionally indulged in a little target practice with my .22 rifle. Pointing at a dead rat lying near a grain bin, my father had asked me the reason for its death. Puzzled, I examined it closely for I had not indulged in rat shooting for some time. The entire top of the rat's head was open and its brains were gone. In addition, its throat had been severed cleanly by some needle-like object.

"Somebody blew its brains out," I hazarded a guess.

My father had patiently shook his head and added, "We'll look for another tomorrow morning."

On the following morning there was another dead rat nearby in the same grotesque condition. And another the next morning. Then we began to find them by the twos and threes. Completely mystified, I had questioned my father.

Carefully he had explained that I was looking at the work of a weasel. No doubt he had moved in under the grain bin and was living on the blood and brains of the rats.

"But won't all the rats leave now?" I had questioned with wide eyes.

"No, son," my father had patiently explained, "it doesn't work that way. In fact more rats will come into the barnyard. The weasel lives off the rats' blood and brains, and to attract them, he gives off a scent that is pleasing to the rats. They'll flock to him like homing pigeons and, in the end, be destroyed by him. He'll sacrifice them one by one to satisfy his greed."

Then looking at me with an odd little smile on his firm mouth he had remarked casually, "As you go through life, son, you will find that there are men like that too."

Sitting there at the table, I thought of how true his prediction had been. I watched the three company officials settle in their seats, stretch their necks, and pass friendly banter across the table. No doubt they were looking for Sayen.

"H-a-r-u-m-m!" Dave cleared his throat and consulted a large railroad type of watch in a vest pocket. "Guess it's about time we kick off."

Di Pasquale stretched about three inches of neck out of his collar and asked quickly, "Where's Sayen?"

"Oh,—Sayen." Dave looked down our side of the table as though missing him for the first time. "Why—," he hesitated for a second, "we had something come up with one of the other carriers that required immediate action." He gave the company members a very serious look.

"I had to rush him back to headquarters to sort of fill in during my absence. You know," he confided, "something always seems to happen that requires immediate action whenever we both get out of pocket at the same time."

The company members nodded sympathetically while they tried to adjust their thinking to balance for this new situation. It was suddenly quite different from what they were expecting. They looked at each other in bewilderment.

"H-a-r-u-m-m!" Dave cleared his throat again and fixed childlike blue eyes on Di Pasquale's brown ones. "Where were we?" he questioned with guile and innocent blue eyes.

"Oh," Di Pasquale was startled, "I believe that we were to conclude our briefing on the Pacific operation."

"And," Dave added significantly, "I believe that we were to give you our position relative to the operation without a contract amendment to cover the pilots."

"They will be covered by my policy letter," Braznell interjected quickly.

Dave nodded slowly, raised his eyes, and studied the thin ribbon of smoke rising from his cigar. He brushed his mustache carefully with his left hand and appeared deep in thought. No one interrupted.

"I keep thinking of something you said this morning, Walt." He fixed his blue eyes on Braznell.

"What was that?" Walt asked quickly.

"That the company took two days to sign a contract with Pan-American."

"Of course," Braznell bristled just a little, but tried not to show it. "Our company had to have a contract before it could go to the expense of readying airplanes, engines, and planning such an operation. It isn't practical otherwise."

Dave nodded slowly.

"Two days," he murmured softly with his eyes on the ceiling. "That doesn't seem very long to me," he added gently.

The company members sat silent with a little nervous fidgeting.

Yet no one else uttered a word while the ol'man studied the wallpaper and ceiling. He was turning on the heat.

Finally Braznell cleared his throat and spoke again.

"We are merely subcontracting some flying from Pan-American. We have obligated ourselves to furnish the airplanes and crews. All operational features will be handled by Pan-American."

"Two days!" The ol'man murmured again. Then he fixed his eyes on Di Pasquale. "It just happens that we can arrange our schedule to give the company two days to conclude a contract with the pilots covering the Pacific operation."

The company members stirred uneasily in their chairs, tried a short whispered conference, and finally excused themselves from the room. When they returned a few minutes later, they were well composed and confident. Di Pasquale stretched his long scrawny neck and thrust his chin out slightly. A smile played on his lips.

"You drive a hard bargain, Dave," he murmured. "However, we are willing to devote two or three days to a contract on the Pacific operation as soon as we can get squared away on the operation. Time is very essential in the war effort and we are bending every effort to rush the program into full schedule."

It was a weasel-worded reply. He had made it appear that the company was agreeing to negotiate a contract covering the Pacific operation, yet he had made it clear that the program was going ahead as the company had planned it and that a contract would be something that would follow along later.

In the event that we didn't agree to one, the company would have the pilots flying the Pacific on a war-effort project and we all knew that they would probably refuse to be placed in the light of holding up the war effort by instigating a 'work stoppage' until a proper contract was signed. It was now or never on a contract.

Dave nodded slowly as though agreeing with everything Di Pasquale had said.

"I'm glad to hear that the company is agreeable to negotiating a contract to cover the projected operation." He spoke softly with his blue eyes holding Di Pasquale's.

"However," he added significantly, "Walt has stated that it wasn't practicable for the company to start an operation before a contract was concluded covering the operation and I can see his point quite clearly.

And it doesn't make sense to let our pilots get started on an operation that will take them flying half way around the world and into many different lands without being able to give them a contract spelling out the conditions under which they will operate, their pay, and their status under most any situation they might encounter—such as being lost at sea, capture, internment, etc."

"My policy letter covers all that." Braznell insisted. "After all," he raised his eyebrows significantly, "they are our pilots."

"Yes," Dave answered evenly and shifted his blue eyes that appeared to have frosted slightly to Braznell's arrogant stare, "and that is all the more reason why we should sit right here at this table and work until a contract covering the Pacific operation is concluded. We on this side of the table are ready to do just that."

I smiled inwardly and nudged Red Cary with my knee over the way the ol'man was twisting and using their own words in support of our position.

"Impossible!" Di Pasquale suddenly exploded, "we have other work commitments. Why—why—," he paused slightly, "there are System Board hearings scheduled for tomorrow. Wayne there, is the chairman and he has served notice on the company that there will be no postponments."

Dave nodded slowly and turned to look at me. "I guess we can carry on two meetings at the same time, can't we? Wayne, do you consider it imperative that you participate in the negotiations on the Pacific operations?"

"Not really." I smiled and noted the explosive storm in Di Pasquale's eyes.

"Impossible!" he snorted again. "I must represent the company on the System Board hearings and on any contract negotiations. I cannot be both places."

"In addition," he continued, "Hamilton here is my assistant; I need him on any contract negotiations, and he has just been appointed to the System Board of Adjustment to serve as a judge. Naturally he cannot be both places tomorrow."

I raised my eyebrows at that one. This was news to me. What a fine situation the company was developing on the System Board. Di Pasquale, as Director of Labor Relations, would represent the company and argue the company side of each case before the System Board while his assistant, Hamilton, would sit on the board as a judge to help decide the case.

How much impartiality could we expect from Hamilton? If he took the pilot's side of a case and gave the decision to the pilot in the face of Di Pasquale's arguments, then Di Pasquale could, and likely would, fire him!

I smiled grimly to myself. No doubt Di Pasquale was packing the court. Tomorrow, I decided, would be most interesting.

Dave's booming voice brought me back to the present.

"It looks as though you might be a little under manned for the projected operations." He spoke to Di Pasquale with almost scorn in his voice.

"One or the other will have to be postponed," Di Pasquale stated flatly. I sensed that he would like for someone to suggest the System Board hearings be deferred. He glanced at me as though trying to pull such an offer from me.

I lit a cigarette and stared at the ceiling while Dave shook his head sadly.

"It would hurt me a great deal," Dave spoke softly to both Braznell and Di Pasquale, "to have to wire all the Amalgamated council chairmen to instruct all pilots to refrain from volunteering for the Pacific operation until we have a signed contract on the operations with Amalgamated."

Braznell's eyes were stormy again, his jaw muscles working slightly. "Then I will have to assign the pilots to the operation in the reverse order of seniority," he declared.

Again Dave shook his head slowly and a bit sadly.

"Now, Walt," he cautioned, "I would hate to see you do that since it would involve a violation of the Railway Labor Act."

"You know," he added significantly, "the pilots' working agreement clearly states that it pertains to flying within the continental limits of the United States."

It looked as though Walt was going to blow his top for a minute. His face grew red, his cheeks swelled, and his little gray mustache fairly quivered while he glared at Dave. I was glad that the wide table separated them. Walt, I remembered, had an explosive temper.

Di Pasquale asked for a short recess and the company members withdrew behind closed doors. We patted Dave on the back. Two tried to compliment him verbally, but I interrupted and pointed at the light fixture in memory of a hidden microphone. At that Dave laughed loudly and slapped his leg in enjoyment.

"Ole Bring-Home-The-Bacon never forgets!" He shook his head in enjoyment of the situation. Thereafter we huddled together in a corner of the room for a whispered conference.

When the company members returned to the table, we were all sitting in a business-like manner with straight faces and our scratch pads neatly arranged for immediate action. Two were painstakingly making notes as though the situation was a routine one.

"Dave," Di Pasquale looked directly across the table into eyes that were mild and gentle, "we have reviewed the situation and find that it will be several days before any of the airplanes are ready to proceed to San Francisco to be placed into operation by Pan-American."

Dave nodded slowly, tender understanding reflecting from his rough features.

"In addition," Di Pasquale continued, "we will suspend the call for volunteers for a few days. Perhaps we can get together around the first of next week and expedite some form of a rough draft that will enable us to get things in full swing, and at the same time, make everyone happy. In the meantime we would like for you to take a copy of the policy letter that Walt is issuing, study it, and see if it can be accepted as a basis for the Pacific operation."

Again Dave nodded slowly, his eyes mild and blue, expressing sympathetic understanding. I marvelled at what an actor and poker player he was. At the same time I wondered if the others on my side of the table fully understood and appreciated the crushing blow Dave had delivered Amalgamated Airlines in defense of its pilots.

The meeting was suddenly over. Everyone was shaking hands with everyone else and I found myself holding Di Pasquale's eel-like fingers and permitting him to pat me on the back with the fondness of a brother. At the same time I reflected that I should look at that patting hand to make sure that it did not hold a knife. Gloomily I thought that his actions boded ill for the morrow. Chicken, rat or weasel, he was, no doubt, looking forward to a feast on pilot carcass!

Yet I slapped his shoulder in true brotherly style and laughed heartily over his attempts at humor. Dave had taught me that a worthy foe always made sure that his actions were the smoothest and his mannerisms the tenderest around the time his blade bit the deepest.

Red Cary and I walked back to the Belmont Plaza together after bidding Dave a hurried farewell just before he and his secretary caught a taxi to the airport to fly back to Chicago. Another source of pilot trouble had erupted on United; the pilots were calling for the ol'man.

And the ol'man was rushing to their aid even though it robbed him of a nice dinner in New York and a leisurely evening. Off to another fray with his blade still bloody from the last. I marvelled at his endurance, his energy, his round-the-clock devotion to the airline pilots, and the twenty-four hour daily access they had to his time and attention.

Red and I strolled into the lobby of the Belmont Plaza Hotel and immediately found ourselves surrounded by several Amalgamated pilots who were loafing around the lobby. It was their normal layover time in New York from bases such as Nashville, Chicago, Memphis, Dallas, Cleveland, and Tulsa. Short and fat Dan Landall, with his thick lips sucking a cheap cigar, crowded close and, unlike Behncke, carelessly blew cigar smoke in my face.

Dan was based at Tulsa and flew the same runs that I frequently flew. However, I never wasted much time with him. I considered him to be a company stool-pigeon; at least he was a pipeline into the company offices and I didn't have much respect for him.

"Well, Allison," Dan questioned, "have you settled the contract yet?"

I shook my head, spoke and nodded to several other pilots and tried to edge away from Dan.

"Do you think we stand a chance of getting any form of a mileage limitation?" Dan asked in a loud voice.

"Oh, sure!" I replied easily.

"How?" Dan wanted to know.

"Whatever path the pilots decide to go." I threw back.

"You mean to strike?" Dan persisted.

I laughed. "Look in the mirror, Dan," I suggested, "and ask yourself that question." Several pilots chuckled for they knew that Dan was strongly opposed to any talk of a strike. He was always very pro-company in conversations, and his face turned a little more red than normal.

"Well," Dan insisted, "how do you feel about it?"

"My calluses are pretty thick," I replied, "from sitting in meetings with the company. So far we have settled nothing, but, I repeat, my calluses are pretty thick."

"What happened today?" Dan changed his tactics.

"The company told us about the Pacific operation," I replied with a smile.

The pilots crowded closer. Tall and lanky Tom Claude pushed his boozed red face near and inquired, "Anything wrong with that deal?"

"Nothing much, except that we do not have a contract on the operation, and, without a contract, the company can about do as it pleases with any group that volunteers to fly that operation." I gave Tom a direct response.

"What'd they say about it?" Tom insisted on something more definite.

Tom was not an association member, he had been expelled a couple of years before for nonpayment of dues. Actually, he was crowded out of the association because of his excessive drinking and his refusal to pay up his back dues just made it easy for the union to pull his card.

Most of the pilots liked Tom because of his rough and sharp sense of humor and his ability to fly, which about matched his ability to drink. Yet, as a group, they had become fearful that his drinking might lead to an accident. It had caused several older pilots to have a quiet talk with him. But it had done little good.

Quietly Red and I told Tom and several other pilots what had happened. Dave insisted that a contract be signed before anyone volunteered, and soon I left Red with the group. He was explaining what might happen without a contract.

By chance I ran into little Ed Graham, who had been my copilot for several months during the war. He was small in stature, with a ready smile that disclosed two tightly fitting squirrel-like teeth. He was probably one of the most humorous copilots I had ever flown with. I had passed many very pleasant hours with him, both in the cockpit and at some layover points.

I shook his hand with pleasure, for I had not seen him for several months.

"Who you flying with now Ed?" I inquired.

"Tommy Claude," he chuckled.

I laughed. "Well, I was just talking a little with him. Does he still tell the stewardesses filthy jokes?"

"Not so much." Ed grinned. "The company wrote him number twenty letter about that a short time ago. I don't know what the letter said, but Tom sure slowed down on that score."

Then he laughed. "Wayne," he asked, "do you want to hear a real funny one about him and Dan Landall?"

"Sure!" I smiled in anticipation, for when Ed knew a funny one on someone, it was usually good. We sat down on a nearby lounge.

"Well," Ed began, "last trip we were going home to Dallas from a Nashville stop in the afternoon. Dan Landall was deadheading with us on a route check flight and sitting on the engineer's seat between Claude and me. Both of them were loafing and doing nothing but talk while I flew the airplane, handled the radio contacts and just about everything else but the stewardesses. They kept the girls busy bringing them plenty of coffee. Suddenly Tom raised up and turned to Dan and asked; 'What number wife you working on now, Dan?'"

I chuckled, for both Tom and Dan had been married and divorced several times.

"Dan admitted that he was working on number three," Ed continued.

"Then Dan asked Tom what number he was sleeping with now. Tom scratched his head, ran a finger around his shirt collar and replied that he was working nights, at home, with number four."

Ed paused to laugh a high-pitched giggle before continuing: "Then Tom asked Dan how much alimony he was paying these days."

I laughed, for everyone knew that Dan was paying considerable alimony because he complained so much about it.

"Dan squirmed a couple minutes and replied that he was paying about five hundred each month." Ed giggled again. "Then Dan asked Tom how much *he* was paying. Tom stretched his long neck and admitted to eight hundred each month."

"There were several minutes of silence," Ed continued, "while they both looked out across the country, then Dan nudged Tom and said in a mournful voice, 'Tom, ain't it a hell of a note how some lucky bastards get a good one the first time.'"

Leaving Ed a few minutes later, I entered the dining room where I found George having coffee with Jinnie and Jean. I joined them.

George explained with a wink, "Jean just started to tell us about last night's gory details."

I noted his hollow eyes and thought his face looked a little thinner than normal. He must have had quite a night, I decided.

"I did not!" Jean blushed and appealed to me with her eyes. Silently I admired her clear blue eyes and rosy cheeks.

"She won't tell us a thing," Jinnie giggled. "We've been trying to pump her a little, and she won't give a hint about what happened last night. I think it's awful to fly with a girl like that, don't you?"

I smiled and met Jinnie's eyes. They were a little bloodshot, either from too much drinking the night before or from sleeping all day. Probably both, I surmised. Her cheeks also had a washed out look beneath the liberal layer of rouge.

"I'll tell you what happened." I volunteered. It was easy to see that these two seasoned party hounds had been giving Jean a rough time.

"Oh, good!" Jinnie squealed in delight. "Tell all!"

Leaning over Jinnie I lowered my voice real low. Both George and Jean had to strain their ears to hear me.

"I made a terrible discovery last night." I looked into Jinnie's eyes from close range. "Promise you won't tell anyone if I tell you?"

"Of course not!" Jinnie pulled on a cigarette and leaned toward me in anticipation.

"It's awful!" I whispered. "Last night I learned that I'm over the hill—over the hill!" I assumed a sad look. "Imagine that! And me in the prime of my youth!"

"Aw, bosh—!" Jinnie laughed suddenly, exhaling a good quantity of smoke.

"Is George?" I questioned soberly in a continued whisper, holding my eyes steady on hers.

It was Jinnie's turn to color and she did it quite nicely. Under my direct gaze the color deepened while she tried to laugh in a careless manner.

"Is he?" I insisted.

"We'd better dress for our trip." Jinnie jumped to her feet in laughing confusion and bolted from the dining room.

George sat laughing with Jean and me. Looking hard at me, he slowly shook his head. "I hope you can put Di Pasquale in that much confusion tomorrow."

I walked with Jean to the elevator and enjoyed it. I felt the eyes of several pilots follow us through the lobby.

"Thank you, Wayne," Jean said gratefully as we neared the elevators. "I didn't know how to handle them."

"In a deal like that," I cautioned with a smile, "always keep the fire in the other fellow's back yard. It's the only defense."

"I'll call you when I get back to Tulsa," I offered. "If I'm still here on your next trip, give me a ring and let me know that you're in town. If you'd like, we'll go out to dinner," I promised.

She nodded. "I would like," was the reply as she smiled and disappeared in the elevator to prepare for their return to Tulsa that evening.

George and I walked slowly to the Lexington Hotel. The cool evening air felt good and I wished suddenly that I was taking flight forty-nine to San Francisco that night. By the time the flight allocation hearings started I could be in San Francisco ready for a nice long day's sleep in the cool air. Glumly I shook my head. There never seemed to be an end to union work.

"Ship and Nat are coming in around six." George interrupted my thoughts. "We invited them for dinner," he informed me with a grin.

That night we four dined in the hotel dining room where we could talk quietly and stay as long as we liked. I related the day's happenings to the trio and it was an occasion for several hearty laughs. Ship was particularly amused at Sayen's attempt to "sell" a form of mileage limitation under another name.

"It's like painting a tiger brown and telling someone that the brown animal is a honey-bear," he laughed. "The long tail doesn't mean a thing, not a thing,"

Then when I told them about Sayen lunching with Braznell and his attempt to work out a 'side-door' deal, I thought both Ship and George were going to bite the waiter. Their anger was quite evident. But both were delighted that the entire negotiating committee had walked out on the deal.

"I'll bet the ol'man fires him for that," George declared.

"He can't," Shipley told him. "The convention resolution provided that Behncke would hire a fulltime vice-president. No authority to discharge one was incorporated. So," he pointed out, "the issue is covered by an old convention resolution passed many years ago and incorporated in the bi-laws of the association that provides that the officers of the association will serve until reelected or replaced by convention action."

I shook my head over that one. Ship had brought up something that neither George or I had realized. The more I considered it, the more I realized that Ship was right. Sayen was immune to a firing by the ol'man. It would take convention action to dispose of him, the same as it would take convention action to dispose of the ol'man. What a situation!

George and I discussed it a good deal that night, long after we had told Ship and Nat good night at the subway and walked back to the hotel. In the lobby we sat for a while and continued the discussion. A vice-president that the president could not fire, especially when it had become evident that his ideas and methods of doing business were quite different from the ol'man's, could lead the association into trouble.

"Well," George concluded at last, "I'm thinking that the ol'man is going to chew Sayen's arse good and plenty over the deal and Sayen is going to suddenly acquire some of the ol'man's ideas about running a union." He smiled at the thought.

"I hope so!" was my reply as we entered the elevator enroute to our room. But glumly I could not help but reflect on a saying that my grandfather had often used in reference to men. "Men are of two types," he had impressed on me, "horsetraders and fighters. Sometime you might see both types horsetrading, but you will never see both types fighting!"

For eighteen years the ol'man had proven to be a real rough and tumble fighter. He gave a good fight for the association and for any member, no matter the location or the odds. And he demanded that all his subordinates conform to the same principle.

On the other hand, this day had proven Sayen to be a horsetrader. Clearly he wanted to avoid a fight, or any show of force. Salesmanship was the weapon he preferred to use, salesmanship, otherwise known as "horsetrading" in another era.

In our room George and I settled down for the nightcap before retiring. It was a time that we both enjoyed immensely, a time of prognostication on the morrow. Relaxed, half unclad and with drinks between us, we eyed each other thoughtfully.

"It's going to be a rough deal tomorrow," George ventured. "They're serious about breaking the union with the simple procedure of floating flight time around the system, robbing a pilot base that happens to be a strong union camp and blessing the base that is weak and willing to accept any and all management decrees regardless of how much pilot-passenger safety is jeopardized."

I nodded slowly and added: "Pilots are too peace-loving; they permit the company to encroach too much on their safety."

"How do we play it tomorrow?" George questioned.

"I gotta plan," I grinned.

"Like what?"

"I gotta plan," I repeated solemnly. "Now you just get real sleepy all of a sudden and pretend to go to sleep. I'll tell you in the morning."

He laughed, set his glass to one side, and dutifully slid into bed.

"I did have a plan," he grinned. "And it worked. Now it's your turn to put one in bed with me."

"Right here!" He patted the pillow beside his head.

"But I won't be as particular as you are." He gazed at the ceiling absently. "Something on the order of Jimmie, or Jackie, or Terry, or even Mary, but say!"

He raised up and looked real serious. "Won't they get mad if you start giving them away?"

"Aw, shut up!" I threw a pillow at him, turned out the light, and then had to lie there and listen to him giggle while I kept thinking slowly of giving Jimmie away, and Jackie, and Terry, and Mary. Then I thought of Jean. He hadn't mentioned her. But I went to sleep thinking about her.

Chapter 9

The Flight Time Grievances

It was fairly early when I awakened, slipped into the bath, shaved, showered, talked to myself a little, and smiled in memory of the previous morning. Then I awakened George and hustled him out of bed.

Leaving him dressing I wandered down to the hotel coffee shop where I ordered his breakfast and mine. About the time it arrived with mine, George came hurrying through the doorway with his blond hair showing the effect of a hurried combing and his eyes still swollen from sleep.

Soon we were joined by tall and rangy Wylie Drummond and stocky Wes King, both of the Nashville council. Then a few New York based pilots trickled in for coffee before the hearings began. A pilots' bull session was soon in progress.

Gene Burns, the Tulsa chairman, came in just as I was finishing my breakfast and pulled a chair up close to me. He was short and heavy set with dark hair that was prematurely gray at the temples. His gray eyes probed mine and his voice, as usual, was soft and low with an apologetic note.

"How are you planning on running these hearings, Wayne?"

George had to bend his head closer to catch the question.

"The first grievance received by the Board is the first one we will hear, followed by the others in the order we received them," I replied. "And that makes you lead off man."

Gene's mouth drew into a straight line. "Okay, I'm ready."

"Have you seen the association attorney?" I questioned.

Gene's firm mouth went into a smile and he chuckled at the end. "We spent half the night last night going over that transfer of flying time from the Tulsa base to the San Francisco base. He now knows the ins and outs of that deal so well that he can argue it like a real pilot."

I laughed with pleasure.

When I walked into the large hearing room the hotel had prepared for us, I was highly pleased. George had done a good job with the arrangements. At one end of the room a large table was turned sidewise with four chairs placed on the side next to the wall. These were for the four members of the board. Along each side of the room and extending down from the board's table were two continuous rows of tables, one for the company participants and one for the pilots.

Between the two rows of tables and near the board's table was a small desk and chair for the court reporter. Near him and facing the board was the witness chair, on either side of which was ample room for the lawyers to move freely. Below the tables and in the lower half of the room were several rows of chairs from wall to wall with two aisles. These were for the pilot observers. The room was well lighted and had a semi-judicial setting.

I complimented George as we took two of the four board seats and arranged our papers in front of us. The several pilots to appear as witnesses picked seats along the side of the room near the association attorney, Lampe, who took the first chair after warmly greeting George and me. He had presented other cases before the AA System Board of Adjustment in our presence.

It was only a few minutes later when Di Pasquale came breezing into the room, followed by his assistant Hamilton. When Di Pasquale dropped his briefcase beside the first chair at the tables opposing the pilots, Hamilton hesitated, then continued up to the board's table.

"Guess one of these chairs is mine," he chuckled in almost a sneer.

"Help yourself, Ed," I invited, and watched Dave Little come ambling up the long room.

Dave was a company member of the board and had been on the board for near a year. Why he was there I could never understand, for Dave was scrupulously honest. He was long and tall and thin, his shoulders were bony and his face was a thin arrangements of lines.

Dave was a line pilot, and a fairly senior one at that. He had quietly flown the line for a number of years until the company found that he knew more about electrical engineering, electronics, radio, and radar than any engineer they could hire. So they gave him a desk job.

And Dave took it; not that he wanted it, but he just couldn't resist the company's plea to make use of his vast knowledge. All he asked was his pilot's salary.

I rose and shook Dave's hand warmly. We were good friends. He knew that I was dealing honestly with the company and the pilots, and he was trying to do likewise, hamstrung though he was with attempts of company officials to dictate the position he would take on each case before the board. That was Di Pasquale's fine finger.

George followed my lead and we three stood talking pleasantly for a few minutes. Seasoned line pilots have a natural respect for each other, and in addition to that, George and I had a great deal of respect for Dave Little as an honest man. During the last year he had been most considerate and honest in his dealings with us on the cases before the board.

Soon the room was pretty well filled, but not before Shipley breezed in with Nat in tow and grabbed the last two seats on the first row. Both Ship and Nat knew all the pilots, most of them by their first names, and they exchanged friendly greetings all over the room. To George and me they gave big waves and Ship found a half minute to step up and thank us for the previous entertaining evening.

Promptly at nine I rapped on the table and called the meeting to order. It was the pilots' court, the place where they could take their complaints of unfair treatment and expect a reasonable settlement. True, the actions of the board were frequently delayed a great deal through company obstructionistic tactics, but the provisions of the Railway Labor Act were quite specific, especially in regard to compliance with the provisions of our labor contract.

Those provisions provided for a four man board, two company and two pilot representatives, to hear the third and final appeal for the settlement of a grievance. The first two hearings were held by company officials, and with Amalgamated, they were a waste of time.

The room became quiet as the four board members settled in their seats. I nodded to the certified court reporter to start the record and began it by reading the company letter appointing Hamilton on the System Adjustment Board as a representative of the company. I stated that this was a special meeting of the pilots' System Board of Adjustment to hear several grievances concerning the company's actions in floating flight time from base to base in an irresponsible and unjust manner.

Then I specifically opened the grievance of the Tulsa council against the floating of four pilot vacancies to the San Francisco base. I read the original grievance, the two company decisions, and the appeal to the System Board of Adjustment. Thereupon I called on the association attorney to take the floor and present the case of the grieving pilots.

It wasn't the best system—that is, to give the floor to the grieving pilot—because this procedure placed the burden of proof upon the grieving pilot, but it was the best we had been able to obtain under the provisions of the Railway Labor Act and the Pilots' Agreement with the company.

This was particularly true in grievances that resulted from company disciplinary action. In such cases the grieving pilots were forced to take the floor and prove their innocence. It also placed the company in the position of being able to sit back and say nothing until the pilots' grievance was completely aired. In short, the pilot was assumed guilty unless he could prove his innocence.

Mr. Lampe, the association attorney, rose to take the floor but was interrupted. Mr. Di Pasquale suddenly demanded the floor. Puzzled, I paused, then repeated that the hearing was provided at the request of the grieving pilot and in accordance with years of past procedure the floor belonged to Mr. Lampe. Again I called for him to take the floor.

Again Mr. Di Pasquale interrupted and insisted on having the floor. This time he was aided by Mr. Hamilton, who nudged me, and in a hoarse voice, insisted that the company should be given the floor.

A sudden inspiration hit me.

"Mr. Di Pasquale," I asked, "do you desire the floor to present the company's side of this grievance?"

Mr. Di Pasquale indicated that he wanted to make a motion.

Thereupon I recessed the board for a few minutes and we four board members held a little caucus in the adjoining room.

Hamilton was insistent that Mr. Di Pasquale be given the floor to make his motion. Dave Little was noncommittal. George, as usual, was quick to see that dirty work was afoot.

Again I called the meeting to order and advised Mr. Di Pasquale that we would not depart from the established procedure; the floor belonged to the grieving pilot. But that did not deter Di Pasquale in the least. With his Adam's apple working overtime, he was on his feet, waving his arms and demanding the floor to make a motion.

The pilots were all leaning forward in their chairs, trying to sense what the company play could be. It was something of importance and each pilot was endeavoring to determine the company's objective. I glanced at Lampe and let him indulge in a little argumentative talk with Di Pasquale over the point of order while I surveyed the situation.

George whispered not to let Di Pasquale have the floor. I glanced at Shipley and Nat to see them both slowly shaking their heads. It caused me to smile a little as I winked at them. It was actually a tense moment throughout the room.

"Mr. Di Pasquale!" I spoke loudly and clearly in order to command the attention of all those present. "Several years ago some very important cases came before this board, cases that became widely known as the screening cases, at which time the matter of procedure before this board was settled. Of course," I reminded him in a tone that brought grins of appreciation from the pilots present, "that was before your time.

"Now," I continued, "with several years of practice during which the board has operated along the lines agreed upon for the screening cases, it appears to me that you now want to change the procedure."

"Mr. Chairman," Di Pasquale gave me an acid smile, "I seek not to change the procedure, but merely to make a motion prior to the beginning of these flight allocations cases, and then, with the disposal of my motion, we will continue the hearings in accordance with the established procedure."

In a flash I saw the situation he was trying to develop, and at the same time caught George's warning nudge. Di Pasquale was evidently wanting to make some motion relative to these cases and then demand a ruling. With two company members and two association members voting according to their representation, we would be deadlocked.

Such a situation would likely take several months for the deadlock to be broken by a neutral from the National Mediation Board. That would greatly delay the flight allocation hearings. It was a sly delaying move and might win the cases for the company through the long delay in a decision.

"Mr. Di Pasquale," I smiled pleasantly at him, "I appreciate your desire to further the work of this board and your eagerness to get on with these hearings."

Several pilots exchanged sly smiles.

"However," I continued, "before you can be given the floor to make a motion, I suggest that you tell us something of the nature of the motion."

"Gladly," Di Pasquale was on his feet in an instant. "The company seriously questions that these flight allocation cases are—!"

"Hold it, Mr. Di Pasquale!" I ordered sternly and then made sure the court reporter had stopped the record. "Mr. Di Pasquale," I smiled tightly at him. Before I could continue, Lampe was on his feet and talking rapidly, angrily, endeavoring to explain to us that Mr. Di Pasquale obviously wanted to delay the function of the System Board, that any attempt to question the power and scope of the Pilots System Board of Adjustment was a delaying maneuver. He was red of face with suppressed emotions, fearful that I would not see through the maneuver.

"You do bring up an interesting thought, Mr. Di Pasquale." I waved Lampe back toward his chair. "However, before we proceed further let us take a look at the Adjustment Board provisions of the agreement between Amalgamated Airlines and the pilots in the service of Amalgamated as represented by the Air Line Pilots' Association, International."

I picked up the small green labor contract, in booklet form, and thumbed through it until I found the page I wanted. Then I read out loud that the Pilots System Board of Adjustment would hear any pilot grievance properly brought before the board. There was no limitation on the scope of the matters to be heard. I closed the booklet. Then I smiled slowly at Mr. Di Pasquale.

"Under the circumstances in which the authority of the System Board is so clearly spelled out to cover all matters properly brought before it, I must rule that you are out of order with any motion relative to the authority and scope of the Pilots System Board of Adjustment.

"I have here before me," I continued to the entire room, "the papers of submission of the question at issue on the flight allocation cases from both the company and the association. No question has been raised as to the propriety of these papers and the board has already ruled that the submissions are proper. Therefore, I again present the floor to the grieving pilot, Mr. Burns, representing Council 62 of Tulsa,

Oklahoma, and his attorney Mr. Lampe."

Again Mr. Lampe started to take the floor but Di Pasquale, his face livid with rage, advanced toward the board waving his arms and talking at the same time.

"Mr. Chairman," Di Pasquale almost yelled. "I demand to make a motion before this board on behalf of Amalgamated Airlines."

"Mr. Di Pasquale," I looked at him coldly. "You may make any motion you desire when your proper turn comes. This board will first hear the grieving pilot." Again I nodded to Mr. Lampe.

It was more than Di Pasquale could take. Again he moved toward the board waving his arms. "Mr. Chairman," he insisted, "if I am denied the right to make my motion at this time, then I will withdraw as company counsel from this case."

The threat was a total surprise to me. I never anticipated such a move. Before I could find words to cover the situation, Hamilton leaped to his feet from the chair beside me.

"And I will also withdraw as a company member of this board," he announced most dramatically.

I glanced at Dave Little sitting just beyond Hamilton. He was looking at the ceiling and pulling slowly at a cigarette. The seamy lines in his face seemed more pronounced than ever. I glanced sidewise at George. "Do you want to go too?" I asked in a whisper and with a smile.

"Yeah, yeah, yeah!" Came the chuckling whisper back. "Now saw them off!"

"Very well!" I spoke to Di Pasquale and Hamilton, turning my head from one to the other. Then to the court reporter I stated: "Mr. Di Pasquale is denied the right to make any motion at this time."

"Then I withdraw from this case," Di Pasquale spoke with finality.

"And I also withdraw from this case," Hamilton echoed his boss.

"Very well." I again spoke to the court reporter. "Mr. Di Pasquale has withdrawn as counsel for the company on this case and Mr. Hamilton has withdrawn as a board member on this case. We will not close the record until they have had an opportunity to depart."

They didn't anticipate such a move. The room was suddenly filled with buzzing conversation, yet everyone kept seated, sensing that the drama was not completed. And, curiously, neither Di Pasquale or

Hamilton made any move to depart. I rose and walked to the back of the room for a drink of water.

The hotel had obligingly placed a table in the rear of the room and loaded it with pitchers of ice water and glasses. To this table I strolled, conscious that many eyes were trying to anticipate the next move. Truthfully, I was thinking of the next move too; the ice water merely gave me a chance to stretch my legs and think at the same time.

Pouring a glass of water, I found myself joined at the table by three chairmen.

"Where do we go to from here, Wayne?" Drummond asked.

"Boy, what a deal!" Shipley exclaimed quietly. "They're trying to gag the System Board,"

"I sure would like a chance to tell them what I think of this deal," O'Connell, chairman of the large Los Angeles council, muttered in my ear.

The suggestion gave me an idea. I rolled it around in my mind as I walked back to the front of the room carrying a pitcher of ice water and two extra glasses for George and Dave. Sensing that the pilots were seething with anger over the situation, for like wildfire, the more penetrating minds had spread the full implications of the company move to all corners of the room, I decided to let them have a hand in the next play.

Taking my seat at the head table after pouring George and Dave Little ice water with slow deliberate moves, I looked the room over and noted that Di Pasquale and Hamilton had both moved over to a side wall and taken seats. They appeared to be ready to invoke the Homesteader's Act and become permanent fixtures. It was quite clear to all that they thought they had completely riddled the Pilots System Board and that it would fall to pieces in a matter of minutes. Naturally they wanted to stay and see the collapse.

Signalling the court reporter, I again started the record.

"Gentlemen," I spoke very clearly for all, "before Mr. Di Pasquale, who has resigned on the record as counsel for the company on these cases, and Mr. Hamilton, who has also resigned on the record as a member of this board, depart, I would like to ask those gentlemen if they object to hearing some pilot views on the action they have just taken?"

Di Pasquale was on his feet in an instant with a statement that he was always glad to listen to pilots, that his door was always open to pilots who wanted to accomplish objectives in a proper manner. Hamilton followed Di Pasquale's lead and agreed that he, too, would always listen to pilots.

Turning to the first pilot on my right I asked him if he had anything to say at this time. It was amazing, he did!

Launching into very colorful language, he told the company representatives in no uncertain terms what he thought of the deal they were trying to pull in gagging the System Board. His delivery wasn't the best, but his points scored like crude arrows well aimed.

The next pilot merely had one line to deliver: "It stinks!" he declared, "and I'm going to do my best to make sure the pilots smell it from one end of the line to another."

Then came Knight of Nashville.

Getting to his feet slowly, he stretched his medium height and stocky appearance a good two inches while he glared across the room at the two company representatives.

"I hope," he began quietly, "that Mr. C.R., the president of the airline for which I have worked for over ten years, and for which I have always had profound respect and unswerving loyalty, may hear or read these words." His eyes flickered to the court reporter who was busy over his machine with his eyes intently fixed on Knight's face and his ears almost pointed in Knight's direction.

"In 1938," said Knight, taking a small green booklet from the side pocket of his coat and holding it out for all to see, "Mr. C.R. Brown signed the first labor agreement with the pilots of Amalgamated Airlines. That agreement provided the pilots with a right to grieve. It provided a method for the company and the pilots, as represented by the System Board, to arrive at a fair decision on any and all problems that might come before that body.

"Today," he held the little green booklet up, "today, through his representatives, he is attempting to abrogate this agreement. Until today, I always had an unlimited amount of faith in Mr. C.R.'s word. I always had a great deal of respect for any communications that bore his signature."

With that, he ripped the green booklet into two pieces with a vicious twist of his wrists, then flung the two pieces across the room in the direction of Di Pasquale and Hamilton. Everyone silently watched as the two pieces ricocheted from the ceiling of the room and fluttered downward. By a strange freak of fate, one piece suddenly changed its course of fall and swerved sideways until it struck Di Pasquale squarely in the face, despite a hand he had raised in a protective gesture.

Several pilots then stood on their feet, one by one, and endorsed Knight's speech, word for word. Then Wylie Drummond, chairman of the Nashville council, stood up and, smiling in an apologetic manner at Di Pasquale and Hamilton, remarked:

"I have approximately fifty men in the Nashville council. Mr. Knight is and without a doubt, the quietest, mildest, and most even-tempered one of the group. So," he added significantly in a voice that was almost soothing in its softness, "if Mr. C.R. and his officials responsible for this action today happen to look out a window within the next couple of nights and see an Aurora Borealis in a southern direction, I hope, gentlemen, they will immediately recognize it as council number fifty of Nashville, Tennessee."

It brought a good laugh from everyone present. Even Di Pasquale and Hamilton appeared to enjoy it, yet with faces that seemed to have an unnatural glow.

Then we came to O'Connell, chairman of the large Los Angeles council. Typically Irish, he stood several inches under six feet, and had brushed-back reddish blond hair. He looked around the room with baby-blue eyes which seemed to bulge from their sockets each time they crossed Di Pasquale and Hamilton.

"Pilots and representatives of Amalgamated Airlines," he looked around the room and popped his baby-blue eyes again, "this situation here today reminds me of a period of my childhood." He gave everyone a big smile.

"In those days," he continued, "it was customary on Saturday and Sunday, in the town where I was raised, for the boys of the neighborhood to gather to some vacant lot, each bringing his glove, bat, or ball. There, when we had assembled and pooled the choice items of our savings, we usually had enough ingredients for a game of baseball.

"And," he smiled at the memory, "at such gatherings there was usually one boy who had either doting parents, grandparents, or an expense allowance far in excess of us newspaper boys. At any rate, such a boy would usually show up with both a ball and a bat.

"Well, as the game progressed," O'Connell continued, "there would usually come a time when the more liberally endowed youth would find that he was not going to be allowed to bat when he wanted to, or, he might be called out at third, when he was sure that he was safe. So, that budding executive would promptly declare that if he was not going to be permitted to bat at that time, or was not safe at third, he would immediately take his ball and bat and go home.

"Mr. Di Pasquale!" O'Connell's voice cut like a whip. "You now have your ball and bat, and you may now go home."

The room was deathly silent for at least three seconds. Then Di Pasquale lunged to his feet and attempted to launch into an oration.

I banged the gavel loud, and I banged it long, and I drowned all with the sound of the little wooden hammer on that wooden table.

"Mr. Di Pasquale," I declared when the room had quieted, or rather when Di Pasquale had subsided enough to hear the chairman, "you and Mr. Hamilton agreed to listen to the pilots. Your official status here is terminated and there will be no rebuttal."

Again I banged the hammer as he started again to speak. "There is no rebuttal!" I repeated emphatically.

"Captain Knight!" I called to Knight who happened to be in the back of the room, "would you be kind enough to open the door? We have two officials here who are making an exit."

Knight opened the door with a flourish and almost bowed as Di Pasquale and Hamilton found themselves swept toward an exit that they appeared to shun.

"What about the hearings?" Di Pasquale raised his voice at the door and half turned toward me.

"We will hold them without you!" I exclaimed emphatically. "The agreement says that a vote by the majority members of the Board shall be competent to make a decision."

Knight pushed the door closed almost gleefully on Di Pasquales's heels. It was the most flagrant showing of contempt for two company officials I have ever seen. And to me, it was a sign, a symbol, a mark on the wall which signified that, once again, we had forced our company officials into the open.

I turned slowly in my standing position and looked down at George and Dave Little. George was chuckling and giggling with his blond hair tousled over a pencil that extended from behind an ear.

Dave just lit another cigarette and with a half smile, as he blew out the match, looked up at me.

"Maybe I'm supposed to walk too, Wayne," he remarked. "But it just doesn't seem right to me for a pilot to be granted a hearing and then permit the company to have the floor ahead of him."

I sat down and lowered my voice.

"What do you want to do, Dave?" I asked quietly.

"I'd like a chance to contact the higher echelon," he grimaced slightly, "and see what comes out of there. Then if you want to go ahead with the hearings, I'll sit through them." He looked me steadily in the eye and once again my estimation of Dave Little rose to new heights.

"And," he added thoughtfully, "I'd appreciate it if you would contact the vice-president of operations and, as chairman of this board, give him an official report on what has happened here. It'll kind of take the heat off me." He chuckled a bit grimly.

Slowly I banged the gavel. Looking around the room at the various faces, I was struck with the many reactions among the pilots; some were thoughtful, some mad, some gleeful and still others reflected grave doubts over the turn of events. Nat Shipley's highly intelligent face reflected somber thought.

"Gentlemen," I paused and looked around. "It is now late in the afternoon. The hearings will resume at nine tomorrow morning, with or without a company representative to present the company side, and with or without one company member of the board. Dave Little has taken the position that a grieving pilot has a right to be heard and he will hear the grievances as scheduled."

The applause was almost thunderous, and it was spontaneous. As it echoed through the room, the five chairmen present rose to their feet. Everyone else followed their lead and soon we were all standing applauding Dave Little. It pleased me greatly.

George and I walked to the subway entrance with Ship and Nat, bade them good-bye and walked a few blocks for exercise in the crowded New York sidewalks. Keeping from getting run over by hurrying New Yorkers was exercise in itself.

"I wonder who's coming in on flight forty-eight this evening?" I mused aloud.

"Just a couple of bags!" George informed me without a moment of hesitation. "I got the schedule before we left Tulsa."

"Shucks!" I complained jokingly, "my fangs feel real sharp tonight."

"Well, don't look at me like that," George grinned, "or I'll get me a separate room."

In our hotel room we showered and cleaned up for a nice quiet dinner together. As George put it, "We had to wash that company crud off before we became contaminated."

Together we picked up Gene Burns and we three went out to a nice quiet dinner where we talked over the day's happenings. We recalled and repeated almost verbatim every word Di Pasquale and Hamilton had uttered. This we did to reexamine the company plays and exchange impressions, ideas, and thoughts. Gene was a good thinker but had not been an ALPA activist as long as George and me, but he was a good recruit.

Much speculation was done on how the company would react to my declaration to continue the hearings. Once Gene leaned back in his chair, chuckled, and with the corner of his mouth drawing down when he spoke in his habitually quiet manner, he remarked: "I used to think Behncke was a thick-headed old coot from some of his letters, but now that I have seen the way he has a pair of roughriders like you two working for the pilots, well, I feel like taking my hat off and bowing in the future whenever the postman hands me a letter from him." He shook his head and chuckled, looking first at George and then at me.

"Manufacture your own powder and be ready to burn it," I admonished. "You'll have plenty of opportunities in the future. It's going to take a lot more roughriders than George and me to make an ethical company of Amalgamated."

Finally, as the evening wore on, we told Gene good night and retired to the privacy of our room. There I put in a long distance call for David L. Behncke, President of the Air Line Pilots' Association. I gave the operator his office number for Dave, I knew, would be working until eleven or twelve on pilot problems. Then he would travel the few short blocks from his office to his home and back again at nine in the morning.

A slave the pilots had, a slave that had dedicated all his assets, including his life, to the promotion of the welfare of airline pilots—God's gifted children. But they failed to see the strong union he had built for them, the protection they had in their jobs, the tremendous battles he was constantly waging with various airlines against encroachments on the pilots.

Yet all the ol'man's accomplishments were ignored as the rank and file of airline pilots complained about his long-winded letters. As the educational level of the airline pilots rose through the many years of his presidency, his letters came under increasing criticism. They had failed to progress above that eighth grade level, even though his speaking ability and negotiating power were matchless.

I hung on the phone and reclined on my bed with my back against a pillow while those thoughts ran through my mind. I could see the ol'man humped over a desk which was piled high with communications, reports, folders, and reference files while he worked.

The phone clicked and I could see him reaching over to the desk edge to switch the little buzzer off which was connected to the switchboard in an other office. I could almost call the second he would speak in that slow, heavy voice that always sounded tired. Then he was on the line with that tired, "Hullo!"

"Dave," I explained, "this is number one."

It was a private joke between us, and one that was shared by almost all the pilots on Amalgamated. It had all started more than three years back when Ralph Damon, then president of Amalgamated, had climbed up the front loading ramp of my airplane in Washington for a flight to New York. Due to a heavy load of passengers, and because he held a cockpit authority card which enabled him to ride up front as an extra crew member, Ralph Damon sat at my elbow on the flight.

This was at a time when the screening cases were very much in the limelight, and before I had briefed him in front of Mr. C.R., the Master Executive Council of Amalgamated and the other system board members. Enroute to New York I had leaned back a little and with a smile on my face had asked:

"Mr. Damon, who is the number one man on your preferential list at this time?"

Puzzled he had asked: "Preferential for what?"

"Firing." I had replied, grinning.

He gave me a brief smile, rubbed his curly grey hair back with the palm of his hand before removing his horn-rimmed glasses and inspecting them for dirt.

"Well," he had replied, "I can't tell you exactly who is number one, because that might hurt the incentive of others on the list, but I can tell you the first four names on that list."

His voice had become edged and a little sharp as he continued: "They are Shipley, Schustman, Cox and Allison."

I laughed in delight, made a slight adjustment on the throttles and then turned to him again.

"Well," I inquired, "is that the order of seniority?"

Chuckling faintly he had given me a sly look of appreciation before replying: "Well, it's possible that I may have turned them around because they rhyme better that way."

At that moment, I had known that he was speaking the truth. I was number one!

Naturally it was too good to keep, I told it to Schustman, I told it to Cox, and I told it to Shipley, and it was soon all over the system. And of course, it got to Dave because Cox protested, questioned my right to be seniority number one. He appealed to Behncke for a decision.

It brought up an issue that tickled the ol'man. It caused him to roar in glee telling about it. Then he appealed to Mr. Damon by letter, a copy of which he sent to each of us "four horsemen of Amalgamated" as the association employees called us, especially the secretaries, who picked it up from Dave.

Exactly what Damon said, or if he ever replied to Dave's letter, I do not know. But it wasn't too long until all the personal correspondence from Dave to me was written with a dash following my name and after that the number one. And Cox much to his chagrin was given number two.

"Huh!" The ol'man snorted. "Oh, yes!"

Then he laughed that loud belly laugh for which he was so famous. It was good to hear it.

Briefly I told what had happened in detail that day. I reported the walkout and what the company representatives were trying to do, that is, dead-lock the System Board. He was amazed when I disclosed the resignations of Di Pasquale and Hamilton on the record.

Dave listened and asked several questions. Finally he concluded that I was handling something that had no precedent on any airline. We discussed the possible directions the company might take. At last we concluded the conversation with him asking me to call him each evening.

"Now I feel better," I said to George after placing the receiver back on the phone. "When the ol'man is satisfied that we are doing the best possible, I can sleep with ease."

But I didn't get a chance to sleep, for the phone rang with a short unexpected blast. George answered it, listened, opened his eyes wide in disbelief, and then did a short dance between the two beds.

"Yeah, yeah, yeah!" He chortled. "I'll be there in five minutes. No, he won't come. He's already undressed for bed and it will be just the two of us."

He winked at me and hung up the phone. Like me he was undressed down to his shorts and under shirt. But in about two minutes he was dressed in an immaculate suite with white shirt and tie. Puzzled I watched him.

Finally, before leaving, he looked at me and grinned.

"That was Jackie. She just came in on flight two and has invited me to go barhopping in Times Square."

"Where's Jimmie?" I asked with sudden interest.

"How should I know?" He seemed to have little interest in my question. "I have a date with Jackie," he informed me as he headed for the door, "But," he added as an after thought, "she'll probably write you a letter!"

Then just before he closed the door he looked solemnly at me and suggested; "You'd better call Dave back and tell him who is really number one where it counts."

I lay there on the bed and looked at the ceiling with the click of the door latch still in my ears. Why had Jackie called, gotten George on the phone, made a date with him, and left me out altogether? She and Jimmie had been flying with me fairly regularly for several months. They were my regular stewardesses, and friends as well.

I thought of a number of times when I had taken the two of them, Jackie and Jimmie, out together. We had always had a good time. Reluctantly I admitted to myself that I would have enjoyed making it a threesome tonight.

But Jackie wanted to go barhopping with George. Evidently she just wanted it to be the two of them.

I didn't like the feeling I had as I lay there and looked at the ceiling for a good ten minutes. Maybe I was just a bit jealous of George and the way the girls seemed to flock to him. It made me consider another before dinner drink, or before bed drink. I was unhappy.

Then the phone gave another short blast. My spirits soared when I recognized Jimmie's sweet tones.

"Wayne," she giggled, "I told Jackie to leave you behind, I need an escort to a movie I want to see. Are you interested?"

Was I interested? I didn't give a damn about the title of the movie and I didn't ask her the title. But I was sure interested in the way she cuddled going and coming in that cab.

We were just having a late drink in the bar of the Lexington when the bartender called me to the phone. George was on the other end of the wire, and he was excited.

"There's been a big airplane accident in Dallas," he told me in a flush of words.

"Who?" I questioned with a tightening feeling inside me.

"Amalgamated, Tom Claude pilot, crashed on landing. There's been a bunch of people killed. I have just seen it flashed on the screen in Times Square," he explained. "I don't know any particulars yet. We're on the way back to the Belmont Plaza, and I thought I'd call the field from there."

"We'll join you there." I told him and returned to Jimmie to give her the news.

We finished our drinks and walked around the corner of the Lexington to the Belmont Plaza just as George and Jackie unloaded from a cab. A quick call to Amalgamated's operations office on the company phone gave us what was known at the time.

The crash had occurred on landing with over twenty known dead. The pilots had escaped. That shocked both George and me. We were unable to picture how it had happened. But the dispatcher explained that the plane had tried to pull out and flattened against the side of a hangar with the nose section, which contained the pilots, breaking loose and sliding across the top of the hangar and off the other side.

Jimmie and Jackie lingered with us to learn what we could tell them. They suddenly had haunting looks in their eyes with the knowledge that both the stewardesses were killed and one was a classmate in stewardess training school. We walked them up to their room with a touch of tender understanding. It was their first experience with the closeness of death on an airplane.

Later in our room George and I sat and discussed the crash and speculated on how it might have happened. The initial information was so meager. Finally we went to bed and I fell asleep wondering if that was the way it would happen to me. The end of the line came quite suddenly at times to airplane crews.

The following morning George and I ate breakfast together and read about the crash in an early morning edition. There was not too much to read, with the exception of the long line of passengers.

Tom Claude, veteran airline pilot of over twenty years with Amalgamated, had encountered difficulty landing the big four engine transport. After a period of struggle, during which the tower operators could see that something was wrong, he had crashed while trying to clear a hangar at the end of the field. The weather had been clear with good visibility.

I shook my head and sipped my coffee in a melancholic mood. "Who was the copilot?" I questioned.

"Ed Graham." He looked at me. "Know him?"

"Yes," I replied, "I was talking with him just the other day; he told me a funny story about Tom Claude and Dan Landall, "is he hurt?"

"Broken back, fractured pelvis, and possibly other injuries," he read slowly.

I thought of Ed, while I sat quietly and sipped my coffee. I thought of the many transatlantic trips we had flown, his cheerful good nature, his efficiency in handling an airplane, and the way he liked to pull a little joke here and there. A slow smile crept across the corners of my mouth as I recalled how he had slipped a raw egg, shell and all, in our navigator's hip pocket while he was standing on a stool making a celestial shot through the Astrodome. That had been funny, especially when Henry had run his hand in his hip pocket and pulled it out with the yoke of the egg clinging to his fingers. But it had caused me to decree to all crew members that there would be no more jokes pulled in the air.

Then I shook myself from the past with the pleasant thought that both pilots were still alive, with Tom Claude suffering only minor injuries. No doubt he would be able to throw considerable light on the reason for the crash. I turned my mind to the business of the day.

We ran into several pilots in the lobby of the hotel where we were holding the hearings. It was early for the meeting, but they were congregating, anticipating more fireworks, for like wildfire the story of the preceding day had filtered through the pilot group and up and down the line during the night. George stopped to talk to a couple of them while I continued to the meeting room with my briefcase under my arm. Preoccupied with my thoughts, I wandered into the meeting room, expecting to find it empty.

There, seated in one of the board members chairs, sat big Hamilton with his face slightly flushed and his mouth twisted in a self-conscious smile. He shook my hand as though he had not seen me for a long time. That amused me and I was sure he knew it.

"Well, well! And how is the chairman this morning?" A voice spoke from behind me. I turned to see Di Pasquale stretching his scrawny neck and smiling his best as he deposited his briefcase in the chair reserved for the company attorney. It was obvious that the company representatives were back again, bright-eyed and primed for something.

Casually I placed my briefcase beside my chair and looked at Hamilton and Di Pasquale with a slow smile on my face.

"Are you fellows lost?" I inquired courteously.

"We are ready for the hearing," Hamilton hastened to advise me.

"But you two resigned from this hearing." I reminded them.

"The company reappointed us last night." Di Pasquale spoke as he handed me two letters signed by the vice-president of operations which were simple letters of reappointment addressed to me as chairman of the System Board.

I glanced at them and back at the company representatives. Laying the letters in my chair, I looked around the room and noted that a few pilots were beginning to drift in. They moved forward at sight of Hamilton and Di Pasquale to catch the drift of the conversation. Shipley and Nat appeared in the rear of the room and, they too, pressed forward with curious looks at me, at Hamilton and at Di Pasquale. Shipley could stand it for only a few seconds. "Well," he exclaimed, "do we have to have a retake because someone left the film out of the camera?"

I raised my hand, just as George took his seat beside me, signalled for silence and then motioned everyone in the room to their seats. On a sudden inspiration I explained:

"I need a couple of minutes to check a legal question."

Then I walked purposefully out the door and down the hallway where I ran into Dave Little just getting off the elevator.

"A word with you, Dave," I requested.

Silently we walked in the opposite direction from the hearing room until we had rounded a turn in the hallway. I turned and faced him, noting the deep lines in his thin face.

"What's the pitch?" I asked abruptly.

Slowly he lit a cigarette while the ghost of a smile played at the corners of his mouth.

"I thought you had it figured yesterday," he smiled at me.

"Yes—on the walkout," I smiled back, "but I don't quite understand the walk-back deal."

"Well—," he studied me thoughtfully. "What else could they do? They couldn't have a three man board holding a hearing, could they?"

"Then why did they walk in the first place?"

"They didn't mean to." Again he smiled at me and I had the impression that he was enjoying the situation. I wondered at the way his wrinkles could move around without something breaking. "You just forced their hand. And, in a pinch, they were sure I would walk too!"

"And someone forced their return?" I hazarded a guess.

"Had to! It would have been stretching the Railway Labor Act a little thin." The thin smile remained while he added: "Don't think they didn't get hell clubbed out of themselves—not for what they did—but for not putting it over."

I nodded as I spoke. "I was sure the top echelon was behind the deal; that's why the walk-back had me puzzled."

"Well," Dave flashed the wiry smile again and added, "I can thank you for getting me off the board as soon as we have finished these particular hearings. You know that I haven't enjoyed that thin ice I have had to skate between the company and my conscience."

I stared at him. "How have I pushed you off the board, Dave?"

"Di Pasquale is using this to show the top echelon that he must have two board members who will take orders. If he loses these cases, he puts over his point. He's playing the middle against both ends."

"You mean he wants board members who will vote as he directs," I corrected him with a snort of disgust.

Dave nodded slowly as we walked back down the hallway, both of us, honest in our thinking and each of us respecting the other's honesty. And, I suspect, that in the back of both of our minds there was a little fear of the future with a company that was showing more clearly, day by day, a complete lack of ethics, a complete lack of respect for the Railway Labor Act, and its own labor agreement with the pilots, both of which guaranteed the System Adjustment Board complete independence and freedom of action to discharge its duties in an honest and forthright manner without fear that such actions would jeopardize the positions of the board members with the company.

Beautiful sounding words, I reflected, as I paused to light a cigarette and puff on it a little, while Dave walked ahead so we could make separate entrances into the hearing room. But the top echelon of Amalgamated did not read these words the way Dave, George, and I, as well as the pilots of Amalgamated, read them.

Mr. C.R., Tom Boyson, Walt Braznell and a few others, including a couple of ex-generals, buddies of C.R. recruited during WW II, were determined to control and rule everything on Amalgamated without regard to right or wrong, honesty, contractual obligations, or federal laws. They believed, I decided, in the divine right of kings with themselves as the kings.

Those thoughts, I am sure, gave my face a solemn, almost bleak look as I walked into the hearing room, a room almost full of pilots in which everyone was sitting quietly, patiently waiting for the takeoff.

Slowly I took up the gavel and looked at the other three members of the System Adjustment Board. I looked at the opposing attorneys and the court reporter with his pointed ears and expression of alertness. Casually I permitted my eyes to sweep the fifty or sixty pilots present as I tapped the table lightly with the little wooden mallet.

"Gentlemen," I began, "yesterday terminated with the company attorney and a company member of the Board resigning from these hearings. This morning they have returned with letters reappointing them to the positions from which they resigned."

Again I reminded all that it had become customary during the years I had served on the Board for the grieving pilot to have the floor. Should a time arrive, I warned all, when the company appealed a case to the System Board, the floor would be granted to the grieving company. Turning to the association attorney, Mr. Lampe, I asked him to present the case of the pilots of council sixty-two of Tulsa, Oklahoma, as represented by Mr. Gene Burns, the council chairman.

This time there was no objection, there was no disturbance. A courtroom quietness prevailed as Mr. Lampe rose to his feet to present the pilots' case.

Thus the flight allocation hearings got under way. Once again, George and I had turned another wave of the tide being sent against the pilots. But there would be more, and more, with an ever increasing tempo as long as the management of Amalgamated preferred to deal unethically.

The hearings lasted three days without much additional fireworks. Three hard days of dirty work for George and me. The pilots, through the association, were methodical and complete with their proof. George and I had engineered that, and it pleased us to watch the planned shots go home.

Like baying dogs after a sheep-killing bear, the pilots pushed and pushed the company into smaller corners. They never let the issue rest. There was small wonder that Braznell and Di Pasquale had wanted to get the flight allocation cases dropped. They had little defense!

On the third day the pilot proof really bound the company in an endless mire. That occurred when Walter Braznell, on the witness stand, was forced to admit that he did not promote pilots at Chicago and Cleveland in accordance with system seniority. And he was forced to admit that he did not demote at Los Angeles and Fort Worth in accordance with system seniority.

There, at that point, exercising the right of a board member to ask a question at any time, I drove another spike into my coffin.

"Mr. Braznell," I asked innocently, "if you did not use system seniority in promotions, and you did not use it in demotions, when do you use it?"

"Uh—er—on layoffs, that's about the only time!" he snapped with his bristling mustache showing signs of the strain he was under.

It was a candid admission of the truth. Cornered, squeezed, and harried, he gave us what we wanted, a simple admission by a senior company official that he had ignored a section of the labor agreement which provided that all promotions, demotions, and layoffs would be in accordance with system seniority.

This was at the close of the third day of the hearings and it brought the flight allocation cases to a close with definite proof that the company had disregarded system seniority and had engaged in, as I had named it, the floatation of flight time. The establishment of that fact brought attention to another point, and that was, the reason the company was engaging in the policy. How could Amalgamated benefit by such a procedure? Labor baiting was the only logical reason.

George and I almost chattered as we made our way back to our hotel. With the System Board adjourned until the certified reporter had time to transcribe his notes and furnish both the company and the association, for George and me, a copy of the record of the hearings, we were free to return home. For a while, at least, we could fly our runs the same as any other pilot.

Strolling along Fifth Avenue with George, I felt a real sense of relief that the hearings were over. Now all we had to do was win a decision on the four man board. Failing in that we would have to appeal to the National Mediation Board for a Neutral to sit with the board and decide the issue.

Now we had several beautiful weeks, at least, before the records would be completed and certified copies made. Of course there was no doubt in our minds about the record, for we had listened intently to every word uttered by a witness, but to satisfy the company, we had established a policy of waiting for the record and using it at the board meetings.

That procedure had proven profitable to the pilots. We had used the record to push the company board members for a favorable decision for, invariably the preponderance of the points established in the hearings would be on the pilots' side. It was a rare occurrence if a company member on the board voluntarily went into the record on any point.

It was a wearing game, a patient pressure game, which at times past had developed into an endurance game, a game in which each side tried to wear the other side out, both physically and mentally. The reason for that was the fact that the company had never voluntarily gone with us to a neutral. And, in the past, we had frequently challenged the company board members to jointly appeal, with us, for a neutral to help decide the case.

George and I had seen quite a number of company officials appointed to the board. Most of them had their instructions. They had been brain washed into believing that a company official could do no wrong, and did not want to review the records of the hearings. In years on the board we had only seen three fairminded officials, including Dave Little. The ones we'd know had a short tenure of office with the board. The company had removed them rather quickly. It was not a popular company assignment.

While George talked, I found myself wondering how Dave Little would skate on the thin ice when we started to write a decision. These cases were extremely important, especially to the pilots. A decision in favor of the pilots would lay the company open for damages to pilots that would run into large figures.

So far Dave had been a square dealer, honest and sincere. And Dave, as he had mentioned, had a conscience. But he had only been on the board for a short year and had not heard any cases of the magnitude of these. He had not represented the company on the screening cases. Dave had been a line pilot then, and strongly on our side.

Now I wondered how Dave would react if the company really applied the pressure to him, with straight talk from the top, telling him what to do. As George put it, he might suddenly develop wing flutter.

Chapter 10

A Copilot in Trouble

Entering the hotel in almost a buoyant mood, George and I were surprised to find a telegram awaiting me. Casually I took it from the desk clerk while George told him that we were checking out, enroute back to the mines, to haul precious ore from coast to coast.

"Read it!" George prompted me as I studied it slowly and wondered if it was something from Jimmie, for I had heard nothing since her return to Tulsa.

"Later," I smiled, "when we can hear four thousand horses dragging us homeward."

"But," he insisted, "it might be from some weak pilot on the back row who finally got up enough nerve to wish us luck."

George gave me the blue-eyed poker face look.

"In that case there would be a hundred of those," I laughed.

"That's right," he conceded. "Then it must be from you-know-who 'cause there's only one of her."

Casually he reached out and snatched the telegram from my hand. "I'll read it," he volunteered, "and if she doesn't say the right things you can shoot yourself. I'll tell you when to shoot!"

Quickly he tore the telegram open and scanned it hurriedly.

"Just as I thought," he exclaimed, "it's for you and I'll tell her about you when I get home."

He handed me the telegram and turned to the cashier to pay his bill.

Puzzled, I followed him with my eyes before dropping them to the short message. It read:

Request you stop by Chicago to see me enroute home.

Behncke

I didn't want to go to Chicago. I wanted to go home, back to my one little airplane, my one little copilot, my one little engineer, and my two little stewardesses. Somehow I felt that they needed me, and soon.

Why did Behncke want to see me, just a few days after spending considerable time with him? Surely it was not about the hearings, for I had reported the progress each night by phone. The question caused me to shake my head in disappointment.

An hour later I parted with George at the airport, waved him on an Amalgamated plane headed for Tulsa, then climbed on a United going to Chicago. The United girls were real sweet and let me talk them out of a couple cups of coffee before eating dinner. After that I dropped off to sleep like any tired businessman is expected to do.

In Chicago it was raining, just as it always seemed to when I arrived in the windy city, in a hurry to complete my mission and run onward. This night the rain caused a slowdown in the approach procedures and one hour behind the advertised schedule I threw my bags into a cab and headed for the rendezvous with the ol'man. It was only nine, however, when the cab stopped at a spot on dirty 63rd Street. I climbed a long flight of rickety stairs and paused to look at a large room filled with rows of dark and silent desks.

This was the Air Line Pilots' headquarters, this was their slave compound, this was where they has kept their willing slave for almost twenty years. I looked behind me at the rickety stairs and wondered at the many times the ol'man had climbed those squeaky stairs with his slow and heavy step.

"Twenty years," I murmured aloud, "how many times?"

But they had not been wasted years, not for the airline pilots. That far-sighted ol'man had built them a strong union, called an association to make it more saleable to a younger generation who fancied themselves to be first cousins to superman. They could not stand the thought of being in a stevedore type of organization or a ditch digger group. They were too well educated, too near the college professor class for that. So the ol'man had called it an association of pilots.

Who ever heard of a strong union of college professors? An association of college professors, yes, but not a union! The old timers, the organizers, understood, having gone through crashes, firings, and strikes on numerous occasions in past years. And it had amused them to have Dave call it an association, one affiliated with the AF of L.

In those twenty years, after repeated rejections, Dave had persuaded a biennial convention to authorize the purchase of a tract of land for a headquarters building. Then with that approved, he had shopped around until he had secured a fine site at the intersection of 55th Street and Cicero Avenue.

Dimly, as I stood there and looked around the central office, I recalled what a time Dave had had in getting that approval to buy a plot of ground, back in a convention in 1940, my first. He had talked and talked of the need for a headquarters building, of the need for the pilots to establish strong roots, save the monthly rent, and invest idle money in property that would grow in value each year. In the end, they had passed his resolution with a bare squeaking majority, after limiting the amount to be invested in real estate to a very modest figure.

Again, at a later convention, he had sought approval to build a small headquarters building when building conditions were more favorable. He had asked for a modest hundred and fifty thousand dollars. But the delegates to the convention, swayed by a number of representatives who were anti-Behncke in their thinking and possibly pro-company in their leanings, refused the ol'man funds for even a shanty.

It was a blow! However, the ol'man had suffered many unjust blows from the pilots in the past, being a slave, and with the patience of one, he just considered it due to their limited vision. He knew they were like children in many respects, simple gifted children, and he believed strongly in each side of a problem being given full expression.

Then, when the vote went against him, the ol'man simply rolled with the punch and waited, and waited, until those with limited vision could see a little further down the road. Finally, at another convention, the issue was brought up again. It had pleased me greatly to be there when Bart Cox, representing the Los Angeles council, sparked the drive and gave it the push it needed to make it seem like a bandwagon. So most all the delegates climbed on the wave and the ol'man suddenly had the necessary authority to build the building, his dream. I could still recall the way his eyes had glistened with moisture.

Now for the last several months the construction had been going full speed with the ol'man, besides doing the regular association work, finding time to check blue prints, installations, and the general construction work. Recently I had heard that the ol'man even found time to sort the bricks that were being used in the walls, to eliminate the faulty ones. I didn't doubt it, for I knew him to be that meticulous.

Giving one last glance at the long row of empty desks, and thinking how very much I would enjoy seeing the ol'man settled in a good office building, his building, I turned a hallway corner and stopped before a door that was leaking light from the top and bottom. Banging it with my fist, I then gave it a quick shove and jumped inside.

"Surround him, men!" I ordered, "and back the padded wagon up to the stairway. Any man who will work all day and half the night for pilots, is bound to be as nutty as a fruitcake."

"Ha!—Ha!" He snorted. "Grab your guns, men," he yelled in response, "Chief Bring-Home-The-Bacon is attacking!"

We both laughed loudly, then paused to shake hands in obvious pleasure at seeing each other again. A pot of coffee was brewing on a small electric hot plate in one corner of the crowded office, the most impressive feature of which were the long rows of pictures of pilots, pilots and more pilots with airplanes in the background dating back to the square-nosed models with the wooden props and Liberty engines which Dave had flown in World War I.

Stirring our coffee and relaxing with our feet on his desk, we didn't waste much time getting down to business. No one ever wasted much time in getting down to business with Dave. He made sure of that.

"I asked you to come by," he apologized, "to give me an opportunity to talk with you."

"Where's Sayen?" I asked nonchalantly, looking around the office.

"I sent him to Miami," he explained. "There seems to be some resistance building up there against a strike on Amalgamated over mileage limitation."

I stared at him.

"Some of the influential Eastern boys are dissatisfied with the way things are going."

"Who isn't?" I commented dryly.

"But they don't want to see the Amalgamated boys strike," he explained.

"It's the only way we'll get a mileage limitation on our flying." I was firm in my belief.

"But they don't want a mileage limitation on their flying." He told me earnestly.

"What?" I could not believe my ears.

"Well," the ol'man looked me in the eye with his faded blue ones, "you know that there are a couple of Eastern pilots who have controlled their pilot voting for years. They shape the policies of Eastern. And they sleep pretty close to the company management."

"Jerry West and Slim Bastitt!" I exclaimed.

The ol'man nodded thoughtfully. "You know them?"

I nodded silently, then added: "They work strictly for West and Bastitt, too!" I reminded him. "What's their beef against a mileage limitation on Amalgamated?"

"They don't want it!" he told me bluntly. "They want the association to drop the issue on Amalgamated. The way I figure it, they don't understand the importance of Amalgamated spearheading an industry wide drive for a mileage limitation. So I have sent Sayen down there to explain its importance to all airline pilots."

I studied the ceiling slowly then looked directly at Dave.

"They understand it," I declared. "And they are against it because their company officials are afraid it will spread to Eastern. That's their beef!"

"That's the way I have it figured," Dave agreed. "But Sayen thinks we can't be sure of that at this time. He wanted to see them and have a talk with them."

"Dave," I protested, "West and Bastitt on Eastern are exactly what we have been fighting on Amalgamated. They are a couple of 'all for me' pilots. They're fence-riders, vultures, hanging their faces first on one side of the fence and then on the other, sleeping with their company management and getting gravy from both sides." I arose and paced the floor while I talked. "Amalgamated's New York council was full of that type before Shipley lowered the boom and cleaned up the council. A couple of our councils are represented by that type right now, the type that insist we can deal with the company like gentlemen—if we would only send in gentlemen to talk with those nice company gentlemen behind the desks—you know what I mean."

He nodded slowly. "Sayen thinks they don't understand," he insisted.

"Hell!" I snorted. "Those two are smart, shrewd, and crafty. If they're against a mileage limitation then it's because they think they can get more for West and Bastitt by blocking a mileage limitation drive in the association then they can get by aiding it. All pilots will benefit if we put it over, and the younger pilots can look forward to a future. If we don't, then the airlines will save millions by pushing fewer and fewer pilots further and further, month by month, year by year." I stamped the floor in anger. "It's a waste of time to send Sayen down there to talk with them. They understand all the angles, and they're working them for West and Bastitt!" I insisted. "Those old wolves will give Sayen a rough time."

Suddenly the ol'man smiled at me. It was a smile that he stretched almost from ear to ear and drew his wide mouth into a long line. His eyes crinkled at the corner and glowed with fondness.

"Well," he admitted, "the kid has to learn. Now if you had tossed your hat in the ring for that vice-president's job, I wouldn't be sending you to Miami to get you out of the way."

I looked at him and watched the smile change to a chuckle as he enjoyed a little joke. He began fumbling for a cigar while he chuckled more and more. Casually I took one from my pocket, suspecting that he had seen the end peeping out, and handed it to him.

Slowly he lit the cigar and drew two or three long pulls before blowing out the match and throwing it at a paper basket.

"In this business," he paused and studied the brand of cigar thoughtfully. I knew by his reflective gaze that he liked the expensive brand I always managed to have in my pocket for him. If it had been a cheap brand of cigar, he never would have looked at it.

"In this business," he started again, "I have long known that it is a good idea to send an old battle scarred warrior in where the going is rough. So I sent him to Miami to give me an excuse for sending you to Dallas."

"Sending me to Dallas?" I questioned. "Why am I going to Dallas?"

He pulled on the cigar while he studied my face with those blue eyes.

"To see that copilot," he explained. "I don't like the rumors that are coming out of there. My two headquarters crash and investigation boys are down there and they have phoned me some disturbing news."

"Like what?" I was all attention.

The ol'man laid the cigar aside and stroked his mustache with the fingertips of one hand while he rolled his eyes toward the ceiling; for a long moment he gazed upward while I waited.

"Well," he began, "you know that the captain, Tom Claude, who was involved in that Dallas crash the other night, is not a union man, so we have no responsibility there. In addition to that, he received no serious injuries in that accident."

I nodded silently.

"The copilot is a good dues paying member and entitled to all the help we can give him. On top of that, he's lying there in that hospital with a broken back, a fractured pelvis, enclosed in a plaster cast up to his arm pits.

"Some Amalgamated officials are putting out the story that the copilot interfered with the controls while the pilot was landing the airplane and they are keeping a watch on his room. My two headquarters crash and investigation representatives phoned that news to me this morning. They haven't been allowed to see the copilot, and as far as I can find out, the company will permit no one excepting his wife to see him."

"What do you want me to do, Dave?" I asked quietly.

"I want you to sneak into that hospital down there and have a little talk with that copilot." He fixed his eyes on me as he continued. "You've done a lot of work for the copilots in the last several years. So I figure you can get the true story out of him."

"You know," he added, "I don't like the way Amalgamated officials always seem to be willing to do anything that will help weaken the association. And I wouldn't be surprised if they concocted some cock and bull story to shift the blame to the copilot simply because he is a union man."

I nodded again and let the ol'man continue.

"The Civil Aeronautics Board will be holding its hearings on that crash within the next few days," he reminded me. "We can't permit anybody to rig up a story that would reflect on a kid who is down flat of his back in a hospital and facing at least six months in that damned cement suit. The least we can do is to see that the entire story gets aired. Then, if the kid was responsible for the crash, we'll do all we can to help him."

"I'll wager that he wasn't, Dave," I spoke quietly with a feeling that I knew what I was talking about. "I know him well, because he was my copilot for several months during the war when I was flying transatlantic. He's a smart boy and a darned good pilot." Then I laughed recalling the raw egg episode with the navigator. It was too good to keep and I took a little time to tell the story to Dave.

At the end of the story we both had a good laugh together. Dave looked at me shaking his head and remarked: "Can't you just feel that damned egg running down your leg."

The ol'man pulled his railroad watch from a vest pocket. Picking up a phone, he called the airport and in a few minutes I had a reservation on Braniff to Dallas leaving Chicago in about forty-five minutes. It would arrive in Dallas around two in the morning.

The ol'man followed me to the head of the rickety stairs.

"Remember," he cautioned, "let that kid know what they're trying to do, get his story and lay the play out for him. He'll trust you."

"And," he added, laying a friendly hand on my shoulder, "give it the same treatment you gave Ardmore when you sneaked in there in the middle of the night like a raiding Apache, set that deal up for those fired pilots to be rescreened under more favorable circumstances, and sneaked out again without the company ever knowing that you were near the place."

I laughed at him.

"You know, Dave." I confided, "I have often wondered how you have been able to keep your faith in human nature while working for self-centered pilots and dealing with Amalgamated company officials who would dance with glee if they heard that Dave Behncke had suffered a major stroke and was not expected to live."

"All airline officials are not like that, Wayne," He insisted, "I can name several companies who have always dealt quite ethically with the association. Their officials have always lived up to their contracts, kept their word, and I have a real respect for them. It is true that they are tough, and hard businessmen to deal with, but their methods are honest and above board."

"That's a far cry from Amalgamated's methods," I commented dryly, "Why?"

"There was a time, a long time ago," he reflected, "when Amalgamated was a straight dealing company. C.R. Brown sat with me, and, flanked by our assistants, we wrote the first labor agreement of any airline. And, for a long time there after, Amalgamated was a most ethical company with which to deal. Then came the war, which changed many men. C.R. laid aside twin stars when he returned to

Amalgamated, and since that time Amalgamated has hit the bottom of the barrel in its dealings. The screening deal was a classical example."

Sadly he shook his head. Then he continued: "I don't understand it! He has been behind one crooked deal after another, and his officials have turned into a bunch of weasels. They lie, cheat, promise anything and do anything. That walkout on the System Board the other day was just another one of their stinking deals. That's why I expect them to come up with something dirty at Dallas. As the top goes, so goes the bottom!" He quoted softly, shaking my hand warmly in parting.

I hailed a cab in the rain and was soon back at the airport. There I purchased a ticket to Dallas and in a few minutes was able to climb aboard the Dallas-bound Braniff plane. It was to be a non-stop flight and I located myself so I could have a nice little sleep.

"As the top goes, so goes the bottom" I reflected. How true it was, how very true!

It was even true in the pilots' union, the association. The ol'man was such a citadel of honesty that beneath him the preponderance of the rank and file of the pilot representatives had always leaned to honest and square dealings. A rat or a weasel occasionally reared a head, but somehow it didn't last long. The two on Eastern, West and Bastitt, were the only ones I could think of who kept thrusting their heads out and squealing against the sweeping current of the ol'man's honesty. I could recall a number in the past who had surfaced only briefly and then been engulfed by the strong current.

"May the current always flow strongly in the same direction!" I prayed feverently as I dropped off to sleep with the subdued cruising throb of several hundred horses in my ears.

The Dallas arrival was on schedule at two in the morning. I left my bags with the Braniff agent and lost no time in catching a cab to the hospital, where little Ed Graham lay in a cast.

It was just the hour that I preferred to arrive at a hospital to see a pilot, a pilot whom the Amalgamated officials did not want me or any representative of the association to see, at least not until they had the story as they desired it. The hour of my arrival was an hour at which close surveillance of the copilot's room would be relaxed.

The main desk was deserted with the exception of one girl. She looked at me questioningly, but did tell me that Ed Graham was on the third floor. Before she could say more, or question me, I brushed up the stairway.

On the third floor I almost ran into the arms of a big buxom nurse as I came through the door from the stairway. She surveyed me critically for a moment and then smiled a surprisingly pleasant smile.

"May I help you?" She continued to regard me with a calculating look.

"Sorry to bother you." I apologized and lied in the same breath. "But I would like very much to see my brother. He was hurt in an airplane accident and I just arrived from Alaska." Then I added: "His name is Ed Graham and I'm Jim Graham." I tried to give her a nice smile, and at the same time look tired.

She studied me another moment, saying nothing.

"It's awful important!" I almost whispered and skated back onto the truth. "We flew together during the war and I know he would feel better just knowing that I had arrived to sweat him out in this ordeal."

"His room is restricted to all excepting his wife," she told me as she consulted her clipboard. "But I know that they didn't mean to keep his brother out."

She gave me a room number, another smile, and indicated the direction down the hall. I gave her a loving pat and left her sniffing a little fresh Alaskan ozone.

Ed was awake when I slipped through the door. He turned his head toward me, expecting to see the nurse, then broke into a big smile that showed his squirrel-like front teeth. The sound of a chuckle originated from down within a plaster cast that came up to his armpits. A sheet covered his lower extremities, but I knew the cast must extend some distance below his hips.

"I've been expecting you!" He grinned and spoke in a low tone as he stretched out a hand.

There was a movement in a big chair beside his bed. His wife of twenty-seven raised a dark head and blinked the sleep from her eyes before recognizing me. Then she smiled with such an expression of relief that it caused my eyes to dim. I had seen her several times during the war when Ed and I were flying together and leaving the states. She was small, good looking, and inclined to be a little plump.

"Oh!" she whispered. "I'm so glad to see you. But how did you get in? They aren't allowing anyone to see Ed."

Her eyes were wide with a questioning look.

"I'm his brother!" I laughed. "Don't forget, I'm Jim Graham from Alaska. When I slip out, forget that I was here."

Ed chuckled again in his cement-like enclosure.

"The ghost of Ardmore!" he exclaimed. "Everyone knew he was there from the tracks he left, but no one would ever admit they saw him."

We conversed together in half whispers for a little while. Then I asked Ed's wife if she would mind letting us talk shop for a little while in private. It caused her to hesitate a moment, but at Ed's nod she agreed to leave us alone. She was an extremely loyal wife and was determined to stay close to her man.

After her departure Ed told me that she had been staying with him constantly, sleeping in that chair and going out for only a few minutes each time to eat. She had been doing that ever since the accident. It caused me to shake my head at such a display of loyalty.

"Is this room bugged?" I asked Ed abruptly.

His eyes widened with questioning surprise while I took a few minutes to search the room. I looked behind the curtains, under his bed, in the bathroom, and even in the little closet while I told him about the time the company had wired a meeting room in New York during a contract negotiating conference. Satisfied that we were outside the scope of the long ears of Amalgamated, I settled in a chair beside his bed.

"How did it happen? I asked.

"We were westbound to Dallas, non-stop from Washington," Ed related. "Near Nashville we had to feather the number three engine because of roughness. Tom decided that we would say nothing about that on the radio and bring it on to Dallas as the company officials always seemed to want us to do without actually telling us."

"Extend the flight," I prompted. "It's against CAA regulations. That's why they can't tell us outright to do it."

"That's right," he agreed. "So we just kept coming to Dallas with the other three purring like kittens. Tom wasn't feeling so good and slept most of the way."

"Had he been drinking in New York?" I asked abruptly.

Ed hesitated. I could see he was making up his mind to tell me all I wanted to know.

"He always does." He smiled apologetically. "This time he was kind of drunk when we left New York. He let me make the takeoff at New York, the landing at Washington, and the takeoff out of there. In fact he didn't handle the radio or do much of anything but nap along and give the stewardesses hell about his coffee being cold. But he's done that before," he recalled. "The engineer and I are kind of used to him, and we just took care of things and left him alone."

"Did any of the dispatchers or agents talk with him in New York?" I asked.

"Matland did," he remembered. "And I heard him tell Tom to gargle something for his breath and leave that stuff alone in the future. He said that if he didn't he would have to report him."

I whistled softly to myself. "And then Matland cleared him on the flight?" I asked in surprise.

"Oh, sure! They always do, I've heard other dispatchers warn him to gargle something and leave that stuff alone."

"Did anyone else smell his breath before the departure?"

"The stewardesses did," he replied. "I remember them asking me if Tom had been drinking pretty heavy."

"But they're dead!" I reminded him shortly. "Anyone else at New York or Washington?"

"Oh, yes!" He waved a hand in sudden recollection. "That real blond agent at Washington noticed it and told me that he was going to file a report with the company."

"What did you say to that?" I quizzed him.

Ed chuckled and then grimaced from pain as he tried to make a move with his shoulders. "I just told him to do as he liked, that I was only a copilot and wasn't going to open my mouth unless I was asked a question."

"Good answer," I conceded. "Now what happened here?"

"It was clear and about eleven at night when we arrived at the Dallas airport," he continued. "I shook Tom and told him that we were home and asked if he wanted to make the landing. He raised up, grabbed the controls, and told me that he would make this one. So I ran through the cockpit check list with the engineer, called the tower, gave Tom the runway to use and got the plane ready for the landing."

"Then I noticed that the number four main tank gas was pretty low for a landing and asked Tom if he didn't want me to cross-feed it for the landing. "He looked at it for a moment and growled that it was okay as it was, and for me to leave it on the main. I did.

"At the start of the landing approach we were too high," Ed explained. "Then we got too far off to one side and Tom slipped it a little to lose altitude, then he banked it up pretty sharply in the slip to get back in line with the runway. Next we got too far over on the other side and he banked and kicked it back until we were in pretty good shape over the end of the runway, but still too high. I remember thinking that the passengers probably were wondering if a cowboy was at the controls.

"I gave him the flaps and gear whenever he called for them. We were about the middle of the runway and still ten feet high and off to one side on the grass when Tom realized that it was going to be a close one. He pulled the nose up to stall it in, then suddenly decided to go around." Ed raised up on his elbow in the excitement of the story as he relived the accident.

"He yelled to me to get the gear up and give him full low pitch." He talked slowly with his bright eyes fixed on my face. It was easy to see that he was straining to remain calm.

"I did both at the same time," he recalled. "And with that I yelled to him to remember that number three was out."

Ed sank back on the bed and caught his breath in short gasps. His face was beaded with perspiration and his eyes flashed back and forth around the room. I picked up a towel, wetted it at the sink, and cooled his face down.

"Calm down, Ed," I admonished. "You went through it once, let's just talk about it now."

He gave me a smile and lay quiet for a full minute without speaking. When he did speak again, his voice was calm and detached; his manner was that of a sick man who suddenly realized that he must remain very quiet for a long time.

"Tom shoved all four throttles open," Ed told me quietly, "and number four started popping and back-firing. The surge of power from one and two turned us sidewise for a few seconds before he got it halfway straightened out, but by then we were headed for a hangar. In a flash I checked to see that the mixtures were in automatic rich. They were. I glanced at the fuel pressures and saw that number four was bouncing on zero. I knew number four engine had sucked air from the steep approach and the near empty tank. I slapped the electric booster pump to number four into the high position and at the same time I glanced forward in time to see the beam of the landing lights climb up that hangar as Tom tried to suck us over it. Then we hit!"

He laid his head back on the pillow with the tears running down the sides of his face. I wiped them again with the cold towel.

"Just as we hit," he whispered, "I heard number four roar into full power and felt the surge of its power, but it was too late."

While I wiped his face again, he fixed his overly bright eyes on me again.

"That's all of it," he declared. "The next thing I can remember is coming to my senses in an ambulance. Later they told me that Tom and I went over the top of the hangar and off the other side in the nose section, which had broken free of the fuselage."

"Lie back and relax," I ordered, pushing his head back on the pillow and again wiping his face with the cold towel.

I sat there quietly for some time, applying the cold towel, while my mind turned the story over several times. It was the truth, I was sure of that. It was so logical.

It was appalling, I reflected, how a little thing, or combination of things, could cause an accident. Flying is truly a most exacting profession.

"Ed," I asked slowly, searching for words, "after you turned the airplane over to Tom, did you interfere with his flying in any manner? Did you try to help him on the controls?"

He shook his head.

"I never touched them," he declared positively. "I just followed orders."

"They're putting out the story that you interfered on the controls," I told him while watching him closely.

"Does Tom say that?" he questioned.

"I don't know," I replied. "But it is entirely likely that Tom will say whatever they tell him to say. After all, he was the captain and he is outside the union. The association has no obligation to defend or even advise him.

"I'm here," I reminded him, "not to see or advise Tom Claude, but to see and advise the copilot, Ed Graham, who is a good pilot. I know!"

He gripped my hand tightly and lay there silently for a long minute.

"You know," he declared hoarsely, "I never realized until right now what it means to carry that little union card."

A light tap on the door interrupted us and I opened it to let his wife back into the room with a reassuring smile. She slipped quietly back into her chair while her eyes silently studied my face with occasional flashes to Ed's white one.

"This is the payoff," I continued speaking to Ed. "This is where you collect for those dues you have paid the association. And the association is determined to see that you are able to keep paying them for many years to come."

"What do I do?" Ed asked quietly.

"Nothing," I replied. "Just get well."

"Yes, but what do I say?" Ed was visibly worried.

"Nothing," I replied. "Until the CAA holds their investigation, tell them nothing."

"But they are going to have a little committee of company and CAA men call on me today," Ed interjected. "They will be asking all sorts of questions. What do I say?"

"Oh—," I studied him thoughtfully. "So they are coming today? I knew it would be soon, but didn't know that I was running that close a race with them."

I smiled at Ed as the humor of the situation struck me. A thought hit me that caused the smile to change into a wide grin and then into a quiet chuckle.

"Ed," I asked, "do you have one of those association representation cards?"

"Some place, but I don't know where, right now."

"Then I'll give you mine."

I thumbed through my billfold until I found my ALPA (Air Line Pilots' Association) representation card. There was no name on it, for I had neglected to write my name in on the space provided when I received it. Actually I had simply stuffed the card in my wallet, never dreaming that I would actually need it.

"Take this," I instructed him, after writing his full name on the card. "When they come in to question you and after all have congregated, but before the questions start, simply dig this card out of some place, under your pillow, or that desk drawer, and give it to someone near you with the request that he pass it around."

Ed took the little card with a curious, questioning look. His wife snapped on the light at the head of the bed and rearranged his pillow while he slowly read: "I, Edward Howard Graham, am a member of the Air Line Pilots' Association, International, and desire not to proceed further from this point without benefit of advice from an association attorney."

Then he saw the humor of the situation.

"Wayne, I love that!" he chuckled with twinkling eyes and the old grin that reminded me of the time of the raw egg episode.

"Will you do it?"

"Will I? You're darned tooting I will." He vowed. Then as an afterthought, he asked: "But what about the attorney?"

"I'll get one down here as quickly as Dave can release one and we'll have him with you throughout any questioning they may undertake, and also during the CAB hearing," I promised.

"Wonderful!" he sighed and I could see from his expression that a great load had been lifted from his mind.

"One thing more." I remembered something.

Taking a twenty dollar bill from my billfold, I handed it to his wife.

"Here's a card for you," I insisted. "Take it and hound the telephone company until you get a private phone in Ed's room. The ol'man is going to want to talk with him frequently, and with it he can get me, the ol'man, or an association attorney in just a few minutes."

Carefully I wrote the ol'man's office, private night line, and home phone numbers on a sheet of paper. I included my own home phone at Claremore where I lived with my mother.

"Use them," I directed Ed while handing him the list, "Use any of them at any time you feel a need. If you don't get me at my home, my mother will be able to tell you where you can reach me."

He grinned at me and squeezed his wife's hand.

"Take care of him," I instructed his wife. "If he gives any sign of worrying, just tell him to call brother Jim."

With that I was gone, out the door, down the hallway, the stairway and disappeared in the misty dawn.

An hour later I called the ol'man from a pay phone at the airport when I was sure he would be up and ready to do battle for some pilot or copilot. Briefly I told him what had transpired in Dallas, the triggered mechanism I was leaving behind, the need for an attorney for a little copilot named Ed Graham. I also suggested to him that it might be a good idea to have the attorney advise Ed to omit the part in his story about Tom Claude being drunk in New York. It was something, I pointed out, that we could bring out later in the form of new evidence if there was any attempt at the hearing to blame Ed for the crash. In the meantime, to bring it out unnecessarily in a public hearing, would only prejudice the public against flying.

Dave agreed with me, then he made me repeat what the ALPA card said, for he had forgotten about sending them out almost two years previously. His rough and spontaneous laughter told me quite plainly that David L. Behncke was going to enjoy that day.

He would enjoy it simply by thinking occasionally about a choice collection of company and CAA officials calling on a poor and helpless little copilot who was in a cast with a broken back, and who would be defenseless from sly, leading questions. Defenseless, that is, except for a little card!

No doubt, I visualized, the ol'man would have one of those cards set on his desk so he could read it each time the thought struck him. Somehow, it seemed like a day I would enjoy too!

Chapter 11

Trading Stewardesses

Three hours later I discreetly deplaned from another Braniff plane and wandered into the Tulsa operations office to check on my schedule before going home. The offices were open and the business day just approaching the lunch hour.

On my schedule I found that I was due out that night, or rather, the following morning, departing at two a.m. on a trip to San Francisco. My copilot and engineer were good competent boys and had flown with me at different times when my schedule required me to make up time lost during ALPA business trips. I knew they would make the trip easy for me. Truthfully, I felt that I needed an easy trip or two. The New York hearings and the Dallas trip had pretty well drained my reserve.

Signing in for the trip, I glanced more closely at the balance of the crew, the girls flying with us. An older stewardess, Beckman by name, whose parents and sweetheart lived in San Francisco, was assigned as one of the two girls.

I felt a little thrill on seeing that the other stewardess was June Tabler, tall, shapely and dark-headed. The thought of her alertness, her beautiful features, and the way she had acted in New York with those little arm squeezes caused my ears to point upward a little. It made me realize how long I had been divorced and how lonely the life of a bachelor could be.

Then I noted that Schustman was taking an extra section to San Francisco, leaving Tulsa just thirty minutes ahead of my schedule. Good! I thought. It'll give me a chance to talk further with George and tell him of the Dallas affair. I smiled at the memory of the little card I had left with Ed Graham.

George had his regular crew. I paused over Shissler's name, sweet little red-headed Mary, and mused over the thought of what a good little wife she would make a man—in a class with Ed Graham's wife. Her flying mate was, of all stewardesses, Jean Thurson. Her name on the schedule sheet caused me to recall the night I had spent in New York with her. That was one for the book, I realized, shaking my head, a story no one would ever believe.

I noticed a little movement in the doorway to the side of the schedule sheet. I glanced over to see the chief pilot's secretary, Margaret Seamore, sorting papers in preparation for posting on the bulletin board. She was a small, mouse-like creature of near my own age, near forty, with a very sweet disposition and an apparent desire to please everyone.

Margaret was the kind of secretary who always tried to make everyone who entered the chief pilot's office feel welcome. In contrast to Joe Anderson's surly nature, she always seemed to be ready to smile or laugh at something. Being the mother of a married daughter in her early twenties, Margaret had little trouble expanding that motherly attitude to include the younger secretaries, youthful agents, and boyish cargo handlers who worked in the vicinity of her office or who came in contact with her in the normal course of their duties. Truly a well liked person, Margaret could not understand the antagonistic feeling with which her boss regarded me.

"Hello, Captain Allison!" she smile most pleasantly. "I'm glad to see you back."

"Thank you, Margaret," I replied. "It's good to be back and headed for San Francisco tonight. Where's Joe?" I asked as an afterthought, for I had long ago learned to try to keep him located at all times.

He had been baying on my trail for three years, and I had learned to be like the fox that had had a beagle on his trail for so long that whenever he couldn't hear him bay or see him busy trying to work out the scent, he would immediately become uneasy, worried, and fearful that something had happened to the poor, slow running little bastard. As a matter of fact, I had pointed to him on my trail so many times to other pilots and called him my beagle, that the story had gone around among the pilot group until the Tulsa based pilots had become aware of my desire to keep him located at all times.

So, they had started helping me! Three times in the middle of the night when I was flying and had reported over check point, I had heard another flight say, "Wayne, we have your beagle."

Even the stewardesses got into the act. Once when in New York on contract negotiations a former Tulsa based stewardess, who had flown considerably with me before transferring to Chicago to be near her ailing folks, had approached me in the lobby of the hotel, smiled sweetly at me and said: "We just brought your beagle in from Chicago, Wayne." I had thanked her and bought her a drink.

"Captain Anderson is in San Francisco," Margaret replied pleasantly. "I think he is coming back tonight sometime." She was not too sure about that.

"Glad to know that," I told myself a bit grimly.

"He is checking Captain Blankenship out on the DC-6's," she volunteered.

"That's good," I replied. "John has been due for that promotion for some time."

I thought of the extra money the company had had to pay to Blankenship, as well as Jewell because of the way Joe had promoted a junior pilot out of line of seniority. Thereby he had laid the grounds for the Jewell grievance, and ultimately, the Jewell decision which had caused the ol'man so much worry, and was now one of his favorite jokes. But well I knew that Joe didn't blame himself for the trouble, and shocking decision to the company. He blamed me. It was all my fault in his thinking.

"How's Joe's health these days?" I questioned with a smile.

"He hasn't been feeling so well the last week," she reported. "Mr. C.R. Brown, Mr. Tom Boyson, and Captain Don Ogden were here a few days ago," she recalled. "There was some talk of transferring Captain Joe to Fort Worth, and he is sick over the thought."

My mind flashed back to the night I had had the two emergencies and the desperate effort Anderson had made in front of C.R. and the others to nail me for a violation.

"They're stepping up the pressure on him," I told myself. "I had better be more careful."

"Well, I sure hope they don't!" I spoke aloud to Margaret and was sincere in my expression for I could easily see that he might be replaced by another who might be a taller, leaner, and faster running hound, a hound that ran silently on the trail. The idea gave me a little chill.

"Yes," I declared, "we would sure hate to see Captain Joe transferred. It wouldn't seem right without him around." She giggled a little. "Captain Allison," she exclaimed, "it's so nice to hear you say that. I do wish that Captain Joe would feel the same way about you, for I think you both could get along wonderfully if you would just try."

"There's no doubt about it, Margaret," I agreed. "Now how about letting me buy your lunch?"

"Oh,—no, I couldn't do that!" she was startled and recoiled almost like I had struck her. "They have warned me against you. I have been ordered to have nothing to do with you except when it is officially necessary. Somehow they think I might tell you something that's an office secret."

"Margaret," I looked directly at her. "I know you would not do that, and I will never ask you to do such a thing. I don't deal that way."

"I know, Captain Allison." She smiled sweetly at me and disappeared back into her office. A moment later she was back with some papers.

"I need your signature on these interrupted flight reports for the CAA on the flight in which you declared two emergencies." She explained. "I had them in your box but Captain Joe took them out for some reason."

The CAA had long required the captain of a flight who had declared an emergency to explain the emergency on a form provided by the CAA. To speed up the submission of such a form, it had been the company custom for the pilot, upon completion of the interrupted flight or a flight in which emergency authority was used, to write out in long hand the nature of the emergency and then sign four blank forms, clip them together, and leave on Margaret's desk. She would then type the report on the signed copies and submit the report to the CAA without further delay.

Because there was a short time limit for the submission of such a report the pilot making such a report seldom ever saw the typed report over his signature. Margaret had the penciled copy I had given to Joe Anderson with the conversation on the flight of two emergencies. But I had not signed the four blank forms and now she wanted my signature on the completed forms.

Quickly I signed all four copies, noting that they exactly reflected my penciled copy. The bottom line on the form stated that the above flight was conducted in accordance with CAA regulations, without which the CAA could revoke my license if a serious infraction had occurred.

I thanked Margaret for her thoughtfulness and in a little while I drove to Claremore where my mother lived in the big two story house on the west side, a short two blocks from the Will Rogers memorial. Mother and Dad had lived in that one location for some twenty years until Dad's death at the end of WW II. During the last year and a half I had lived with her.

Mother was slim, alert, and good looking with grey hair and a youthfulness she had always maintained from the time she and Dad had come to Oklahoma from Missouri, as little more than teenagers, the year Oklahoma became a state, back in 1907.

There, at the big house, I found my boy of ten playing around the yard. He had left his mother's home on the east side of Claremore, which I had given her in the divorce, and decided he wanted to move in with his Dad. The little rooster had packed a bag and lugged it across town to his grandmother's house and was waiting for his dad to return.

But then, he just wanted to go swimming at the nearby pool. With that major issue settled, he was quite willing to play at the pool and let me sleep the afternoon out, for I had begun to feel the need for a good bed.

That evening I took him home, after he had eaten his fill of his grandmother's cooking. He was content to stay a few more days with his mother, while his dad went flying again. When I returned, he insisted that we would go to the farm, as we had done in the past. It was most difficult trying to explain to him that the farm was a thing of the past, that his mother had recently sold it and we would have to play at the swimming pool.

Returning home I sat for a long time on the front porch, thinking about how gifted a man might be in his profession, and how well he might fight battles for others, but when it came to making a success of a marriage, what a wash-out he could be.

Truly I wondered if a pilot, an airline pilot, had any business taking the marriage vows. So many seemed to fail, and so many had two or three marriages behind them. It caused me to think of Ed Graham and the story he had told me in New York about Tom Claude and Dan

Landall.

What was the reason airline pilots seemed to make such poor husbands? No doubt Dan's remark reflected the thinking of an egoist. And pilots were, generally speaking, egotistical and inclined to be conceited, first cousins to Superman, to put it in terms of their own thinking.

But didn't airline pilots have a right to be conceited? Well, I studied that one for a while. True, they had excellent jobs with good pay and short hours of work which, in consideration of the faster and faster equipment, had a rather bleak future. But lots of men had even better jobs, and they did not have to buck an exacting physical and flying examination each six months, year in and year out, to keep that job.

Really, I decided, an airline pilot did not have much to be conceited about.

"Guess it's just that relationship to Superman!" I acknowledged with a wry expression before going back to bed.

Some pilots have sleep routines they go through to get the necessary sleep before a late hour flight. As for myself, the war flying had caused me to form the habit of sleeping wherever and whenever I had the opportunity. I learned to sleep sitting in a corner, on the floor, or at a vacant table. I even learned to catnap in the airplane, flying, with my shoe off, my leg hung over the control pedestal in such a manner that my big toe rested on the up or down button of the automatic pilot and a touch of the toe would readjust a sudden tilt of the plane, requiring only one eye to give the artificial horizon a brief scrutiny.

At twelve-thirty the alarm went off. I arose and dressed rapidly in the blue uniform of AA. Then placing my bags in my car, I drove leisurely to the airport. Long ago I had formed the habit of having a little reserve time in the event of a flat, trouble along the road, or some other delaying factor. This enabled me to arrive at the airport some fifteen minutes ahead of the due time, and it permitted me to catch George and his crew some twenty minutes before they were due to board their plane.

No airplanes were at the ramp when I walked toward the operations office, but I knew, as I looked up into the star-studded sky, that two big giant conquerors of time and space, some thirty minutes apart, were homing on Tulsa with unerring accuracy. Soon one would roar in, unload sleepy passengers and a tired flight crew, take on more sleepy passengers, a fresh crew plus nearly three thousand gallons of gasoline, and several thousand pounds of cargo and mail.

Then it would roar out again to conquer time and distance enroute to San Francisco for an early morning arrival. It was a fascinating profession, I admitted to myself. Each flight always seemed to have a separate taste of adventure, a sense of a vague promise, always kept, of some new, hidden thrill and assurance that it would be different from any other. And the taste of adventure, the promise of some new hidden thrill coupled with the knowledge that each would be different, had always eliminated any sense of boredom.

Glancing at the stars my eyes sought and found Polaris, the north star, the star more used by aerial and sea navigators than any other. Somehow, I felt that we were old friends, for through more than three long years of war-flying, Polaris had never lied to me. Always, when asked, he had given me my latitude, my distance from the pole over which he kept constant vigil.

I dropped my bags at the corner of the operations office where others were already stacked. Shoving the door open, I entered with my cap shoved back. Inside me I knew that I was about to embark upon another adventure, another flight, to make another sojourn into God's Heaven. And I was happy!

My crew had not yet arrived, but I found George's clustered around George in the snack bar, enjoying early morning coffee. They greeted me warmly, with the exceptions of little red-headed Mary, who had a quiet and sweet little smile for me, and Jean from Minnesota, who gave me a blue-eyed questioning look as though trying to decide whether I was a man, or a beast with undiluted timber wolf blood.

Taking a cup of coffee, I carefully selected a seat at the table, managing to squeeze in between Mary and Jean. Casually I mixed my coffee and looked up into George's eyes with a sly grin on my face and remarked, "I'll trade you even." I looked directly at him, knowing that he would understand.

"What's the matter with ol'man Behncke?" George looked around the table, ignoring me. "He called me long distance in New York to ask if there was some little favor he could do me, to sort of keep me speaking to him. I wouldn't have said anything, but he was so insistent on doing me some small favor that I just mentioned that I would like to have a nice trip with Mary and Jean without having that big overgrown timber wolf there, running around and frightening my little chickens with his lousy flying and poor approaches." He indicated me with a wave of his hand. "So he promised to call Allison to Chicago and keep him in a cooler for three days." He shook his head in disgust.

"Honest to Pete!" George explained, "I've tried to teach him to drop his nose slowly and carefully set his flaps to the trail and be gentle and smooth on the approach until he gets in landing range." He shook his head sadly, "But he keeps trying to come in like a raiding chicken hawk. Some of these days," he prophesized, "he's going to hit so hard that he will tear his gear clear off and scatter his tail feathers down the runway."

George chuckled in his coffee and glanced around the table with his bright eyes to see how many had followed. His engineer laughed loudly while Jewell, his copilot, chuckled and smiled while Mary, who had flown with George for three months, calmly sipped her coffee as though the throw had been so high and wild that she had not even heard it whistle. Only the lightning flash of her eyes at me told me that she had followed. Jean said nothing, but glanced around with a questioning look and decided that she had better just listen to this conversation for a while.

"He's so rough," George continued, "and so exhausted from over-controlling that I have to frequently put him to bed, with or without."

It was Jean's cue with George looking directly at her with twinkling eyes and she could not stop the slow blush that crept over her face. George's intent look did not help.

"I'll trade you even," I insisted again, more to divert the attention from Jean's blush than anything else.

At that moment June Tabler came into range of the group with a smooth rolling walk that caused George to stop his cup halfway to his mouth and sit transfixed while he tuned in on her every move. She was worthy of note too, with her black head high, her rosy cheeks glowing and her eyes bright from several hours of sleep. It was easy to see that she knew she was adventuring.

"It's a deal, with delivery in San Francisco." George exclaimed with alacrity as he leaped to his feet to pull a chair for June up close to his own.

Everyone understood his actions, but he and I alone, I thought, understood that we had traded stewardesses in San Francisco. It caused me to take another look at what I had traded off. I muttered a little to myself.

"What did you say, Wayne?" Mary leaned her red head close.

"I was just remarking that a two for one deal is pretty good." I smiled and spoke in a low voice to her.

"Only if the merchandise is of equal quality," she answered in an equally low voice and looked directly into my eyes.

"There's no comparison," I hastened to assure her. "He just traded two beautiful gold pieces for a gold brick."

"Thank you, Wayne," she murmured as she arose to respond to the loud speaker announcing the arrival of the extra section going to San Francisco.

I stood at the window of the operations office and watched George roar out on a west takeoff. That brought him by the window just before he slanted the nose upward to clear the hangars on the west side by a good safe margin. The roar of those four mighty engines seemed to vibrate the office for a few seconds, then all was serene and quiet in the early morning hour with the muffled roar of George's engines fading rapidly westward.

"Flight forty-nine is in range," a radio operator stuck his head through a small window of the radio room adjoining the operations office to notify the agent.

"That's our buggy," I spoke to June who had been standing close to me watching George's takeoff. She was quite fascinated with the wonderful world of flying.

"How can you be so matter of fact about it?" She regarded me with shining eyes. "It's wonderful!"

I looked at her again, from head to foot while a slow smile crept across my face.

"You'll get used to it," I told her, "you'll even learn to gripe about it."

"Oh, no." She protested. "I'm so fascinated by it all that I can hardly pass the time between trips."

"I have that trouble too," I replied, thinking of the farm that had once occupied so many pleasant hours of my off duty time. Now it was gone and I was dreading those days off with little to do.

"Maybe we should sort of pool our problems together," she invited with her head tilted to one side while she regarded me with glowing black eyes. A nice smile accompanied the invitation.

"That's a thought." I gazed down at her, knowing that she was tempting me, encouraging me.

"But let's talk about our time in San Francisco now," she suggested. "It's ahead of us. Then when it's behind us we can talk about how we will spend our time in Tulsa."

She puzzled me. I had never seen a girl quite like her, so direct in the way she had homed on me, like I was a transmitting station. Actually, I had not given her any encouragement that I could recall. It just seemed that she had selected me and tuned in like a homing pigeon. Now she was making it plain that she was ready for the approach.

I thought a little shamefully of the way I had referred to her as a gold brick while I smelled the delicious aroma of her perfume and looked down into her challenging eyes. It was so hard to think clearly and look into those eyes at the same time. She was truly a beautiful woman.

"How old are you?" I asked suddenly.

"I am twenty-seven," she declared and smiled a red-lipped smile.

"Most girls are between twenty-two and twenty-five when they come with the company," I mused.

"And they leave sometime between that and thirty," she informed me. "I've checked into that. They want to get rid of a stewardess before they get much beyond that thirty mark."

"How does it happen," I questioned, "that you have waited until twenty-seven to start?"

"I was dumb for a long time," she smiled. "I worked as a private secretary for a big lumber company in Oroville, California."

"A private secretary?" I studied her closely. "Did it not pay more than a stewardess job?"

"I was making three times a stewardess's starting salary when I left," she replied.

I whistled softly.

"I don't understand why you left that sort of a job." I was frankly puzzled.

"The reason is real simple." she informed me waving a shapely hand. "I wasn't meeting the right people. Day after day, week after week, month after month, all I met was a bunch of old fuddy-dudds who were only interested in lumber. You know what lumber is, that's wood! And every time I exposed a leg accidentally they would automatically think about a two-by-four."

I laughed, enjoying her frankness.

She tilted her head at a more saucy angle before continuing: "I finally came to the conclusion that I wasn't meeting any eligible men there, and that I'd better get out."

"So—," she smiled, "I went to New York and worked as a model for a while. That didn't seem to help much until one day I met a stewardess, and here I am."

"There's no better hunting ground in the world," I told her frankly while watching her closely.

"That all depends," she smiled in a provocative manner.

"On what?"

"On the way our schedules match." She touched my arm in a friendly gesture.

Further conversation was cut short by the arrival of flight forty-nine. It swung into the gate directly opposite the operations office. June picked up her bag and hurried out to be ready to board. Beckman was already out at the gate, eager to reach San Francisco and her lover as well as her folks. That meant, I realized, that June would have a stewardess room all to herself. George already had that figured, there was no doubt.

Outbound stewardesses were supposed to be standing on the ramp when the passengers unloaded so that they could be of assistance to anyone who needed help. And too, I guess they were meant to serve as a sort of added attraction for any traveling wolves.

I remained in the operations office a few minutes longer and spoke to the incoming crew. The captain was a short, slender man of about my own age, with stringy blond hair and a receding chin. Like many little men, he was as pompous and cocky as a banty rooster. Sam Ballard by name, he lost no time in buttonholing me about the lack of any action from the negotiating committee. Patiently I explained that way the company was refusing to agree to any section of the contract as long as we insisted on a mileage limitation.

He didn't buy that, claiming that ol'man Behncke was the problem, that if we replaced him, we could make progress. Sam was full of ideas. He knew we could get a mileage limitation if the ol'man would do something besides write long-winded letters about how hard he was working. He remembered, too, that we needed a good retirement plan for men getting along in age. Something had to be done about that, he was sure.

Then he got on the subject of the new headquarters building the ol'man was building just to have a monument, a temple with a throne for him to sit upon. A terrific waste of money!

I listened as best I could and tried to get in a word here and there, and did point out that the land we had purchased a few years back for the building was now worth almost double the price we had paid for it. In addition, I insisted that the new office building would be worth, upon completion, three times our total investment in the project.

Both our copilots were listening as I explained his erroneous thinking with great patience, not expecting to make any headway with him, but I wanted the copilots to understand. To me Sam was a lost cause, one of a group of pilots I called the 'vulture army.'

When I had first used that term in front of the ol'man he had stopped me and asked for an explanation of the term 'vulture army of pilots.'

"Well, Dave," I had replied, "that is the group of loud mouth pilots who are always dissatisfied and urging you on in their behalf. Then when the shooting starts, Golly—Damnation, it's amazing how fast they disappear."

The ol'man had laughed at that.

"Then," I had continued, "when the shooting is over, and you have actually won something, they are the first there with their hands out, screaming for a major portion of the booty." That explanation had caused the ol'man to stroke his mustache and study the ceiling for some minutes after the humor of the explanation had worn off.

When my copilot nudged me, I was glad to break off the conversation and hurry out to my airplane. Well, I knew, it was a waste of breath trying to talk to Sam, and, it required too much self-control to listen to the conceited little bastard.

Taxiing out down the long runway to the east side of the field to follow George out on a west takeoff, I felt a glow of happiness bursting inside me at the feel of the big ship under me. It had been several days since I had flown and my desire to fly was keen within me. Smoothly and gently I touched a toe brake and held the nose steering steady as the big plane flexed its shocks over the little swells in the runway. Positively, I reflected, there was no other occupation that gave a man such a sense of responsibility, or a sense of accomplishment, as taking a big airliner, loaded with precious, living cargo, up into the cleansing and pure atmosphere and depositing it gently and undamaged at a far distant terminal.

On the run-up the engines tugged and strained at the wings while they demonstrated their power on the cockpit instruments. Then, with each one checked to my satisfaction, I released the brakes and headed westward after George. It caused me to think of the many stagecoach drivers who must have cracked whips on hard pulling horses as they dragged their heavy loads westward.

Easing the throttles forward in one slow, continuous movement, I found myself wondering what one of those old stagecoach drivers would think if he were alive and could visualize how many thousands of horses I was snapping the whip on as I eased those four little levers into the full forward position. And the stagecoach driver, I mused to myself, what would he think of it? What would he think of the place where I placed my feet in comparison to the foot rest where he braced his feet when he strained at the lines?

Leaning forward I watched and felt the swells of the runway pass under with rapidly increasing speed. A flick of my eyes at an air speed indicator told me we were climbing past seventy and I lifted the nose wheel free of the earth and held it steady until the tandems floated off the ground. At that moment I signalled gear up and flattened out ten feet above the runway. It caused the air speed to build up more rapidly which shortened the critical engine-out period.

When the distant hangars began to loom up in the landing lights, I gave the stabilizer wheel a half turn and lifted the nose into the dark blue of God's Heaven. It was exhilarating to feel that big giant respond and bore upward and upward and upward.

Out of Oklahoma City after a brief stop we climbed and climbed and watched the stars grow brighter and brighter as we forged up through the polluted air. At twenty thousand we leveled off and pulled the power and propellers back to that slow, long distance throb that devoured the miles at a rate of more than six a minute. Trimming the controls, I engaged the automatic pilot and was ready for coffee as well as interesting conversation from a good looking black-headed girl who had admitted that she was hunting.

Our arrival in San Francisco was a little ahead of schedule but only fifteen minutes behind George, for, as we learned later, he and his crew had gone sight seeing up Death Valley, as soon as the morning sun caught their big giant. Always a fascinated tourist at heart, George enjoyed teaching others the art of going sightseeing with the aid of an Amalgamated airplane.

The passengers loved it too, especially when they found that it was a little extra consideration being thrown in by an accommodating captain. So, they never reported such irregular flights.

It was nearly eight o'clock when we found George and his crew ordering breakfast in the dining room of the hotel in which the company maintained hotel rooms for the layover crews. There we found another crew also having breakfast in preparation for departure of an eastbound extra section with the airplane that George had brought in.

Gene Burns, the chairman of the ALPA council at Tulsa, greeted me warmly. We had not had a chance to talk since the grievance hearings in New York, so George, Gene, and I pulled over in a corner away from the noisy crew members. There I told them of the Dallas affair and the two really enjoyed a laugh over it. It struck Gene as especially funny.

"You know," Gene looked directly at me as he spoke, "there ought to be a congressional investigation into the way the airlines are using influence, bribery, and favors to get the various local CAA agents to do their bidding. We haven't had any real accident investigations with concrete preventive recommendations since Congress, acting on a presidential request, washed out the Independent Air Safety Board. The Civil Aeronautics Act of 1938 set it up and it really became something in a few years. We had some real honest accident investigations. Then when it was found that politics could not influence it, the airlines spear-headed a drive to get rid of it. And Roosevelt helped them."

George and I nodded.

Again Gene laughed aloud in glee.

"Wouldn't you," he asked laughing, "loved to have seen those bastards passing that little card around and looking at each other with real intelligent looks?"

"I'll bet the ol'man enjoyed that one," George offered.

Then I had to tell in detail exactly what the ol'man had said.

Gene and his crew left us shortly to take their trip back to Tulsa. George and I gathered our two crews together at a big table. I guess it was good that the dining room was deserted, for we sort of took it over. It isn't often that two crews have an opportunity to get together away from the home base with a long layover ahead of them, especially at San Francisco. All crew members soon made it evident that they were planning on enjoying it.

"Now," George suggested, "we've got to get real scientific about this." He looked around the table at the three girls. We had lost one in my crew for, true to my prediction, Beckman had hit the ground running and looking like anything but a tired chick. "Wayne and his crew are not due out until tomorrow night around midnight and thirty minutes behind us," George continued, "that gives us lots of time to sleep today, dinner and drinks tonight, tomorrow and half of tomorrow night to sleep it off."

"So—." George looked around again. "Shall we meet in the lobby and go to dinner around six with preparatory drinks being served in the bar starting anywhere between five and five-thirty, depending on your thirst?"

Everyone laughed acceptance of the plan and we soon finished breakfast and wandered off to bed. The sandman was fast catching up with us.

On layovers the stewardesses had two double rooms adjoining with a connecting door. They could either keep the door open and be chummy or close it and have privacy. The pilots had a similar arrangement on another floor. It was to these company rooms we all strolled, laughing, talking, and enjoying the mental and physical let-down that always follows a tiring flight—and all flights are tiring.

George and his copilot followed my copilot and me into our room for a little drink from a bottle which I kept tied to a short string and hung behind the curtain about two feet from the curtain rod. It must have looked good from the building across the way.

Anyway, it was still there, so I unhooked the string with its attached hook from the curtain rod and was ready to pour. As George put it: "There's nothing that will soothe frayed flying nerves or sharpen pointed ears like alcohol."

Chapter 12

The Warning of the Whistling Bird

Around five my copilot and I awoke, showered, shaved, and dressed in street clothes. It had been a nice cool day for sleeping, as usual, and I had really relaxed. Somehow the San Francisco air could relax me better than any other. Or maybe it was the greater distance between me and the company offices that did the trick.

At the bar we found George and his copilot together with our engineers. Everyone had a drink and was enjoying it. But I refused to order anything more than a plain soda. The CAA had long published a regulation prohibiting an airline pilot from drinking intoxicating drinks within twenty-four hours prior to a scheduled flight. We were legal as far as that regulation was concerned.

Recently Walter Braznell, the Director of Flight, had issued a company regulation increasing that time at layover stops to include the entire layover, regardless of its length. It was a complete ban on drinking away from home. But hardly any flight crews paid any attention to it. It was considered to be too asinine. They respected the CAA regulation, but few paid attention to the new company regulation. Few, that is, with the exception of Allison.

I watched the company regulations like a hawk. I made sure that I complied with them to the letter, for somehow, I had the feeling that such sleepers as that new drinking regulation were written for Allison, or any strong union official whom they had a desire to liquidate. From experience, I had a very low opinion of company ethics.

It was a known fact, by both company officials and pilots, that David L. Behncke was a teetotaler and much disinclined to raise a finger of protection to a pilot involved in illegal drinking; that of course meant within the CAA twenty-four hour period prior to taking out a flight. And when such a drinking pilot, if married, was also involved with a stewardess, well, the poor devil might as well throw himself on the mercy of the company, for Dave would have none of him.

So I refused to drink, even when the three girls joined us looking like three luscious, but thirsty peaches. They accepted the drinks George and I bought for them and the party began to throb. George tried his best to talk me out of staying on the wagon, but I was hearing a little birdie whistle. I had heard it from the time I first read the new company regulation written by Braznell. So I refused to consider any other course. As I explained it, I was too involved in ALPA representation to take a chance.

June, with bright eyes, glowing cheeks, and urging lips, insisted on my joining the party. She wanted so much to have me drinking with her, even to the point of shaking loose from George and squeezing in close to me to try to get me to drink from her glass. But, I would have only soda water.

"I'll have a bottle in my room when we return from dinner," June promised me with a laugh. It caused George to give me a look of reminder of the two-for-one deal we had made in Tulsa. Mary was clad in a neatly fitting knit suit, giggled, and whispered something to Jean. The two then turned away, laughing between themselves.

The dinner was a big success. We went to a favored spot in the International Settlement and secured a large table, large enough to accommodate the two crews and all the food we ordered. It was a delightful meal. We ate until we could hold no more.

Then we went to see a couple of shows of the waterfront variety. To make sure everyone saw those shows in the right frame of mind, George kept ordering drinks for everyone, except me. He wanted everyone well lubricated.

Finally we came back to our hotel in a body where the group split up. There the engineers and copilots took off to bed. They were invited to a nightcap at the bar but declined. When I refused again to drink at the bar, June insisted on buying a bottle at the bar, which George paid for, showed it to me and offered to pour me and everyone drinks in her room.

So we adjourned to the stewardesses rooms where the girls promptly opened the adjoining door between the two rooms. I ordered up ice and a set-up for everyone and served as the bartender. After another drink, during which I made sure that Mary and Jean had light drinks, at their repeated requests, June became rather intoxicated. Throughout the evening she had shown signs of having a thirst for strong drinks and had once ordered a double shot.

Now she began to show a definite thirst for a little loving. Once she dragged me into the unoccupied room on the pretense of telling me a little secret where she promptly rolled into my arms. She scared me and I beat a hasty retreat to Mary and Jean, much to her amusement.

They thought it was real funny! Giggling to each other, they dragged me into the unoccupied room and closed the middle door with George and June in June's room, at the same time telling George that they had traded him off. He didn't seem to mind.

So we talked for some little while as the girls finished their drinks and I killed another soda. Neither Jean or Mary wanted life of the fast variety. However, it seemed to be a certainty in the adjoining room, for we heard nothing more from there. Smiling, Mary once mentioned casually that all was quiet on the western front.

After asking them to have breakfast with me I finally told them good night and slipped out the main door. They were half in bed when I departed and I knew they would not waste any time crawling between the covers. We were all getting sleepy.

I wandered leisurely to my room and prepared for bed. My copilot was sleeping soundly and I thought I could join him, but by the time I was ready to crawl into bed, the desire for sleep had left me. After a time in the bed I turned the light on in the short hallway to the bathroom, seated myself in a chair, and proceeded to read a little while I thought of June Tabler, Mary Shissler and Jean Thurson. It was funny, I reflected, on the difference in women.

June was quite a dish, or rather, had given that appearance. Yet tonight she had given me the impression of being something entirely different, a party girl, a woman who would get sloppy drunk, maybe a call girl. If you watched long enough, you could find all kinds on an airline.

Now Mary Shissler, I mused, was a quiet and sweet woman of twenty-five, little more than a girl and a fine one for any man. But she had been overlooked for almost three years by the men looking for wives. There was no doubt that she would make a man, almost any man, a wonderful wife. Yet she had been passed by, or, she had discouraged suitors. I wondered which, as I acknowledged to myself that she had shown signs of liking my attention, even encouraging it. But was I imagining? Was I dreaming?

Last, I thought of Jean Thurson and confessed to myself that I did not know her very well, even though I had spent the night with her in New York. That realization caused me to smile quietly to myself and make a correction. She had spent the night with me.

Jean, I knew, was a well-educated girl with a brain. She was pretty, exceptionally easy to look at, and she was looking, looking at the world, at people, and at men. She had looked me over carefully in New York. She had traded beds with George because she wanted to hear me talk to myself. Thereby she had moved unflinchingly up close to a precipice, one I was sure she had never crossed, and she had expected me to let her go unmolested. And I did! In so doing she had moved in near to me, studied me, and made a close appraisal of the animal, Wayne Allison.

On this trip she had continued that study. That I could tell without half trying. She and Mary, I was sure, had held a conversation about me. Throughout the evening she had appeared very attentive, almost fascinated. I found myself well pleased at the respect I had given her and Mary throughout the evening.

Suddenly I came to my senses. Why was I analyzing every good looking girl with whom I came in contact? What was the reason I was taking each one apart as a jeweler might do to a fine watch? "Hell," I snorted, "it looks like you are looking for another wife."

"Is that true?" I asked myself aloud and turned to a mirror.

I looked into the mirror and studied the lean face, the dark hair, with the little sprinkling of gray at the temples. I looked at my straight figure, the strength of my shoulders, my sturdy arms, and thought gratefully of the years in the oil fields. Then I thought of my past marriage.

"No, sir!" I exclaimed emphatically. "I am going to play the field for a while. The next one is going to make me so certain that she is the right one that it will take me a lifetime to raise a single doubt."

A few minutes later I was just crawling back into bed, after giving up the idea of reading, when there was a light but insistent knock on the door. At first I wasn't sure of it.

Chapter 13

The Hotel Raid

Then it came the second time, followed almost immediately by George's whisper.

"Wayne, Wayne!" he called softly with almost a pleading note in his voice. "Open up quick, I want to talk to you!"

I slipped into my trousers and opened the door. There George stood, lipstick still on his face, his hair disheveled and uncombed. His clothes looked as though he had thrown them on and then slept in them. In fact, his oxfords were not even tied. But little George was cold sober even though his eyes were bloodshot.

"Come in!" I urged and shut the door behind him,

Quietly I closed the door to the bedroom and we stood in the short hallway to the bathroom and eyed each other. It was easy to see that he was shaking as though chilled.

"Want a drink?" I invited for he sure looked as though he needed one.

He nodded and sank down on the floor to lean against the wall with eyes half-closed while I poured him a stiff drink. There was no doubt about his needing it from the way he grabbed the glass and gulped it down straight. I didn't get an opportunity to give him another glass with water. He just poured the drink down like it was water without any facial contortion. I know it must have burned all the way down. But he didn't show it.

"I had a hell of a narrow escape tonight." he began. "That girl is no damned good! I think she's a decoy," he volunteered. Then his words started coming in a torrent.

"Start at the beginning," I ordered, knowing that George had to be given direction when upset.

He sat for a full minute without saying anything. I could see he was trying to regain his composure while I waited.

"Well," he started again, "you know how she was, so eager, willing, and hungry acting?"

"So," he continued as I nodded, "I locked the door after you steered the other girls out. We had two or three drinks together on the edge of the bed while we talked and loved each other. Then she got pretty drunk, started to peel off her duds, claiming she was hot. So I helped her."

He paused with his head down, and I sat on the rug beside him in silence.

"Then I took some of mine off," he admitted with his head still down. "And she started helping me. After a few minutes we crawled under the bed sheet, or rather, I pulled it over us while we were loving. We were pretty bare. Honest to Pete, I was never so scared in my life," he whispered.

"But what happened?"

"I think we had been asleep for a little while. There was a hell of a knock on the door all of a sudden. It paralyzed me for a second. Then a loud voice spoke up: 'This is the hotel detective. We want to inspect this room.'" He shook as though experiencing a bad chill.

"A joke," I laughed. "Someone pulled one on you."

"No!" He shook his head fiercely at me. "They started fumbling with the passkey."

"What?" I couldn't believe it.

"That's right," he insisted. "I heard them fumbling."

"We both jumped up," George admitted. "She seemed to be a little more sober, then fell back on the bed. So I whispered to her to stall them."

"I ran over to the door to the other room, opened it, and then ran back, grabbed my clothes and ran into the other girls' room. I wasn't a bit too soon." He was positive. "June told them to give her a minute, but they didn't. They just came rushing right in. I hardly got the middle door shut when I heard the other door open and someone say. 'Where is he?' I heard them looking around the room. There were three of them and one of them mentioned your name. Said he knew you were there."

"What?"

He nodded. "I'm sure of that." He insisted before continuing, "Mary and Jean were both awake and were sitting up in bed with a light on between them, looking at me as though they couldn't believe their eyes."

"What did you have on?" I questioned with a grin, beginning to see the funny side of his predicament.

"Just my shorts," he admitted.

"What did you do?" I began to chuckle as the full scene began to unfold.

"I whispered to Mary and Jean to hide me," he recalled, shaking his head and looking at the floor. "I was really scared! Jean pointed under her bed and before I knew what I as doing, I was under there with my clothes, trying to put them on."

He looked at me with a half-smile. "Did you ever try to put your pants on under a bed?" He shook his head at the memory.

I laughed at him. His sense of humor was always near the surface. "Then what happened?"

"They looked in the bathroom and shower, I guess. Then they tried to come in where Mary and Jean were. Mary jumped up and held the middle door almost shut while she called to Jean to call the police. The guy with his foot in the door and his head halfway in kept trying to tell Mary that he was the hotel detective and the manager was with him and they were inspecting the rooms at the request of Amalgamated Airlines. But he had to push her backward with some help from the others.

"All of a sudden the three of them were in the room and trying to quiet the girls down. Jean had the desk and asked for the police while telling the desk clerk that some men had forced their way into their room and they needed protection.

"The three guys got nervous with Jean getting through to the police and Mary telling them over and over to get out before she screamed.

"So," George concluded, "they backed out, apologizing all over the place to Jean and Mary, but they didn't say a word to June in the other room. She had passed out as slick as could be. I checked her later after Jean had called the police back and cancelled the call."

"Who was the third guy?" I asked.

George looked at me a long minute before answering. "The San Francisco station manager for AA," he replied.

"What?" I was a little stunned.

George slowly nodded and continued to look at me. "Boy, are they after you!" He breathed.

"Me—you mean me?" I feigned surprise.

"I mean you!" He was dead serious.

"Well, now isn't that a surprise?" I smiled to cover up my own feelings. "It just goes to show you can't trust your own company officials."

"You know," he shook his head in doubtful thought. "I was wondering if you weren't yelling wolf unnecessarily when you refused to have a drink at the bar or out where anyone could see, but now I am beginning to see more to this. That June was a plant to get you to drinking with witnesses. No wonder she was being so cozy with you. It was probably a paid performance."

Abruptly he grinned at me. "Guess you really are number one," He conceded.

I studied George in thought for a little while.

"Could you have been wrong about hearing someone mention my name when they were searching the room?" I questioned after a little thought.

Again he shook his tousled head. "Not a chance! My girls heard it too." He was emphatic on that point.

"And about the identity of the manager of operations here in San Francisco?" I questioned further.

George chuckled in a self-conscious manner. "I got a good look at him," he declared, "right out from between Mary's legs."

I laughed.

"Besides," he cinched the point, "Mary knew him too."

I had a drink with George. Somehow, I felt a need for it. And George thought it would do us both good.

The next morning I had breakfast with Jean and Mary. They were not up when I called them at eight, but they decided that they could make an eight-thirty breakfast with me. So we three met in the dining room for a nice cozy breakfast mixed with funny conversation. It was funny because, in the early morning sunlight of a beautiful San Francisco morning, the happenings of the night before seemed like slapstick comedy.

The dining room of the hotel was so located that the early morning sun came streaming in on our table to do wonders with the dark red hair on one girl and the reddish blond hair of the other. I kept looking from one pair of brown eyes to the other pair of blue eyes. Both noses seemed to be upturned. Freckles adorned Mary's nose and went well with her brown eyes. Jean's nose and skin were peaches and cream.

I knew from the way I kept turning my head from one to the other it was clear to all that I was more than pleased with my company. They verified everything that George had told me. Also they gave me a few verbal candid camera shots of the night's happenings that George had omitted.

I laughed heartily at the way they likened George's entrance into their room to that of a tow-headed boy making a hurried exit from a forbidden swimming hole. They were real descriptive about the way he was hugging his clothes, all in one big bundle. But they couldn't remember whether or not he had shorts on when he came into their room. Both were sure he had them on when he came out from under the bed.

After the three intruders had departed and George had dressed in their bathroom, the three had cautiously opened the adjoining door into June's room. There they found June, clad only in her slip and sprawled, sound asleep across one bed. George had shaken her and shaken her, and kept telling her to wake up and take her girdle off before she strangled, until she finally woke up enough to say: "It's already off—what happened?"

To that George had replied, "Nothing—the shot went wild!"

We took a long walk right after breakfast, at the start of which we spoke a few words to the incoming crew on flight forty-nine for that morning. The girls were game for several hills, at the end of which we found a convenient cable car, and were glad to ride it back near the hotel.

There, in the lobby of the hotel, I found George. He was ready for breakfast after a long, late sleep. I had coffee while he ate. All our crew members had come and gone from the dining room so we had a nice quiet little conversation, while Mary and Jean took off on a shopping tour.

George looked pretty good when I considered the rough night he had been through. And it was quite evident that he considered himself a pretty lucky individual, but as he expressed it, they were not after him. Of that we were both certain; however, had they snared him in the noose it is extremely unlikely that they would have let him go with less than six months or a year as a copilot. Or they might have fired him outright. They certainly could have done it without any back-wash from the union, we both knew quite well.

"Do you know," George stirred his second cup of coffee and looked at me, "the more you think about last night, the bigger it gets?"

I shrugged. "How do you mean?" I had always liked to consider carefully any wild bee that might be buzzing around in George's bonnet. I had learned that they were well worthy of examination.

"They were shooting at you. Without any doubt you were the buck they had the sights set for. But me, little George, had to come stumbling along just as they were squeezing the trigger." He chuckled at the thought.

"Maybe that'll teach you to let my girls alone," I warned him.

He raised his right hand and looked me in the eye solemnly. "Never again!" he promised with all the sincerity of an alcoholic swearing off for the hundredth time.

It was my turn to chuckle.

"Just the same, it's bigger than you think!" George insisted.

"I'm listening," I reminded him.

"Well," he squinted his eyes at me and glanced around to be sure we were alone, "do you remember that time we briefed Mr. Damon in New York on the screening deal, in front of the entire master council of Amalgamated?"

"Of course."

"Then you recall how, in getting to his office, we got lost on the elevator and ended up on the wrong floor, talking to the real pretty receptionist for about ten minutes before we would concede that we were on the wrong floor?"

I snapped my fingers and stared at George.

"George, is that the girl?" I demanded to know.

"That's our little June!" He conceded. "I've been trying to figure out where I had seen her before. Last night when she started telling me about living in New York and working as a model for a while, it suddenly came to me. She never admitted she ever worked for Amalgamated before, but she kept dodging the subject and I finally got enough drinks in myself to remember. By that time it was too late."

"I knew from the way she took after you that it was for some other reason than your sex appeal," he grinned and declared. "She's a paid decoy. Sorry to puncture your ego."

I sat quietly watching him and listening.

"They thought they had it all figured," he mused aloud. "They were sure you would grab her like a hungry fish—and bang. They meant to set the hook in you last night. The only thing they didn't figure," he grinned again, "was that she would get so drunk she didn't know just what was going on, or who, and that I would beat you to the bait." He chuckled at me as he finished.

"They who?" I quizzed while I slowly nodded my agreement that the little tow-head had the angles figured pretty close.

He shrugged and guessed. "It might be a long line of connections directly into one high office on Park Avenue. Again, it might not go that far. Last night it was the station manager of San Francisco trying to spring the trap. The night before your beagle, Anderson, was out here, and we know he is after you. But just a few nights before that he was with Ogden, Boyson, and even 'C.R.' himself. So take your pick or simply say that it's coming from Park Avenue. That's my guess."

Slowly I whistled. At the conclusion I conceded. "You're right, George. It might well be coming from the top."

"Another thing," George added, "Di Pasquale's attempt to gag the System Board came from high up, and when he failed to put it over he was clubbed good, according to Dave Little, and sent back to eat crow in front of all the pilots. That had to be coming from real high up. So," George continued, "the way I figure it, your days are numbered. They'll stoop to anything to get rid of you."

I sat silent looking at him, for I could see he had more to say. After stirring his coffee a little more he continued: "I have already penned my resignation from the System Board to the ol'man."

"Don't get yourself upset, George." I cautioned.

"I'm not." He countered. "It is simply time that little George dissociated himself from any more union work. When I can't 'shack' a little with some girl who wants to play without having to grab my clothes and run and hide under some good girl's bed, then I quit. That is giving too much for the pilot's union, especially when you stop to remember that we receive no extra compensation for our work. Dave just guarantees us pay for time we lose on union work."

"Now George," I soothed.

"I'm serious," he continued. "For years I have watched you fronting for the pilots, taking the shock load of this shady deal, that crooked play and digging until you uprooted the stinking mess for all to see until the pilots on Amalgamated have begun to take you for granted."

"But you've always carried your share of the load," I reminded him.

"Oh, no!" He denied it. "I've just ridden along on your coattails— to watch the fireworks. But," he emphasized, "I've begun to feel the heat. If I get any closer, I'll get burned. Oh," he hastened to add, "I'll help you finish the flight allocation grievances, get a decision on them—if we can, and that's all. No new cases, nothing else. Little George is going to let them keep thinking that he just got in bad company for a while."

He sat quietly looking me in the eye for several minutes. Deep within me a strange feeling of uneasiness took root. I sat quietly studying his face and thinking while a long montage of thoughts flashed through my mind. Anderson, Ogden, Boyson, and C.R. paraded by. I recalled the warning words of a friend—the station manager at Phoenix—about a price on my head.

"What do you think about telling the ol'man about this deal?" I questioned.

George laughed mirthlessly.

"How," he questioned, "do I tell him that, although married, I shacked with one girl and hid under the bed of another, clad in only my shorts?"

"I'm afraid he wouldn't understand." I laughed, conceding the point.

"Oh, he'd understand." George hastened to assure me. "He'd understand that C.R. had a right to fire a worthless pilot like me. Dave, you know," he finished emphatically, "runs a clean union."

Slowly I nodded in silent agreement before adding, "and that's the reason I've worked so many years for the pilots."

"Yeah," George grunted and glanced at me over his coffee. "That, plus a desire to make Amalgamated an honest company. I know your dedicated purpose," he reminded me.

Suddenly he grinned a wide grin at me and added with his eyes twinkling, "just a modern knight on a shining horse. Ride on Sir Galahad, I must tarry with the lady fair."

"Aw, hell!" I snorted. "I thought you did that last night."

"I did," he readily agreed, "and got badly jousted."

Then we both laughed together with our eyes steady on each other. We had a great friendship.

Late that night I stood at the window of Amalgamated's operations office and watched George's blinking lights disappear out over the bay toward Oakland as he lifted his nose upward to point it over the western peaks and to a home in Oklahoma where he had a nice wife and two fine boys in the grade school.

"Men are no damned good," I told myself, "especially pilots."

My eyes caught a glimpse of a sleek blue uniform hurrying out to that tall-tailed monster sitting to one side of the operations office and I focused them on June Tabler.

"Women are no better!" I muttered to myself.

Idly I thought of how carefully June had avoided both of us, George and me, since last night. No doubt she didn't want us to pin her with questions, questions about last night, questions about her connections, and more questions.

Watching her climb the steps to our airplane, I thought of the San Francisco operations manager. On the spur of the moment I turned to the agents at the counter and asked one to get the operations manager on the phone.

He hesitated a moment and reminded me of the late hour.

"Get him!" I ordered, giving him a hard look.

With the phone in hand I listened to the stuffed shirt manager—the chicken—sleepily answer the phone.

"Bill," I informed him quietly, "this is Allison."

Then I listened to him fake a friendly greeting and inquire what he could do for me,—the two-faced chicken—!

"Bill," I repeated, not allowing the least bit of friendly tone to enter my voice, "I want to see you on my next trip into San Francisco.

"It's about a girl." I told him in response to his casual question. "It's about a girl named June Tabler."

I hung up the phone after that remark knowing that it would be months before I would see that operations manager again, months during which he would make a point of being out of town, away someplace.

A half hour later I was looking downward at Oakland and pointing the nose upward toward the ridges of the Rockies, toward a home in Oklahoma where I did not have a wife. The courts had said so.

I polished the throttles with my hand and thought about that a moment. When did a man cease to be married? What right did a man have to cease living with one woman and start hunting for another? And why?

Acutely I became aware that I wanted a cup of coffee. Before thinking I buzzed the stewardesses and lifted the receiver off the hook. Then I remembered June and the Mexican plover in the rear. Hastily I handed the phone to the engineer and signalled coffee to him while I made a pretext of being busy with the radio. Somehow I didn't want to have anything more to do with C.R.'s pussy cat.

Then I found myself thinking of the two stewardesses just thirty minutes ahead of me, Mary and Jean. I wished seriously that they were with me now and that this hussy was with George. That thought made me chuckle to myself. The idea of George and June after last night's episode, being in one airplane, even though it was a large one, hit me as a humorous situation. I laughed aloud.

Taking my cup of coffee from the engineer I ignored the questioning looks from the copilot and the engineer and settled back in the seat to fly manually while I thought of Mary and Jean. I had promised to take them home on arrival at Tulsa. It didn't seem right that they should have to wait very long for me, so I took a good look at the upper wind reports and decided that at about twenty-three thousand feet we could readily set sail for Oklahoma.

At twenty-three thousand I leveled out again. To make sure of a good speed I inched the throttles open to the full authorized horsepower and settled back to listen to the rumbling roar of those hard running horses. Occasionally I looked out the wide glass at the moonlighted mountain ridges, the cooling desert land and mentally clocked the speed with which they faded under that skinny wing, a wing too damned skinny for the fat load it was required to carry.

"About four hundred per hour," I guessed to myself and smiled at the thought that we were walking up on George who was loafing along at fifteen thousand with light winds helping him. My plan was to hit the ground about ten minutes behind George. It wouldn't be right, I decided, to keep the girls waiting more than ten minutes, for they would be tired, sleepy, and weary from walking up and down that long fuselage all the way from California to Oklahoma.

We hit the ground at Tulsa just ten minutes behind George. And I mean hit! I was still lecturing to the copilot on his failure to level off properly as we taxied up to the terminal, but cut the lecture short when I saw Mary and Jean standing at the operations window to watch our arrival.

It was nearly eight in the morning when I walked into the operations office, gathered my mail, the two girls, and hurried our exit. I guess it was mean of me but I didn't offer June a ride because I sort of figured that C.R. would pay her cab fare. George neglected her too, but not because his wife was there to pick him up.

I drove Jean home first as she lived the nearest in a small bungalow where she, a classmate named Rosemary, and another girl had set up housekeeping in a furnished home. Seeing her to the door I promised to call later.

Mary lived in an apartment with two other girls, one of them being Terry. They had lived together for over a year and frequently flew together.

At one time, in a teasing frame of mind, I had accused them of exchanging dating information and placing eligible males at a disadvantage. To this they had given me a coy smile but did not deny it. So I went up with Mary to see Terry.

Terry was glad to see us both. She was alone and expecting Mary at any time. But she had not expected me and quickly excused herself to tidy her face and hair up a bit, but not before thanking me for the flowers in Amarillo.

She was having to wear a heavy and stiff back brace under her pajamas and robe. She really didn't need to tidy up for I thought she looked pretty darned cute for so early in the morning. I wondered if the fact that she was a shapely little blond had anything to do with that early morning good looks.

So I helped the two girls with breakfast. Then I took them out shopping for groceries and drove them around for an hour just to get Terry out of the apartment for a while. I think she appreciated that because they did not have a car. In consideration of the many cups of coffee she had brought me in the last two years, I felt that it was the least I could do. Funny, I thought, I had never really noticed before how really cute they both were.

While driving around I persuaded Terry to tell me a little of the Amarillo accident, how Ellis had been cruising with the seat belts off in smooth air, then a little choppy air, then terrific violence.

She recounted how passengers had been floating around, lunging in to each other and being heaved from the ceiling to the floor along with scattered luggage from the luggage racks overhead. She had injured her back when thrown across a seat near the stewardess station while trying to help a passenger back into his seat belt. Thinking her back to be broken, she had clung to the stewardess station in a huddled position on the floor.

She told us of having the Superintendent of Stewardesses call and ask her a lot of questions relative to the trip and passengers. Then the matter had been quietly shelved, as far as she knew. Ellis was still flying and had not been given any time off, for he had not missed a schedule, according to the other stewardess roommates of theirs who had recently been flying with him and was presently out on a trip with him. I shook my head over that and wondered what would have happened if the captain had been Allison instead of Ellis. The mere thought made me shudder a little.

We did not dwell on the subject long for both Mary and I could see it was bothering Terry to recall the scene and again hear the screams of pain from the passengers. To change the subject Mary launched into the story of the hotel raid in San Francisco. It improved with each telling.

Chapter 14

The Wild Flight

An hour later found me in Claremore. I pulled into the driveway to the big two story house where Mother had lived alone since Dad's death shortly after the end of WW II. She was waiting with a little lunch and information that my boy of ten wanted me to call promptly. He answered the phone on the first ring and led me to believe that he had been waiting by the phone for my call.

"Daddy," he gushed, "I've been thinking, if we can't go to the farm, why can't we go down to the river lease and run the bird dogs for a while, and maybe I can fish a little." He referred to an oil lease that Mother owned and which I had been pumping periodically since Dad's death.

It was located in an isolated section of the Verdegris River that was subject to flooding and overflow. As a consequence there were no homes or houses in over two miles of the flat river bottom land. It was river land, especially fine for raising corn, but the overflow character-istics of the Verdegris River made such a project similar to rolling the dice at Las Vegas. Many corn crops in tassel and roasting ear stages had, in past years, been swept down the river.

"That's a good idea, son," I declared. "Ask your mother."

"She's gone downtown," he acknowledged, "and I'm having to ba-bysit Kathy. But I'll call as soon as she gets back."

I turned from the phone to my slim and gray-headed mother.

"He wants to go to the river lease," I explained, "and will call back as soon as he asks his mother."

Mother shook her head. "She hasn't been very cooperative."

I acknowledged that, but reminded her that we had a joint custody deal which I had purchased with most of my assets. It provided that if we could not agree on a problem related to the children then either of us could appeal to Doctor Gordon who would settle the issue based solely on what he believed to be best for the children involved.

Doctor Gordon, a lifelong friend, had agreed to settle any dispute, in consultation with his wife, who was a very close friend of Betty, my ex-wife. Already they had decided two disputes contrary to Betty's wishes.

I sat down with Mother to the lunch table in her big house, feeling a little tired and sleepy from the night flight, but knowing I could enjoy going to the river lease, getting it to pumping and have the boy fishing and probably swimming before the afternoon was over. Also, I thought, it would be a good opportunity to run my two bird dogs a while. I had been keeping them in a pen back of mother's garage.

"Oh," Mother recalled. "Mr. Behncke wants you to call him. He called this morning about eight."

I reached around and pulled the phone over on the table next to my lunch plate. Carefully I dialed the ol'man's private number which no one answered but the ol'man, and filled my plate at the same time. It caused Mother to laugh as she sat down.

I listened to the phone ring three times and then the ol'man came on with a pretty healthy "hello." I liked the way it sounded.

"Secret Agent number one reporting," I disguised my voice.

"Oh—ha, ha!" He exclaimed. "Just a minute, #1, while I clear my office." I could see him putting his feet on the desk and waving Miss Forrest, who had a corner desk, out of the office.

"All right, #1, I called to tell you that AA has called for a meeting tomorrow on writing a supplemental contract for the Pacific operation. I would like to have you there if you wish to participate," he explained.

"Skip me, Dave," I requested. "If you want some pilot help, I suggest Red Carey and Shipley. They live in New York. I'm too far away and need to make up a little flying time I've lost this month."

"I thought you'd feel that way," he acknowledged. "Okay, but while you're on the line I want to tell you that I sent an association lawyer, Maurice Schy, down to Dallas to be with that little copilot in his cement nightgown. The CAA and AA were pretty reasonable with a lawyer at that boy's elbow. The CAA was especially pleased to get the boy's story even though AA didn't act pleased about not getting to grill the boy and then have him confirm the report of an agent in

Washington that Tom Claude had appeared to be drunk. When the CAA came out with that, Schy let the boy confirm it. So, I guess AA is on the hot seat with the CAA. It may open up some lawsuits for AA."

"Good!" I exclaimed. "AA has it coming."

"Another thing," the ol'man continued, "Sayen didn't do any good with that Eastern bunch. In fact I sort of have the feeling that they've influenced him to the point that he is only lukewarm about a mileage limitation for pilots."

"I hate to hear that, Dave," I replied, "but I've had that impression all along. No doubt Jerry West and Slim Bastitt gave him a real snow job."

"I'm afraid so," Dave ruefully admitted. "He has tried to talk to me about putting off this mileage limitation drive on Amalgamated."

"Dave," I felt the grimness in my own voice, "slap him down fast. We've enough weak sisters in the field, which I call the 'vulture army' without having one in headquarters."

"I'm giving it a lot of thought," he admitted, "and I expect to discuss it with Shipley in New York."

"Good," I replied and we closed the conversation.

Immediately I was back in the lunch plate but hadn't finished when the phone rang. I answered and found a little boy of ten crying on the other end of the line. I felt something deep inside me tearing.

"Mother says I can't go," he cried loudly. "Daddy, I want to come live with you." That something tore some more and I felt sick inside.

"Son," I whispered gently, "you're a little man now and I want you to act like one; mind your mother and be a good boy this evening. Maybe I can take you with me tomorrow."

For a long five minutes after he hung up the phone, I sat and stared into space. Finally I shook myself out of the trance and remarked to a gentle and understanding woman, "Mother, let's drive down and pump the river lease this afternoon, and I'll let the bird dogs run a while."

That night I had been asleep a scant two hours when the phone awakened me. It was the AA operations and they sounded real urgent. Kelly, the operations clerk, breathed a sigh of relief when I answered. Another clerk was also calling for a pilot alongside of Kelly. I could hear him along with Kelly.

"Boy, I sure am glad to get an answer, Wayne," he confided. "Not a single captain in Tulsa answers, including the chief, Anderson, and we need a captain for flight 49 tonight."

"Who is scheduled?" I know I sounded sleepy.

"Stan Younger," he replied. "But he just called in to say that his left eye is swollen shut from a bee sting last evening. He says he has been keeping ice packs on it, but it is still swelling and it's now shut. He couldn't fly that way, could he?"

"Not legally," I replied, "and you want me to cover?"

I glanced at the clock as he answered in the affirmative.

"Be careful," he admonished me. "It is raining here and the roads are wet."

Hastily I shaved and dressed, beginning to hear the light rain on the roof. I would have preferred two or three more hours of sleep, but long years of training had me awake and feeling good as I threw an always-packed suitcase in the car with my flight kit, which I seldom unloaded.

I drove leisurely to Tulsa in light rain with a heavily overcast sky that appeared to be lowering as I approached the airport. "This is sure good for the country," I mused aloud, as I thought of how dry and hot it had been the last month.

"I hope it's not another one of those tornadoes." I talked to myself while parking near the operations' side door. I hurried through the door, only slightly damp from the exposure in the light rain. There appeared to be no lightning, thunder or wind, just what is termed a good ground soaker—if it continued all the rest of the night. I studied the smooth layer of clouds through an operations window and estimated the ceiling to be about a thousand feet with good visibility.

"Well, well, the old war-horse himself!" A friendly voice spoke at my elbow and I turned to greet little Dunc, as he was called, short for Don Duncan. He was slight in stature with very light blond hair, blue eyes, and a friendly approach that seemed to never meet a stranger.

I knew him well, for he had flown several months with me in the last two years during which we had become good friends. In fact, I knew him so well that I had dubbed him Amalgamated's 'covey dog' from the way he always seemed to be with more than one stewardess. Single, at thirty, he appeared to be most relaxed with more than one stewardess, and ill at ease with a single. He was famous for meeting newly assigned stewardesses at the airport and driving them around to help them get settled in an apartment or a house, as long as there were more than one. He quickly deserted the singles. So I had dubbed him the 'covey dog' and the name had stuck. Even the stewardesses caught on to the name and seemed to get a big kick out of my story that Don Duncan only worked the coveys.

That was until Rosemary appeared on the scene with Jean Thurson. Classmates in stewardess school, they had come to Tulsa together, and settled in a house together with another girl. Little Dunc had given them his customary cab service and quickly learned that Rosemary had a boyfriend in Korea to whom she was engaged, didn't want to date anyone, and was true-blue to 'John in Korea.' And she told it to all who would listen.

Little Dunc listened and liked the idea. Evidently he decided that he was safe with her and would listen to her latest letter from John and soon got around to making suggestions of things she could write John to keep her in his thoughts. That seemed to be her major concern, keeping in John's thoughts.

At that time little Dunc was flying steadily with me as he was the senior copilot at Tulsa and consistently bid the same monthly runs I bid. So we became real good friends, for I enjoyed his company.

However, the last month he had bid the trip schedule that Rosemary was assigned to fly so that he could furnish her transportation to and from the airport, and help her with her "Dear John" letters in San Francisco when they were having dinner together. That put him with another captain, but it didn't matter, especially with me gone so much on contract negotiations and grievance hearings. Besides, he was flying with Rosemary. She liked to bring coffee up to him and he started to liking the idea too.

Rosemary, whom I had never met, appeared in the doorway to the coffee shop and beckoned to little Duncan before abruptly disappearing back into the coffee shop. Duncan and I finished looking the weather over, I signed the flight plan he had prepared, and we wandered into the coffee bar several minutes behind Rosemary.

There in the coffee shop, I was both surprised and pleased to see Jean Thurson sitting with Rosemary and the flight engineer. I had taken her out to a movie a few nights before during which I had learned much about Rosemary. But I was much more interested in learning more about Jean. She had proven to be even more attractive than on our first encounter.

Jean introduced me to Rosemary while little Duncan went for an extra chair for the table. I found myself looking into a pair of innocent blue eyes between which a rather pointed nose extended. I thought her lips appeared a little thin.

But Rosemary was a very good-looking and shapely blond, somewhat shorter than Jean with fluffy hair that boiled from under her flight cap in almost the same way that Jean's did. I could not help but compare the two as they sat side by side, across the table from me. Jean's hair had a reddish glint while Rosemary's was considerable lighter, with almost a peroxide touch.

I soon found that Rosemary had a cute habit of looking very intensely at you when she spoke to you, or anyone, as though she was not going to fail to see the effect of her words. At the same time she had a special way of leaning forward toward you when she spoke and focusing those probing blue eyes with that intense look. The way she would lean forward to speak gave the impression that her shapely breasts were looking and probing too.

After sipping a little of my coffee and listening to the chatter around the table while I studied Rosemary discreetly, I arrived at the conclusion that little Duncan was in good hands, or going to be before long. Rosemary, I decided, had little Duncan deep in her sights while she talked about 'Dear John.' All she needed, I concluded, was a good opportunity to rape him. But first, she had to allay Dunc's shyness. He had had no experience.

Shortly I excused myself and went back into operations to look at the latest weather on the teletype machine, read the company forecast again, and think about it. I was troubled with a vague and uneasy feeling about the weather.

Outside the rain had increased in intensity as flight forty-nine called in range, ten miles out with restricted visibility and shifting over to the tower for landing clearance. A few minutes later I stood at the window and watched flight forty-nine park close to a gate where a long canopy of canvas sheltered the walkway from the terminal to a very short distance from the airplane.

A thoughtful porter with an umbrella took my girls that short distance and brought back another pair, tired from a night's work. He even managed an umbrella for the rest of the arriving crew before helping the outgoing passengers board with their carry-on luggage.

I spoke a few words with Dan Landall, the incoming captain, and thought of Ed Graham's story of Dan and Tommy Claude while I watched Dan's upper lip curl in a sneering smile as he told me that number two engine had a lot of time on it and seemed a bit sluggish on the takeoffs. I thanked him and turned toward the airplane.

The rain was heavier now and seemed to raise a little fog from striking the pavement in large drops. It was becoming a real downpour. I managed an umbrella to go up the front loading ramp and stay out of the way of loading passengers. But with the umbrella covering me I sat down in the pilot's seat feeling like my uniform had lost a few of its creases.

Little Duncan was there ahead of me with the engineer, Marty, and they were going through the cockpit check list. I joined in the parrot-like procedure that was so important on a complicated airliner, yet so boring at times.

Soon the ramp was away and the doors closed. With four engines idling, we headed for a taxi strip at the tower's clearance to taxi which was required, even at two in the morning. The rain was making a real fog now and we could feel and hear it on the fuselage above the idling engines. It was just heavy, heavy rain that appeared to be coming straight down in sheets, making visibility very limited.

Duncan asked for a west takeoff as I had instructed him to, so that if we encountered any little surprises on the takeoff, we would be facing them. We had a little trouble finding our way to the east side of the east-west runway and had to rely on the flush-type lights the tower turned on to assist us. The visibility was more in yards than in miles, but the official weather was still a half mile visibility. Maybe it was from the tower, which was considerable higher than our chariot.

We were running up the engines and cleaning them out with heat when a very sharp bolt of lighting flashed to the ground about a half mile west of the field and illuminated the entire city of Tulsa along with the field and the surrounding countryside. It was blinding and we could see nothing for a few seconds.

"Tell the girls to keep themselves tied down until we phone them," I yelled to Duncan. "It may get kind of wild."

With that I turned the airplane on the runway, headed west, very carefully set the gyro compass to the runway heading and cracked the whip on the eight thousand horses hitched to the chariot. In fifty yards we could see nothing ahead as the flashing windshield wipers could not handle the deluge. My eyes flashed back and forth from the gyro compass to the flush type lights on the left side of the runway while the airspeed climbed past a hundred. It was a blind, blind, instrument takeoff.

The tandem gears were fading on the runway when we hit something akin to driving into an underpass at a high rate of speed and finding a foot or two of water. Our bodies surged forward momentarily in our seat belts. In a split second the air speed was reading two hundred and fifty. I pulled back sharply on the wheel and felt the big plane respond, then we were in turbulence, wild shaking and shuddering turbulence. I was fearful of hooking a wing on the ground and kept pulling back on the wheel. I wanted away from that runway with a little wrestling room.

The two hundred and fifty on the airspeed gauge was authentic and we rose like a balloon with the nose almost vertical, shuddering and shaking with severe buffeting from either side. Up, up and up we rose, vertical from the point of leaving the runway. The two hundred and fifty on the air speed gauge persisted and I kept pulling the nose higher and watching the rate of climb indicator needle wrap two or three times around the dial.

Then slowly, with gear and flaps up from the time I had first pulled off the runway, the violent upthrust began to fade until the plane flattened out at normal climbing rate, but we were above five thousand feet and barely west of the end of the runway. The sky was now full of fire, with bolt after bolt of lightning showering the city of Tulsa, the airport, and surrounding area like huge sparklers. They kept everything as light as day and made the wet runways and streets of Tulsa look greased.

With the throttles reduced to hold the air speed down, we shuddered then shook across Tulsa until we were through the front and the air began smoothing out. In a few minutes the girls could move around and bring us coffee. But Rosemary looked apprehensively at Duncan when she delivered the coffee and was a little white around the collar of her uniform.

"It's okay," Duncan reassured her, smiling. "Our captain was getting a little sleepy and the Ol' Man had to wake him up."

I switched the interphone on and jingled the rear of the plane.

"Are you okay, Jean?" I inquired softly.

She responded instantly. Her voice had that cheerful good morning tone as she exclaimed: "That was fun, let's do it again sometime!"

I shook my head and smiled as I gave the controls to little Duncan for the Oklahoma City landing. He was sure right about one thing. The Ol' Man had sure been able to wake me up.

"That was quite a takeoff." Duncan leaned toward me as he spoke. "I've never seen a storm like that on takeoff before, have you?" He flashed his eyes from the instruments to my face. I could see his features lightly illuminated in the instrument reflection and occasionally clearly illuminated by dwindling flashes of lightning, now behind us.

"Once," I replied, leaning a little toward him for better hearing. "During the war in a takeoff at Santa Maria Island in the Azores I had a similar deal. It practically tore up the airport, wrecked several planes on the ground, blew doors and roofs off the hangars, and did a half million dollars' damage."

He shook his head. "That one seemed pretty wild to me," he volunteered.

On the ground at Oklahoma City in a light rain while picking up a half dozen sleepy-eyed passengers, we learned that the Tulsa airport was out of operation with considerable damage due to hurricane force winds.

Out of Oklahoma City Duncan gave the engineer his seat so he could do a little enroute flying, for he was a qualified third pilot. Duncan promptly went back in the cabin to see if he could help the girls, namely Rosemary. I settled back in my seat and watched the plane climb up through the overcast and out in a starry sky, poaching again in God's Domain.

A couple of hours slipped by and the gray dawn of early morning began to light up the country from behind us. We were north of Phoenix on a direct route to San Francisco. I was back in the front lavatory washing the sleep from my eyes when the number two engine began backfiring.

I rushed back into the cockpit and followed the manual of operations by putting heat on the engine and richening it at the same time. With a little adjusting on the heat and mixture the engine settled down so that it was running normally at a slightly reduced power setting and with greater fuel consumption on the flow meter to number two. Looking out at the engine from my seat I could see that it was slinging a little oil from the prop hub. But it was operating normally on the instruments.

Picking up the mike I called Los Angeles and asked: "Where do you want a three engine airplane landed?"

I knew we did not have any spare equipment at Phoenix or San Francisco and AA officials had been very specific in verbal instructions about extending the flight to a base with spare equipment when one engine was inoperative. I anticipated that I would soon be on three engines.

Immediately Los Angeles came back asking if we had feathered an engine, which one and where?

I responded in the negative and requested an answer to my question. Then we were advised that we could land at Phoenix or proceed to Los Angeles at the captain's discretion.

I knew the company had no spare equipment at Phoenix. So I replied, "We are proceeding toward Los Angeles, operating four engines with one at slightly reduced throttle. Do not believe it will stand another takeoff."

Los Angeles acknowledged, then a few minutes later gave us another clearance. "Flight forty-nine from Los Angeles, you are recleared to Los Angeles with landing at Los Angeles, weather permitting, alternate Burbank." I repeated it back as required and then spoke to Duncan.

"I hope they have a spare airplane for our arrival. Those passengers are not going to be happy at the delay of landing at Los Angeles and changing airplanes." Then with an added thought I asked Los Angeles, "Advise equipment."

Soon we had a reply. "Will have reserve airplane available on your arrival."

I hung up the mike and began thumbing through the manual of operations.

"We had better read up on the latest in three engine operations," I told Duncan and the engineer with a smile. "I can't afford to have them catch me in violation of the bible."

The latest CAA regulation stated that, with one engine inoperative

on four engine aircraft we were required to land at the nearest suitable
airport. I read it to Duncan as he sat flying the airplane manually.

"What is considered suitable?" Duncan questioned with a grin.

"That's the bone of contention," I acknowledged. "When the CAA
first came out with that new regulation nearly two years ago it was
made quite clear by the CAA that a pilot, with one engine inoperative,
was to consider getting the airplane on the ground, safely, in the
shortest period of time.

"Then the airlines," I continued, "through the Air Transport Association, which is an association of the air carriers, tried to dilute the
word 'suitable' by taking in a number of other factors such as passenger comfort, other available equipment, altitude and the next scheduled
landing terminal. But the CAA was adamant and wanted the pilot to
consider nothing but getting the airplane on the ground safely.

"Of course the airlines, especially Amalgamated, began encouraging the pilots, verbally, to give the regulation a broad interpretation so
as to advance the flight."

"I remember that," Duncan recalled. "I think I was flying with you
at the time. Didn't you write a letter on it to the company when you
were chairman?"

I nodded with a smile.

"Did you get an answer?" Both Duncan and Marty asked at the
same time.

Again I nodded. Then I laughed at the recollection.

"I wrote Anderson a letter asking him for the company's interpretation of that CAA regulation," I recalled. "I thought some pilot would
likely get in trouble on that point before very long."

"I'll bet they didn't answer that letter," Duncan guessed.

"Yes, they did," I corrected him. "Anderson forwarded it with a
letter of his own and asked for some clarification."

Again I laughed and took a good look at the number two engine.
It was slinging a little oil but was okay on the gauges.

"A week or so later," I continued my story, "when I was taking this
flight out in the middle of the night I found my letter, his letter, and an
answer signed by the assistant superintendent of flying, W.H. Dunn.
He specifically stated that the company wanted to give the word
'suitable' a broad interpretation in order to advance the flight. Attached to that was a handwritten note from Anderson asking that I

return the correspondence when I had reviewed it."

Duncan's blue eyes were wide as he took them off the instruments to look at me. Marty was also watching me and listening.

"Did you?" Duncan was impatient for the full story.

I looked ahead for a moment, then smiled at the two. "I'm still reviewing it." I explained, as they both laughed.

"Did he ever ask for it back?" Both boys were curious.

"No. I surmised he must have forgotten about putting it in my mailbox. He never mentioned it and I didn't either. And as long as that regulation isn't changed, it might save some poor pilot's job sometime."

"The last sentence," I recalled, "in that letter from Dunn stated: 'Of course we cannot publish this policy.'"

Duncan whistled softly, shook his head, and gave me an appreciative look before adding, "That will take some digesting if the CAA get hold of it."

"I like it in my file," I explained.

Approaching Palm Springs in clear weather with the early morning sun rays illuminating San Jacinto and the San Gorgonio mountains, we took another reading on the number two engine. The oil consumption was getting excessive, even though all instruments indicated normal. But the outside of the engine was beginning to look as though it was taking an oil bath.

I gave the order to shut the engine down and feather. Soon it was a dead hunk hanging on the wing.

"Now I guess we extend the flight?" Duncan smiled at me.

"That's what they want," I concluded. Then I called Los Angeles and advised the flight dispatcher we had feathered #2 as a precautionary measure.

West of San Gorgonio we could see the blanket of sea fog from the Pacific ocean lying like a smooth blanket and extending inland as far as Riverside. Descending toward Riverside, I could see March Field to the south, considerably higher, enough to be out of the fog. I glanced at it and recalled the year I had been stationed there, long ago, after graduating from Kelly Field. The recollection brought back some very pleasant memories.

On top of the fog approaching Los Angeles International Airport we received clearance to make a standard instrument approach as the ceiling was reported at five hundred and the visibility given as a half a mile.

I was flying the airplane and descended into the fog with all radio facilities guiding us down. We became contact at about three hundred feet, which was the limit for an instrument approach, with our gear and flaps extended. The visibility from the cockpit was quite poor.

The airplane had a very sluggish feeling, slowed down and on three engines. Suddenly I realized that I was tired. My instrument work was not as keen as normal and when we saw the airport we were practically on top of it at three hundred feet and not perfectly in line with the runway. I had a flashing thought of Tommy Claude's crash at Dallas and his attempt to maneuver a big airliner like a pursuit plane.

"Let's get out of here," I yelled to Duncan and the engineer as I opened up the three good engines. As they roared in, the gear came up and the flaps followed.

Back on top of the fog we advised Los Angeles that we had abandoned the approach due to poor visibility. I told the boys in the cockpit that it was too close and not enough visibility to take a chance on three engines. We would wait and let the fog dissipate some.

"Still limits reported," the flight dispatcher replied, "if you care to make another approach."

I shook my head to Duncan. No way was I going to get that airplane down in that restricted visibility again and take a risk of being another Tommy Claude.

"Tell them we'll hold on top for better weather," I instructed.

A short time later, probably twenty minutes, the fog began breaking up and the visibility improved. We were able to make another approach and land without incident. I was glad to get that wallowing bastard on the ground.

It took about a half hour to change planes, during which time the girls, Jean and Rosemary, were busy with the passengers. During that time Duncan and I were in operations where I filled out a F-27 form as required by the CAA to cover declared emergencies, engine failures in flight, and cases where a scheduled flight was rerouted after takeoff or landed at a field other than the one cleared to at the time of departure. It was considered a very important form by the CAA and required the signature of the captain under a statement that the above flight was conducted in accordance with CAA regulations.

By the time we had the paperwork completed, the passengers and cargo had been transferred from the crippled plane to a good one, and we were ready to climb back into the cockpit. Soon we were cleared out with the other morning traffic and enroute to San Francisco. It was a short flight and we were tired, tired from the long trip and glad to unload in San Francisco.

We were all glad to settle into the cushions of the limousine and let someone else worry about the traffic. Rosemary, for once, was quiet and permitted her head to rest gently against Duncan's shoulder. I guessed that she was making sure he smelled her perfume. It smelled real nice too, I realized, and wished that Jean would give me the same treatment.

We slept soundly all that day. Tired as we all were it was easy to do. There is no fatigue that compares to flying fatigue.

Late that afternoon, after a refreshing shower, I wandered down into the lobby to the pin ball machine until Jean appeared. She had agreed to have a leisurely dinner with me as Rosemary had made it clear that Duncan was going to help her with another 'Dear John' letter.

When Jean appeared she looked so fresh and lovely in a short-sleeved dress and carrying a light sweater, that I knew my eyes were glowing with appreciation as she came down the stairway from the balcony. There is no better way to appraise a girl than to watch her descend a stairway from below.

We had a nice dinner about a block from the hotel and spent a couple of hours getting better acquainted. I was amazed at Jean's maturity at age twenty-two. She had been the last of four children, some eight years behind, and had been associated with older people most of her life.

Raised on a lake in northern Minnesota with a retired father and mother, she had spent considerable time by herself, fishing, boating, and tramping through the woods with her dog in search of grouse. I was surprised to learn that she had a shotgun and had actually had experience shooting grouse on the wing. But when she told me how many times she had missed before she finally killed one on the wing, I knew she was not just talking. Her eyes glowed too much as she talked about hunting. I could see that she was an avid hunter.

In turn, I told her of my bird dogs, my love for quail hunting, and how good the hunting was in Oklahoma. I had hunted the ruffed grouse in Maine and New Hampshire before WW II and when home between overseas flights during the war. She was a good listener and studied my face closely while I talked. She didn't miss anything.

We walked back to the hotel, arm in arm, real buddies. I found myself promising to take her bird hunting when the season opened in about a month. In turn she promised to send home for her gun, her boots, and hunting jacket. In the meantime, we decided, we would do a little fishing together. I knew a spot where we could catch some bass and channel cats.

That night we were off from San Francisco on a midnight schedule departure with nothing but clear weather to Tulsa. The hurricane force storm and rain had moved out toward St. Louis. So we leveled out at twenty-three thousand altitude with a full moon in our faces and hazy mountains, dim and distant in a smoky blue-like atmosphere, far below. The four props were glowing in the moonlight and seemed to be keeping time with the full-throated beat of the engines in perfect synchronization.

In the glow of the moon I looked down at the mountains below, and with mountains in the distance barely visible, I thought how nice it would be to be able to fly on and on to that land where all companies were honest and treated their employees with fairness—Utopia. My eyes repeatedly swept the hazy horizon, and the dimmed instrument panel, while my mind dreamed and enjoyed the poaching, high up where thought was cleaner and more pure.

Within an hour all the passengers except two were asleep. I think Jean was up front in the cockpit and sitting on the engineer's vacant seat almost as much as Rosemary. But we didn't talk much, just sat and enjoyed the beauty that was created, just for us to see. Finally Jean leaned forward with her face glowing in the moonlight, a half smile on her face and a radiant look in her eyes as they drank in the horizon.

"I see what you mean, Wayne," she murmured in my ear, "about poaching in God's Heaven." It was a picture, a scene, a flight I was to recall with her many, many times, to again and again taste its beauty. God felt extremely close.

Soon Rosemary came up with coffee. Jean went back with the passengers and the spell was broken. Rosemary wanted to lean against Duncan's shoulder and talk low, probably about "Dear John."

In the early morning arrival at Tulsa, I did not lose any time getting

Jean into my car and taking her home. It seemed that Duncan and Rosemary were satisfied to have me take her home and I didn't think Duncan would want us to offer Rosemary a ride. It was very nice to have Jean slide into the front seat close to me. We didn't need Rosemary's chatter.

It was near noon when I arrived at mother's house. She held the side door open while I carried my baggage in and listened to her tell me she had a lunch on the table.

"Oh, yes," she recalled, "Mr. Behncke called early this morning and asked to have you call him back when you arrived."

I sat down at the lunch table with the phone in my hand, wondering what new problem the ol'man had in his lap. After several rings he answered, sounding real tired. And I didn't try to josh with him.

"Wayne," he spoke abruptly and I knew his office must have been empty, "both Braniff and Eastern pilots have passed a resolution against our pushing for a mileage limitation in the Amalgamated contract. They insist it isn't necessary. And," he added significantly, "they refuse to back a strike on Amalgamated."

That didn't sound good. It sounded like the fine finger of Bastitt and West trying to undo a convention resolution which had authorized a strike and which the Amalgamated pilots had voted for by an overwhelming vote. Since the Amalgamated pilots were carrying the ball on jet equipment, I reminded Dave that such resolutions coming from Eastern and Braniff were sabotage.

I suggested that it was the management of Eastern working through Bastitt and West with possible help from Braniff management. It made me wonder if Sayen, who had been with Braniff, was involved. However, I refrained from suggesting such a thing. Dave had enough worries.

But, still, it made me wonder about something like that coming out of Eastern and Braniff right after Sayen had made a trip to see them and to convince them to back a mileage limitation drive. He had stopped by to see the Braniff boys on the same trip. I shook my head at the thought.

I was toying with a cup of coffee when the phone rang again. I answered to find Chief Pilot Joe Anderson on the phone. He sounded gruff.

"Allison," he came abruptly to the point, "I'm going to pull you off schedule until I investigate your last trip." There was nothing friendly about the beagle. He was baying on a hot trail and I thought I could see his teeth. I wasn't sure about his hot breath, maybe imagination.

"Fine," I responded like a good poker player. "You'll see that I followed the book all the way." Then, as an afterthought I added, "In the meantime I'll be fishing."

I found myself wishing, as he hung up without saying more, that he had asked to go with me. Probably I could find some excuse to throw his arse into the river.

Then I called Jean to ask if I could pick her up early the next morning and take her fishing. She was delighted and sounded more than pleased when I told her that I wanted to take my mother along. I wondered if she had a lingering fear of a big timber wolf on a lonely river bank. But, I explained that mother was an avid fisherman, and too, she would fix the lunch.

Chapter 15

The Bite of the Beagle

Early the next morning I picked Jean up at her home. She looked real cute in blue jeans, a long-sleeved blouse, and tennis shoes. We stopped at a diner for a quick breakfast and returned to Claremore to pick up Mother, the fishing gear, and the lunch. It was a full basket.

We drove northwest from Claremore up the Caney river where I knew a good spot to catch channel catfish. It was a late summer day, cool at night, but warm in the day. The mosquitoes and flies were still around but easily discouraged with a bug repellent.

In a little while I had Mother sitting on a blanket in the shade and fishing over an old log with a long cane pole. Casting reels were unfamiliar to her.

It was different with Jean. Raised on a lake in Minnesota, she handled rod and reel like a professional. She was a little puzzled when I insisted that she would do no good with a lure. Instead, I outfitted her with a sinker, a hook, and a live crayfish I picked out of my minnow bucket. I hooked it through the tail so it could crawl around and swim a little.

"Now cast out there near the middle, let it sink to bottom, sit down and be patient," I directed.

Dutifully she obeyed, watching me do the same a few feet away. But from her expression I knew she had misgivings about the procedure.

I had hardly seated myself comfortably when Mother let out a cry of surprise. I looked around to see her with a badly bent cane pole hoisting a one pound, fourteen inch channel cat out on the bank. She didn't believe in wasting time.

While I was stringing Mother's fish on a stringer and getting her another crayfish, Jean had two rods in her hands with one suddenly alive with a catfish. She had trouble discarding the idle rod. It was fun to see.

Two hours went swiftly. The string of catfish grew longer with a couple of two pounders. In between the fish, we worked on the lunch. It was a very pleasant day.

Just as we began to talk about going home, Jean hooked a two pound bass and had her hands full for several minutes. I just watched and laughed, especially when in her excitement, she stepped into the river. Her enthusiasm was so real and her delight so genuine that I knew she would be ready to go fishing any time.

Then Mother hooked a five pound catfish and wrestled him in with little delay, cracking a good cane pole in her haste. That ended the day's fishing. We had plenty on the stringer.

A week went by during which I had little to do but pump the river lease and get my bird dogs in condition. I wasn't accustomed to having a lot of spare time. In that week Gene Burns called to find out why I had not been on schedule. I could tell him nothing. He related that he had had a long talk with George Schustman and learned of the San Francisco episode with the decoy, June Tabler. But he had to laugh as he told me of the conversation. I guess little George's description of putting his pants on under the bed hadn't lost any flavor.

Gene was worried. George had convinced him that the company would stop at nothing to get rid of me. He was inclined to agree with George's thinking. I had done too much for the pilots.

Also, in that week Mother had showed me a deed she had found in Dad's papers. It was a deed to the mineral rights on a hundred and sixty acre tract of land in the Bird Creek river bottom near the Caney River. It wasn't a deed to the land, but a deed to the mineral rights under that tract of land. Dad had purchased those rights during WW II.

Mother related that she had had two calls from oil men wanting to lease her mineral rights which they had checked out on the courthouse records. That had caused her to hunt for the deed.

After terminating the conversation with Gene, I suggested to Mother, to have something to do, that we go locate that tract of land and look the country over. She was delighted to get out of the house on a nice day.

THE BITE OF THE BEAGLE

Using one of Dad's old maps we were able to find the location of those mineral rights. Then we drove around in that area looking for signs of drilling machines or pumping wells. We found both. There were active pumping wells within two miles of the land. More wells and two active drilling rigs that were working we found in another direction. I was quite surprised at what we had found, for I had expected to find nothing but river bottom land, farmland, and pasture land.

On the way home I found myself speculating about Dad's old drilling machine and drilling equipment stacked in a vacant lot next to Mother's home. She had refused to sell any of it and did not have many opportunities. It still remained where Dad had had it stacked while sick and unable to work. That had been near the end of WW II when I was flying overseas.

When we arrived back home I walked over to the old machine to give it a look over. I was surprised to find it in such good condition. Bits, bailers, and drill stems were stacked on blocks with pins and boxes coated with grease. Dad had always preached to me about taking care of the equipment.

I felt a wave of nostalgia sweep over me. It had been so long! Then in the doghouse, full of tools, I found a sledge hammer. I handled it gingerly at first, then took a few good practice swings at an imaginary stake with that fourteen pound hammer. It immediately began to suck on my insides. There was no doubt, I was not in condition for that kind of work. It would take a while.

Mother had been watching me from the kitchen window and had a question when I returned to the house. "Are you thinking of drilling on that Bird Creek land?"

She had been Dad's partner in oil and gas drilling for many years during which they had raised a family, drilled many dry holes and some oil wells. I sensed that her wildcatting blood was stirring.

"It's a thought that looks interesting from all the oil wells in that area," I responded, and caught the pleased look on her face. Men, I decided looking at her, were not the only ones with wildcatting blood.

"Oh," she exclaimed, "you have a special delivery letter that came while you were over at the machine. It's from Amalgamated Airlines and I had to sign for it."

A foreboding passed over me as I opened the letter. It was from the beagle, Chief Pilot Joe S. Anderson. But he had not written it. Of that I was positive on the first reading. He had signed it as my immediate superior, but I was sure that was all. He did not have the ability to write such a letter.

On the third reading, I surmised that it was written by some smart lawyer in New York. I immediately thought of Di Pasquale and how he would love to compose such a letter. The distribution list went all the way up the ladder to L.G. Fritz, General Fritz in World War II, whose desk was now next to C.R.'s It read:

Captain Wayne Allison
From: Asst. Supt. Flight - Tulsa
Subject: Flight 49 of September 6, 1951
With reference to my letter to you dated September 12, 1951 subject "Removal from Schedule."

After investigating the circumstances in connection with Amalgamated Airlines Flight 49 of September 6, 1951, I find that:

As Captain in command of Flight 49 of September 6, 1951, you elected to continue flight on three engines to Los Angeles International Airport and there attempted landing despite the fact that the Los Angeles International Airport official weather was reported as 500 feet-5/8 mile. In your conduct of this flight you made an unnecessary compromise with safety and exercised unusually bad judgment. Throughout the period of continuing flight to, and attempted landing at the Los Angeles International Airport, the official U.S. Weather Bureau weather was reported as CAVU at Phoenix, unlimited and 2 miles at Burbank.

Due to the reasons outlined above and the fact that you have been previously warned concerning your deviation from standard practices and procedure, you are hereby notified that effective September 29, 1951, you are dismissed from the employ of Amalgamated Airlines, subject to hearing rights as provided for under the agreement between Amalgamated Airlines, Inc. and the Air Line Pilots' Association, dated July 1, 1948.

Your attention is called to the fact that it will be necessary for you to turn in all Company furnished equipment to this office. Both your personal and expense accounts must be properly balanced by the

Treasury Department at New York before final pay check will be delivered to you.

An exit interview has been arranged for you with Mr. John Mole on September 29th or earlier.

J.S. Anderson

cc: L.G. Fritz
    G.K. Griffen
    W.W. Braznell
    W.P. McFail
    D.S. Ogden

It was quite a shock! The little beagle had been baying on my trail so long that I had grown accustomed to him, almost fond of him. Now he had taken a bite, a big bite. I looked again at the distribution list to see who was hissing him along.

Then I recalled the night I had had the two emergencies, the night Ellis had put a bunch of people in an Amarillo hospital and severely damaged an airplane. But he was a company man, a weak sister. No penalty had been given him, not even a day off without pay. It caused me to recall the exchange of conversation with C.R. It had to be coming from the top.

But there was nothing wrong with the flight the beagle had seized upon for an excuse to fire me. No passengers had been hurt, no damage done to the airplane, and I knew that I had followed the company bible to the letter. In so doing I had taken in account the letter from the director of flight about extending the flight. It was a policy they could not publish. The letter had admitted it.

Gloomily I thought of the time it would take to get the case before the System Adjustment Board. Now that I was fired, I was no longer on that board. In the years I had sat on the board, it had usually taken nearly a year to get a case through the three hearings to a final decision. They were, the first hearing, the second appeal hearing, and the final appeal hearing before the System Adjustment Board.

The company had always delayed as long as possible, taken the full time for each hearing, and the full allotted time for rendering a decision. Never had a decision been favorable to the pilot involved in the first or appeal hearing. It had to be in front of the System Adjustment Board for a pilot to get a favorable decision. Sad, but true.

The gloom deepened as I thought of the farm and most of my assets that I had given Betty, just for a joint custody deal over the children. Now she had gone back into court claiming the joint custody wasn't working, just because she had received a couple of adverse decisions from Dr. Gordon and his wife. The judge had listened to her, ignoring my attorney, and given her full custody. In addition he had barred me from seeing the children for two months because she had claimed that it disturbed the children too much and she needed time to establish better discipline.

Quickly I went upstairs to my room for almost a half hour. Have you ever seen a man cry? I hadn't until I looked at myself in the mirror.

A short time later, after discarding the self-pity profile, I seated myself at the telephone and slowly dialed the ol'man's number in Chicago. There was no answer and I knew he was out of the office. Then I dialed George Schustman in Tulsa to give him the news. He was most sympathetic, but had been expecting it. When I gave him the particulars on the flight and also the discharge letter, he became very angry at Anderson, the distribution list on the letter and all the top management of AA.

"You are as clean a a hound's tooth," he declared and added: "Wayne, I had a long talk with Behncke a few days ago and told him I expected them to fire you on some pretext or other, and possibly me too. I let him know that I was very worried about you. Now I am worried about little George. It has me shaking in my boots," he confided.

That was news to me for George had not mentioned talking with Dave, but, I had not seen him for some time.

Then he chuckled: "Just think where I would be now if they had caught me, little George, in that room in San Francisco."

It was good to hear his little chuckle and I knew immediately that his wife was out, otherwise he would not have mentioned that room in San Francisco. George was not the household boss.

I shared the laugh with him, for I had the mental picture again, as Jean and Mary had painted it, of little George coming through that hotel room in his shorts, carrying his clothes, and begging them to hide him. It was refreshing and lifted my spirits considerably.

Then I called Gene Burns. He was home and insisted that I read the letter to him. After I gave him the particulars on the flight, he, like George, became very angry. He insisted on calling Behncke and, as chairman of Tulsa, give him the information. I thought that was a good idea for he had some other points he wanted to give Dave that pointed up my discharge as being quite unfair. Also, he wanted to get out a letter to the Tulsa pilot group on the matter. I asked to be left in seclusion for a few days.

In spite of that, within thirty minutes I began getting calls from other pilots. They were most sympathetic and pledged me the utmost in support. They wanted details, more details than George had given them. Instead of being in seclusion, I felt I was in Grand Central Station. Their calls extended through the dinner hour. I finally left the phone off the hook for a while.

The next morning I typed out a letter of grievance to Amalgamated Airlines, Inc. and sent it registered mail from the post office, requesting a hearing. I knew that it would be at least ten days from the time of delivery before I could expect a hearing.

Then Mother and I sat down at the dining room table to discuss the situation. Her black hair, streaked with gray and combed back, with a middle part, together with her dark eyes and finely chiseled features gave emphasis to her ancestry.

I had told her what the lawyer had reported regarding the children. We discussed this for some time and she was firm in her opinion that the children would make Betty's life miserable if she persisted in keeping them away from me for over a week. The children thought too much of their daddy, she insisted.

It made me feel better to think the ban would not last long. With time on my hands, I thought how good it would be to have them around the house and over at the swimming pool across the street. I could tell that Mother liked that idea also.

Next we discussed the idea of my trying to get a temporary job flying. I knew that there were possible flying jobs with oil companies in Tulsa, but a temporary job that I could leave if reinstated would be hard to find. We decided that I should give it a try. So several days later I went looking for a job.

It gave me a strange feeling to drive into the Tulsa airport in civilian clothes and park in a public parking place. So many times in the past I had parked in the AA parking lot and strolled into the company operations office that it was difficult to keep from doing it again. But not this time. I was not welcome. I was a fired pilot.

I went to three different oil company airport offices, Sun Oil Company, Helmrich and Payne, and Gulf Oil. I visited with the official in charge of each office and talked with the pilots who were there. Most of them knew me or had seen me previously, in uniform taking an AA flight out. One of them recalled that I had, a few months earlier, taken him through a DC-6 cockpit and explained many of the plane's features. He again expressed his thanks and appreciation.

They listened respectfully to my story of being fired and that it was subject to the grievance procedure, about which they knew little. Slowly they all shook their heads. There was no need for a temporary pilot, or even a permanent one at that time. All jobs were filled, and, at present there was a surplus of Air Corps officers furloughed from active duty who were out looking for jobs. They painted a rather bleak picture of the employment situation.

It gave me a chill to listen and think about it. After sixteen years with Amalgamated, I confessed to myself, I was not prepared to hit the pavement looking for a job even though my qualifications were spotless, sixteen years of airline flying with never an accident, not even a busted tire. It was hard to take.

I was walking back past the terminal to the public parking lot when two of the Tulsa based AA pilots spotted me and swung their car in to stop. Gene Burns was driving and Freddy Mills was his passenger. Both were strong ALPA members with Gene being the chairman of the local council which he had represented in the flight allocation grievances. They were close friends and frequently spent an occasional day off together.

Gene leaned out the car door and with eyes hard and penetrating and the right side of his mouth turning downward as he remarked, "Wayne, I heard the CAA lifted your license." It was both a statement and a question.

"Not to my knowledge," I responded. "They have no grounds."

"Get in." Gene swung a rear door open. "Let's get away from the field for lunch where we can talk."

In a nice quiet little truck stop on a major highway we settled at a table and ordered lunch.

"That's the story going around all over the system." Gene continued. "You are supposed to have signed a flight irregularity report to the CAA that allotted the flight was not performed in accordance with CAA regulations."

I laughed. "Of course not."

Freddy Mills, a slim towhead near Gene's size added, "They say you feathered the engine just north of Phoenix and kept going on to Los Angeles."

"No," I replied and told them the exact point of feathering near Palm Springs. "Who told you that?" I questioned.

"Joe Anderson." Freddy answered with his mouth a hard line. The right corner of his mouth almost imitated Gene's.

"That's real interesting, don't forget that," I requested.

"We had just been discussing that before we saw you," Freddy added. "Joe sort of went out of his way to tell me that and we were wondering about it; now we are wondering who is putting out the story that your license has been revoked."

"I've heard nothing from the CAA," I stated emphatically, "and I'd be the first to know, for they'd call me in immediately and ask for my ticket."

Slowly the other two nodded in agreement.

There was quite an empty feeling in my stomach and it was not hunger as I drove back to Claremore, thinking of the long delays before a decision would be forthcoming. I thought of the many cases I had chaperoned through the System Board. I thought of the seven fired pilots whose reinstatement and return to the company with full back pay I had engineered. That thought gave me a warm feeling. Now I could use some help.

Chapter 16

My Runaway Children

Lost in thought I pulled into Mother's driveway without seeing what was before me. Kathy and Wayne, Jr. were playing in the front yard while Mother sat in the porch swing and kept an eye on them. Kathy's tricycle was sitting on the sidewalk.

At sight of me Kathy came flying into my arms, hugging and kissing me and almost crying at the same time. I sat in the car with the door open and held her close while Junior draped himself over the swinging door.

"What are you kids doing here?" I asked between Kathy's kisses.

"We ran away and came to see you, Daddy." Kathy, barely four years in age, hung to me like a little leech.

"Yes, Daddy," Junior added: "We just decided to come see you while Mother was taking her afternoon nap. Kathy rode her tricycle and I walked to help her across the side streets."

"My gosh!" I exclaimed, "that's a mile and a half across town."

"I know, Daddy." Junior was proud of the feat. "I took good care of my little sister and helped her with the tricycle and watched for the traffic. She wouldn't stay home."

"Did anyone you know see you?" I was still stunned at the enormity of what they had done. Claremore was a busy little town of some ten thousand people.

Mother had left the swing and was standing near the car with a smile on her face and an "I told you so" look in her eyes. "Oh, yes," Kathy insisted in answering me from a close distance of six inches, "we saw Doctor Gordon and his wife. We saw Mrs. Bilbrie, we saw Joe Ellis, and we saw the preacher where Mrs. Bilbrie and Mr. Bilbrie take me to Sunday school."

She referred to Betty's next door neighbors who frequently babysat with Kathy when Betty would permit. They especially liked to take Kathy, a beautiful little blonde girl, to their church and for a walk on Sunday.

I shook my head in amazement.

We were on Mother's spacious front porch when the phone rang. Kathy was still in my arms and junior was hanging on to one of them. He quickly turned loose and hurried to the phone, answering it a little breathlessly.

"Hello, Mother," he repeated after the initial hello. Then he was silent for a little while.

"Mother." he appeared to interrupt his mother. "Daddy did not kidnap us! We came to see him. Yes, Kathy is with me and we came over to Daddy's by ourselves. He didn't know we were coming."

"No, Mother," he denied. "Daddy did not put us up to running off. We just decided to come visit Daddy."

"Well," he continued, appearing to answer another question, "I walked and Kathy rode her tricycle. I helped her across the streets and watched for cars.

"Yes, Mother," he answered another question, "we saw quite a few people coming over to see Daddy. We talked with Dr. Gordon and Mrs. Gordon. We told them that we were running away like kids do in the movies."

Mother was standing near me and the open door Junior had left ajar. Her eyes met mine and I was suddenly very happy that Junior had answered the phone. Finally he handed me the phone, saying that his mother wanted to talk with me. It wasn't difficult to make arrangements to keep the children all night. She was, for a change, trying to be cooperative.

The next day, a Saturday, we three were in the swimming pool for most of the day and a good part of Sunday. Then they were content to go home to see their mother for a little while.

The rest of the week slipped by slowly during which Mother and I went to the river lease a couple of times and made another trip to look over that acreage at Bird Creek. I even took the deed to the courthouse to determine if it was legitimate. It was, and had been recorded. A bee began to buzz in my head. I looked Dad's old machine over a couple more times.

That Saturday morning when I picked up my mail at the post office I had a letter from Amalgamated Airlines setting my initial hearing on September 27, 1951, at the Tulsa Hotel. I was glad to receive that and was surprised to have the date set within the time prescribed in the labor agreement.

I promptly called the ol'man, David L. Behncke, for a chat. As usual, on Saturday, he was in the office all morning and a part of the afternoon. I had not talked with him since my discharge, for Gene Burns had given him a full report.

I was pleased to find he knew a lot about my case and attributed the company's action to my union representation of the pilots. He promised to send me the best ALPA attorney in headquarters. He was very reassuring.

Later I called Gene Burns and informed him of the hearing date. He promised to get out a letter to all Tulsa members. We had a nice chat on the phone.

I had a dinner date with Jean that night and was jubilant at the turn of events with my children. I was looking forward to having them meet her and get to know her.

When I parked my car at Jean's home, I noticed that little Duncan's car was already there. That gave me a smile and a thought that he was probably over there to help Rosemary write another letter to "Dear John."

Jean met me at the door and invited me in. She had such a nice warm smile and the way her cheeks glowed caused me to mentally hope that a portion of that beautiful glow was for me.

Duncan was his usual friendly self and wanted to know the latest on my case. Rosemary was sitting near him and there was one other stewardess there with her date. When I told them the hearing date had been set for the 27th, I could not fail to note that Rosemary and Duncan exchanged glances. It made me wonder.

Later when Jean was in the car with me and going to a good dining place she began laughing and had difficulty controlling her mirth. Finally she was able to talk and wipe the tears at the same time. Rosemary had confided to Jean that morning.

The day before, Rosemary and Duncan had returned from a trip together, arriving home in the early afternoon. As usual Duncan brought her home, and, as usual, she had invited him in for a cold drink. With everyone else out on trips they had first sat on the edge of her bed, then lounged across it while they talked and talked.

Jean paused to laugh some more. She slanted her eyes at me as she wiped them again. She was greatly amused.

"Now this is the way Rosemary told it to me." She emphasized the point. "Little Dunc, with no provocation, suddenly grabbed her in his arms. He kissed her repeatedly and at the same time begged her to marry him," Naturally, she finally consented. Again she slanted her eyes at me.

"Oh, brother," I murmured more to myself than Jean, "I wonder who raped who?"

Jean shook her head and added: "Anyway, they have written the last 'Dear John' letter and are planning to be married at noon on the 27th."

Chapter 17

The First Appeal Hearing

I had taken a room in the Tulsa Hotel in order to be available to the association attorney, Maurice Schy, the night before the start of the hearing. He had arrived about three in the afternoon and I had met him at the airport. He was a young man of thirty with a good athletic build and a love for the outdoors. When I learned that he loved hunting, we soon found we were talking about some subjects other than my case.

In the quiet of our rooms, for I had reserved an adjoining room for him, we were soon deep into my case. In a little time we were joined by Wylie Drummond and Wes King of Nashville, who had come over to sit in on the hearing. They were very concerned about my welfare and desired to brief Schy on the flight allocation cases and the jack-box we had the company in with the contract and Railway Labor Act violations. They also brought extensive notes as the certified record was not out at that time.

In addition they briefed him on some of the things I had done for the pilots in the past, even giving him a case history of the screening program. They were warming up to their subject in the middle of the evening conference and I was beginning to squirm in embarrassment when George Schustman arrived.

I immediately excused myself to get away and have private coffee with George. He apprised me of the conversations, rumors, and lies that were being floated up and down the line. He insisted that it was being consistently and repeatedly released from a company office that I had had my license revoked. That would kill my case, for, without a license, there could be no reinstatement.

"That's the fine finger of AA," George charged. "I'll bet they are putting a lot of pressure on the CAA to lift your license, and they are laying the groundwork for such an action."

Invariably that was being spread by pilots who were pro-company in their leaning, generally pilots who were a little weak in their flying and weak in the association. It amused me at the way George had them all characterized, catalogued, and cross-filed. He even felt that he knew the company officials feeding the field.

"They are all good members of what you call the 'vulture army,'" he laughed.

A short time later George departed for his home. I rejoined the conference with the attorney. He had thoroughly acquainted himself with the letter of discharge and other information Drummond and King gave him. Now he wanted to go over the flight, step by step. This we did. Wylie Drummond and Wes King were good at pointing out company and CAA regulations as I verbally described the flight. It was midnight before the attorney was satisfied with the review.

I slept well that night, probably because I had acquired a lot of confidence in Maurice Schy. Behncke was right. He was a sharp attorney.

The hearing was to be held in the Oklahoma room of the Tulsa Hotel. It was a rather large meeting room which could accommodate eighty to one hundred people. Ten minutes before the time set for the start of the hearing there were forty pilots congregated, probably all who were in town plus three from the Dallas-Fort Worth council and two from the Los Angeles council, not to mention Drummond and King from Nashville. All those from out of town were there to take back a report to their councils. I was impressed with the turnout, and I think the company officials there were also surprised.

Those officials consisted of Assistant Chief Pilot Joe S. Anderson, Chief Pilot Don Ogden, Anderson's superior, Samuel B. Gates, the company attorney, and W.B. Whitacre of Chicago, the hearing officer. They were clustered in one corner of the room in idle conversation and trying not to notice the flow of pilots who quietly eased into the room and found seats in the rows of chairs. A few spoke to the group but mostly they just passed them by. It was noticeable. It was also noticeable the number of pilots who stopped by and wished me luck along with a slap on the shoulder.

Whitacre, the hearing officer, was of medium height and rather heavily built. He had been a station manager for Amalgamated for several years before the war, during which time he was an Air Corps officer in the Reserve. When the war broke out, he was called into the service for active duty. I have no knowledge of his contacts with C.R. during the war, but rumors persisted that he had ridden C.R.'s coattails into a brigadier general rank when C.R. collected his second star. There was no doubt about his being one of C.R.'s generals.

The fact that he was appointed hearing officer assured all that he was high on C.R.'s reliable list.   Hand picked is a better way of expressing it. There was little question what his verdict would be. The evidence didn't matter.   At least, until that time, no company hearing officer had given a verdict favorable to the pilot.   And I didn't expect one, not for Allison.

Whitacre, of course, would make a big show of being fair, but in critical rulings on issues between the attorneys, he would favor the company attorney.   I had seen it happen many times before in quite a number of cases in the first and second stage hearings. That is why the System Board had had so much business in the five years since the close of World War II.

The important thing for my attorney and me was to establish a good record, show a well-executed flight to refute the shotgun allegations in the letter of dismissal.   A neutral, sitting with the System Adjustment Board would, in all probability, decide the case.   I thought gloomily of the long year ahead.

The company attorney, Samuel E. Gates of New York City, was a slim, dark-haired man of medium height and about forty years of age. I caught him looking me over about three times before the hearing officer called the meeting to order.   He had been well briefed, I was sure, and I wondered idly if he was a good friend of Di Pasquale or Hamilton.

My speculation was cut short by the hearing officer.

Then the Hearing Officer commenced: "We are about to open a hearing on the appeal grievance filed by Captain Wayne Allison against his discharge from Amalgamated Airlines.   I have been appointed hearing officer and before the hearing starts, or we get officially into the record, I would like to ask if there is any one here that does not work for Amalgamated Airlines or is not connected with the Air Line Pilots' Association."

"Yes, sir," a voice spoke from the audience of pilots and a big man stood up. "I believe you have my name—Tibbs, with the CAA."

I knew immediately that the company had asked the CAA to attend the hearing, probably confident that I would be shown in violation of CAA regulations, lose my license, and that would be the end of Allison. Whitacre was making sure he was there. Amalgamated, I knew, was capable of such maneuvers.

The hearing officer then read into the record, which was being taken by a certified reporter, my letter to Joe S. Anderson requesting a hearing under the labor agreement in effect at that time. He then offered the letter to the reporter and asked it be marked for identification as the Hearing Officer's exhibit #1. Thereupon he called on me or my representative to present the case justifying my appeal. In other words, I was given the burden of proving my innocence.

The two attorneys immediately became involved in an argument, with my attorney insisting that the burden of proof was on the company. In the five years I had sat on the System Board of Adjustment we had always had that argument. The pilot was considered guilty of the company charges unless and until he could prove his innocence. As I have said before, it was the best we could do.

And, as in the past, we had to be satisfied with taking the burden of proof and showing that the company's charges were false. That meant we had to take the flight in question and show that it complied with all existing regulations, both company and CAA.

I was then called as the first witness by my attorney. The company attorney immediately asked that I be sworn in. That was a new wrinkle. In the five years I had sat on the board the company had repeatedly refused to put its officials under oath, even though the pilots had always been quite willing to take the oath. Now the situation amused me.

I knew from the way the company attorney Gates looked at me he was expecting me to refuse. But, since I had nothing to hide, I willingly took the oath administered by the reporter, a Notary Public of the State of Oklahoma. I hoped that company officials in the future would comply with this precedent.

My attorney, Maurice Schy, then had me reconstruct the flight from the time the engine began backfiring. Numerous questions were asked by the attorneys as to the time of broadcasts, the place the engine was feathered, etc. Much time was consumed in going back over the radio reports of positions and times.

My attorney asked a number of questions to bring out the points that the landing was uneventful, the passengers and crew unharmed and the airplane undamaged. A missed approach, or an abandoned approach, he brought out in my testimony, was a frequent happening with changes in weather conditions or a captain's dissatisfaction with the perfection of the approach. It was nothing unusual and occurred frequently in instrument weather.

Then he dug into my background with Amalgamated, asking when I was first promoted to captain, which was in 1939. He extracted the fact that I had never been involved in an accident with Amalgamated. He also brought out that I had never failed an instrument check, never been suspended or had my license revoked or suspended by the CAA.

Next Schy began questioning me about my union work, about positions I had held with the association and the number of years I had held those positions. I replied that I had been the chairman of the Boston council, which consisted of all AA pilots domiciled at the Boston base, for a period of two years, and had served as chairman of the Tulsa council for another two years. I had served on three separate contract negotiating committees, in addition to having been on the System Adjustment Board for over five years.

It was an impressive record over the years, and it was quite evident that the listening pilots were surprised to hear such an extensive record. I had always been around, representing pilots whenever a representative was needed, and the pilot group had sort of taken me for granted, never really thinking how much I was in the forefront of any pilot problem. They had always taken it for granted that Allison would be there, he would look after the pilot's interests.

They just voted me into any pilot representation job that required a representative. They did not really think about how much work it had been for me, in addition to my job as an active flying pilot. The enormity of the company's action began to come home to them.

Next Schy asked me how many cases the System Board had heard during the time I was on the board. It was an impressive number of near thirty, which I listed from a sheet of paper.

Mr. Gates, the company attorney, kept protesting that my union work had nothing to do with the conduct of flight forty-nine for which I was discharged.

Finally Schy gave him a good haymaker.

"Mr. Whitacre," he explained to the hearing officer, "we contend that Allison's conduct of the flight doesn't have much to do, if anything, with his discharge. His discharge was actually motivated by reason of enmities incurred by him among company officials which were the result of his representation of pilots as an officer, or an office holder of the Air Line Pilots' Association."

"Captain Allison," Schy turned to me, ignoring Gates sputtering, "calling your attention once again to Flight 49, did you at any time consider a procedure which you felt to be in jeopardy of the property of the company or of the lives and welfare of the crew and passengers?"

"No sir," I replied.

"Did you, to the very best of your ability, conduct that flight in a safe and efficient manner?"

"Yes sir," I replied.

"Thank you. I have no further questions at this time," Schy concluded.

A break was taken for lunch.

After the lunch period the cross-examination commenced.

Gates, the company attorney, apparently surmised, probably from assumptions by Anderson and Ogden, that I had feathered the engine when I first asked the question of where they wanted a three engine airplane. He approached that from several directions and finally produced a map and asked me to spot our exact location when the engine was first feathered. That was easy. But it took a little calculation from position reporting times before and after the feathering. He could not extract any questionable answers from me.

He tried, however, by asking such questions as the airplane's position when I feathered the engine the first time. A little later he wanted to know the position when I feathered the engine the final time. That was asked two different times and it amused me and caused me to give him a big smile and head shake as though I did not think he had been listening.

It caused a snicker to ripple through the pilot audience, followed by grins of approval.

"There was only one feathering," I finally insisted, "and that was reported immediately to Los Angeles." I emphasized the point.

It was difficult for him to accept that, and he made it plain that he thought I was hiding something. Finally he took a new approach.

I quote directly from the certified record:

Mr. Gates: You filed a form F-27 report with the company, did you not?

Answer: Yes sir.

Mr. Schy: Now just a moment, I object to that. There is nothing in his testimony on that point. If he filed a form and the company has it, will the company introduce it?

Mr. Gates: We will introduce it; I just asked him if he filed one.

Mr. Schy: I object; this is cross-examination, and cross-examination is confined to his direct testimony.

Mr. Gates: Mr. Examiner, are you going to conduct this thing as one of these hypertechnical cases or are you trying to get the facts?

Mr. Schy: Mr. Gates, you know...

Mr. Gates: If we are going into that I am prepared to go into it that way too, but we will be here for a week if we do it that way.

Mr. Schy: That is not a hypertechnical point, Mr. Hearing Officer. Counsel, I am sure, will be the first to admit it. Cross-examination is confined to the subject of the examination by its definition, and by its purposes, that will be the effect. If Captain Allison testified to anything that the company thinks is inaccurate or untruthful and they want to bring it out through questioning, we certainly have no objection, but he wasn't asked if he filed an F-27; there is nothing in his direct testimony that indicates or suggests that he did and I submit it is improper for counsel to cross-examine him on it.

Mr. Gates: If we are going to have to go into a legal argument I am not sure that our Hearing Officer is himself a lawyer or a judge, it is perfectly appropriate for the purposes of testing the credibility of the witness to ask him certain questions which are not directly concerned with the direct examination.

Mr. Schy: Well, that is a little bit preposterous, Mr. Hearing Officer. Mr. Gates, do you intend to attack the credibility of this witness by asking if he filed an F-27?

Mr. Gates: I am going to find out what the facts are; that is what I am going to try to find out.

Mr. Schy: That's right.

Mr. Gates: And that is what you should attempt to do.

Mr. Schy: And that is what I am attempting to do.

Mr. Gates: You should not be objecting about my question, asking the witness questions about whether or not he complied with company procedure.

Mr. Schy: I object to any question that was not gone into on direct examination.

Hearing Officer: The witness has answered the question and has stated that he did. Can I ask, Mr. Gates, if you intend to offer that F-27?

Mr. Gates: Yes, I do, because I will have to find out what it means. Let me ask a preliminary question. Captain Allison, did you follow the company procedures with which you said you were familiar?

Mr. Schy: Objection for the obvious reason it calls for a conclusion on his part. It is like the question, when did you stop beating your wife? If he says, 'yes,' and counsel has something to show that he did not, he apparently has impeached him. If he says, 'no,' then he says, that's the reason we fired you. Now we are trying to conduct this thing in a fair manner and I want, Mr. Whitacre, for you to consider once more the nature of my objection. Captain Allison has been on the witness stand for some hours and some minutes and I asked him questions covering a number of subjects, and any question that was covered in direct examination I will not object to counsel's examination, but I certainly object to his cross-examining him on a subject that was not touched upon in direct-examination—maybe he was a juvenile delinquent, and I didn't bring that out, and I would object to counsel going into that subject on cross-examination.

Mr. Gates: He talks a lot about the ALPA though.

Mr. Schy: Yes, question him about it! I won't object. Besides, he is asking him about a document, which, if it exists, is a part of the company records, and which the company is in a position to produce. Now if he did—.

Mr. Gates: I intend to produce it.

Mr. Schy: Then he will put it on as a part of his case?

Mr. Gates: I certainly have a right to cross-examine him about it; I never heard of such a suggestion from a competent lawyer.

Mr. Schy: I have stated my objection. I don't think anything further will be gained by laboring the point.

Hearing Officer: Mr. Gates, will you drop the F-27 matter until you introduce it?

Mr. Gates: Well, I have to have this witness on the stand to ask him about it, Mr. Whitacre; I am prepared to introduce it right now as far as that is concerned as my exhibit, but all we are going to do is to take time enough to call Captain Allison back to testify about it.

Hearing Officer: Do you have any objection to that, Mr. Schy, when the time comes?

Mr. Schy: No sir.

Hearing Officer: Can we proceed that way then?

Mr. Gates: I am not sure I understand what you want me to do; I want to accommodate you any way I can.

Mr. Schy: Mr. Whitacre, I wouldn't have any objection if he wants to introduce the document now as a company exhibit.

Mr. Gates: I intend to; I just asked a preliminary question.

Mr. Schy: Okay, drag it out.

Mr. Gates: I have only one copy of this, and this is the company's only copy that I have been able to find, Mr. Schy. Will you agree that I may substitute a true copy of this?

Mr. Schy: Would the true copy not have the signatures, is that it?

Mr. Gates: Not as such, they would be typed in.

Mr. Schy: I have no objection.

Hearing Officer: It is Captain Allison's statement anyway: he can verify it—he made the report.

(Thereupon the instrument tendered was marked by the Reporter as Amalgamated's Exhibit #2.)

Mr. Gates: Captain, there is Amalgamated's Exhibit #2. I will ask you if that is your signature which appears on the exhibit?

A It is not my signature—it is my signature; it is; not as I signed it.

Mr. Schy: Answer the question, Captain Allison.

A That is my signature.

Mr. Gates: Now you said it was not as you signed it; what do you mean by that? Do you mean that Mr. Anderson has put his signature on it since?

A No, I mean that—you see, at the time it was made out I was on the ground at Los Angeles and I executed a pencil copy with the pertinent notations—on the pencil copy of the F-27 and signed the required number of F-27 copies in blank—may I see my pencil copy of the F-27 with my writing on it that I left in the Flight Dispatcher's office at Los Angeles at the time I signed the blanks?

Mr. Gates: You may, Captain. I will show you what appears to be a pen and pencil copy of the Captain's Irregularity Report form, F-27, on which there appears to be your signature and ask you if that is the paper to which you refer?

A That's the paper.

Mr. Gates: All right now, will you compare that?

Mr. Schy: Wait just a minute, that is not in evidence.

Mr. Gates: Wait a minute, let me ask the question before you start objecting.

Mr. Schy: Well, I want it marked for identification in some way; the testimony is going to deal with it and we have got to refer to it.

Mr. Gates: May I ask my question, Mr. Whitacre?

Hearing Officer: Go ahead.

The Witness: It—.

Mr. Gates: Go ahead.

A As I recall, I made the original one out in pencil.

Mr. Gates: Is that your handwriting?

A This is my handwriting. I believe we rewrote it then. This is the original—not the original one, but second, I guess, that we wrote out at that time.

Mr. Gates: Do you have the original?

A No sir, I do not.

Thereafter there were numerous exchanges between the lawyers and it was finally established that the penciled notations on the F-27 form were done by me but not the pen insertion of "not" that changed the whole report and made it appear that I was signing a report that admitted the flight was not in conformity with CAA regulations.

The CAA man, Tibbs, made it quite obvious that he was very interested in that aspect of the case. The comparison of my handwriting with the writing of the "not" was so different that there was no question but that someone had altered my F-27 report after I had signed the form in blank with penciled insertions to be typed in to the blanks.

A recess was taken during which there was much buzzing in the room. Several pilots asked to see the altered form. Tibbs was with them. No one could disclose, or would, the identity of the person who had made the alteration. There were no confessions. Mr. Gates appeared much mystified.

Before the recess was over, Jim Jewell came around to me with a half smile on his face and confided that he had just had a little conversation with Mr. Tibbs as Tibbs was departing.

"Tibbs," Jim related with the smile deepening on his good-looking features, "remarked to me going out the door that the CAA did not have anything against you, Wayne, that it looked as though you were flying their regulations and that this is a company fight."

"You see," he continued with a knowing look, "I have been teaching his daughter to fly and Tibbs has become sort of a friend." He gave my arm a reassuring slap before heading for his seat. "I guess," he concluded as he departed, "that kills the idea of your license being revoked."

Then for over two hours, Mr. Gates grilled me on CAA regulations, company regulations, and the responsibilities of the captain of a flight. My attorney, Mr. Schy, did a good job of side tracking his pointed attacks and made him clarify his questions, questions that in many instances could not be answered with a "yes" or "no" reply. It was vicious!

Finally Mr. Gates attacked the subject of an emergency operation, a captain's emergency authority, and my use of it. I steadfastly insisted that I did not have an emergency, that never was the flight's safety in question and that I was advancing the flight in accordance with the company's policy. I referred to the unpublished policy.

Mr. Gates did not like any reference to an unpublished operating policy and tried to insist that no such policy existed. He was quite taken back at my quoting the policy—which they could not publish—and he denied that it existed.

When my testimony was concluded that night, I had been on the hot seat for eleven hours. I felt like a grilled cheese sandwich.

It had been an exhausting day, but Maurice Schy seemed to be quite pleased with the conclusion of my testimony. We settled in my room for a good drink to relax and discuss the day's events. Schy kept turning back to the F-27.

"Who did you suspect wrote that 'not' in the F-27?" he finally asked.

I had also been puzzling over that point. On a sudden inspiration I suggested that Margaret Seamore might know.

"Do you think she would tell you?" Schy asked.

I was already thumbing through the Tulsa phone book while Schy sat in thought. "We'll find out," I exclaimed as I dialed Margaret's number.

The phone rang twice and then Margaret was on the line.

"Margaret," I explained, "This is Captain Allison."

"Oh, Captain Allison, I am so glad that you called. I have been considering trying to reach you." She seemed relieved that I had called her.

"Captain Allison," She continued, "I heard some of the pilots talking out at the field this afternoon, telling about how your F-27 had been altered after you signed it. They told of how the meaning of a sentence of the F-27 had been changed by the insertion of the word 'not' and it didn't match your handwriting.

"Captain Allison," she confided, "I feel so badly about it that I'm sick. I feel that I am to blame. When I typed up the F-27 report over your signature Captain Anderson put that 'not' in the sentence saying that it was necessary.

"Oh, Captain Allison, I am so sorry! I know that you have tried so hard to get along with Captain Joe Anderson. And what he did was so wrong."

"Just a minute, Margaret." I turned from the phone and related to Schy what Margaret had just said.

He was on his feet in an instant. "Let's go interview her," he insisted.

Margaret agreed to see us and in a matter of a few minutes we were driving out to her home. With very little trouble we found her home, a tall two-story house on the north side of Tulsa which she shared with a daughter and her husband.

Margaret met us at the door where I introduced Maurice Schy as my attorney. She was most gracious and we settled in the front room. Schy, with charming manners, soon had her telling all she could about the falsification of my report to the CAA. It was quite revealing and Schy kept drawing her out about the way Anderson reported to Ogden and above on each and every incident pertaining to Allison.

She told about how Anderson kept a special file on me and that I was the only Tulsa pilot on which such a special file was maintained. Repeatedly she apologized for her part in the affair. We both felt sorry for that sweet, honest and innocent woman.

Finally Maurice Schy explained to her that what she had told us would have to be revealed at a later hearing before the Pilots System Board of Adjustment. He asked if she would be willing to relate everything later in front of that board if the association paid her travel and expenses. She agreed, indicating a strong desire to do anything to straighten the matter out.

The next morning the hearing officer, William B. Whitacre, convened the hearing at nine. The hotel had furnished a good supply of coffee along with a few dozen rolls so the hearing started with many cups of coffee, especially with late arriving pilots. I was relaxed with a cup of coffee in my hand, especially when I found that there were no more questions for me. I was finished. It was on the record.

Don Ogden was then called to testify as superintendent of flying at Fort Worth which included Tulsa. The high sounding title actually meant chief pilot and was probably designed to make him feel better without a raise in salary.

Naturally he was most critical of my conduct of the flight in question. But he could not point to any company or CAA regulation I had violated. All he could do was harp on bad judgement referred to in the letter of discharge. He testified that I had had an emergency even though I had not declared one. To hear him, the flight was in jeopardy from the time the engine first started backfiring.

When Mr. Schy had an opportunity to cross-examine him, his testimony became shaky, for being on the hot seat is quite uncomfortable. Also, the pilots attending the hearing were making it evident that they were in sympathy with me. I really began to enjoy my coffee.

Schy, by his questioning, brought out the fact that neither he, Ogden, or anyone other than the pilot in command and the flight dispatcher on duty had the authority to declare an emergency over a given flight. The fact that one had not been declared indicated that the flight was not considered in jeopardy by either the dispatcher or me. Arguments between the two lawyers consumed over three additional hours.

Then Schy took up the subject of the company's unpublished policy with respect to extending the flight. Ogden denied knowing anything about it. Schy showed him the letter over the signature of the Assistant Director of Flight who was above Ogden on the official ladder. Gates threw a fit and insisted that no such policy existed. The exchanges over that point were hot and heavy. Even the hearing officer had to drop his cloak of neutrality and get into the fray to assist Gates in keeping the unpublished policy out of the record. It too throughly justified my execution of the flight.

Schy had to temporarily drop the matter. Then Ogden's testimony relative to the flight clearance by the dispatcher did not coincide with that which Whitacre wanted in the record and he quizzed Ogden repeatedly, insisting that Ogden did not understand the question, until Ogden finally came up with the right answer. Some of the pilot spectators shook their heads in disgust with little smiles of disbelief. Even Schy rolled his eyes at me with a smile as though asking me: "Did you see that snake's tail?"

Then the questioning went into proficiency checks. The following is taken from the record:

By Mr. Schy:

Q The company had certain provisions, does it not, for checking the proficiency of pilots?

A Yes sir.

Q Is it a part of your duties to administer those proficiency checks.?

A Yes sir.

Q Do you, at the present time, have under your supervision any pilots that you consider not proficient?

Mr. Gates: I object to that as being immaterial and outside the issues of this proceeding.

Mr. Whitacre: Sustained.

Mr. Schy:

Q Did you on September the 6th, 1951, consider Captain Allison proficient?

A Yes sir.

Q Did you consider him proficient on September the 7th, 1951?

A Yes sir.

A Do you consider him proficient now?

A No sir.

Q What's the reason for the change of your opinion?

A The flight 49 of September the 7th.

Q Did you, prior to the Dallas Accident, consider Captain Claude proficient?

Mr. Gates: That is immaterial and outside the issues of this proceeding.

Mr. Whitacre: Sustained.

Q Did you, at any time, consider Captain Claude not proficient as an airline pilot?

Mr. Gates: Same objection.

Mr. Whitacre: Overruled. He can answer that.

A No sir.

Q Did you give Claude the last flight check prior to the accident?

Mr. Gates: I object to that as being immaterial, irrelevant, and outside the issue of this proceeding.

Mr. Whitacre: Overruled, the witness can answer if he remembers or knows.

A I don't remember.

(Odgen was plainly ill at ease. It had been widely circulated among the pilots that he had done just that.)

Q Can you find out?

A No sir.

(This caused the pilots in the audience to look at each other in disbelief. All chief pilots had to maintain a written record of each check; a copy of the check was placed in the pilot's personnel file, and it was quite apparent that Ogden did not want to disclose that he had checked Claude and passed him only a short time prior to the accident.)

Q Did you ever give him a flight check?

A Yes sir.

Q Who gave him his last flight check?

A It could have been Anderson; I called him down there to give them occasionally, it would be one of my assistants if it was not me.

Q Did one of your assistants refuse to pass Claude on a flight check prior to the accident?

Mr. Gates: I object to that as being immaterial and irrelevant.

Mr. Whitacre: Overruled.

A Sometime prior to the accident he was taken off of schedule for being not proficient, and he was given training time and then rechecked, yes sir.

Q Who rechecked him?

A I don't recall.

Q You did it yourself, didn't you?

A I don't know.

Q Did you ever check Claude.?

A Yes sir.

Q You don't know whether or not you checked him in the last check prior to the accident?

A I don't remember, no sir.

(That caused a little stir among the pilots at the hearing as they looked around at each other with little smiles at the way Ogden again could not remember if he had checked Claude and passed him just prior to the accident. It was widely known that he had.)

Q Did you personally reprimand Claude?

Mr. Gates: I object to that, it's immaterial.

Mr. Whitacre: Sustained.

Mr. Schy:

Q You testified that you had a conversation with Mr. McFail relative to Claude, both before and after the time the medical department advised him that he should stop flying, didn't you?

A Yes sir, I did.

Q Will you tell us what that first conversation was about?

Mr. Gates: I object to that as immaterial.

Mr. Whitacre: The witness does not need to answer, it has no bearing on this case; it was a private conversation.

Mr. Schy: Well, I object to the ruling that it was a private conversation. It was between two company officials relative to an airline pilot who had just had a major accident, but I won't argue about the ruling.

(It was obvious to all that Whitacre was doing all he could to assist Gates in protecting Odgen.)

Mr. Schy:

Q Now after Claude had been removed from the line for lack of proficiency, he was reinstated, wasn't he?

A Yes sir.

Q Was it your opinion at the time he was removed that he should have been removed?

A Yes sir.

Q Was it your opinion at the time he was reinstated that he should have been reinstated?

A Yes sir.

Q Approximately how long after he was reinstated was it that he had his accident?

A That I can't remember.

Q Was it a year?

A I don't know.

Q Was it less than a year?

Mr. Gates: He stated he didn't remember. What more can he say.

Mr. Schy: He can tell me if it was less than a year.

A Yes sir.

Q Was it less than six months?

A It would have to be, yes sir.

Q Now you told me that you didn't remember whether you had reprimanded Claude as a pilot under your supervision, did you not?

Mr. Gates: I don't think he did. I think I objected and the objection was sustained.

Mr. Schy: I see. Did you reprimand Claude within the six months period prior to the accident?

Mr. Gates: I object to that on the grounds that it was irrelevant and immaterial.

Mr. Whitacre: Sustained.

Mr. Schy: Did I understand that you will object to any questions that I may ask as to whether or not Captain Ogden reprimanded Claude?

Mr. Gates: Yes sir.

Mr. Schy: And will those objections be sustained?

Mr. Whitacre: Yes. Of course, you may take exception.

(That caused additional looks of disbelief by some pilots in the audience. The company wanted no comparison of my treatment with that given Claude.)

Mr. Schy: Captain Ogden, do you know whether Claude was a member of the Air Line Pilots' Association or not?

Mr. Gates: I object to that as being immaterial.

Mr. Schy: It is not immaterial. As you know we allege that Allison's discharge of his Air Line Pilots' Association duties is in question, and there is no secret about it; it was to show that there was a completely different standard of safety which applied to Allison and which applied to Claude, the dispatcher and others.

Mr. Whitacre: Mr. Schy, I was going to overrule the objection. I'll now sustain it. You took it a little too far for the Hearing Officer.

(It was evident that Schy was building a real defense for me, and Whitacre did not like it. I am sure he knew what his decision would be when he was selected as the hearing officer.)

Mr. Schy: Do you know whether Claude was a member of the Air Line Pilots' Association or not?

Mr. Gates: I will have to object.

Mr. Whitacre: And I will sustain it.

Mr. Schy: Do you know whether or not Claude was not a member of the Air Line Pilots' Association?

Mr. Gates: I offer the same objection.

Mr. Whitacre: I sustain it.

Mr. Whitacre: I would have agreed with you, Mr. Schy if Mr. Claude had received a disciplinary discharge, but the testimony in the past has indicated that he resigned for medical reasons.

Mr. Schy: I would be glad to put in the testimony.

Mr. Whitacre: I mean Ogden testified—his testimony along that line—I can't—I can't agree that there was any question as to his Air Line Pilots' Association activities having any bearing on the case.

Mr. Schy: We're prepared to prove that he was reprimanded for a number of things, but if counsel is going to object, and I'm going to be overruled, I won't take the time to do it.

Shortly after one, Ogden was excused as a witness. The Hearing Officer ordered a luncheon break for an hour.

After the luncheon break my engineer on the flight was called to testify. He made short work of verifying my testimony in every detail. The location of the feathering of the malfunctioning engine, the altitudes, my conduct, and all the happenings, including the testimony of flying with our manuals on our laps, was again recounted. Soon both lawyers were satisfied that he was telling the truth. My testimony was completely substantiated.

My copilot was not called as he had taken off on an assigned vacation and honeymoon. Neither lawyer considered his testimony essential in view of the engineer's verification of my original testimony.

Mr. Gates then called Joe S. Anderson to the stand, had him sworn in, state his name, point of residence, and official capacity. The two lawyers had stipulated a number of things in the record as exhibits.

Among those exhibits was my captain's irregularity report, the F-27, with the "not" inserted in pen.

Mr. Gates, probably to save time or, more likely, to take some of the fire out of the issue in front of the pilots, stipulated that Anderson had inserted the "not." He insisted that Anderson had not intended it to be the statement of Captain Allison.

Whitacre, the hearing officer, had to get into the fray in an attempt to whitewash the matter, and finally agreed that Anderson could admit that making such a change on the F-27 was in accordance with AA company policy, as he understood it. In effect they were admitting, through Joe Anderson, that the company was editing the pilot reports to the CAA. I was sorry that Tibbs had not stayed longer in the hearing.

Under questioning, Anderson claimed that he had made the decision to fire me after conferring with Captain Ogden several times and going over all available records. He also claimed that I had an emergency and with emergency powers had directed the course of the flight. Los Angeles, according to him, had merely concurred and exercised as much cooperation as possible.

He testified that Captain Ogden had sent him to New York to see Braznell and put the matter to him. In a three hour meeting Braznell had concurred with the decision to fire me. Probably it had been cut and dried from the top down. It explained why Joe Anderson had been a beagle on my trail for so long. It explained the look General C.R. had given me in the Tulsa operations that early morning when he and his "yes" men were delayed in Tulsa.

My mouth felt dry thinking about that and realizing that Joe Anderson probably had instructions down the line from the very top, to get something on me that would substantiate a firing. The distribution of the firing letter told a lot. Larry Fritz, listed as L.G. Fritz on the distribution list, sat next to C.R. He was another recruit during the war.

In an increasingly serious frame of mind I recalled the station manager at Phoenix, who had made a trip out to the field at two in the morning to see me when he learned that I was making an unscheduled stop for gas. I had not seen him for months, or had an opportunity to stop. My flights were all fly-over trips.

"Wayne," he had said looking earnestly at me, "there's a price on your head. The word is out that anyone who can get something on you to fire you, will receive a promotion."

"You did me a favor once," he continued, alluding to the time I had loaned him the money to pay for Cappie's operation, "and I'm trying to pay the interest now."

Our eyes had met in a clear understanding and mutual respect for each other.

"I know, Ed, and thank you." I had temporarily matched his seriousness and then gave his shoulder a friendly slap as I went off laughing into the night to that airplane guzzling gas.

Under questioning by Mr. Schy, Anderson admitted that he had gone into my file and considered each and every item at the time he had decided to fire me. Each little notation on a check ride or an instrument approach check was considered, even though I had passed each test. I had never failed a check ride or any test.

Mr. Schy than took up item by item separately in my file and the more he quizzed Anderson about each item the more evasive Anderson became and crossed himself up in his testimony. In one letter in which he criticized me for declaring an emergency in order to land for gas in bad weather, he disputed the fact that an emergency existed, then had difficulty trying to explain why he was insisting that I had an emergency on flight forty-nine in good weather even though I had not declared one. The pilots listening seemed to be enjoying his squirming.

I quote further from the record:

Mr. Schy: I show you this document over your signature, addressed to Captain Wayne Allison, subject engine out, four engine aircraft, dated January 30, 1948, and ask if you signed the original to that?

A I assume so.

Q Did you send it to Captain Allison?

A I assume that I did.

Q Now you write—'please note the attached letter from Dunn'— I now show you Dunn's letter dated January 26, 1948, and ask if that was the attachment?

A Yes.

Q May I question him on it now, Mr. Whitacre?

Mr. Whitacre: Yes sir.

Mr. Gates: May the record show that I'm still interposing an objection. There is no indication as to what it is a reply to.

Mr. Whitacre: He's questioning him on the letter to Allison now and the attachment.

Mr. Gates: The attachment is the letter from Mr. Dunn which is a reply to the letter of January 19th, and there is no indication as to what questions were raised in the letter of January 19th.

Mr. Whitacre: Well, the supervisors in this case saw fit to use it and I'll admit it.

Mr. Schy: Now Mr. Dunn's letter refers to an unpublished policy, does it not, Captain Anderson?

A Yes.

Mr. Gates: No, it doesn't, excuse me, but that isn't what the letter says. I ask you to read the last sentence, Captain Anderson, before you answer the question.

A We cannot, however, publish this policy. I will have to take my statement back on that.

Q The letter refers to a policy which the company cannot publish, does it not?

A I don't know.

Q It says, "we cannot publish this policy," it says that?

A That's right.

Q Did you understand it when you got it?

A I think so.

Q Do you know whether at that time the company had any other operation policies which the company could not publish?

A I do not know.

Q Do you know whether the company at the present time has any operational policy which it cannot publish?

A Not that I know of.

Q Do you know whether the unpublished policy referred to by Mr. Dunn...

Mr. Gates: Just a minute, he does not talk about an unpublished policy, and I am going to object to that and the characterization of it.

Mr. Schy: Do you know if the policy to which Mr. Dunn's note refers is still in effect?

A No, it isn't.

Q When was it revoked, if you know?

A I don't know.

Q Do you know whether it was revoked or not?

A The policy was changed by—by a change in the CAA regulation on that—an addition to the present CAA regulations.

Mr. Whitacre: This might save time. Captain Ogden testified yesterday and it was agreed that we had a liberal policy back in 1948, or the policy was somewhat different than it is now. He introduced a couple of CAA interpretations and instructions from the company saying we must not do this and that. I think it is well established that there was a definite change in the thinking between 1948 and 1951.

Mr. Schy: I think there is a definite change in the thinking regarding the published policy, but I don't know of any evidence that the unpublished policy...

Mr. Gates: Just a minute. There is not a word in this record about unpublished policies.

Mr. Schy: Five words in Dunn's statement that "we cannot publish this policy." That's what the letter says.

Mr. Gates: I'm through with the subject, Mr. Whitacre.

Mr. Whitacre: All right.

(Whitacre stopped the testimony. It was getting too sticky for the hearing officer, considering the verdict he knew he was going to give. It completely vindicated my conduct of flight forty-nine of the 7th of September.)

Thereafter the hearing wound down with both lawyers waiving summation due to Gates pleading a need to catch a late plane to New York. He sounded as though New York would soon stop dead unless he returned shortly. So the hearing terminated near eight that night.

Over a dozen pilots were still an attentive audience when the hearing ended. They all came forward and congratulated Schy on the presentation. Not many had ever sat in on a discharge hearing before. Only a couple had sat in on at least one of the screening hearings which had been held in 1947. All were quick to assure Schy and me that we should not have to worry about a verdict, that we had proven that I had been "framed."

I looked around quickly to see if Whitacre was a part of the audience. But he was nowhere around. He had slipped out along with the company attorney.

The pilots remaining were very complimentary to Schy on the way he had handled the "Unpublished Policy" letter by Dunn. They could not understand why Whitacre had cut off the examination of Joe Anderson on that subject. They had really been enjoying it, for all knew the company had an unwritten policy encouraging a pilot, when experiencing an engine out with four engine equipment, to extend the flight. But they had never seen it in writing. They could not understand having the company disclaim it when confronted with it in writing. It would make good juicy conversation up and down the line for the next few days.

Later in my room Schy called Dave. When he had finished giving Dave a brief summary of the hearing, I took the phone and thanked the ol'man for sending Schy down to help me.

Neither of us had any expectations about a favorable ruling, in view of the company's past record on grievances. Dave was kind and thoughtful enough to remind me what a fight we had had on the screening cases and that we would survive this one also. It helped bolster my spirits a little.

An hour later I took Schy to the airport and saw him off on a late flight to Chicago. We had become good friends. In fact, he promised to take a couple or three days of his vacation before Christmas and help me shoot a few quail. I made it sound as though they were about to take the country over. At the same time I resolved immediately that Jean would not be available to go with us. Maurice Schy was too good looking and was only thirty. A man that is just turning forty has to be careful when he introduces his best girlfriend to a good looking bachelor.

I checked out of the hotel and headed home late that night with my mind too full to consider any sleep. I had wanted to talk to Jean as soon as the hearing terminated but found that she was out of town on a trip to New York. I guess it was near four in the morning before I finally dropped off to sleep. The hearing had drained me and I slept until noon.

That afternoon Jean was home when I called and I made a date to take her out to dinner. Her response and eagerness to go out with me gave me a real glow. I temporarily forgot about my troubles with Amalgamated, something that had been constantly on my mind ever since receiving the beagle's slobbering bite.

Now, with the first hearing concluded and what I believed to be a good record established, I felt my natural good spirits returning. Schy had done a good job and devastated both the company attorney and the hearing officer Whitacre with that unpublished policy letter of Dunn's.

It clearly supported my entire conduct of the flight, which had been to advance the flight in accordance with the company's wishes. I firmly believed, and Schy had agreed, that we had won the first round.

That afternoon I received three calls from pilots who had spent at least a part of their time at the hearing. All were quite elated at the way the hearing had gone. They had been quite attentive and surprised me with the way they had analyzed it. Clearly they could see that the insertion of the "not" in my report to the CAA was designed to cause the CAA to pull my license. Then without a license, I could not fly any airliner and the entire hearing with subsequent appeals would be just a matter of rhetoric.

"Joe's a pretty crude worker," one of them offered. "He was my copilot out of Chicago for a little while, maybe two or three months. His flying was rough as hell and I finally managed to trade him off."

Schustman had missed the last day of the hearing, due to being out on scheduled trips and wanted me to give him a blow by blow description of the last day. We had several laughs together in the discussion.

It was so refreshing to talk with him and when he mentioned that he was going to call the ol'man and thank him for sending such a good attorney which George described as the 'best we had had in the last five years.' I decided that I should also call Dave again. It was a good excuse for me to talk a little more about Schy.

When Schustman had finished, I called Dave and thanked him again for Schy. That pleased him.

"I knew you would like him," he boomed in my ear. "He is the hardest working attorney I have ever had work for us. And he asked for your case."

"Better keep him, Dave," I encouraged. "He is better than anyone we have had on almost thirty cases I have sat on.

"It might be a problem," he acknowledged in a musing tone. "There are a couple of big law firms that have made him offers."

"But," he added, "when he came with us he promised to stay two years to get some labor relations experience, and we have almost a year to go. I've already started thinking up ways I can entice him to reenlist for another hitch."

We both laughed at his characterization of the situation. ALPA work was about as demanding as military service and few knew it better than I.

"Dave," I confided, "I would like to give you an added suggestion in that respect. Schy confesses to being thirty and is still single. A few months before his enlistment expires, why don't you get a real good looking secretary and sort of assign her to take care of Schy's paper-work as a first priority and fill out other work as a second priority?"

"Haw-haw! Are you talking about a fringe benefit?"

"That's the idea, Dave," I admitted. "A fringe benefit with a really attractive figure."

We both laughed together before concluding the conversation. It pleased me to hear the ol'man feeling so good.

It was such a nice fall evening when I picked Jean up early at her home. Rosemary was gone on her honeymoon with 'little' Duncan and Jean was lonesome. She moved in close to me in the car seat before many words had been exchanged. It was a very pleasant feeling.

"Who did you fly with yesterday?" I inquired as I guided the car out on a little drive.

"Jim Bell. He is doing relief flying from New York." She smiled and gave me a glimpse of those white teeth and clear blue eyes.

"The first thing he did was ask about you. He insisted that he knew that I was your girl." She laughed that throaty laugh with its musical note.

"He said the word was out up and down the line that I was your girl and that I can expect to have many inquiries about you and receive messages to you. He confessed to being one of the 'screened' pilots who were fired four years ago and all he wanted to talk about was you and what you had done in getting him reinstated with Amalgamated along with six other pilots. He could not praise you too much.

"He said," she continued, "to tell you that he knows what you are going through and to remember how you counseled him to have patience and let ALPA do the worrying."

She turned sidewise in the car seat to face me squarely.

"Jim Bell told me how, after ten months of being fired and out of work, he was about to give Amalgamated that letter of resignation in exchange for a little letter of recommendation that might help him to get another job."

I nodded slowly and thoughtfully. "Jim Bell was awfully blue when I ran into him in Nashville about then," I recalled, my eyes on the road ahead, not wanting her to see the moisture in them.

She was studying me intently as she continued. "Jim Bell said that you offered to loan him some money to eat on for a few months."

"I don't recall." I changed the subject.

We stopped in at the Hammet House in Claremore for a nice leisurely dinner. Several times during the dinner I caught her studying me with a half smile on her face. It was disconcerting.

Then I think she realized that her looks were making me uncomfortable and promptly launched into easy conversation. She told me that she had received her shotgun from her father along with her hunting boots, jeans, and hunting jacket. Laughing as we climbed into the car for a long drive in the moonlight, she told me that her father had even enclosed her Minnesota hunting license.

That provoked a laugh from me and hunting conversation as we drove. She was so easy to talk to and seemed to understand my thoughts and feelings.

Soon she had me telling her about the hearing, and what I had kept bottled up inside me came out in almost a torrent. Much later that evening I took her home. I had talked and talked, with pent-up emotions from the hearing, as we drove and drove in the moonlight. She was a good listener and helped me unload my innermost feelings. They had been bottled up so long.

Once again, at her home, she mentioned Jim Bell to tell me what I had advised him on the completion of his final hearing in Memphis before the System Board.

"Jim," she quoted me as saying, "I realize how rough the firing and these hearings have been on you. When I first talked with you, you were about ready to buy that little two-bit letter of recommendation from AA with your resignation. I talked you into filing a grievance and soon the hearings will be over. Your case looks good to me, and I feel sure we will eventually win your job back.

"David Behncke," I had continued, "the president of the airline pilots organization, the only one we have ever had, is a firm believer that an airline pilot's job is almost sacred. He has fought so many unfair discharge cases on many airlines and secured so many pilots' reinstatements to their jobs that he considers a pilot's job as the most precious thing the association can protect.

"The day," Jean kept quoting me in my talk to Jim Bell, "of

companies being able to discharge a pilot on some official's whim is about over. They must have just cause for such a drastic disciplinary action. Protection from that, an unfair firing, is the greatest benefit your dues can buy."

I opened the car door for her at her home listening to her quote me through Jim Bell. It was almost as though she had memorized the speech.

"Now Jim," Jean continued quoting, "it may take a year to win your case and the others, but we will not give up until we have you back on the line. Be patient, find a job of some kind, even if it is digging a ditch, and trust the association where you have paid your dues."

Quietly I walked her to the door in deep thought. I wished sincerely that I could be as sure now as I was then, four years ago. As I started to kiss her good night she stepped back a step and faced me with a big smile.

"You know," she exclaimed, "you are the first man I have ever met that I thought I might like to marry."

Then she kissed me a tender good night while I murmured, "Little girl, you might get that opportunity."

I drove home that night, in the cool fall air, thinking first of Jean and next about the advice I had given Jim Bell. It seemed about time that I took my own advice. Resolutely, I decided to do so.

Chapter 18

Back in the Oil Field

Two weeks slipped by during which I contacted an old driller, Russ Forsythe, who had worked for Dad, about helping me repair Dad's old machine. Russ was in his sixties and had a little heart problem, but as he said, "I'm tired of sitting on the front porch and fanning myself. It would be fun to do something that would give me an excuse to sweat a little."

I think he remembered my working with him in the oil field when we used boilers and steam for power. With his wry sense of humor he seemed to enjoy telling me that the oil field had improved greatly in the time I had been away from it. As an example, he pointed at the big industrial engine that served as the power unit for the drilling machine and related how that had replaced the steam boiler and the coal shoveling that went with it. Then he picked up one of the sledge hammers and made me heft it, explaining that it was still the main instrument used to drive stakes and dress out white hot bits pulled from the forge.

He even insisted on my lifting some newer pine blocking and timbers while reminding me that all the earlier blocking used in the oil field was made from native oak and was twice as heavy as the pine.

We spent two weeks working on the machine. He was a good worker and had been very familiar with the machine in past years, for he could remember many items that needed servicing.

Together we poured several babbitt bearings that appeared worn, rebuilt a sand reel pulley, and had a local machine shop make some brass liners for several other pulleys, including the derrick crown sheaves, which as Russ pointed out, were a lot easier to get to with the derrick lying on blocks than when fifty feet in the air.

We worked in a vacant lot where Dad had stacked the machine, a short distance from the house. Mother could call me whenever I had a phone call.

That worked pretty well, for several members of the pilot group at Tulsa called at various hours. Also, my boy Junior insisted on coming over after school and spending time with us. I think the proximity of Grandma's cookie jar had a lot to do with his visits.

Finally I received the letter from William B. Whitacre with the decision on my grievance. Of course it found the company was justified in my discharge. All first and second hearings since WW II had been given the same treatment.

Before that time the grievances, if there were any, had been disposed fairly in the first or second hearings by company officials who wanted to deal fairly with the pilots. Ralph Damon had seen to that. And the pilots were satisfied. They could still walk into an official's office and talk out a fair solution with the official having jurisdiction over the problem.

But since the war, things were decidedly different. Unfair disciplinary actions by any junior official, regardless of how unfair, were rubber stamped with approval all the way to the top. Top management suddenly did not give a damn about cooperation from the pilots. They were peons, privates and expendable.

That attitude by company officials had kept George and me pretty busy on the System Board since shortly after the close of the war. Senior pilots had returned from overseas flying for Uncle Sam and a surplus of pilots was created, plus war veterans looking for jobs.

I had already typed out an appeal of the decision by Whitacre and had it ready for mailing. It went to the vice president of operations, L.G. Fritz, another WW II general, and the last official on the distribution list given on my letter of discharge. He was the one whose desk stood next to C.R.'s. I mailed the appeal as soon as I received Whitacre's decision.

The appeal hearing was just a formality, a step required in the labor agreement, enroute to the System Board. No additional evidence had been offered in past cases, and none was planned in mine. It was just a case of walking into the vice president's office at the appointed hour and advising him that we were standing on the record of the first hearing. Since his office was in New York, on Park Avenue, I had arranged for Shipley to represent me and had given him an Authorization-to-act letter.

During the time I was repairing the old machine I had three dates with Jean. We had gone out to dinner once in Tulsa, once in Claremore, and one time we had dinner with my sister, Erma, who was two years younger than I and was happily married to an executive of Mid-Continent Oil Company,

Leonard Prickett by name. He was a big man, inclined to be overweight, quiet spoken and tremendously interested in my problems.

Leonard wanted to hear all I could tell him about my problems with AA. He would listen, shake his head at related evidence brought out in the hearing and exclaim, "I never heard of a company doing such a thing."

He could hardly believe Anderson altered my report to the CAA. If a company official on Mid-Continent did something like that, Leonard insisted, he would immediately be dismissed.

Erma and Jean were quite drawn to each other and seemed to enjoy each other's company. It didn't take Sis long to get around to telling me that Jean was a jewel.

Sis was a good contact for Jean, had her own car, and loved sports. When she and Jean learned that they both liked tennis, they soon made a date for a game.

Then the subject came up about the coming opening of the quail season, the forthcoming weekend. Neither Leonard nor Erma were hunters, but both dearly loved to eat those little birds. Erma could hardly believe that Jean had never tasted quail, they were so common in Oklahoma. So she invited Jean back for a quail dinner with my furnishing the quail. When I told Erma that Jean was a hunter, she shook her head in disbelief.

That made me tell her the story of Jean roaming the north woods of Minnesota with her shotgun and shooting partridge without any male assistance, not once, but repeatedly after school and on weekends, and had done that from the time she was a sophomore in high school.

That coming Saturday Jean was home and off schedule. I was after her early in the morning, about seven. She was ready with her shotgun and hunting clothes. Her bright eyes were flashing blue with anticipation while she laced her boots in the car. My bird dogs were in the back of the station wagon, restless and eager to go. They had seen the guns and knew this was no exercise run. It was what they lived and dreamed. They leaned over the back seat as though pushing the car down the road.

Soon we were in the fertile quail country that stretched for miles east and west of Claremore and along the river bottoms of the Verdegris and Caney Rivers. I chose to take Jean up on the Caney where I was acquainted with most of the farmers. We had planned to hunt all day with a lunch Mother had prepared.

"Did you get my license?" Jean questioned, pausing in lacing her boots. At my nod she smiled in appreciation, for she had been out of town for a couple of days. I could tell that she was liking my attention.

Quail hunting was a new experience for her. She wasn't sure what they looked like and had quizzed me repeatedly about how they flew, how fast, and if they dodged in flight. I had enjoyed giving her a complete briefing on the bobwhite quail. All she knew was ruffed grouse in the heavy timber of northern Minnesota.

The use of bird dogs was also something new to her. She had never seen one hunt or work a covey. In Minnesota she had had a pet terrier, named Stubby, that had accompanied her in her hunting, but was more mindful of the little piney squirrels than he was of the grouse. She had to resort to the task of walking them out of the timber and brush.

In the first quarter of a mile we strolled along together and watched the dogs sweep the fields, brush, and creek banks with almost effortless ease. I explained what they were doing as we enjoyed the easy walking. She would not believe that dogs could move so rapidly, so gracefully, and with such unerring instinct.

In a short while we had a point in the edge of scattered sumac bushes. The second dog honored the point while we closed in to the prime point. Jean's eyes were wide with the excitement. She did not know what was happening but she was eager to learn. I cautioned her that there would likely be a number of quail on the rise, that they could be noisy and to calmly pick out one and try to kill it.

Despite my briefings on quail rises, she was not prepared for what happened. I had moved over to one side to be in the clear to shoot while talking to the dogs to steady them.

As I had instructed her, Jean moved slowly toward the prime point with her gun at the ready. Then it happened! Nearly twenty quail rose around Jean with a sudden roar. She had walked into the middle of the covey and they literally wrapped around her on the rise.

I was able to get in three quick shots and brought down two birds. The dogs quickly retrieved both for me while I turned to see Jean standing, shaking, and laughing.

"I couldn't shoot, I couldn't move," she confessed as she laughed. "They paralyzed me. I thought a grouse was noisy, but these little birds simply roar." Her blue eyes were sparking.

It was the beginning of a perfect day. We strolled along with the dogs and went from one point to another. Finally, near one, we were back at the car and enjoyed a sandwich on the tailgate of the station wagon. She had progressed to being able to get off a shot on a bird rise, especially on singles. And in the middle of the afternoon she downed a bird. A few attempts later she had another. By late evening she had killed four. So we called it a day with fourteen birds between us.

I cleaned the birds while Mother was getting the dinner on the table. She had anticipated our coming in near dark or after, for she knew the best hunting was after sundown. However, I did not clean the birds alone. A Minnesota grouse hunter began learning how to skin those plump little quail that so closely resembled the ruffed grouse of her home.

But there were more than fourteen birds between us that evening. There was a comradery between us, an understanding that we had a bond being forged more fine than gold filament. We became hunting buddies! We were more than that, we were man and woman with a great desire to be together, to partially satisfy that hunger that was building between us.

After the dinner with Mother, we wrapped up six birds for Jean to take back to Tulsa for a good dinner with her roommates. Enroute we stopped for a little loving. She had been so enticing, so lovely looking all day with that beautiful reddish blond hair billowing from under her hunting hat, those flashing white teeth and questioning blue eyes, that I could hardly keep my hands under control. But those blue eyes were not questioning when I stopped in an isolated spot. She met me in the middle of the car seat. A wolf, she had decided, was a pretty nice animal!

A few more weeks slipped by, weeks of bird hunting twice a week with Jean, and drilling activity during which I forgot about being an airline pilot. At least I tried to forget. Shipley had carried my appeal through the vice-president of operations and, as expected, the decision had been adverse when it finally reached me. Mr. Behncke, when advised, promptly appealed it to the System Board of Adjustment.

In those weeks I became an oil field hand again, working, sweating, handling heavy timbers, some of them oak, and heavy steel tools as Russ and I moved Dad's old machine out on the lease where Mother owned the mineral rights. Once again I became friends with that fourteen-pound sledge hammer.

It was slow and laborious, dirty, greasy work that went with rigging an old machine up on a well location. Struggling with tangled guy-wires, drilling lines, together with frequent trips up and down the derrick became common exercise for me.

Russ was a better man than he thought, and I wasn't as good a man as I had thought. We both lost weight as we struggled on the job. Russ's heart problems disappeared and I became hardened and more athletic while the contents of the ice can disappeared daily.

I thought occasionally of that nice, cool, clean cockpit with a good looking girl frequently handing me a cup of coffee or tea. Somehow, the ice water tasted better. There had always been an invisible crud in that cockpit that I was beginning to see clearly for the first time. I wondered if other crooked companies gave off the same tainted flavor.

Sometimes Jean's schedule would interfere with a planned bird hunt and I would work at the machine. Then we would make up the day someplace along the line. Those hunting days were wonderful days of being together until late at night. Frequently she had short notes for me from some pilot friends on the line, along with verbal correspondence to me. A copilot here, a captain there would sometimes hesitantly approach her and ask if she was going to see me soon, before sending a message or encouraging note. I had a lot of friends, even though some belonged to the 'vulture army.'

Wylie Drummond of Nashville, the one who sent the message to Mr. C.R. of the impending aurora borealis at Nashville during the flight allocation grievances, frequently sent notes via Jean. Also, J.J. O'Connell of Los Angeles who had popped his blue eyes repeatedly at Di Pasquale and invited him to take his ball and bat and go home, left notes for me in Jean's company mail box as he flew through Tulsa. Those two had been appointed by Mr. Behncke to replace Schustman and me on the Pilots System Adjustment Board. They were loyal friends.

Between hunting quail with Jean and helping Russ with the drilling machine, I worked down through December into January. That ended the quail season. I took a little time off for Christmas with my children, Jean, and Mother.

Jean was over as much as possible before Christmas and after, during which she spent a good deal of time with Mother. Mother did like to go some but hated to drive as it gave her a very insecure feeling. She was not a very good driver and knew it. So, with Jean doing the driving, they started doing some running around together, shopping in Tulsa and elsewhere while I was at work. Jean showed Mother the back road to the Tulsa airport to stay out of heavy traffic and Mother started using it to pick up Jean when I was not available.

Sometimes, on nice warm days, they would come out to the machine during the middle of the day and have lunch with Russ and me. My children found out about that and insisted on being included on Saturdays when they were available. Betty couldn't stop them, for they quickly became very attached to Jean, probably due to her sunny disposition and youthful understanding, in contrast to Betty's moody and irritable spells. It was years later that I learned that Betty had a drug problem, a dependence on strong tranquilizers.

Two times, right after Christmas, I had taken time to go to Tulsa to check on a possible flying job, but had been unable to find even a temporary one. It made me realize how very discouraging and despondent it must have been for the boys, including Jim Bell, who had been eliminated in the company's screening program a few years earlier. My qualifications were much better than theirs had been, but the results were the same. There was an over-abundance of pilots.

Dad's old drilling machine became a haven for me, but an expensive one. Russ's salary was eating into my meager savings that had not gone to Betty for the child custody deal. Mother, however, was enjoying seeing me off to work, as Dad had done for so many years. In her way of thinking she was back in the oil business and we had a well going down. That, was a nice feeling, even to me.

But I couldn't keep from waking each night near midnight and wondering who was taking my trip to San Francisco. It haunted me. I dreamed about flying so realistically that I was sure I was in the cockpit and pulling the nose up, up, and up. Then, sometimes, in a very realistic and vivid dream I would have a fire, up high where the air was clean and I was a long way from earth, a poacher where I did not belong, with a fire on board.

They were dreams I had never had before, and they disturbed me so that I would lie there and think about them for a long time after waking. Occasionally I had a dream so vivid, and had been enduring the dream so long, that my under clothing would be wet and I would feel almost exhausted.

It caused me to wonder if the Ol' Man, the Great Spirit to the Indians, or the Great Creator, as many referred to him, was sending me a message. Was I being told that my "poaching days" were over, that my flying career was ended? It would be so thought-provoking that frequently it would take over an hour before I could get back to sleep. Then, I would slumber only fitfully.

Twice I called Dave Behncke to see how he was getting along. The first time he was pretty busy and only responded briefly to my questions. The second time I called late in the evening when the office was deserted and he was working late.

Dave appeared glad that I had called and we talked for some time. I knew something was not right, for I was having difficulty getting that old belly laugh. Finally he confessed that he was not doing too well, not feeling like doing much work. That was something new for Dave.

Gradually I drew out of him some of his problems. Sayen was giving him lots of trouble, differing with him at every turn of the road. Many pilots seemed to be questioning the need of a mileage limitation with the coming jets. Sayen was siding with them and the field seemed split. It looked, Dave admitted, that with so much dissension, the mileage limitation would likely be dropped. He was sick about it for I knew he wanted to achieve that for the pilots, along with the new headquarters building.

I was saddened to learn of his problems, problems that he did not deserve. It had been my strongest wish that a young and hard working vice-president would lighten his load, be able to coordinate and implement actions that would further Dave's thinking.

During the many years he had been president of the Air Line Pilots' Association his judgment and decisions on far reaching matters relative to airline flying had been unerring. But he did need someone to edit and smooth out his letters to the field. That I had to concede. No one could improve his thinking for the pilots.

"Oh," Dave suddenly recalled, "we have a System Board hearing set up on your case. I have just had a discussion with Schy, who by the way, has asked to present your case to the System Board."

"Good!" I exclaimed. "I like his work."

"Well," he expounded further, "I do too, but just to make sure we have an able presentation, I am sending Henry Weiss with him. They will work together. Henry, you know, has been the association's chief attorney for years. I think highly of his work."

I had heard considerable of Henry Weiss in past years, and had once met him in conjunction with a pilot problem, an accident. I liked Dave's consideration and felt that Henry Weiss along with Maurice Schy would be a team hard to beat. I told Dave as much.

"But, Dave," I asked, "won't that be pretty expensive?" I had heard that his fee was in the range of a thousand dollars per day.

"Don't worry about it," he boomed in my ear. "Schy tells me we have a good railway Labor Act violation to prosecute in your case. Those flight allocation cases and your case are good grounds on which to seek a federal conviction. Amalgamated has been asking for it ever since we let them off the hook on those screening cases by being satisfied with the boys going back to work with full back pay. If Ralph Damon had not been caught in the middle on that deal, I think I would have turned the crank on that one. We had them cold," he explained, then added, "thanks to you and Schustman."

Dave went on to tell me the board hearing would be in New York at the Lexington Hotel on January 23rd. Schy had just finished all the details, even to the point of sending Margaret Seamore an air ticket to New York and making reservations for her in the hotel. Her testimony was being kept a tight secret by all.

Chapter 19

The Pilots' Court

January 22nd was a cold and rainy afternoon when I deplaned from the Amalgamated plane and rode into the Belmont-Plaza hotel with the flight crew. There I took my luggage and walked around the corner to the Lexington hotel and checked in for my reservation. The room I had requested by phone was in order, and I lost no time in washing and cleaning from the trip.

I was just drying my face when Wylie Drummond and J.J. O'Connell appeared at the door with a heavy knock. I admitted them and we all enjoyed a handshake together. It was good to see them.

They had come in earlier in the day, and, due to the weather were a little worried about later flights. My first concern was for my attorneys, Schy and Weiss. However, they informed me that they were already registered and busy at work in two adjoining rooms. That satisfied me after I had called them on the phone and advised them of my location.

Drummond and O'Connell settled down in my room for a discussion on the hearing. They had never served as judges and were seeking information on past procedures.

I was quite surprised when they told me that the company members of the board were Carl S. Day and Howard Tiffany. I had expected that Hamilton would still be representing the company and someone else of Di Pasquale's selection.

Both Drummond and O'Connell wanted to know all I could tell them about the company members of the board. There was no question about the situation. The company had upgraded the company members of the board.

I explained that they were a couple of smart company officials whom I had known for years. They had enjoyed decent reputations as training school instructors. Carl Day had once been a pilot about the time Amalgamated Airlines was organized, but due to a physical defect had to give up flying. However, his knowledge of flying was good, along with his ability to talk it. Howard Tiffany, on the other hand, was very quiet, seldom said anything, and it was most difficult to follow his thinking. When he did speak, he was very brief and to the point.

In our discussion of procedures in front of the system board I did think to remind them that, according to the system adjustment board provisions of the agreement, the chairmanship would be evenly divided. In other words, the pilots would chair the hearings one year and the company members would chair the next year. This was the company members' turn. Naturally we concluded that Carl Day would be the chairman. I was delighted to find that they had thoroughly familiarized themselves with the adjustment board section of the labor agreement.

Further discussion was delayed by the phone. The caller was Maurice Schy, and when he learned that Drummond and J.J. O'Connell were with me, he promised to come to my room and bring Henry Weiss. Within a couple of minutes they were with us and I introduced Henry Weiss to the pilot members of the board.

Henry Weiss was of medium height, a couple of inches, maybe three, shorter than Schy. He was dark, with black hair, turning almost white at the temples and silvery on top. He could easily pass for an aging airline pilot who had kept physically active and looked to be in the best of health. Henry was probably fifty years old, and was delighted to talk with the pilot members of the board. The pleasure appeared to be about evenly divided.

Both Drummond and O'Connell had gone over the record of the first hearing at Tulsa and wanted to discuss it with Schy. Weiss wanted to sit in on the discussion as he had gone over the first hearing with Schy in Chicago. So for a time the conversation was all about the Tulsa hearing. I said very little in the discussion, feeling that Drummond and O'Connell wanted to absorb the attorneys' thinking. Finally I excused myself to go get a cup of coffee.

It was raining moderately, as I looked outside from the lobby. The clouds appeared to be drooping around the building only a few stories above. I could almost hear the air traffic stacking up over New York and the Traffic Control Center assigning approach sequences and holding positions. It was going to be a busy night in the air over New York and I wished I were a part of it.

Going to the lobby phone I called the Shipleys. I wanted to talk with someone. Nat's cheerful voice greeted me with considerable enthusiasm. Ship was flying today, on a trade so he could be in for the start of my hearing, she informed me. He would be in late tonight— maybe, she added with a laugh.

We both laughed at the prospect while I recalled the time she and Ship had met me, along with George, at the airport for the start of the flight allocation grievances. I could see her so vividly hanging on to Shipley's arm with one hand, her hand pressed on her head with the other and at the same time laughingly complaining: "Throttle back, Desmond, before I soar out of my girdle." It was a memory of a happier time and it still brought a smile to my face.

Nat told me that Ship had sent out a letter to all the New York members of his council advising them of my hearing date and asking for a strong showing of pilot interest. That was nice to hear and I thanked her. We talked a while longer and were just concluding the conversation when I saw the system board pilots, Drummond and O'Connell, show up in the lobby with Schy and Weiss. They were going to dinner and I joined them, feeling like a lonely goose with four happy, quacking ducks.

The hearing before the system board was set up to begin at two in the afternoon, probably with the idea of giving all who had to partici- pate, ample opportunity to congregate at the Lexington. So I had nothing to do. Schy and Weiss had made it clear the night before that they were going to be working on my case throughout the entire morning. Neither thought I would be called back to the witness stand. They were concentrating on my legal defense and I felt that I would not be much help there. They didn't ask for my help either.

Wylie Drummond met me in the dining room of the hotel for an eight o'clock breakfast. J.J. O'Connell had decided that hour was too early as he lived on the west coast and insisted that it was only five in the morning on his watch. Wylie and I had to laugh again at the way J.J. had popped his blue eyes at us during the dinner and told us in no uncertain words that he wasn't even considering having breakfast with us at five.

We had a very leisurely breakfast, then at Wylie's suggestion we walked to a couple of sporting goods stores so he could shop for a new shotgun. According to him he was missing too many quail on the tail end of the Tennessee bird season and, he was sure, it was not all his fault.

It was nearly noon when we sauntered in to the dining room of the Belmont-Plaza. We were quite surprised at the pilots, some with wives who wanted to get a taste of the hearing, and others who were using it as an excuse to come downtown shopping while their husbands attended the hearing. They all appeared glad to see me and were most friendly, even joshing me about being with Wylie Drummond, obviously handshaking for his vote.

That made us all laugh because there was nothing in the System Adjustment Board provisions of the agreement that said anything about the members of the board being fair and impartial. It merely stated that two members of the board would represent the pilots and two would represent the company. The words fair and impartial were not in that section.

Several friendly pilots had to tell me how good I was looking and how much the vacation was agreeing with me. When I admitted that I had been bird hunting all fall, a couple expressed wishes that they could spend a fall doing nothing but bird hunt. They were trying to make me feel good. Little did they realize, and I refrained from mentioning it, the heavy work I had been doing at the drilling machine and how close to that sledge hammer I was living. But, I was tanned, lean and fit with a rough and big hand in the handshakes.

Shipley and Nat waved to me from the other side of the dining room and I quickly joined them with a hug for Natalie and a handshake with a shoulder slap for Shipley. Wylie went to join some Nashville boys at another table. It was almost a holiday atmosphere in that dining room.

Sitting and talking with the two, I realized how very much I missed being a part of a throbbing airline. It was a way of life, a business that seldom, if ever, had a flat spot. I had been a part of it for a long time and I felt a keen longing to be back, hauling ore from coast to coast. I knew that the trip to New York for the System Board hearings, and the meeting with old friends would disturb me for some time.

Then Shipley bombed me. "You know about Behncke's ouster?"

he asked. At my mute head shake and reminder that I lived about thirty miles from Tulsa and had been busy out in the oil fields, he explained.

"Dave and Sayen have been feuding back and forth in court for some months, each trying to get rid of the other. Sayen has been apple polishing with the pilots of Eastern, United, Braniff and Pan American. He has been very critical of the ol'man in letters to the executive board and finally was able to engineer a vote by the executive board to move the ol'man out. Behncke went into court and got a stay order awaiting convention action. Everything that went out of headquarters was supposed to be signed by both Behncke and Sayen, especially paychecks.

"A self appointed group of 'revolutionaries' as they called themselves, sat right on top of headquarters and practically hog-tied Behncke and worked in conjunction with Sayen."

He paused, stirring his coffee before glancing at Nat and back at me, then continued.

"At the recent convention, the vote overwhelmingly approved Sayen for president and threw the ol'man out. A lot of the convention members, delegates from each pilot council, were younger and had little background in association affairs. The old-timers were very much in the minority and the younger members would not listen to them. All were charmed by Sayen and his smooth college professor smile, his good looks, and his nice easy command of the English language.

"The younger chairmen and copilot representatives were much better educated, more polished, and mostly former military pilots. I think they thought they were up-grading the association. They didn't want a stevedore labor organization. They wanted an association of college professors."

Shipley paused to chuckle and pour himself another cup of coffee from the pitcher on the table and suggested that we order lunch before he continued. It seemed like a good idea and it didn't take long before getting back to Shipley's story.

"I think," Shipley continued, "half of the delegates at that convention actually believed that if they got rid of Behncke and sent in a gentleman of the college professor class to deal with the companies, everything would be rosy."

His dark brown eyes peered deep into mine as I studied his eyes intently. Shipley was a graduate of M.I.T. but I thought I detected a note of scorn in his voice. However, he had been a 'fired pilot.' He knew what job security and freedom from harassment by irresponsible company officials really meant. That had been the battle cry in organizing the airline pilots association.

I remained silent thinking about the last convention I had attended and the fight I had led to re-elect Dave Behncke. At the convention two years later I had not attended but sent George Schustman in my place. He had never attended one.

It was at the convention George had attended that eleven potential candidates for the vice-presidency were nominated. I had always enjoyed the thought that I had been nominated even though I wasn't there politicing to be nominated. All the others nominated, including Sayen and Shipley, had been present and campaigning for the nomination. It wasn't that they wanted the job, just the prestige of being nominated. I think Sayen was the only one that really wanted the job.

"Go ahead," I urged Shipley.

"A delegation at the recently concluded convention offered to double Dave's salary if he would go into retirement voluntarily and remain in an advisory capacity." Shipley recalled. "But Behncke refused, called it a bribe. Finally, after it was obvious that they were kicking him out, he agreed to accept his regular salary for the rest of his life."

I felt Nat's sympathetic eyes on me while Ship talked. I was shocked to the point that I was speechless. It couldn't be, I kept thinking, after eighteen years of slaving for the pilots, twenty-four hours a day when necessary, then kicked out. Was that what an educated society did? My mind reeled as I thought of the big, rough diamond that had always belonged to the pilots. Now they had thrown it away!

"Where does that leave me?" I finally asked.

"Oh," Shipley explained, "Dave set this hearing up with Wylie Drummond and J.J. O'Connell appointed to the System Adjustment Board just as you and Schustman had recommended. He also arranged for Schy and Henry Weiss to push your case to a final conclusion. It's all set," he reassured me.

We ate our lunch in silence while my mind was full of thoughts of David L. Behncke.

The New England room of the Lexington Hotel was a large room with many chairs, several tables, one in the back of the room with water pitchers and glasses. Separate tables for the lawyers were provided near the middle of the room, with a certified reporter's table and a witness chair in between the two layer tables. The room could easily accommodate a couple of hundred people.

It was a surprise to Shipley, Nat, and me to see the room over half full of pilots, a few with wives. All were seated and quietly waiting for the show to begin with a little subdued conversation here and there. Shipley and Nat joined the pilots and found chairs in the fore part of the room.

I joined my attorneys who had just entered. I moved a chair in behind them at one of the tables. Samuel E. Gates, the company attorney at the first hearing, with an assistant, were busy arranging some papers on their table. The four members of the System Adjustment Board, Drummond, O'Connell, Tiffany, and Day, were already seated at a table with four chairs on one side of the table so that they were facing the attorney tables. Carl Day, as I expected, picked up the gavel and rapped the table until quiet prevailed.

Chairman Day: All right, gentlemen. The Amalgamated Airline Pilots System Board of Adjustment is now in session to hear the grievance of Captain Wayne Nelson Allison, as submitted by the Air Line Pilots' Association on November 30, 1951.

Mr. Schy: Gentlemen of the board, this is a proceeding pursuant to the agreement between the Amalgamated Airlines and the pilots in the employ of Amalgamated Airlines. The issue is whether or not the company was justified in terminating Wayne Allison as an airline pilot for the reasons given by the company in its letter of termination. The letter was executed by Captain Joe Anderson on September 19, 1951.

The procedural requirements of the agreement have been followed, and in September, 1951, there was a first hearing of this matter with Mr. William Whitacre sitting as a hearing officer. That hearing was conducted in Tulsa, Oklahoma. A record was made of the proceedings, a number of exhibits were introduced, which are attached to the record, and it has been agreed between representatives of the company and representatives of the association and of Captain Allison that that record will be submitted to this board for their study and evaluation as part of the record.

The purpose of that stipulation, I am sure is obvious to you, is to avoid the time, the expense, and the mutual inconvenience of both parties in duplication substantially the testimony that is already on the record. However, that understanding was made subject to the right of both parties to introduce any new or rebuttal or clarifying evidence that it may choose.

We would like to make clear at this time that the stipulation, which we have made, does not restrict us in any way from introducing rebuttal or new or clarifying evidence. We realize that the board is under something of a disadvantage in that there has been a long proceeding that the members of this board haven't heard in detail. We feel confident that you will study the record and evaluate the exhibits, together with whatever evidence and testimony is added to that record in these proceedings that you are about to hear—if, for example, you want to get some continuity to the testimony of any witness—we invite you to stop the proceedings and ask questions, and I am sure Mr. Gates, Mr. Weiss, and myself will do everything we can to present to you the factual situation which led to this hearing.

That was all I had by way of prefatory remarks, Mr. Gates. If you have anything, you can say it now; if not I will call our first witness.

(Certain exhibits were introduced into the record for the board's perusal, such as Whitacre's decision and L.G. Fritz's decision. Then Mr. Weiss took the floor.)

Mr. Weiss: I call Captain Anderson.

Mr. Gates: Let's be clear about this now, Mr. Weiss. You are calling Captain Anderson as your witness. You are bound by his testimony and you will, therefore, conduct your examination by direct examination rather than by cross-examination.

Mr. Weiss: I don't so concede that is the position at all, Mr. Gates.

(Several pages of argument followed between my attorney, Mr. Weiss, and Mr. Gates relative to the binding character of Captain Anderson's testimony and the burden of proof which the company had, as I have said before, pushed on the association. This was anticipated by Schy and Weiss, but they decided to, in the end, accept Anderson for direct examination in order to get a repeat of his testimony at Tulsa and lay a trap for Anderson with the testimony of Margaret Seamore. Schy and I had been very tight-lipped about her testifying and, as far as I know Mr. Behncke was the only other one who knew. I had not even told Schustman.)

Mr. Weiss: Captain Anderson, I want to make this quite clear to you in fairness to yourself: I, although not present at the previous hearings, have read your testimony, so the questions I may ask you, while in some instances may touch on your prior testimony, it is not because I am unaware of what you have previously said, do you see?

Q Captain Anderson, when did you first become aware of any situation with respect to Captain Allison's flight of September 7th?

Mr. Gates: What do you mean by "any situation?"

Mr. Weiss: Anything out of the routine, or anything which you considered out of routine order.

A When I saw the F-27 on my desk.

Q When was that, sir?

A I don't remember the exact date at this time. I think I can refresh my memory here. I am not sure as to the exact date, maybe I said it here. The 10th or 11th of September.

Q Am I correct in supposing that you received that F-27 from Los Angeles by mail? Is that right?

A I presume so, I don't know how it came.

Q And then when did you first speak with Captain Allison after having seen the F-27?

Mr. Gates: Do you mean face to face?

Q Either by telephone or face to face?

A I don't remember the date. To the best of my recollection I talked with Captain Allison on the phone. I don't remember the date exactly.

Q And when you spoke to him on the telephone, were you at your office in Tulsa?

A I believe so.

Q Did you call him or did he call you?

A My memory is that I called him.

Q Do you recall where he was when you called him?

A I believe it was Claremore.

Q Claremore, is that what you said?

A I believe so.

Q Would you know how long in time after you received the F-27 on—I think you said September 10th or 11th—it was that you called him?

A No, I don't recall.

Q At that occasion did you discuss with Captain Allison the matter of this flight? What was the flight number in question, Captain Anderson? Do you recall?

A Flight 49.

Q Did you discuss Flight 49 with Captain Allison?

A Since you have been asking me these questions it seems to me that I called Captain Allison in San Francisco while he was on a trip.

Q At that time did you discuss Flight 49 with Captain Allison?

A Not in detail.

Q What was the purpose of your call?

A I removed him from schedule pending investigation.

Q Did you call him to advise him that you had removed him from schedule?

A Yes.

Q And you did advise him that you were removing him from schedule, is that right?

A Yes.

Q Before you advised him of that in that telephone call, did you discuss with him any of the matters relating to Flight 49?

A Not in detail.

Q Did you discuss it at all?

A Naturally I discussed it because that was the subject of the telephone conversation, but the main purpose of it was to advise him that he was being removed from schedule pending an investigation, and that was about all that was said, as I recall.

Q That was about all that was said?

A As I recall.

Q When you said you didn't discuss it in detail, in effect you mean you didn't discuss what occurred on that flight?

Mr. Gates: That isn't what he testified to.

Mr. Weiss: Let's find out.

Q What did you discuss with Captain Allison other than to tell him he was removed from flight schedule?

A As I recall that was the substance of it. He was advised to deadhead home pending an investigation.

Q Is that the entire substance of your conversation?

A I don't recall the whole conversation.

Q As far as you recall?

A As far as I recall, yes.

Q Did there come a time after that when you saw Captain Allison face to face?

A I don't believe I saw him until the investigation.

Q Where was it that you saw him?

A In my office in Tulsa.

Q Who was present there?

A There were some six or eight people there. I don't recall all of those present at the time.

Q Company officials other than yourself?

A There were some six pilots in Tulsa and one Assistant Superintendent of Flight from Fort Worth.

Q Who was the Assistant Superintendent of Flight?

A Clyde McCall.

Q At that time did you go into Flight 49 in considerable detail?

A Yes.

Q Did you have copilot Duncan present?

A No, he was not present.

Q Did any of the other pilot personnel or the ones directly connected with the flight—or were they there as listeners and observers?

A Observers.

Q How long a time did you spend on that day, on the 14th in that investigation?

A I would estimate some two or three hours.

Q In the interim between the time that you had received the F-27 and the time that you met with Captain Allison in your office on September 14th, had you done any other investigatory work? Had you checked into the records or seen anybody?

A Yes.

Q Tell us what you did in that connection?

A I obtained the radio contacts from the various stations.

Q They were mailed to you, were they?

A Yes.

Q What else did you do?

A I talked with Captain Fagin in Los Angeles in part of it.

Q Captain Fagin, who occupies what position?

A Superintendent of Flight of the Western Region.

Q Was Captain Fagin, do you know, at first hand familiar with this flight?

A He had knowledge of some of it.

Q What was the nature of your inquiry of Captain Fagin? What did you ask him?

A I don't recall what I did ask him now.

Q Do you recall what he told you?

A He told me the weather at the time and that the approach was missed by Captain Allison.

Q Did you get any written record of the approach procedure which occurred at that time?

A Approach procedure?

Q Yes, any record of the approach, did you get any written record showing what happened on that approach?

A I don't recall if I did now or not.

Mr. Gates: I take it you are still talking about the period up to September 14th?

Mr. Weiss: That is right, up to September 14th, yes.

Q Is there anything other than that that you did? You remember what you told us you did. You said you got the radio records, that you spoke to Captain Fagin. You had previously received the F-27, is that right?

A Yes.

Q What else, if anything, did you do to investigate this flight up to September 14th?

A I don't recall doing anything else at the present time.

Q Is it fair to assume, therefore, that when you spoke with Captain Allison on September 14th that you had in front of you, in the nature at least of documents, the F-27 and the flight contact records. Were those the only two documents that you had in front of you?

A I am not sure whether that is all I had in front of me or not.

Q Had you, before the hearing, or the investigation of September 14th, by that time altered Captain Allison's F-27 to insert the word "not"?

A No.

Q When did you do that?

A At some later date, I don't remember exactly the date.

Q Can you give us an estimate of time when after September 14th you made that alteration?

A   On or about the 18th.

Q   On September 14th is it a fact that you requested Captain Allison to give you a further or supplementary statement in connection with the F-27?

A   Yes.

Q   When did you get that from Captain Allison?

A   That day.

Mr. Gates: I think it might be well, Mr. Weiss, to insert that that is Exhibit 4, I believe, in that transcript you are referring to.

Mr. Weiss: The F-27 or the supplementary statement?

Mr. Gates: The supplementary statement

Mr. Weiss: Let the record so indicate.

Mr. Gates: Yes, it is Amalgamated's Exhibit no. 4 for the record to which Mr. Weiss is making reference in his examination, and the F-27 is Amalgamated Exhibit 2 and 3.

Q   After September 14th what did you do next in connection with this matter of Flight 49 or Captain Allison?

A   I can't recall what I did next.

Q   You don't remember?

A   No, not at this time.

Q   You don't remember what you did or when you did it?

A   I don't remember when I did it.

Q   Can you, perhaps, take it in order what you next did? You know that you had a hearing or an investigation in your office on September 14th. Can't you tell this board what next occurred as far as you know in this matter?

A   At some time, I don't remember the sequence, I made a trip to Los Angeles to investigate further the circumstances.

Q   With whom did you speak in Los Angeles in connection with this flight?

A   Mr. Fagin.

Q   Anyone else?

A   Mr. Pereira.

Q   Mr. Pereira is the flight dispatcher, isn't he?

A   Supervisor of Flight Dispatch.

Q   Anyone else?

A   I probably talked to twenty or thirty people out there, I don't know how many people I talked to.

Q I assume you will tell us those people you talked to whom you think of importance or significance?

A All right.

Q Am I to judge properly that Mr. Fagin and Mr. Pereira are of significance?

A They were two, yes.

Mr. Gates: Speak up a little, Captain, so you can be heard.

Q When you spoke to Mr. Pereira, did you go over with him the flight contact records?

A Sometime previous to that he had sent me a resume of the contact records.

Q Of course, that wasn't my question, was it, Captain? Will you answer my question?

A I probably did.

Q You don't recall whether you did or not?

A I don't recall.

Q Is it fair to assume that if you did it, you didn't do it so intensively so as to cause you to remember it now; is that right?

Mr. Gates: I object to your characterizing the witness's testimony. His testimony speaks for itself.

Mr. Weiss: Mr. Gates, it may speak for itself, but it is not sufficiently clear.

Mr. Gates: That is a matter of argument.

Mr. Weiss: Just a moment. It doesn't speak with sufficient clarity so that I can understand it. I asked the witness whether he recalls having gone over the flight contact records with Mr. Pereira.

Mr. Gates: He said he didn't recall.

Q I am asking you, Captain Anderson—let me put it this way; did you have the flight contact records with you when you went to Los Angeles?

A Yes.

Q Do you have any recollection of sitting down with Mr. Pereira and examining those flight contact records?

A I discussed them with him, whether I took the contact records and actually went down in detail I just don't remember.

Q All right.

A They were discussed.

Q You do remember having discussed the flight contact records?

A Yes.

Q You said before that you received Captain Allison's supplementary report on September 18th?

A No.

Q When did you receive it?

A On the 14th.

Q I am sorry. I meant to say September 14th. You then also said that you went to Los Angeles and saw various gentlemen including Mr. Fagin and Mr. Pereira. Then what did you next do in regard to this flight or Captain Allison?

Mr. Gates: Mr. Weiss, I am sure you are not trying to mislead the witness. I think he testified that he could not give you these things in sequence and you said, "what did you next do," and I think that is what is bothering the witness.

Mr. Weiss: I think the witness said that he couldn't tell us the time when he did these.

Mr. Gates: The sequence.

Mr. Weiss: Time, when he did them, but I would expect that the witness most assuredly, being a man technically trained, would know the order in which he did them. I didn't ask him a date. He didn't fix the date of his trip to the coast. Of course, if Captain Anderson cannot tell us that, I will have to accept that as an answer.

Q Do you know what you did?

A Not in the proper sequence.

Q You have some recollection of what you did, don't you? Give it to us the best you can.

A After I had gotten what I considered sufficient facts together, I called Captain Ogden on the telephone. This was before the investigation, understand.

Q You called Captain Ogden before the investigation?

A Yes.

Q What did you tell Captain Ogden and what did he tell you?

A I gave him as much detail as I had at the time concerning the conduct of the flight.

Q Did either of you gentlemen or both of you come to any decision or agreement at that time?

A Yes.

Q What was that decision?

A To remove Captain Allison from schedule pending an investigation.

Q Was that before you went to the coast to speak to Mr. Fagin and Mr. Pereira?

A Yes.

Q What did you next do that you recall, or what did you do if you can't recall it in sequence?

A You mean in connection with the investigation—in connection with the incident; is that correct?

Q Yes.

A I went to Fort Worth to see Captain Ogden.

Q Before going to Fort Worth, had you come to any decision as to the question of discharge of Captain Allison?

A Yes.

Q And that decision, I take it, was your personal decision? You had not yet consulted or advised anyone of your position?

A No.

Q Can you tell us, please, when you came to the decision that you would recommend discharge of Captain Allison?

A I don't recall.

Q Do you know about how much before it was that you went to Los Angeles that you made this decision?

A No.

Q Did you reduce your personal decision to a memorandum? Did you put it down in writing before going to see Don Ogden?

A You mean, did I write it on paper?

Q That is right.

A No, not that I recall.

Q If you did would you recall?

A Possibly.

Q You might not or might recall?

A I may or may not have written it down. I don't think I did.

Q When you went to see Don Ogden, had you by that time been to the west coast to see Mr. Fagin and Mr. Pereira?

A I had been to the west coast.

Q To see Mr. Fagin and Mr. Pereira?

A No.

Q I asked you whether you had been to the west coast for that purpose?

A You asked two questions in one.

Q I am sorry if my question was confusing. Had you, before seeing Don Ogden'been to the west coast to see and actually having seen Mr. Fagin and Mr. Pereira?

A Repeat that again?

Q Before going to see Don Ogden, had you seen Mr. Fagin and Mr. Pereira as you previously testified?

A No, I hadn't seen them.

Q When you saw Don Ogden did he concur in your decision to recommend the discharge of Captain Allison?

A Yes.

Q Was that decision reduced to writing, was there a memorandum made of your mutual agreement on that?

A No.

Q What next did you do in connection with this flight or Captain Allison?

A I went to New York.

Q Is that the occasion on which you went to see Walter Braznell, Captain Braznell?

A Yes.

Q What was the purpose of your going to New York?

A To make known the facts in the case.

Q To advise him of your decision and Don Ogden's decision?

A He had previously been advised of that by phone.

Q Did he concur as well?

A Yes.

Q Did you speak with him by phone or did Don Ogden speak with him by phone.

A Captain Ogden.

Q And Captain Braznell concurred; is that correct?

A Yes.

Q Was that telephone call to Captain Braznell made at the time when you were in Captain Ogden's office in Fort Worth?

A No.

Q Was it made before or after you saw Captain Ogden?

A It was made while I was with him.

Q With whom, Captain Ogden?

A Yes.

Q Perhaps you didn't understand my question. In other words, if I understand you correctly, you went to see Captain Ogden, you advised him of your decision in Captain Allison's case—I am summarizing of course—he concurred in that decision and, as I understand it, he, Captain Ogden, telephoned Captain Braznell and advised him of your mutual or joint decision?

A That is right.

Q And secured at that time Captain Braznell's additional agreement of concurrence; is that right?

A I don't know that Captain Braznell concurred at that time.

Q I thought you said a moment ago that he did?

A Not at that time.

Q Perhaps I misunderstood you.

A That was the purpose of my trip to New York, to advise him of the facts.

Q Then, you got to New York. Did you eventually secure Captain Braznell's agreement to this discharge?

A Captain Braznell in his capacity—I went there to check precedent and not necessarily—or I did not go there to get his concurrence.

Q I see.

A It was more to make known the facts to him before we took action.

Q Is it fair to assume, therefore, that it was your view and it is your view that you and Captain Ogden singly or jointly had the authority to effect the discharge without getting Captain Braznell's approval or concurrence; is that correct?

A That is right. There was one other step through Captain McFail, who was the regional operational director.

Q Had you seen Mr. Fagin and Mr. Pereira before going to see Captain Braznell?

A No I hadn't seen him.

Q In other words, this visit about which you were telling us before had not occurred; is that right?

A That is right. I believe that is correct.

Q You said you went to see Captain Braznell in New York City to check the precedent, I think that is the way you put it; is that right?

A Yes.

Q Will you explain to the board what you meant by "checking the precedent"?

A The authority to discharge rests with the regions of the Amalgamated Airlines. Mr. Braznell has no authority to discharge. We do, however, make known the facts to him in case of disciplinary action before we take it.

Q Is that what you mean by "checking the precedent"?

A Yes.

Q So that to all intents and purposes, as far as authority was concerned, the persons having the power to discharge had already come to a conclusion, which was effected within the tabled organization before you saw Captain Braznell?

Mr. Gates: Wait a minute. That certainly is a leading and compounded question. If you want to testify to that and characterize it that way I haven't any objection, but I don't think you ought to ask the captain to do that. That isn't what he has testified to at all.

Mr. Weiss: The captain said "yes," at least he nodded his head.

Q Is it a fact, Captain Anderson, that as you understand it, you had the authority to discharge Captain Allison; is that correct?

A I have the authority to make the recommendation.

Q Who has the authority to approve that recommendation?

A Captain Ogden through Captain McFail.

Q Having cleared that recommendation through Captains Ogden and McFail, though, there is complete power to effect a discharge at that point?

A Yes.

Q So it is a fact, is it not, that the persons having the power to effect the discharge of Captain Allison had determined upon his discharge prior to your going to see Captain Braznell?

A Yes.

Q What record did you take with you when you went to see Captain Braznell?

A Captain Allison's file.

Q Did you take the F-27 in question?

A Yes.

Q Did you take the flight contact records?

A Yes.

Q I believe those flight contact records are in evidence, aren't they?

Mr. Gates: They are Amalgamated's Exhibit No. 5.

Mr. Weiss: Mark this for identification. (Summary of flight contact records marked Association's Exhibit No. 21 for identification.)

Q Did you prepare this summary of flight contact records, which is Association's Exhibit No. 21 for identification?

A I believe they were prepared in my office.

Q Was it prepared under your direction?

A I think so, yes, as I recall.

Q Did you give the instructions for its preparation?

A Yes.

Q Do these flight contact records represent duplicate transmissions received at different bases?

A I don't know what you have there.

Q I have the flight contact records.

A That is true and there were three flight stations.

Q And they would be duplicates; is that correct?

A They should be.

Q Would you look at those, Captain Anderson, and pick out for us the transmission which bears the time 0643?

A All right, I have two of them. This is 0742, which is about 0743 as we show here, and 0744.

Q Did you understand me to say 0743 or 0643?

A 743.

Chairman Day: That is all Pacific time.

Q I didn't realize you had corrected this to the time. May I see them? How long had you been based at Tulsa, Captain Anderson?

A Four years in November.

Q During that time how many pilots were based at Tulsa, Captain Anderson?

Mr. Gates: Do you mean different ones?

Q No, I mean what are the total number of pilots at the base?

A The number I have now?

Q No, I will say in September of 1951.

A Approximately forty-four, forty-five.

Q Were you the official of the company who had, so to speak, the most direct or immediate dealing with the pilots?

A Of the pilots in Tulsa.

Q That, of course, includes Captain Allison doesn't it?

A Yes.

Q During the time that you conducted or at the time that you conducted this investigation or investigatory hearing on September 14th, did you inquire of Captain Allison why he went on to Los Angeles?

A Yes.

Q What did he tell you?

A He said he thought it was a safer procedure.

Q Did he give you any other reasons?

A Not that I recall at the present time.

Q Was there any discussion at all, Captain, as to the question of availability of equipment at Los Angeles?

A You mean did I question him?

Q Was there any discussion at that time as to the consideration of passengers that were on the plane?

A I am not sure.

Q Captain Anderson, before coming to the decision that you made to recommend the dismissal of Captain Allison, did you consider what reasons may have existed for Captain Allison's continuing on to Los Angeles?

A Other than what he told me.

Q Did you take into consideration any reasons of convenience for the company or for the passengers?

A I did not.

Q Have you flown the line, Captain Anderson?

A Yes.

Q For how long a time?

A For how long a time? You mean how long have I been with Amalgamated?

Q No, how long did you fly the line?

A Approximately two years.

Q You, of course, are aware, are you not, that considerations existed and do exist now which might make Los Angeles, let us say, more convenient and appropriate than some other base in which to let the airplane down?

A You mean convenience for passengers?

Q And for the company.

A That is not to be considered in this case.

Q Sir?

A That is not to be considered.

Q That was not my question, was it, Captain?

A Would you repeat the question, please?

Q I said are you aware that there are such considerations?

Mr. Gates: I am going to object to that question. I thought I would let you go into it once, but not twice. Let us quit leading the witness and ask him questions. If there are considerations, what are they?

Mr. Weiss: Mr. Gates, I have this rather curious feeling that I will ask my questions and you may ask yours.

Q Captain Anderson, are you aware of any considerations which affect company policy or determine at what base you let a plane down?

Mr. Gates: Under what circumstances?

Mr. Weiss: Let the Captain answer the question and then we will get more specific.

A I wish you would.

Q You are troubled by that question, are you?

A Yes, I am.

Q Let's put it this way: Before you made your decision in the Allison case, your own personal decision to recommend discharge, did you consider that it might have been to the interest of the company with respect to equipment availability to put the plane down at Los Angeles?

Mr. Gates: Objected to as being completely speculative.

Mr. Weiss: I fail to see how it is speculative. I have asked the Captain whether he considered that. Now, if he did consider it, he may say so. If he did not, the Board should also know that.

Chairman Day: Answer the question. Did you consider it or didn't you?

A In my decision to release Allison you are asking me if I considered company convenience, was that your question?

Mr. Weiss: Would you repeat my question, Mr. Reporter?

(The question was read by the reporter.)

A No.

Q Before coming to your decision to recommend the discharge of Captain Allison, did you take into consideration any company policy with respect to the advancement of a flight, notwithstanding the fact of one engine being out?

Mr. Gates: I will object to that until you show there is such a policy.

Mr. Weiss: I think the Captain certainly should be qualified to state.

Chairman Day: Ask him if there is such a policy.

Q Is there such a policy? Is there such a policy of advancing the flight? Do you understand what I mean by the policy?

A Yes, I have heard it before.

Q Are you aware of such a Policy?

A There is none in existence to my knowledge.

Q I didn't ask you whether there was one now in existence. I am asking you as of that time.

Mr. Gates: As of September, 1951.

A No.

Q Was there ever such a policy, Captain Anderson?

A Not that I know of.

Q May I understand that your answer is that you say under oath that you are aware of no such policy of advancing the flight in the event of an engine malfunctioning?

A No, sir, I know of no policy.

Q Obviously, since you knew of no such policy and know of none, you couldn't consider it; is that correct?

A Yes.

Q That didn't even come into your mind; is that right?

A That is right.

Mr. Weiss: I would like to have this marked for identification.

(A photostated document consisting of four pages was marked for identification as Association's Exhibit No. 22 for identification.)

Q Captain Anderson, I show you the first page of Association's Exhibit No. 22 for identification, which bears on the top of it the date 16 December, 1947.

Mr. Gates: Just a minute, I am going to object to this because you are seeking to impeach your own witness. He has testified that he didn't know of any such policy and now you are seeking to introduce in evidence some kind of a document by which you are seeking to impeach and discredit him.

Mr. Weiss: Mr. Gates, I think you are doing a very unfortunate thing. May I point out to the Board that this is one of the natural consequences that Mr. Gates was arguing for in the first instance. In other words, we are now going to presume that this witness is for all purposes ours and to use it as a basis of excluding from this Board proper evidence for its consideration, then, I strenuously object to any such proceeding. It is our purpose to get everything before this board that is proper, and, moreover, I may say this: Mr. Gates well knows, as an attorney, that under any interpretation this man is regarded as a hostile witness. It is my purpose to continue to introduce it.

Mr. Gates: Mr. Weiss, there has been no showing that Captain Anderson is hostile.

Mr. Weiss: I think a reading of the record will indicate his complete hostility.

Mr. Gates: Not at all.

Mr. Weiss: I don't think you seriously mean that, Mr. Gates.

Mr. Gates: You can read my mind better than I can?

Mr. Weiss: I may say to you that we advisedly will go further to demonstrate it. I have asked the question and I ask for a ruling of the Board.

Chairman Day: You are asking the witness to identify that?

Mr. Weiss: Actually I started to call his attention to the first page of this exhibit for identification, consisting of four pages, and I was going to proceed further and question him upon this paper.

Chairman Day: The Board rules that he can identify that.

Q   Captain Anderson, I am gong to read to you the first page of Association's Exhibit No. 22 for identification and ask you whether or not you have any recollection of having seen this or heard or read it previously. It is addressed to the chief pilot from Captain Wayne Nelson Allison and is headed: "Engine out operation."

"Out of Washington, on Trip Two, of December 9, 1947, pressure on No. 4 went to 30. Tested gauge—"

Chairman Day: What is the date of that?

Mr. Weiss: December 16, 1947.

Mr. Gates: I object to that as being immaterial and irrelevant to this proceeding.

Chairman Day: I think that it is relevant. Mr. Weiss is trying to establish—

Mr. Gates: Let's not waste time, go ahead.

Mr. Weiss: "Out of Washington, on Trip Two of December 9, 1947, pressure on No. 4 went to 30. Tested gauge and found it OK.

Feathered engine. Requested three engine clearance from Philadelphia to New York. Clearance was refused by Flight Superintendent at New York. We landed in Philadelphia with fifty passengers in compliance with company regulations. Some time later cleared to New York, after discovering loose oil line as cause of low oil pressure."

Under the line for the signature is: "W.N. Allison."

Q Do you have any recollection of having seen that or heard of it before my reading it to you just now?

A I think so, I remember it.

Q I ask you whether with respect to the second page of this, which is under date of December 23, 1947, on the interoffice correspondence the letterhead of Amalgamated Airlines, addressed to Superintendent of Flying from Assistant Chief Pilot and is headed: "Engine out operation."

"Attached please note engine out report from Captain Wayne Nelson Allison.

"In this case I feel it would have been entirely in order and a reasonable operation to proceed to New York. However, the regulation as written, does not leave any choice. I would appreciate some clarification on this matter. Joe S. Anderson, copy to Chief Pilot and Captain Allison."

Q Do you have a recollection of having seen that?

A Yes.

Q Is that actually a memorandum which you sealed, signed, and transmitted?

A It seems to me it is, yes.

Q Then, I wish to read to you from the third page of this Exhibit under the date of January 30, 1948. It is also on the interoffice correspondence letterhead of Amalgamated Airlines to Captain Wayne Nelson Allison from Assistant Chief Pilot, subject "Engine out — 4-engine aircraft."

"Wayne: Please note the attached letter from Dunn. Seems that the flight superintendent was not up on his policy when he ordered you into Philadelphia. Kindly return this for my future reference. Joe S. Anderson."

Q Do you recall having written that?

A Yes.

Q I want to read to you the last page of this exhibit under date of

January 26, 1948, on the same letterhead of Amalgamated Airlines to
Assistant Chief Pilot - Tulsa, from Superintendent of Flying. Subject:
"Engine out — 4-Engine Aircraft."

"With reference to your letter of January 19th on the above subject,
we should like to advise that the proper interpretation relative to this
matter requires that aircraft land at a suitable airport. We have briefed
all of our dispatchers and requested that they give this a liberal
interpretation, thereby permitting the captain to use discretion in the
selection of a suitable airport. This interpretation means that the pilot
may select an airport which will advance the flight. We cannot,
however, publish this policy. Signed, W.H. Dunn."

Q   Do you have a recollection of having seen that, Captain
Anderson?

A   Yes.

Mr. Weiss: I offer these in evidence.

Mr. Gates: I object. They are immaterial to this proceeding and
have no bearing whatsoever upon a case which arose in 1951 in the
month of September unless it shows that that same piece of paper is
still in effect.

Chairman Day: The objection is overruled. It is up to you to show
that it still isn't in effect. It is admitted in evidence.

(Association's Exhibit No. 22 for identification received in evidence.)

Q   Captain Anderson, are you aware of any other memoranda or
communications by the company or its officials having to do with the
policy of advancing the flight?

A   No.

Q   You testified previously that you knew of no such policy; have
you forgotten about these letters or memoranda which are now in
evidence?

A   No, I hadn't forgotten about them.

Q   You had them in mind?

A   Yes.

Q   Do you now say that no other memoranda or communications
issued by the company having to do with the policy of advancing the
flight exist?

A   If I understand you correctly, no.

Q   Is there any doubt in your mind as to what I am inquiring about?

A Yes, there is.

Q What is that doubt?

A I don't know exactly to what you are referring.

Q By that do you mean that you don't know what I mean when I say a policy of advancing the flight; you don't understand that part of it?

A No, not exactly.

Q Then, will you be good enough to look at the last page over the signature of Mr. Dunn and see whether you can understand it from your official's statement?

A Yes, I previously testified that I had cognizance of this letter.

Q I asked you not that, Captain Anderson. You said there was some doubt about what I was talking about. Do you now understand what I mean by advancing a flight and a company policy in that connection?

A I know of no policy, this letter is the only reference to anything of that nature that I am aware of.

Q Having received this letter, you did receive it, didn't you?

A Yes.

Q You then became aware, did you not, that there was, at least, an unpublished policy of advancing the flights?

Mr. Gates: Wait a minute, that isn't what it says. It says the policy can't be published, but doesn't mean that there is an unpublished policy.

Mr. Weiss: Sometimes, Mr. Gates, unconscious humor is the best of all.

Mr. Gates: Isn't it, though; let's all laugh.

Q How about that, Captain Anderson, having received that memorandum did it mean to you, as an official of the company, that the company in that memorandum at least, was declaring that it had an interest in advancing the flight and that it had an unpublished policy to that effect?

A It had an interest in advancing the flight.

Q How do you interpret the phrase: "We cannot, however, publish this policy?" Did that mean that they had a policy to that effect? How did you interpret it?

A I interpreted it that they didn't want everybody outside of the company getting hold of that—

Q Did it mean, however—

A And some people within the company.

Q And some people within the company.

A Yes.

Q But was there any doubt in your mind when you saw this memorandum that there was such a policy, whether it was published or not?

A No, I don't think so.

(During the afternoon, from the time that Captain Anderson was called to testify, the semi-full room of people had remained seated and gradually became quieter and quieter as Weiss extracted this important disclosure from Anderson. The slightest sound would carry throughout the room. Now several rose to find restrooms, shaking their heads in disbelief. Mr. Weiss then took up another subject.)

Q What type of personnel files do you keep on the pilots in Tulsa?

A Standard personnel files that are set up for pilot personnel.

Q Were they kept under your supervision?

A Yes.

Q Is it part of your job to maintain personnel files?

A That is right.

Q Am I correct in assuming that those personnel files covered all the pilots based at Tulsa; is that correct?

A That is right.

Q Will you describe to the Board physically how they were kept and were they kept in filing cabinets, were they kept in paper files?

A In filing cabinets and paper files within the filing cabinets.

Q One file for each pilot; is that right?

A That's right.

Q Did you ever recommend any disciplinary action against Mr. Pereira?

Mr. Gates: Objected to as being immaterial and outside the issues of this case.

Chairman Day: Sustained.

Mr. Weiss: I will tell the Board now that we will have definitely established its materiality and bearing upon this.

Mr. Gates: What is its materiality?

Mr. Weiss: I don't believe I am required to state the ultimate purport of my inquiry.

Chairman Day: I don't see any connection with it to this case. What he recommended to Mr. Pereira.

Mr. Weiss: It very often happens and this is one such instance in which counsel must be permitted preliminary questions in order to lead up to a point and it would obviously destroy the validity of any series of questions to divulge the ultimate object I have in mind.

Chairman Day: Off the record.

(Thereupon a short recess was taken.)

Chairman Day: We will resume the record. Mr. Weiss, the Board rules that in the form in which you have phrased your question it is not material. It is not Mr. Anderson's function to recommend disciplinary action for any people except those that are under his control, and Mr. Pereira is not under his control.

Mr. Weiss: All right.

Q Who was Mr. Pereira's superior at that time?

A Mr. Mace.

Q Where in the echelon of command did Mr. Fagin stand?

A He is also under Mr. Mace.

Q Is he the immediate superior of Mr. Pereira?

A Mr. Mace?

Q Mr. Fagin.

A Yes, he has authority over him.

Q You spoke of Mr. Fagin; didn't you?

A Yes.

Q And speaking of Mr. Fagin, you discussed flight 49, did you not, you have already told us that.

A Yes.

Q In discussing flight 49 with Mr. Fagin I think you already told us that you already had in your possession at that time the flight contact records, did you not?

A Yes.

Q I ask you if in your discussion with Mr. Fagin did the question of disciplining Mr. Pereira come up in any way in that discussion?

A No.

Q Did you directly or indirectly suggest to Mr. Fagin that Mr. Pereira be disciplined?

Mr. Gates: Objected to as being immaterial and outside the issues of this proceeding.

Chairman Day: Sustained. It is the same question.

Q Did Mr. Fagin indicate to you that there was any disposition on his part to discipline Mr. Pereira?

Mr. Gates: Objected to as calling for a hearsay answer.

Mr. Weiss: It can scarcely be hearsay.

Chairman Day: Sustained.

Mr. Gates: What Fagin told him.

Mr. Weiss: May I be permitted to finish my explanation?

Chairman Day: Go ahead.

Mr. Weiss: I am asking Captain Anderson what he personally heard. He is going to relate, if he is permitted to answer the question, what he heard of his own knowledge and that is not hearsay.

Chairman Day: Do you still wish to object?

Mr. Gates: I certainly do.

Chairman Day: Off the record.

(Discussion off the record.)

Chairman Day: Resume the record. You asked him if he heard Mr. Fagin say.

Mr. Weiss: That is correct.

Mr. Gates: May I be heard on that? He is seeking to prove by his statement, not the fact that Mr. Fagin may have made some statement, but he is trying to prove the truth of that statement.

Chairman Day: He asked the question; did he hear him say anything about it.

Mr. Gates: There is no showing that he did make such a statement.

Chairman Day: Read the question again, please.

(The question was read by the reporter.)

Mr. Gates: He is assuming facts not in evidence.

Mr. Weiss: I am not assuming anything; I am asking whether those facts existed.

Chairman Day: Read the question to the witness.

(Question read by the reporter.)

A I think I can.

Chairman Day: I think he can testify to that.

Mr. Gates: It is hearsay testimony, I submit.

Chairman Day: Go ahead.

A No.

Q What connection can you tell this Board Mr. Pereira had with the conduct of this flight 49?

A He came on duty some time after the difficulty existed. I believe it was around eight o'clock, I am not sure about that time. I could check the records. He relieved the flight superintendent who was on duty initially.

Q What did he do in connection with the flight?

A I don't know other than what is in the record.

Q Let's discuss what is in the record.

A What do you wish to know?

Q I want to know what connection Mr. Pereira had with this flight 49? Do you understand my question?

A He was flight superintendent of the flight dispatcher on duty.

Q As such is it the fact that he received the transmissions and in turn caused transmissions to be sent to the flight?

A Yes, indirectly.

Q I don't mean direct, but he did cause it to come about; isn't that so?

A Yes.

Q On the summary of the flight contact records, which was prepared under your supervision, you have that in front of you; don't you?

A Yes.

Q Will you examine that and tell the Board whether you find anything in the record which indicates that the flight dispatcher recommended any redirection or instructed any redirection of the flight.

A No.

Q In coming to your conclusion, your personal conclusion to recommend the discharge of Captain Allison, did you consider the provisions of the company manual, Section 4822, dealing with redirection of flight—I will read it to you Captain Anderson, accurately, which says: "Consistent with safety the captain shall comply with any redirection of flight requested by flight dispatcher."

Q Did you consider that?

A What was the reference again?

Q Section 4822.

Mr. Weiss: Read the question.

(Question read by the reporter.)

A No.

Q Captain Anderson, in coming to your personal conclusion to recommend the dismissal of Captain Allison, did you take into consideration the rule of the company manual, Section 4894, dealing with clearance, which provides: "Flight shall not continue toward point cleared to if either captain or flight dispatcher feels that the flight cannot be continued in safety."

Q Did you consider that?

A No sir.

Q Captain Anderson, in coming to your personal conclusion to recommend the dismissal of Captain Allison, did you consider the provisions of the company manual, Section 4006, which provides: "If the flight dispatcher does not agree that the Captain's procedure is the best possible, he shall so advise the captain."

Q Did you consider that provision?

A No sir.

Q Captain Anderson, when you discussed the matter of your recommendation for the dismissal of Captain Allison with Captain Ogden, did you take those three provisions into your considerations and discussions?

A No sir.

Q Were those provisions discussed with Captain McFail?

A No sir.

Q Were those provisions discussed with Captain Braznell?

A No sir.

Q Were you aware of the existence of those provisions?

A Yes sir.

Q Were you present at the time that Mr. Pereira testified?

A Yes sir; I believe part of that time.

Q I read to you, Captain Anderson, from Mr. Pereira's testimony: "Sometimes we find it advisable in most malfunctions to reroute the air flight, to have the plane land and have the equipment changed, particularly where its destination may be a point where it may be turned around for another flight; at the larger fields it might be repaired, as they don't have the equipment at many of these small airports."

Q I ask you whether or not you agree or disagree with Mr. Pereira's statement?

A Not entirely.

Q With what part do you disagree?

A Mr. Pereira's duty is advisory.

Q I asked you what part of that statement you disagree with?

A If I interpret correctly what he is saying, he is implying that he has the sole authority to direct flights. I don't agree with that.

Q Do you concede, Captain Anderson, that he had any authority or responsibility in the direction of flights?

A He can only suggest.

Q Do you find any suggestion in the flight contact record?

A Yes, there is some suggestion there.

Q Will you point out, please, what suggestions were made?

A The contact 0858, Los Angeles to ship.

Q Will you read what that suggestion is?

A "Believe best to hold here."

Q "Here" means where?

A He was over the outer beacon marker, I believe, at the time.

Q At Los Angeles?

A Yes.

Q Is that the sole suggestion that you find?

A That is all, yes.

Q So that as you read the flight contact record, the sole suggestion that you find in that record made by the flight dispatcher to Captain Allison was: "Believe best to hold here"?

A That is right.

Q I read to you from page 43 of Mr. Pereira's testimony—

Mr. Gates: Excuse me, I think that the reference you just read from was page 43.

Mr. Weiss: 42 is what I have. In any case, if you are reading from the inner marker I will read from the inner marker as well.

Mr. Gates: Fine.

Q I read to you from page 44, the next succeeding page, in any case Captain Anderson, of Mr. Pereira's testimony in which he states: "Our responsibility is to give the pilot all the information that we can, that we have available that will aid him in deciding on which route or which airport he wants to proceed to with a 3-engine aircraft."

Q Do you agree with that?

A Yes sir.

Q Now, then, I read to you from page 46 in which the question is put to Mr. Pereira as follows: "In this last case would you have authority to redirect the flight?

"Answer: Not while the captain was exercising his authority to proceed to the point of his landing. I could redirect if, in my opinion, I thought redirection might be helpful to the captain in his arriving at a better decision or election of another airport, but I could issue nothing to the captain that he would have to abide by."

Q Do you agree with that?

A I will repeat: The superintendent of flight dispatcher's authority is advisory.

Q I am sorry, but I must ask you to answer my question, Captain Anderson. Do you agree with his statement?

A Not entirely, no.

Q Let's see, Captain Anderson, as you conceive the flight dispatcher's authority. Is it your understanding that he is charged with any responsibility to suggest, let us say, to the captain that the plane be landed at a destination other than that which the captain has elected to use?

A Yes, he may suggest.

Q I asked you whether he had any responsibility to make a suggestion?

A I would say yes.

Q Would you also say that he would be charged with such a responsibility if, in his opinion, the course which the captain elected was not safe; would he have a responsibility to suggest to the captain a different place for landing?

A Yes sir.

Q Do you find in the flight contact records any such suggestion?

A No.

(In this course of questioning Mr. Weiss brought out that I had followed the wishes of the company as disclosed in Mr. Pereira's testimony by taking the airplane where other equipment was available and at the same time "advancing the flight.")

Then Mr. Weiss began questioning Anderson relative to his filing system on the pilots based at Tulsa. He was laying the foundation for our surprise witness, Margaret Seamore.

Anderson acknowledged that the cabinets containing the folders on the Tulsa-based pilots were only two or three steps from his desk, but he did keep a separate folder on Captains Allison and Schustman in the bottom drawer to his desk, insisting that it was used for the separate incidents as they came up. He acknowledged that he started the file when I began filing grievances, which, as chairman of the Tulsa base, I was doing on behalf of the pilots at Tulsa. He became very evasive as the questioning continued.

At five-fifteen that afternoon the hearing recessed until nine-thirty the following day, January 24, 1952. I went to dinner with Schy and Weiss and then spent a couple of hours going over records and reports with them, in preparation for the next day.

The following morning the hearing was resumed and Captain Joe S. Anderson continued as the witness. Over a hundred pages of testimony then went into the record with Mr. Weiss going into Anderson's filing system, investigation into the flight 49 of September 7th, changes made in some of the messages and the fact that my file only contained critical items in Anderson's possession. Somehow, he did not have a letter of commendation to me from a company vice-president and claimed he had never seen it before it was shown to him on the witness stand. But it was in my file with a notation that it was going into my personnel file and I had received a copy of it. Anderson did not have it.

Much time was consumed in direct testimony, cross and recross examinations by the attorneys. Finally, in the afternoon, Captain Anderson was excused from the witness chair.

Chapter 20

The Surprise Witness

Mr. Weiss asked for a few minutes recess to call a surprise witness. Mr. Schy left the hearing room while the audience stirred, buzzed in anticipation. Mr. Gates, Captains Anderson and Ogden, who had come in shortly after the noon hour, huddled at the attorney's table. It was easy to see that they were completely mystified.

Mr. Schy returned in a few minutes escorting Margaret Seamore who was dressed in a trim business suit. Her small shoes with low heels made her look insignificant alongside Schy's tall frame. In a very attentive manner he guided her to the witness chair after having her sworn in by the certified reporter. I could see Mr. Gates asking Anderson her identity as Margaret settled in the witness chair. A few of the pilots who had been flying in and out of Tulsa knew her and the word was flashed around the room.

Mr. Weiss approached the witness chair with a smile and began the questioning in direct examination.

Questions by Mr. Weiss:

Q Miss Seamore, were you at one time an employee of Amalgamated Airlines?

A Yes sir.

Q When did you come into the employ of Amalgamated Airlines?

A December 7, 1947.

Q How long did you continue in their employ?

A Until September 29, 1951

Q On or about or shortly prior to September 28, 1951, is it a fact that you were discharged by Amalgamated Airlines?

A That was the date.

Q While you were in the employ of Amalgamated Airlines, what was your job?

A Secretary for the Chief Pilot.

Q Was that secretary to Captain Anderson, specifically?

A Yes sir.

Q Miss Seamore, although I address you as "Miss Seamore," you are married, are you?

A Divorcee.

Q Have your expenses been paid to come to this hearing?

A Yes sir.

Q And who paid or has assured you that your expenses will be paid?

A All I have received so far is a round trip ticket, but I have been told my hotel bill will be paid.

Q Have you been told that the Air Line Pilots' Association would pay your expenses?

A I assume they are the ones, that is right.

Q And have you been promised or assured of any payment of any kind for your attendance here as a witness or otherwise other than your actual expenses?

A Not in any manner.

Q Miss Seamore, after your discharge from Amalgamated Airlines, did you make any effort to secure reemployment by Amalgamated Airlines?

A About four or five different times and ways. I said—she raised her low voice—at least three or four times I have asked to be reinstated.

Q Has it been your desire and intention to secure reemployment by Amalgamated Airlines?

A Yes, definitely.

Q Are you conscious of the fact, Miss Seamore, that by reason of your being a witness here that you may be prejudiced seriously in securing reemployment by Amalgamated Airlines?

Mr. Gates: I object to that as being immaterial and being outside the purview of this case.

Chairman Day: I will sustain that.

Q Miss Seamore, how does it happen, you tell the Board how you were contacted and were requested to be here as a witness?

Mr. Gates: I don't understand that question: "How does it happen." You mean who contacted her, what do you mean?

Q Miss Seamore—

A I will answer it—

Q Just a moment, there is an objection. I will put it this way:
When did you first meet me, will you tell the Board?

A The day before yesterday.

Q And when we met, did we discuss the matter of your testimony
at this hearing?

A Yes.

Q Now before you and I met, did you discuss the matter of your
testifying with anyone else?

A With this attorney here.

Q This gentleman on my left, Mr. Schy?

A Yes, Mr. Schy.

Q Did you discuss it with Captain Allison?

A Yes sir, at the same time; they were together.

Q Can you tell the Board briefly how you were contacted as a
possible witness in this hearing?

A When the hearing on the release of Captain Allison ended at the
Tulsa Hotel, that was in October, just immediately after it was over,
why, I had guests at my home that were members of the flight division,
and one of the gentlemen came in and said—I mean his wife was with
me at that time—and he said, "Well, they have released Wayne
Allison." That is the first time I knew that he had been meant to be
released from the company. So, shortly after that, we sat there and
talked for an hour, probably, of what had happened at the hearing with
this pilot. And shortly after that the telephone rang and Captain Allison
said, "Margaret, in the hearing Captain Anderson has testified that you
made some changes on a report that has come up in the hearing, and
would you mind if we come out and talk to you a few minutes?"

I said, "I will be glad to see you." When he came out, why, there
was a discussion on it.

Q Who was it that came out, Miss Seamore?

A Mr. Schy and Captain Allison.

Q Did they discuss with you what you knew about that matter?

A Thoroughly.

Q At that time, did they indicate to you that they might want you
as a witness in this proceeding?

A They asked me if I would be willing to state what I had told them, and I told them I would.

Q Miss Seamore, in your job as secretary to Captain Anderson, did you have any dealing or contacts with the personnel files of the pilots of the Tulsa base?

A I was the only one who did have anything whatsoever to do with any of the pilot files, and I was the only one who held a key to the cabinet except Captain Anderson, and he had given me specific orders, several times, to never let my key go to anyone else, until just shortly before I was released, and I was told then that another member of the employees out there would have a key to the personnel files and he would take care of the pilot files from that day on.

Q These pilot files to which you held a key, where were these files physically located?

A In Captain Anderson's office. They were locked at all times, and any time I left the office I always locked the cabinets and locked the door.

Q Will you describe for the Board how far away in Captain Anderson's the files were from Captain Anderson's Desk?

A My office was, we'll say where that exit door over there, and then you took about—well, there was another small office that led through there. I had to walk through that small office that led through there, and through a very short distance in a hall to his door. I would say that would be twenty feet.

Q I don't think you quite understood my question; but in any case, that is all right. Let me ask you again; the personnel files were in these locked cabinets or filing cabinets in Captain Anderson's office, weren't they?

A Yes sir.

Q Captain Anderson, I assume, had a desk in that office, did he not?

A That is right.

Q How far was his desk, approximately, from the personnel files which were in his office?

A Not over six feet.

Q In the personnel files which you have just described as being in locked cabinets for which you had a key, do you know whether or not there was a file or more than one file in those cabinets relating to Captain Allison?

A His personnel file was thick as was some of the older seniority captains, and it was kept in three different folders, which each of them were from that thick to this thick, and his was the thickest one of anyone's.

Q Captain Allison was one of the most senior pilots on this base, wasn't he?

A I believe so.

Q In any case, there were files, one or more, folders, let us say, relating to Captain Allison in the personnel records which were contained in this locked cabinet; is that correct?

A Right.

Q Were there also folders or a folder relating to Captain Schustman in those locked cabinets?

A Yes sir, I believe his only contained three folders, all of his personnel papers.

Q Was it the practice in that office to take all memoranda—

Mr. Gates: Just a minute. I am going to object to the form of that question. It is a leading question.

Q Where were all the memoranda or communications with relation to any pilot placed?

A Every piece of material that I filed was kept in the file cabinets with the exception of one small individual folder for materials that were collected.

Q Miss Seamore, did there come a time during the course of your employment when you became aware of the fact that a folder containing papers relating to Captain Allison was being kept in Captain Anderson's desk?

Mr. Gates: Again, I will object to the form of the question. He is leading the witness.

Chairman Day: Do you want to rephrase your question?

Mr. Weiss: All right.

Q Miss Seamore, did you ever become aware of any folder containing papers relating to Captain Allison kept in a file other than in the locked personnel files?

Mr. Gates: Just a minute. There is no indication that there was such a file in existence, and I must object upon that ground.

Chairman Day: Do you want to start at the beginning?

Mr. Weiss: All right.

Q Miss Seamore, did you ever become aware of any folder relating to Captain Allison other than the folder or folders concerning Captain Allison in the locked personnel files?

Mr. Gates: Same objection.

Chairman Day: She can answer that.

A Yes.

Q Now, will you tell the Board, please, where that other folder was kept?

A It is in the right hand bottom drawer of Captain Anderson's desk.

Q When did you first become aware of the existence of such an other folder?

A Early in my employment; I don't know what month.

Q Can you assist the Board and place as nearly as you can the approximate time of when you first became aware of the existence of that other folder in Captain Anderson's desk relating to Captain Allison?

A Captain Allison was going to other bases quite often for ALPA—

Q I don't mean to interrupt you. Just listen to my question. I asked you to give us your best judgment, Miss Seamore, of when it first came to your attention that there was another folder relating Captain Allison, which folder was kept in Captain Anderson's desk.

A It was early in my employment; I would say in 1948.

Q Can you tell the Board how long that folder relating to Captain Allison, which was kept in Captain Anderson's desk, continued to be kept there?

A I think it was there when I left the company.

Q You left the company when?

A September 28, 1951.

Q Did you ever have occasion to go to that folder in Captain Anderson's desk, the folder concerning Captain Allison?

A Frequently.

Q What were those occasions; how did that come about?

A That folder was strictly what I would call "reprimand folder."

Q How did you happen to go to that folder?

A Anything that we could compile or get together of a nature that wasn't complimentary and anything pertaining to notices or memoranda, why, we put in this particular one and sometimes I was asked to make several copies. These were extra copies.

Q   When you went to that folder, did you do so under the instructions of Captain Anderson?

A   Yes sir.

Mr. Gates: May I have that answer?

Mr. Weiss: The answer is "yes."

Q   Can you tell this Board whether or not that folder was continually kept on Captain Allison in Captain Anderson's desk from the time you first became aware of its existence until the time of your discharge?

A   It was.

(This was a complete violation of the contract provisions of the System Adjustment Board section of the contract agreement.   In addition it was a violation of a section of the Railway Labor Act pertaining to air carriers.   The disclosure caused those pilots in attendance to stretch their heads a little higher and listen more attentively to Margaret Seamore's testimony.)

Q   At any time did Captain Anderson instruct you to make extra copies of papers which went into the personnel folder of Captain Allison in the locked cabinets for the purpose of inserting those extra copies in the separate folder in Captain Anderson's desk?

A   That is right.

Q   How often was that done, Miss Seamore?

A   Not any definite lengths of time.   It was just whenever any certain paper came up that would be good material for that kind of a folder and, why, then I made extra copy for it.

Q   Did that folder have on it the name of Captain Wayne Nelson Allison?

A   No.

Q   What name did it have on it?

A   It did not have any name on it.

Q   Were papers or memoranda relating to any pilot other than Captain Allison kept in that folder in Captain Anderson's desk?

A   George Schustman.

Q   Were papers relating to any pilot other than Captain Allison and Captain Schustman kept in that folder in Captain Anderson's desk?

A   No.

Q   Are you positive of that?

A Positive.

Q Can you describe that folder for the Board? What did it look like?

A It was just like this, and it once had a blue label pasted on it, and that blue label had been torn off. We often reused the same folders for other things, and this particular one had been torn off at the corner to designate, rather than write a name on it.

Q Miss Seamore, were there other folders in that same desk drawer?

A Probably fifteen.

Q In the course of your duties, did you have occasion to use those other folders?

A I put materials in those quite often.

Q Can you tell the Board whether or not the other folders contained material relating to specific pilots?

A No.

Q Will you tell the Board generally what was the nature of the material in the other folders?

A Some of them were old material that Captain Anderson had had for a long time, things that didn't concern me. It was all his personal chief-pilot business. One was a folder that was called, "Tips to Pilots," and anything pertaining to tips we would put in that one.

One was "Pilot Meetings," and through the six months until another pilot meeting would be due, why, we would collect materials. And one said, "Annual Vacations," where I had set up a vacation folder for all the flight personnel.

Q Miss Seamore, you are conscious of the fact that you are under oath, are you not?

A Yes.

Q Being aware of that, are you positive that no papers relating to other specific pilots other than Captain Allison or Captain Schustman were contained in the specific folder or the other folders?

A Nothing, no other.

Q Was the folder, which we have been talking about containing papers relating to Allison and Schustman and kept in Captain Anderson's desk, kept current and up to date?

A Well, anything, like I said, there wasn't any special time to put anything in that, but anytime we would get a paper that was on that order, why, we put it in that file. Even though a copy was in the personnel file, this was an extra copy file.

Q Was that done at Captain Anderson's instruction?

A Yes, sir.

Q Do you recall an occasion on which there came to the attention of Captain Anderson, in your presence, a letter of commendation with respect to Captain Schustman?

Mr. Gates: I will object to that as being immaterial.

Mr. Weiss: The materiality of that is this, gentlemen I intend to lead up to a point of proof to show this Board that the witness, Captain Anderson, took an attitude of extreme bias and prejudice as a part of a patterned plan directed both against Captains Schustman and Allison.

Mr. Gates: Captain Schustman is not at issue in this proceeding, I submit.

Chairman Day: I think you can confine this to Captain Allison.

Mr. Weiss: The difficulty is this: Where you prove a plan or a pattern, you can not possibly establish that until you bring all the bits into the picture. I have no desire to involve anyone else, but I must do it in this way to get the evidence before the board.

Chairman Day: Answer the question.

A When I was new in the company, I didn't know one pilot from another or much about any of it, and we received a very nice complementary letter naming George Schustman, captain of a certain flight. And it was from, I believe, a man from operations. I am not sure, but it said, we wish to commend this captain helping on a delayed flight. It was on the ground, and he loaded baggage personally with his own hands, and worked well to get the flight off the ground. And it said that we want him to be thanked for it.

I was very new there, and I saw the letter being discussed. And so someone else, that wasn't Captain Anderson, made the remark saying, "It is time he is doing one good thing," And so I know I asked the question "I don't know who he is," and Captain Anderson said, "You don't know George?" And I said "No." Then he said, "Well, you will know him, you just watch."

So then I still didn't know him for a little while after that until he came in to sign a paper one time, and I looked at him and remembered him.

Mr. Gates: I am going to have to ask that this testimony be striken as non-responsive to the question. It related to a letter of commendation.

Mr. Weiss: In any case, Miss Seamore, at the occasion of this letter of commendation having come up, you told me that the comments were that Captain Anderson made with respect to Captain Schustman to you. Now, did there come a time when Captain Anderson further expressed his view with respect to Captain Schustman?

A He made the remark to me shortly—

Mr. Gates: You can answer that question yes or no, Miss Seamore.

A Yes.

Mr. Weiss:

Q Tell us, please, what was said and when it was said and under what circumstances.?

Mr. Gates: Who was present?

A There were some F-27's written—

Mr. Gates: Just a minute!

Mr. Weiss: I have asked her the circumstances under which this came about, and let her tell it.

Mr. Gates: I want to know, and I have a right to know, when, where, and who was present.

Chairman Day: Break it down.

Mr. Weiss:

Q Who was present, Miss Seamore?

A Captain Anderson was holding—

Q Just listen to my question. Don't be confused by all this legal garbage that flows around. Who was there at the time?

A Captain Anderson and I.

Q What was the occasion of this comment or this conversation, something to do with an F-27, you mentioned?

A He was talking about an F-27.

Q Just a moment. Can you fix, as best you can, the time when this occurred; About when?

A Yes, it was, maybe two or three months ago. I don't remember the date, of that F-27 that George Schustman had turned in.

Q Will you tell us, please—?

Mr. Gates: When was it?

Chairman Day: When was it, 1947 or 1948?

The Witness: No, I mean in 1951.

Mr. Weiss: Will you tell us, please, what was said by Captain Anderson and what was said by you?

Mr. Gates: I submit that the conversation about Schustman hasn't got anything to do with this proceeding, Mr. Chairman.

Chairman Day: We have ruled on that, Mr. Gates. Go ahead.

A Captain Schustman had written—filled in all the space that was on the front of this form. He always printed his remarks, and then he had turned it over on the back and made a few more lines of comment on his flight, or whatever it was. He had some difficulty or something. So Captain Anderson crossed that out on the back and was angry, and he threw it down and he said, "I will fire him if it is the last thing I do."

Mr. Weiss:

Q Miss Seamore, do you remember an occasion when Captain Anderson expressed himself in your presence concerning Captain Allison on the occasion of an F-22 being involved?

Mr. Gates: What is an F-22?

Mr. Weiss: It has to do with a physical.

The Witness: That was a monthly route qualification sheet.

Q Can you fix the approximate time of when this occurred?

Mr. Gates: Who was present?

A No one was in the office except Captain Anderson and I. There never was usually because his office is private.

Q All right, go on, please, and tell us that happened?

Mr. Gates: When was this please?

The Witness: I would say at least a year before I was away from the company.

Mr. Gates: That would be September of 1950?

The Witness: It was during 1950.

Mr. Gates: Thank you very much.

(Gates was doing all he could to interrupt the direct testimony of Margaret Seamore and confuse her as much as possible.)

A Each month in advance I would make up what was called a "Work-load card," with five columns on it for each pilot. That was for the certain forms for each pilot to turn in that month. Captain Anderson had all the time shown prejudice.

Mr. Gates: I object to the characterization. I don't object to your testifying to the facts, but I must object to your testifying that he showed prejudice.

Mr. Weiss: The objection has been made, Miss Seamore, but the Board hasn't ruled on the objection.

Chairman Day: I will sustain the objection.

A We were in the habit of giving him the first notice to turn in a form if it was due, and then say on the next time "second reminder." And I know one time he picked up this card and said, "hasn't Allison given you this?" That was my check sheet—I will take it back—that was not the work card, that was my F-22 check sheet.

Mr. Weiss:

Q To see whether they had come in?

A Yes, that was on my check sheet. He said, "hasn't Allison given you his yet?"

I said, "No, I will give him another reminder." He said, "just let him go; he will learn."

Q Did you have something else to add?

A Well, we wouldn't have done that if it had been another pilot.

Mr. Gates: Did he say, "We wouldn't have done it?"

The witness: No.

Mr. Gates: I will ask that be stricken.

Chairman Day: Strike it.

Mr. Weiss:

Q Miss Seamore, having been in that office for a number of years under similar circumstances, was it done to another pilot?

A We had several pilots who were habitally delinquent in getting in reports and they had to always be reminded that we needed this report. They couldn't fly a trip if their physical examination, F-16, were not taken. If they had not taken their physical, they were not supposed to go out the first of that month, and if their trip was due, they were supposed to miss that trip. To my knowledge, I don't know whether anybody had ever missed a trip for that or not, but one time when—

Mr. Gates: That is hardly responsive to the question, and I am going to object to your testifying further.

Mr. Weiss: Miss Seamore, are you coming up to answer my question of whether it was done on other cases?

A When you said F-22 though you meant a F-16 physical report, because an F-22 is a different form to a physical. But I remember two or three occasions on different things of those cards and those forms.

Q All right. Miss Seamore, let me ask you this: Do you remember an instance concerning Captain Allison in which there was brought to Captain Anderson's attention a note which Captain Allison had written to crew schedule?

A Oh, yes.

Q Will you fix the time as best you can of that occurrence?

A I think that was 1951.

Q Tell the Board, please, your recollection of that incident?

Mr. Gates: Was this another case when just you and the Captain were present?

The Witness: I don't remember anyone else being with us.

Mr. Weiss:

Q Who brought that note in to Captain Anderson?

A The note wasn't written to Captain Anderson. It was written to another man.

Q Who brought the note in to the office?

A This man that it was addressed to had shown it to me and made some remark, and I didn't comment. So when Captain Anderson came into his office, he, the man, carried it in and put it on Anderson's desk. Evidently they had been in there talking about it, because that is when I walked in.

Mr. Gates: Do you know whether they were talking about it?

The Witness: It was being handled when I walked in.

Mr. Weiss: Go ahead.

A So this man that it was addressed to left the room and Captain Anderson was still looking at it and reading it. So he threw it down and he waited just a minute and he made a remark about it.

Q What remark did he make?

A He said, "Just give him enough rope," and he threw it down on his desk. He didn't address his remark to me. He made the statement and that was all.

Q Miss Seamore, in the course of your duties as secretary in that office, did you have occasion to write memoranda or also of communications to the pilots at Captain Anderson's request?

A Yes sir.

Q Where you present at any time when Captain Anderson, either by telephone or in person, spoke with the pilots about some operational problem concerning the pilots?

A Quite frequently.

Q Can you tell this Board whether or not Captain Anderson in the instance of Captain Allison being involved habitually reduced all such matter to writing and sent them by letter or communication to Captain Allison?

A On printed memoranda form, not in U.S. mails, but he would make more note of anything that was addressed to Wayne Allison than I think to anyone else, and they were always signed by Captain Anderson's name.

Mr. Weiss:

Q Miss Seamore, the matters which were reduced to written memorandum in Captain Allison's case, were similar matters conveyed to other pilots by telephone or in person?

A Sometimes.

Q So that in the instance—.

A I mean, after he would call the pilots by telephone or just a very small little "AOI"—I think what the question would be is, for the same kind of material he would write formal memorandum to Captain Allison whereby the same thing maybe to another pilot, would have been a telephone conversation or a brief "AOI."

Mr. Gates: Brief what?

Chairman Day: Avoid oral instructions, pencil memorandum.

Mr. Weiss:

Q In the instance of the memorandum, would those memoranda find their way into the files of Captain Allison?

A I made copies of everything. I mean, everything that I would type that Captain Anderson would sign, I was always throughly advised to have copies of it.

Q What I am asking you next is: Were those memoranda placed as a matter of consistent practice in both the personnel file in the locked cabinet and in the other files maintained by Captain Anderson in his desk?

A Whether it was put in the personnel file or in the cabinets, we would have a copy made for this little private folder.

Q Miss Seamore, you were employed under Captain Anderson for a period of how long a time in all?

A Three years and ten months.

Q Are you able to tell this Board from your observation whether or not Captain Anderson during that period of time demonstrated or showed an attitude of hostility toward Captain Allison?

Mr. Gates: Just a minute, Miss Seamore. I object to this as calling for the conclusion of this witness. I have no objection to her testifying to facts.

Chairman Day: I will sustain that. That calls for an opinion.

Mr. Weiss: Mr. Day, let me say this on that point: There are certain conclusions which any lay witness may give. In other words, if you and I have feelings on each other over a period of time, it is entirely proper in a proceeding for a witness to say that you acted friendly or unfriendly, you are hostile or otherwise toward me. There is a proper observation to which a witness may testify.

Chairman Day: The Board rules that the objection is noted and the witness may answer.

Q Will you answer please?

A Do you want me to name the specific instances?

Q No. Did he demonstrate an attitude of hostility toward Captain Allison?

A Yes.

Q Miss Seamore, with respect to the irregularity report, that is an F-27, isn't it?

A Yes.

Q Will you tell the Board what the practice was in Captain Anderson's office during the period of time you were there with respect to their making out and the execution of the F-27's?

A Captain Anderson told me that when they were coming in from a flight that had an irregularity to always put a notice in their box together with five blank forms and attach a sheet of paper like this, was my procedure, just a blank sheet, and I would type up here: "Please give us your report on your irregularity, sign these five blank forms in ink and state if you landed overweight. Thank you." And just above those two lines is what I would put on all of them, and put them in their mailboxes.

Q Then, when an F-27 had to be filed, what was the actual practice, will you tell us, please, were the five F-27's filled out by the pilot and left with you?

A Yes sir.

Q Did they fill all the F-27's out or who did that?

A No, the pilot would take this sheet or maybe one blank form, or maybe sometimes on this blank sheet that I attached for their convenience, and they would take their fountain pen or pencil and write their report. Then, they would take these five blank forms and sign their names down here in the corner and give it to me like that.

Q When it was given to you like that, what did you do with it?

A I carried it to Captain Anderson.

Q Then what was done with it?

A After he agreed with what they had written, or after he had inspected what they had written, I was to take it back to my desk and type on these forms what they had signed in the report.

Q In doing that, did you type—

A And the pilot didn't see these forms after they had come back to me.

Q In typing the five signed, but blank forms, did you type the precise language that was written in the form by the pilot?

A Usually, yes, occasionally, no.

Q Tell us, please about the occasions when you did not type the precise language written by the pilot. Where would you get the change from?

A Captain Anderson would pencil out, mark lines through what they had said, and then he would write an extra line or a change here and there.

Q And in that state, with the change, would you then use that as the paper from which you would type the final form, which was signed in blank,?

A Yes, that was what went out of our office to New York and to the places they were directed to.

Q Did there come a time—I withdraw that. Did you or did the office keep the original F-27's?

A You mean the one the man had penciled in his own writing?

Q That is right.

A It wasn't the habit to keep them. I began to notice that—

Mr. Gates: Just a minute. You have answered the question.

Q Did there come a time when they were kept?

A I kept them of my own accord.

Q I didn't hear that.

A I kept the one that the man penciled of my own accord. I never was told to keep them.

Q What did you do with the original F-27 that you kept?

A Besides the five forms that had been signed, because it took five for distribution, I usually made two carbons on onion skin paper, and I always took a copy of my own typing, a copy of the report that had gone out, and stapled it to what the man had penciled in his own hand and put it in his personnel file.

Q So that if I understand you correctly, there came a time when the original penciled F-27 made out by the pilot found its way into the personnel file of that particular pilot?

A I was very careful to always put it in their personnel files.

Q Did it ever come to your attention, Miss. Seamore, that the original F-27's, about which you have just been telling us, were removed from the personnel files?

A Yes.

Q Tell the Board when that happened and who was present.

A On the 20th of September, in the middle of the afternoon, I walked in Captain Anderson's office; he was out of town. He had been out of town all that week, and he came in that day. Another official of the company, it wasn't Captain Anderson, and there were two men in the office, and one of them—they were preparing the files to send to Fort Worth. From then on they were to be located, these personnel files, in Fort Worth. They had a lot of them stacked up on Captain Anderson's desk. One was sitting in the chair and one was standing in front of the desk.

Q Pardon me, were both of these gentlemen officials of Amalgamated Airlines?

A They were getting the files ready to send to Fort Worth while Captain Anderson was out of town. They were opening the files, and the waste basket, I noticed, was just beginning to fill up, and I stood there a minute to see what was being done. And one of the gentlemen was pulling off these penciled originals of F-27's and throwing them in the waste basket, and I said: "What are you doing that for?" because I knew why I had put them in there, and no one but me, unless Captain Anderson had been noticing it, knew that I was keeping all of those and had been keeping them for a long time. I mean not any particular one, but every one.

Q What was said to you?

A I said, "what are you taking those out of there for?" He said, "you don't need to keep all this crap." He said, "That is why the files are so overstuffed now," and he just kept on throwing it in the waste basket.

Q Miss Seamore, do you remember an occasion when you were called by Captain Anderson to come to his office on a Saturday in 1951?

A Yes sir.

Q Will you fix the time, please, what date was that, if you remember?

A The 15th of September.

Q What time did you get to his office?

A He called me at eleven and I arrived a few minutes before twelve noon. He had told me the night before to be ready to come, so I had been ready all morning.

Q At that time who was present in the office?

A No one but Captain Anderson.

Q Was that a regular working day for the office?

A No, I made the remark that I wasn't supposed to come out as I had been told not to come out on Saturdays any more to do my work, and he said, "I already made arrangements for you to come."

Q When you got there, did you receive some instructions from Captain Anderson as to what to do?

A When I walked in the office, he had a lot of folders out on his desk. His desk was full of papers, and he smiled and he said, "Are you ready to do business?" I said, "Yes sir, I am ready to do whatever you want done." So he said, "Well, let's get busy on this. I think this will do it." That is what he said.

Q All right, then, what did you do; what did he give you and what did you do?

A I sat down in the chair for a minute to see what I had come for, and he collected a group, no he told me then to get out to my desk and get a radio communications typewriter. I had never used one and didn't understand them. So I went into the communications room and asked one of the boys in there if they would carry a typewriter in to my desk for me and change my typewriter to one of the weather symbol typewriters. And then Captain Anderson came in and laid a lot of stuff on my desk for me to start working on. They were radio-contact messages and pages of lined tablet paper that he had written some work on.

Q   You say there were pages of lined tablet paper. Will you describe to the Board just what that tablet paper looked like?

A   It was a tablet like that.

Q   Such as is in front of Mr. Day?

A   Yes.

Q   On that, did he give you the entire tablet or just a sheet of paper?

A   No, I don't remember that definitely, but his usual procedure— yes, he didn't hand me the whole tablet.

Q   Try and recall what he did on that occasion. Did he hand you the tablet or the sheet of paper?

A   There were several sheets of tablet paper because he writes in a large hand.

Q   Did you recognize the handwriting on those sheets of paper?

A   Yes sir.

Q   Whose handwriting was it?

A   Captain Anderson's.

Q   In addition to the sheets of tablet paper that he gave you, did he also give you other papers?

A   A large group of radio contact messages.

Q   Are you able to tell the Board in connection with what flight those radio contact messages were or what they related to?

A   It was the flight that had caused the hearing on Captain Wayne Allison.

Q   What instructions were you given by Captain Anderson; what were you told to do, what did you do?

A   He said, "Now, the first thing, take all of these radio contact messages and make me a summary of them on copy paper with several copies. I will need about five copies of it."

So, on these radio contact messages, I never had worked on anything like that before. It was my first experience. I never used that type of typewriter before, and on them—may I make this statement?

Q   Make it, and if it is bad, we will tell you it is bad.

A   If it hadn't been for that I wouldn't be sitting here now.

Q   Go ahead and tell us your story and tell us what happened.

A   On these radio contact messages, why, over here on his penciled tablet, why, he had made a lot of writing and weather symbols and things, and then he would take these or a few of them, and he said, "When you get down to here," and he made little notches, "you type this right here now."

Q When you used your hand, you said, "When you get down to here;" what piece of paper was that?

A On the radio contact messages.

Q When you get down to here?

A He said, "Type this here."

Q Did you do that?

A Yes sir.

Q In the course of doing that, did you prepare a list or a statement which was made up of the writing of Captain Anderson, on the tablet, combined with the radio contact messages from which you were reading?

A Yes sir.

Q Did you pursuant to Captain Anderson's instructions insert, at various points designated by him, his writing?

A I did.

Q While you were doing that where was Captain Anderson standing or sitting?

A He stayed in his office. It was on Saturday afternoon and it was very conspicuous that I was there at my desk working, and he came out of his office around to my shoulder several times during the two or three hours that I was there to see if I was getting the things put in there, and he told me once, he said, "Don't let anybody look over your shoulder now."

Q Don't let—

A Don't let anyone look over your shoulder.

Q Did you complete that work that afternoon?

A Yes sir.

Q You said before, Miss Seamore, that were it not for that you would not be here today?

A That is right.

Q Will you explain to the Board what you mean by that?

Mr. Gates: I object to that.

Mr. Gates: That is just a voluntary statement of the witness. She has already testified to the circumstances under which she came here.

Mr. Weiss: I will ask the question a different way, Mr. Day, and it will make the problem of the Board a little simpler. I will rephrase the question. Before doing so, I think I should advise the Board that my question may be objectionable, but I am trying to get everything before the Board.

Q Miss Seamore, during the course of the afternoon's work on Saturday, September 15, did you personally come to the conclusion that you were participating, at the instruction of Captain Anderson, in a falsification of the radio contact records?

A I know I was. Besides, the remarks that he had been making—

Chairman Day: I can't hear you.

The Witness: I said, I know I was doing that kind of work and besides, the remark that had been made.

Mr. Weiss: No further questions. You may examine.

Chairman Day: Off the record.

(Discussion off the record.)

Chairman Day: On the record. We will resume at 9:30 tomorrow morning. This meeting is adjourned.

(Whereupon, at 5:35 p.m. the meeting was recessed to January 25, 1952, at 9:30 o'clock a.m.)

The room was suddenly in a noisy turmoil with the termination of Margaret Seamore's direct testimony and the prospect of her further testimony under cross-examination. Those forty or fifty pilots still attending the hearing had sat too quietly and too long listening, straining to hear, Margaret's quiet confession. They wanted to move around and stretch their legs. Some had stayed longer than they had planned and hurried out toward the elevators like stampeding steers.

I heard one say: "I've got to get a move on, I'm due out to Chicago at eight." Another was heading for Nashville.

Some few lingered to speak to Mr. Weiss and Mr. Schy and at the same time give me assurances of their support. I had a warm feeling toward them as I continued to sit at the table and gathered up my notes at the same time. I was in no hurry. I would let the crowd scatter while I idly thought how much I would like to take a trip out that night. It seemed so long ago that I had pulled the nose up off the runway.

A sudden slap on the shoulder and three familiar voices, all talking at the same time, brought me back to reality. Little George Schustman continued to beat on my shoulder with Nat and Shipley trying to tell me that we were all going out to dinner. Ship was buying!

"I just had to get here. I had to sit in on at least a part of this hearing," little George explained. "I even took a few days vacation and bought a ticket. I'm a 'revenue rider,'" he grinned at me. "I expect deluxe service."

"George!" I exclaimed in pleased surprise and pumped his hand in pleasure while smiling at Nat and Shipley. They were such nice friends.

"How much did you hear today?" I questioned.

"I arrived just as Margaret took the witness chair." George replied. "Boy, but she is great!"

"We've been here all the time." Nat explained. "Ship took a round trip to Chicago last night and we've heard it all so far."

"I guess I flew a round trip last night." Ship grinned with his agate eyes sparkling. "I don't seem to remember much about it. But Margaret Seamore kept me wide awake all this afternoon!"

"That's more than I've ever been able to do." Nat laughed while hanging fondly to one of Ship's arms.

Soon we settled at a table in a nearby bar and with drinks in front of us began a serious discussion of the case. The question in all of our minds was whether or not Margaret Seamore could withstand the onslaught from the company attorney in the cross-examination.

It would be most vicious. I could attest to that and it had me worried.

Nat with her legal mind and training in legal research, writing legal briefs, studying depositions and outlining case studies, was most optimistic.

"The way I measure her," Nat explained while toying with her drink, "is that she is a stubborn woman that has a very strong sense of right and wrong. She knows she participated in something that was not right and wants to rectify the matter."

Both Ship and George nodded their agreement.

"The way I see this case, right now," Nat continued, "is this way: Wayne Allison is suddenly no longer on trial. Amalgamated Airlines is now on trial! An official of the company falsified an official report written by Wayne Allison to the CAA. Margaret Seamore has testified that there were other such falsifications by that official on other pilot reports. And there is that matter of the unpublished policy which the company now disowns. It makes the whole company stink! The pilot's union should expose the entire matter to the CAA and the press. It would create a first class investigation."

Three pairs of admiring eyes turned on Nat in appreciation of her analysis of the situation.

"That's my legal counsel," Ship boasted. "Where do you think I find all the legal goodies I come up with?" He grinned at George and me. "She just seems to manufacture them."

We four had a nice dinner together and drinks later. It was like old times to me, especially when George and I walked with them to the subway, bid them good night, and then slowly sauntered back to the Lexington. The weather had cleared out of New York City and we enjoyed the clear and crisp air with stars faintly visible between the tall buildings.

"I have a room next to yours," George offered as we entered the hotel lobby. "We have a connecting door, if you care to help me a little with a bottle in my suitcase."

I laughed with pleasure, then added: "Don't ask me to put one in bed with you."

"That reminds me," George chuckled as we took the elevator to our floor and our two rooms which soon became one. "I saw her this morning just before I left. She had come in on a flight and said she would be in for the next two days, if you care to call." He studied me closely with his keen blue eyes.

"Has she gotten over her fear of timber wolves?" he asked carelessly with blue eyes twinkling. "I thought I sensed a longing for one when I talked with her."

There were probably twenty-five pilots already in the hearing room with more trickling in when I walked in with the association attorneys. Ship and Nat had come up with George from breakfast in the coffee shop and settled in empty chairs to one side of the room. I caught Nat's wink of greeting and acknowledged it with a smile while finding myself wondering why a girl's freckles always stood out more in the early morning.

Promptly at nine-thirty Chairman Day banged the gavel and called the meeting to order. At the same time Maurice Schy, who had disappeared, reappeared escorting Margaret Seamore.

Chairman Day: Miss Seamore, will you take the witness chair and be sworn in, please.

That took only a couple of minutes and Margaret Seamore quietly settled into the witness chair, looking a little nervous.

Cross-Examination by Mr. Gates:

Q Miss Seamore, I wonder if you would go back and tell us exactly what transpired on this night in October when you had some guests at your house?

A They were having a hearing at the Hotel Tulsa.

Q The hearing was still going on?

A It had been going on that day and then it was postponed until that night, I suppose seven o'clock maybe. I had some friends at my home.

Q Just let me interrupt you there for a moment. This is in October, I believe you said?

A Yes.

Q Is that right?

A Well now, I don't know. It was after I was out of the company.

Q It was after you were discharged from the company?

A That is right. Whether it was October or November, I am not certain on that. It is whenever the hearing was.

Q Do you know whether the hearing was concluded; by that I mean, whether we finished taking all the testimony or whether we just stopped for one night?

A They told me it had ended that evening.

Q Can you fix the date any more exactly than you have?

A Well, I remember I was out of the company and they were still having this hearing going on; so I assume that might have been—well, let me think now—was that November? I don't know, I wasn't with the company.

Q Would you know what day of the week it was?

A No.

Q Could it have been the 17th of October?

A I wouldn't have any reason—

Q You don't recall? You don't really have very much of a recollection of when this took place?

A I would think it would be later than the 17th of October.

Q As late as the 28th, perhaps?

Mr. Weiss: I don't mean to interrupt your cross-examination, Mr. Gates. Let me suggest this to you, sir: If your purpose is to secure the substance of when this first thing occurred, I may tell you that I am in a position to supply that by proof right now under oath, if you want it.

Mr. Gates: I would appreciate it—

Mr. Weiss: Let me give you my offer of proof.

Mr. Gates: I would rather not because I am cross-examining this witness. I am just trying to find out when this was.

Q Was it as late as the 26th of October?

A I think.

Q Who was present at your house that evening?

A I won't need to state?

Q You won't need to state?

A That is my personal—

Q I think if you are going to testify about this, you should tell us who was there.

A I would not answer.

Mr. Weiss: Just a moment. I object to this because, quite frankly, there is no reason to involve individuals in this transaction needlessly, and the Board will note that Miss Seamore on some occasions, and this is of her own volition, had not named other individuals who in those cases were part of the company so as not to draw into this controversy any other persons more than necessary.

Mr. Gates: Mr. Chairman, we are going to get all the names into the record on this particular situation.

The Witness: I refuse to answer this.

Chairman Day: Are you trying to test her memory?

Mr. Gates: Yes, and I am also seeking to impeach her.

Chairman Day: Answer the question.

Mr. Weiss: I want to be heard upon that.

Chairman Day: It has been standard procedure when this Board disagreed on a ruling that we would note the exception and let the material go into the record. The Board disagrees on this ruling, but in view of the possible personal connotations to that answer, the Board feels, therefore, following the standard procedure rules, that the question should be answered, but that the witness can avail herself of any witness's right to refuse to answer on the normal grounds.

Mr. Weiss: Mr. Day, before you come to the ruling, may I suggest this: I am conscious of Mr. Gates's prerogative to attempt to cross-examine the witness for the purpose of testing her credibility or the substance of her story. We are all conscious, I think, of the reasons which motivate the witness. Now in order that we can, with all fairness, supply Mr. Gates with a test of credibility, I offer now to produce a witness—I make no secret about it, Mr. Schy—who came to the home of Miss Seamore the very night that this conversation took place between some employees of the company and the witness, and I make that offer so that there will be no doubt in anyone's mind that we are trying in all good conscience to supply the Board with, at least upon this point, some touchstone of credibility and veracity.

I urge the Board not even to go so far as to put the witness in the position of having to say that she refuses to answer because her motives cannot be regarded as having been impugned. She prefers not to involve other people, and I think all of us should share that desire.

Mr. Gates: Mr. Day, the testimony of this witness is very serious testimony, if it is given full weight, on the basis of where it stands right now. I think that under those circumstances this witness should be required to answer such questions by the board. I think the Board is entitled to know all the facts surrounding this situation. I am interrogating her to find out bias, prejudice, interest, as well as the other matters that I have already mentioned.

Chairman Day: This Board will let the ruling stand; in other words, that the question should be answered and the witness can refuse to answer on whatever grounds she has.

The Witness: I do. I wasn't an Amalgamated Airlines employee and the guests in my home of an evening are my friends, and I would not name names of who comes to my house or who doesn't.

Mr. O'Connell (Board member): You may say: "I refuse to answer."

A I refuse.

Q Was George Schustman there?

A I told you I would refuse to answer.

Q You make the same answer there?

A George Schustman was not there.

Q Were any of the pilots of Amalgamated Airlines there?

Mr. Weiss: Just a moment. I think, in all fairness to this lady, she had been asked the question and she had stated her position.

Chairman Day: She has answered the question and she refuses to answer.

Q Was Captain Jewell there?

Mr. Weiss: I object to the pressing of this.

A I am not answering this.

Q I want you to so state, Miss Seamore.

A Captain Jewell was not there, but you don't need to name any more names; I won't answer yes or no.

Q You won't answer yes of no to anyone else. Will you tell us what it was that one of the gentlemen guests said about this case?

A Very soon after he came in he said, "They really—." I don't remember the exact words.

Q The best you can.

A But he said that Captain Allison was released from Amalgamated Airlines.

Q He said he was released. Was that all he said?

A That wouldn't have been all.

Q What else did he say?

A There was a general discussion.

Q I know, but I asked you what this fellow said. We will call him "X" for the moment; is that right?

A Yes.

Q All right. What did "X" say for the moment?

A I don't remember.

Q You don't remember anything else except what you have just stated?

A Leave it at that.

Q Is that your testimony? I would like a yes or no answer. You don't remember anything else?

A I would not say I don't remember. I have already said that, but there was a discussion of things that had happened at the hearing.

A All right, I am asking you what did Mr. X say?

Mr. Weiss: Just a moment. I now object to the question because it has no bearing, materiality or relevancy to what the discussion was that evening because the Board will recall that I brought that out for the sole and limited purpose, and which is the only bearing it can have here, of indicating to the Board how this lady came to be a witness here. Now, what may have been said in the privacy of her parlor certainly is not evidence before this Board.

Mr. Gates: Just a minute. This witness testified that one of the guests made at least one statement. If she wants to open up the conversation by making that statement, we certainly have a right to have the entire conversation in the record.

Mr. Weiss: That statement which she referred to, Mr. Gates, we all know, was not a statement upon the merits, it cannot reflect upon the merits of this controversy, and we all should realize, being over twenty-one, that the only possible significance that could be attached to it is how she came to be attached to us.

Mr. Gates: That is your position, but that is not mine.

Mr. Weiss: I will tell you now, that is the only purpose for which that testimony has been offered, and as far as I'm concerned, the Board shall consider it only for that purpose.

Mr. Gates: I am asking the questions at this moment. I would like a ruling on my question.

Chairman Day: I think the question is pertinent to establish the credibility of the witness. The question should be answered.

Mr. Gates: May we have the question, please?

(Question read by the reporter.)

Mr. Drummond (Pilot Board Member): In other words, did you have a general discussion? You are from Oklahoma, aren't you, I am from Tennessee, and I think you have reason to believe that both these attorneys are Yankees. I believe you will find that they will be a little bit more blunt and direct than you and I might be with each other.

A I still feel, though, that when I have personal friends in my home that I don't have to come in here and talk and repeat the things that are said, because that didn't have anything to do with this case here. When I said that that was the first that I had ever known that the company was firing Wayen Allison was when he came in the door that evening and said that and, naturally, there were others in the room, and it turned into a general discussion and it lasted until late in the evening.

Mr. Drummond: Your conversation could have included other things?

The Witness: Why, certainly.

Mr. Gates: I will limit the conversation to that which pertains to Mr. Allison.

Mr. Weiss: I renew my objection. It goes beyond even the appropriate limits of impeaching a witness.

Chairman Day: I think the witness should answer the question about what this person said relating to Mr. Allison. I think counsel has the perfect right to attack the credibility of the witness and I don't know any other way he can do it.

Mr. Weiss: I think he has the right to attack the credibility.

Mr. Gates: Thank you for that concession.

Mr. Weiss: I think Mr. Gates should state to this Board and to me how this can possibly affect the credibility of this witness. I think he should demonstrate that. The Board is supposed to direct an answer to that basis. Let us find out if there is a basis for that.

Chairman Day: Do you want to answer that, Mr. Gates?

Mr. Gates: I don't think it is called for at all.

Chairman Day: I will answer it. The witness has testified to one statement that took place in her home on this evening. Now, I think it is pertinent to know whether she can remember any other statements affecting this case. I think that very definitely reflects the credibility of the witness. If that is the only statement she can remember, I personally would be—in my evaluation, or the weight I would give her testimony would be affected if she could remember other statements, it might be affected otherwise.

Mr. Weiss: Mr. Day, the witness has said upon the record quite plainly that she does remember other discussion. She had indicated her reason for not wishing to disclose the balance of the discussion. How then will your judgement of her memory be improved?

Chairman Day: She hasn't demonstrated it.

Mr. Weiss: By the demonstration of that memory, we are opening the door to a discussion on the merits of the Allison case, which has no part in this case.

Chairman Day: I don't think we open any door to that at all. I think the question, as I understand the question, is designed to test the credibility of the witness.

Mr. Weiss: I don't want to become argumentative. I say to you, sir. That there is no legitimate purpose that I can see served by such a question because if the purpose is to test her credibility, then, if that is made in good faith, then my offer of proof would be accepted, and I have offered to put on an attorney.

Chairman Day: You offered—.

Mr. Gates: Of another conversation.

Mr. Weiss: Let this be clear. I have offered to prove through another witness, an attorney, that he went there as a result of this conversation and he went there that night, so if there can be any question as to whether or not the incidents took place or not—.

Chairman Day: I don't think there is any question about that. I think it is to test the memory of this witness.

Mr. Weiss: If counsel wished to test the memory of this witness, this witness has testified at some length, and I suggest that the discretion of this Board should be exercised that it be tested on other subjects which will not bring into this case matters extraneous to it. One might as well permit counsel to ask this witness matters about which she hasn't testified to at all, about her own personal life in order to test her memory.

Chairman Day: She has testified that there was a general conversation and that she remembers some of the conversation. Counsel is asking her to demonstrate that memory. I think it is a perfectly legitimate question.

Mr. Weiss: I have to beg to disagree with you, Mr. Day.

Chairman Day: Mr. Gates, as I remember it, you said you were confining your question to matters at to what was said regarding Allison and the Allison case?

Mr. Gates: Obviously, I don't have any interest in anything else.

Chairman Day: I don't see that there is anything involving her personal life that is going to get involved in this.

Mr. Gates: I hope not to get into it in that regard.

Mr. Weiss: You see, if this witness had testified about a series of talks that evening, you know, at her home and then if Mr. Gates wished to explore these series of conversations and play one against the other and see whether they ring true I could say that is understandable to me, if he wished to test her recollection. But since she has not testified to that, let us be realistic whether she says this and this was said or was not said is testing nothing because there is nothing against which to test it.

Chairman Day: She has testified that she remembers other things. She has not demonstrated that she can remember other things. Let her demonstrate them. Go ahead.

Mr. Gates: There is a question pending at the moment.

Q Are you refusing to answer the question, Miss Seamore?

A Do I have a right to refuse to answer that?

Q You have been doing so.

Mr. Weiss: She refused to answer one question, Mr. Gates.

Mr. Gates: She refused to answer four or five.

Mr. Weiss: I ask that the Board be the appropriate body to instruct the witness to answer.

Chairman Day: I think the witness can refuse to answer any question which might reflect or that would tend to incriminate her, reflect, degrade her or involve her, or anything of that sort.

Mr. Weiss: May I ask, is the Board conscious of the fact that her refusal, which is in the record, was made by her own statement upon the basis of not wishing to involve others? I think that should be entirely clear, in fairness to all of us. Maybe she is ill advised, maybe she should throw all the names in the pot, but nevertheless I would like the record to be clear that her refusal is about naming names.

Chairman Day: She has refused to name names. This question doesn't involve anybody's name. It involves what was said.

Mr. Weiss: Off the record for a moment.

Chairman Day: Keep it on the record.

Mr. Weiss: All right. I would request a short recess to talk to the witness.

Chairman Day: All right.

(Short recess taken.)

Chairman Day: Are you ready to resume?

Mr. Weiss: Yes, Mr. Day. I would like to make a statement for the record. I have talked with the witness, Miss Seamore, and have personally asked her to answer Mr. Gates' questions concerning the conversation which was at her home that evening, to which she was given her consent upon this understanding, if we can have such an understanding: that counsel will not make any effort, directly or indirectly, to elicit the names of the individuals therein.

Chairman Day: Is that satisfactory to you?

Mr. Gates: No, I would not make such a concession. I cannot.

Chairman Day: I guess we will have to meet those incidents as they arise.

Mr. Weiss: May we go forward with this, and I would prefer that the Board do this: That you know, because I have told you, that she is willing to testify as to the conversations; that the Board instruct her, or maybe regard this as her instruction, that insofar as any conversation which may come up during the course of the examination might perhaps directly or indirectly disclose or point to the disclosure of names, that she has the right to refuse to answer that particular question.

Mr. Gates: Just a minute, Mr. Day. I hope you would not give that kind of instruction.

Chairman Day: I was not. I will instruct the witness that she has the same right to refuse to answer questions, any questions that may be addressed to you, as you have to the questions that have already been addressed to you. In other words, you have the right to protect your own personal affairs by any questions that you feel might incriminate or degrade you. Are you ready to go ahead?

Mr. Weiss: I am going to take the opportunity to instruct the witness, Miss Seamore, to this extent; I have asked you and you have consented, to testify in response to Mr. Gates' question concerning the substance of the conversation at your home, or concerning the conversations, and I want to advise you that in fairness to you and your conscience that you may elect your option to refuse to answer a question which may disclose directly or indirectly the name of any individual present at your home.

I now address myself to the Board and respectfully point out that just prior to this recess it was commented by the Chairman of the Board that the questions being asked were being permitted to be asked by the Board upon the question of credibility, and you specifically pointed out to me that no names were being asked, and it was frankly upon that basis that I discussed this matter with Miss Seamore.

Chairman Day: That is right.

Mr. Gates: Mr. Day, before we go back to the question, I am not at all sure that Miss Seamore understands what I am trying to get at. I know you are in a difficult situation. Every witness is. I am not concerned at all in my questions with any conversations you may have had with people concerning your activities in a club or church, or your family, or anything like that. You can leave all those out, and I hope that you, in answering the question, will make a differentiation between those things which are not connected with the Allison matter and those which are. I am not sure that that was clear to you before.

Q Now, I will ask you what else Mr. X said, other than the statement that you have just made, that you made a little while ago?

A All right, when I told you that I didn't remember, I do, but I just didn't want to involve the particular people.

Q I appreciate that.

A He said that the pilots down at the hearing were in an uproar and that he was sure it would be appealed and they would not let it stand as it was at that time.

Q What else did he say?

A Really, I don't remember any particular statements.

Q Do you remember the substance of anything else?

A Just in general like that. It all went on and on, and I got upset.

Q You got confused?

Mr. Weiss: She did not say "confused."

A I got upset. I got very upset and I said I don't see why they would fire him, if they had used nothing but facts to go by; that I went out there on last Saturday. I think I said "last Saturday," and that is why I am thinking now that it must not have been October because it was right at that time that I had been out there to work on Saturday afternoon, and that was the 15th of September, I remember, because there was an anniversary in my family.

Q You were discharged on the 28th, weren't you?

Mr. Weiss: Let her finish the answer.

Mr. Gates: I thought she had.

A I made the statement, I said, well, the—I don't remember my words; maybe it was not an honest thing that they used against him because I typed some things that were dishonest, and I will repeat that, that was taken to New York to use as the evidence to get him released from the company.

Q You were discharged on September 28th, weren't you?

A That is right.

Q And this incident of which you spoke occurred on September 15th.

A That is the day I did the typing.

Q That is thirteenth day, isn't it?

Mr. Weiss: Which incident have you reference to?

Mr. Gates: The one she has just been testifying to, the Saturday when she went out to work.

Mr. Weiss: When she was at Captain Anderson's office?

Mr. Gates: Yes.

Q When you said to Mr. X that you went out to the office last Saturday, you weren't quite speaking the fact, were you?

A Now, let's see. I said I was out there on a Saturday recently.

Q That is what you want to testify now; is that right?

A (No response.)

Q What did you say?

A I told you now that I maybe don't remember my exact words, but I told you I was out to the office on a Saturday afternoon compiling material that was to be taken to New York to be used on this case.

Q Did Mr. X say that Captain Allison had been released that day?

A He said they are really getting him released, or something to that effect. He said they are really—let's see.

Q Give us your best recollection.

Mr. Weiss: Give her a chance.

A He said they were to fire him, and I thought if they do fire him—

Q I am not interested in what you are thinking about. I am asking what was said, to the best of your recollection; that is all anybody can testify to? What did you say, to the best of your recollection?

A You mean my comments about what happened?

Q Yes.

A I said there was some work that I typed out there on the 15th.

Q It was on the 15th that you said you did it?

A That I typed it.

Q And that is what you told Mr. X?

A Yes.

Q Did you say, "Saturday, the 15th?"

A Yes, sir. The reason I remember that date is because of some other reason.

Q You had an anniversary, I think you said?

A Yes.

Q Miss Seamore, were there also Mr. Y and Mr. Z?

A There was a Mrs. X, I think that is what you are wanting to know, isn't it?

Q Actually not; I was trying to avoid that. There was a Mrs. X, was there a Mr. Y and Mr. X?

A If you call this individual we are discussing Mr. X, why, his wife was present.

Q That is right, I assume that Mrs. X would be Mr. X's wife. Was there a Mr. Y present? I am just trying—

Mr. Weiss: Why don't you ask her if there was anyone else present?

A I don't need to say how many people were visiting me.

Q I am trying to find out whether there were any other people there and whether there was anything else said?

Was there anyone else present besides Mr. and Mrs. X?

A I think I have a right to say I refuse to say how many people were at my house that evening.

Q So you refuse to answer?

Mr. Weiss: Miss Seamore, why don't you answer that question?

A No one else was there at that time.

Q No one else?

A No.

Q I believe you also testified that—strike that, please.

A Listen, I will say this: In my home there was another man and woman and child that lived there, but they weren't in the room with us while this business was being discussed.

Q That is not relevant.

A You said anyone else in my home, that is what you asked me.

Q That is correct. Can you think of anything else that Mr. X said?

A I don't believe I do.

Q Didn't you state on direct examination that Mr. X stated that Captain Anderson had testified that you changed the F-27's?

A Will you repeat it, please?

Q Yes, I will be glad to. I said, didn't you state, in answer to a question from Mr. Weiss, that Mr. X also said that you, Miss Seamore, had changed some of the F-27's?

A Yes.

Q That is what you were told by Mr. X? Did he tell you any more than that?

A Listen, I know that was a little while later; I will say thirty minutes or an hour, thirty minutes after that, I had a telephone call and Captain Allison said, "Margaret, do you mind if I come out to your house and bring a lawyer with me. Captain Anderson has testified here in the hearing tonight that you changed reports that went out on me and are in my case—in our case?" I said, "That will be fine, if you want to come out," something like that.

Mr. Weiss: Mr. Gates, may I make a comment for the Board? I think in fairness to the witness we should all be clear, on the record, of course, and I didn't want to object; it does not disclose, from my recollection, that this so-called Mr. X told her that, but she did say, I think she started out by using the words, "Margaret, Captain Anderson has testified," and has said so and so.

Mr. Gates: My next question, Mr. Weiss, was to ask her if she hadn't been in error when she said Mr. X had said that?

The Witness: I don't know—I know before Captain Allison and his attorney came I had already told them that I went out there and I typed that stuff that Saturday afternoon.

Q You worked for Captain Anderson between three and four years, did you not?

A Yes.

Q Captain Anderson was a pretty good friend of yours, wasn't he?

A He was very nice to me.

Q Isn't it a fact that he kept you in your job for quite a while?

A For a year.

Q At least a year?

A Yes.

Q When other people were suggesting that maybe you should be released?

A That is right—not other people, one other person.

Q Captain Anderson had never done anything wrong to you personally, had he?

A He hasn't yet, and listen while I am—

Q Now, just a minute. Did Captain Allison and Mr. Schy have a copy of what Captain Anderson had actually said in the hearing with them when they talked to you?

A I didn't read it, if they did.

Q I am going to ask, Miss Seamore, if you will look at Captain Anderson's testimony in connection with his statement as to what you did, which appears at page 274 of the record of October 17, and ask you, please, to read about a page and a half and tell me whether that is a correct statement of what Captain Anderson asked you to do?

Mr. Weiss: Just a moment. I object to that. I see no possible purpose to be served by that. This lady was not present at that hearing, and whether Captain Anderson testified correctly or incorrectly at that hearing is not something to which she should testify. It is not proper cross-examination. What purpose is served by this inquiry?

Mr. Gates: The purpose is to show the interest of the witness one· way or another in this proceeding.

Mr. Weiss: How will her reading this testimony aid that inquiry?

Mr. Gates: It is preliminary to other questions.

Mr. Weiss: I object because I can see no possible connection.

Chairman Day: I see no reason why she should not testify as to whether or not that is a correct statement of what he asked her to do.

Mr. Weiss: Just a moment. I object to that. We are now attempting to evaluate Captain Anderson's testimony in a proceeding in which this lady was not present by having her read his testimony and then having her pass judgment on it.

Mr. Gates: I am asking her if that is what she was instructed to do.

Mr. Weiss: I haven't finished. If you want to ask the witness what she was instructed to do by Captain Anderson, then the proper way, as you must surely know, is to ask her what did Captain Anderson instruct her to do. We are not concerned with what Captain Anderson may have said in the hearing.

Chairman Day: I think there are two ways of doing this. One is that Mr. Gates could read the testimony and say, "Is that what he asked you," and I cannot see what practical difference there is. I think we can shorten this thing up by letting her answer the question.

Q Miss Seamore, did you read the top of page 275 or just page 274?

A You had better let me read it again. I thought you were dismissing it. Now, what is the question?

Mr. Weiss: Since that is a part of the question, I have to read it to know what the question is. To what pages did you make reference?

Mr. Gates: Page 274 and over to the top of page 275.

Mr. Weiss: There are a series of statements and questions contained on those two pages, and I submit to the Board, if counsel wants to find out whether her testimony is accurate, he needs simply to ask: "Did Captain Anderson tell you to do this, this and that;" but perhaps fifteen questions out of a record which has no bearing is simply the most difficult way I can see of getting at this problem.

Chairman Day: It seems to me that the way we can save time is to ask her a blanket question of finding out where she disagrees.

A What is your question?

Q My question is: Does the handling of the F-27's, as disclosed by the questions and answers which you have just read, substantially correspond with the instructions which Captain Anderson gave you with respect to the F-27's.

A Right here I read it says that if I changed anything on it I was supposed to check with the pilots. I didn't check with the pilots if I changed anything, because from the time I typed what was on it, why the pilots never did know what went out.

Q Is that all you disagree with?

A This is almost in reverse of the procedure. The pilots usually brought their report in and laid it on my desk and then I carried it in to Captain Anderson, but it is about the same, and then I typed it.

Q So that except for the fact that it came on to your desk or his desk, it is substantially correct as far as your instructions were concerned except as you have pointed out in that one instance?

Mr. Weiss: The witness hasn't said that. She actually has said that this is the reverse of the procedure, and I object to counsel's characterization. We whittle away 99 percent, and except for the 99 percent it is accurate; if that is what you mean, perhaps it is true. You shouldn't characterize her testimony like that Mr. Gates.

A Here is a question down at the bottom of the page that I disagree with. It says "You are positive that the only time you changed a body of an F-27 was in that one instance, that of Captain Schustman, is that correct?" The answer is "That is to the best of my knowledge, yes. At times we changed a word on them."

Q You disagree with that?

A There was more than one. That is why I said I would disagree with the page.

Q Can you tell us what the other ones were?

Mr. Weiss: What other ones?

Mr. Gates: She has just testified that other F-27's were changed.

Q Now, can you tell us what other F-27's were changed?

A I don't believe I could say any specific one, because I typed many, many of them, and it was occasionally, as I have said before, that there were little changes, sometimes sentences and sometimes words.

Q Did those changes about which you have just testified change the meaning, in your opinion?

A In my opinion?

Q Yes.

A May I answer you like this: That I don't know enough about navigation and enough about mechanical problems, that I didn't know whether they were changed for better or for worse.

Q You don't know what the effect of the change was?

A That is right, I didn't know.

Q They were changes other than changing, for example, the tense of a verb in order to make it correct English?

A No, that is not what I mean. Occasionally, the man would write several lines and it seemed that Captain Anderson liked brevity, and sometimes he would cross out quite a bit of that and he would write above it or on another sheet of paper, and whether it meant the same, I wouldn't know because I didn't understand those things.

Q You are unable to tell us of a single instance by name where that kind of a change was made other than Captain Schustman?

Mr. Weiss: I object to that simply upon the grounds that she has answered that and I don't think we should harass the witness.

Mr. Gates: I am asking the questions, and I would like an answer.

Mr. Weiss: The question has been asked and answered just two questions back. The question is legitimate, but asking it a second time does not make it less legitimate.

Chairman Day: Answer the question.

A You want a yes or no, but may I make a comment?

Q No, I want a yes or no, please.

Mr. Weiss: Miss Seamore, I think if the Board cares to instruct you, you may be instructed that if you cannot answer a question yes or no, you have the privilege of offering a comment.

Mr. Drummond (Pilot Member of the Board): That is correct. He cannot instruct you to answer yes or no if you cannot.

Q Will you first testify that you cannot answer the question I have asked you yes or no?

A For a specific F-27 one time?

Q That is right; I asked you could you give me one case where this change—

A There were several cases, but I cannot name the date or the flight of any.

Q Can you name the pilot?

A I might if I would think a while, but right now I cannot think.

Q Will you think, please, and try to recall.

A I wouldn't be able to name a certain flight or a certain captain, but would you let me go ahead and say one more thing?

Q No, I am not asking you to answer anything except that one question.

A I have answered it.

Q I appreciate that. Now, in those cases where you say the changes were made, do you know whether or not Captain Anderson talked to the pilot concerned before he made the change?

A No, I don't know.

Q So it is entirely possible that Captain Anderson talked to the pilot concerned before he made the change, isn't it?

A He could have.

Q In which case certainly the change should be made, should it not?

Mr. Weiss: I object to that.

Chairman Day: Don't answer that. Off the record.

(A discussion was held off the record and the meeting was recessed until one-thirty for lunch.)

Chairman Day: The hearing will please come to order and we will resume.

Mr. Gates:

Q Miss Seamore, did you tell us yesterday all that Mr. X said the night that you received the telephone call from Captain Allison that you can remember?

A I didn't tell you all because we visited for a few hours.

Q I mean all in connection with the Allison case?

A The major part, the important part.

Q I wish you would tell us the minor parts, if you will please?

A I know when he came in he said that it looked like Wayne Allison was losing his job, I mean words to that effect; I don't remember words.

Q I appreciate that. It is a long while ago.

A But he said the pilots were in an uproar and that they didn't think they would stand for that and that they would appeal it, and that is the gist of the whole conversation. That was in his opinion; he didn't know they would. He was just talking.

Q That is all the detail of that conversation that you can now recall?

A Yes.

Q So that you and I will understand each other, because I am going to ask a lot of questions this afternoon, we are talking about the Allison case unless I indicate otherwise?

A Yes sir.

Q About what time of night did Captain Allison call you?

A I don't remember. It must have been as late as nine or nine-thirty.

Q Nine or nine-thirty?

A It must have been because I know my guests came after dinner and it was quite a while after that. This man had returned from the hearing down at the hotel, so, whatever time the hearing ended, he came back to my house immediately where his wife was.

Q You mean Mr. X came after the hearing?

A Yes sir.

Q And then it was after that sometime that Captain Allison called you?

A Quite a little while, yes sir.

Q What did Captain Allison say to you on the telephone? As nearly as you can recall?

A He said, "Margaret, I have a lawyer with me, and I would like to come out, if you don't mind, to your home and talk to you a little bit about this hearing that is going on." He said, "Captain Anderson brought your name into the hearing, that you were making some changes on some reports for the pilots, and if you will talk to my attorney, I would like for you to do so; would you do that?" I think he said as a favor. I said, "Yes, I will."

Then I asked: "What is this that he said that I did?" He said, "Some changes on some forms that you turned in."

Q This was all in that telephone conversation?

A He said that on the telephone, and then they were up to my house in about thirty minutes.

Q He asked if they could come to your house and you said yes?

A Yes.

Q And they came to your house?

A Yes, sir, and that was the first time he had ever been to my house.

Q The first time Mr. Schy had ever been there?

A The first time Mr. Schy or Captain Allison had ever been to my home.

Q When they came, were Mr. and Mrs. X still there?

A Yes sir.

Q And Mr. Schy and Captain Allison came into the living room.

A Yes, I have another sitting room too, and I think Mr. and Mrs. X sat there.

Q You then had a conversation with Captain Allison and Mr. Schy?

A Yes sir.

Q Were Mr. and Mrs. X present at that time?

A Mr. X and Mrs. X were sitting back in my sitting room. My house has several rooms to begin with, but after I sat in the living room a few minutes and talked to them, why, then I spoke to the others and said, "Why don't you all come in here?"

They came out into the living room, and we just visited then, no business talk.

Q Informal things, personal matters?

A Yes.

Q There were five of you at that point, weren't there?

A Yes sir.

Q Did the five of you discuss the Allison case?

Mr. Weiss: I object to any continuance of this line of examination. It is not cross-examination. I have not asked the witness to describe what was said between her and Captain Allison or Mr. Schy, and insofar as counsel wishes to test the credibility of this witness, it is true I introduced a statement by her to the effect that someone who had been at this hearing came down and spoke with her, but that is as far as we went. I think it is highly improper for counsel to attempt to go further into this matter.

Mr. Gates: Mr. Chairman, that is the most remarkable objection I have ever heard made: When counsel put a witness on the witness stand and talks about a conversation and then says that on cross-examination you cannot go into the whole conversation because it is objectionable.

I submit I am entitled to find out exactly what happened at that conversation, who said what to whom, and I propose to go into it at great length.

Mr. Weiss: I propose that counsel shall not for this reason: Because Mr. Gates knows that I did not go into any conversation which took place between Captain Allison and Mr. Schy at this lady's home. I simply went so far as to indicate how she happened to be introduced to us and how we happened to know about her. I did not have her relate any part of any talk between Captain Allison and Mr. Schy while they were at her home.

Mr. Gates: I submit the record will show that, at that time, by Miss Seamore yesterday that Captain Allison or Mr. Schy said, "We may want you to serve as a witness." If that isn't part of the conversation, I would like you to tell me what it is.

Mr. Weiss: That, Mr. Gates, you know has nothing to do with the discussion of the merits of this controversy—wait until I am finished.

Mr. Gates: I don't have to wait for you.

Mr. Weiss: No, you don't. Are you finished?

Mr. Gates: I would like to continue.

Mr. Weiss: I will wait until you have finished your argument.

Mr. Gates: I submit, members of this Board, that this witness had made some very serious charges against Captain Anderson, which, if substantiated, might well mean his discharge, and I submit that this witness should undergo cross-examination to find out exactly what happened in connection with this entire transaction. If I am not entitled to it, I think her entire testimony should be stricken from the record and disregarded by the members of this Board.

Mr. Weiss: Captain Anderson has made very serious charges in this proceeding and prior to this time; that did not alter the fact or deed. I suggest that it altered the rule that examination of Captain Anderson shall be held within reasonable limits, and this Board held me within reasonable limits. The same rule shall apply in each direction equally.

This lady has told us on direct examination her conversation of which she was introduced to this matter, her consent to be a witness and her willingness to testify. We did not pry out any discussion or any substance of the conversation between Captain Allison, Mr. Schy and Miss Seamore.

Moreover, had we attempted to do so, to go into the merits on either phase, it would have been highly improper and Mr. Gates would have objected, I assume, and he would have had a right to object in relation to that type of conversation. In any case, it was not brought out, and this is not proper cross-examination under any analysis.

The fact that the charges that are being made are serious, and they are serious and we treat them very seriously, and that this lady's testimony should be seriously taken, we agree with that. As to the consequences of that testimony, Mr. Gates' surmise is as good as anyone's. That doesn't mean we can roam at will.

Chairman Day: Mr. Weiss, the Board has ruled that so long as the questions pertain to the Allison case the witness should answer.

Mr. Weiss: Will the Board consider this: I necessarily must accept the Board's ruling although I except to it; that insofar as these questions now being put to the witness relate not to matters which I brought out upon direct examination that this witness is now being questioned upon new material and necessarily becomes counsel's own witness.

Chairman Day: Mr. Weiss, we considered that when we were discussing the objection, and we all remember that there was testimony yesterday as to the conversation which took place at Miss Seamore's home. I believe that the questions are in respect to what conversation there was—I think the questions by Mr. Gates, at least so far, has been confined to what discussion there was of the Allison case at her home.

Mr. Weiss: I am in agreement with that as far as it goes, but there is one thing we must bear in mind, that actually we have two events, so to speak, which took place. There was a conversation between this Mr. X and Mrs. X, as the case may be and Miss Seamore. That was the conversation about which we had some "to-do" as to whether she would or would not testify. That was gone into.

Since I did not bring it out, and quite deliberately, I didn't think it was appropriate to go into it, any more than it would be appropriate for me to have this witness relate what she told me, for example, in the preparation of this case. It would be a highly improper thing for me to do. Having avoided that, but in order to inform this Board about how we came to know Miss Seamore, that is where we stopped, and cross-examination must necessarily stop at that point, otherwise we will be in a very improper field, which I don't think this Board should venture into. It would be otherwise if I had gone into that.

Chairman Day: Mr. Weiss, the Board has ruled that as long as the questions are confined to the matters pertinent to the Allison case she can answer.

Mr. Weiss: I want to make this further inquiry: Has the Board in that ruling or does the Board make any ruling as to whether or not this witness, now being asked to testify upon matters which I did not bring out upon direct, becomes counsel's witness, Mr. Gates' witness, which is the rule, you recall, that was applied to me?   Now, what is the Board's ruling on this?

Mr. Gates: I would like to be heard on that, if there is any question in the Board's mind.

Chairman Day: Let us hear what you have to say.

Mr. Gates: It is very clear that whether he opens the conversation, even if it is only by one question and one answer, that on cross-examination I have the right to go into the entire conversation and get as much of the information as I can.

Mr. O'Connell (Pilot Board Member): Mr. Gates, in our discussion up here we have figured that there were two events that took place, perhaps to some extent simultaneously; one was a social event, and one was what we have called a business event. As long as your questioning is confined to the business event, we think that the questioning is proper.

Mr. Gates: I am trying to keep it to the business.

Mr. O'Connell: Where the social matters are concerned, Miss Seamore is able to say she refuses to answer.

Mr. Gates: I suggest to the Board that if you think I get off the reservation then interrupt and say, "I think you are getting off the reservation." I think that ruling is proper. The last question which I asked, if you will recall, Captain O'Connell—

Chairman Day: Just a minute, please.

Mr. Gates: I am sorry.

Chairman Day: Mr. Weiss, the Board feels somewhat overdepth in trying to decide as to whether or not the witness is your witness or Mr. Gates' witness, but it seems to us as laymen that this is legitimate cross-examination. We will so rule.

Mr. Weiss: I am frankly less concerned with whose witness the witness is than the propriety of going into the question at all.

Chairman Day: That is the answer to the best of our ability.

Mr. Gates:

Q Miss Seamore, rather than go back to the record, I think the last question I asked you was: During the time that there were five people present, Mr. and Mrs. X, Mr. Schy, Captain Allison and yourself, was the Allison case discussed?

A Not in the presence of Mr. and Mrs. X.

Q It was not?

A No, because they sat back.

Q You just answer the questions, please.

A No.

Q The entire conversation, when all five of you were present, was with respect to matters unrelated to the Allison case?

Mr. Weiss: Will the record indicate the witness has said "yes" by a nod of her head.

Q Now, will you tell us, please, what the conversation was between Captain Allison, Mr. Schy and yourself? Who introduced the conversation, Captain Allison?

A I don't remember definitely which asked the first question, if that is what you mean, but they began to talk business immediately when they came in.

Q I take it Mr. Schy was introduced to you?

A Yes.

Q You knew Captain Allison, of course, beforehand?

A Yes.

Q Will you tell us in your own words in just as much detail as you can exactly what the conversation was and who said what?

Mr. Weiss: I just wish to point out to the Board, I am not even raising an objection, but you are permitting testimony to go into the record relating to conversations in Captain Allison's presence and with his attorney present, at which time he was attempting to secure a defense from the charges leveled against him. I want to call that to the Board's attention specifically.

Mr. Gates: Are you suggesting that this is a privileged communication?

Mr. Weiss: I made my observation and I am standing on my observation.

Mr. Gates: I want the record to show that this is not a privileged communication in any view.

Q Will you please answer the question if you remember it or I will ask the reporter to read it to you.

A I don't remember words, but I can tell you the gist of the conversation, the general subject of it.

Q Will you do that, please?

A They asked me if I had been changing F-27's that were mailed out of Tulsa, and I said I had made changes, but not on my own accordance; why would I? I don't understand navigation, meteorology, I don't understand the mechanical parts of airplanes. But I have made changes on a lot of F-27's through the penciled changes that Captain Anderson had laid in front of me or handed to me to type. I mailed them out exactly as I was instructed, because they didn't mean anything to me.

I don't understand whether they were better or worse when they were sent, and like you said yesterday, I don't know whether he had conferred with the pilot before the changes were made. I wouldn't know that.

Q Did you tell Captain Allison and Mr. Schy that on the night of this conversation?

A I don't remember if I made those statements or not.

Q What else did you say about these F-27's, if anything?

A I wouldn't remember anything further.

Q You don't remember anything further?

A Not at the moment.

Q Was there any discussion of Captain Allison's F-27, which was filed in this proceeding?

A The main one that was discussed was the Schustman F-27.

Mr. Gates: I will move to strike that answer as non-responsive.

Chairman Day: Strike it.

Q The question I asked you—

A Not a particular F-27 which Allison had signed. What we were—

Q Just a minute. I asked you a question which you can answer yes or no. I wish you would confine your answers to that, and then if you want to make an explanation we will have that.

Mr. Weiss: I object to counsel's scolding the witness. The witness has already answered his question. She said, and the record will disclose, that she did not discuss a particular F-27 of Captain Allison's. She just testified to that.

Mr. Drummond (Pilot Board Member): I quite agree.

Chairman Day: Go ahead, Mr. Gates.

Q Did you discuss an F-27 filed by Captain Allison?

A We didn't discuss—you want me to say "no," then, don't you.

Q I want you to give me your answer. I don't know what it is going to be.

A We didn't discuss an F-27 signed by Captain Allison, but we did discuss—

Q Just a minute. You have answered the question.

A All right. We discussed F-27's in general.

Mr. Weiss: Let the witness finish her answer.

A We did discuss the communication radio contacts that had been written on the 15th of September that I had made several changes on, with several comments added, that Captain Anderson evidently had carried to New York on the following Monday morning. That is what we were discussing chiefly that night. The F-27 wasn't important that night. What started it—

Q Just a minute, Miss Seamore.

Mr. Gates: I submit, members of the Board, that when I ask a question which can very simply be answered, that we don't have to have all of the other things brought in until I ask the appropriate question.

Chairman Day: Miss Seamore, will you please confine your answers to the substance of the question.

The Witness: I will. I am not trying to be arbitrary.

Mr. Gates: I appreciate that, but we will get along a lot faster if you will try to confine your answers to the questions I ask you.

Witness: I don't mean to do that.

Q You say you did discuss the F-27 of Captain Schustman?

A Yes sir.

Q How did that subject come into your conversation, if you recall?

A I said—

Mr. Weiss: I object to that on the ground that Counsel has limited himself to the discussion only of the Allison matter.

Chairman Day: Sustained.

Mr. Gates: Just a minute, may the Board please. I have objected consistently through this proceeding to any conversation or any testimony or any evidence with respect to Captain Schustman, and this Board equally consistently has ruled against me on the ground that it is a part of a pattern. I submit that this is a two-way street, and I am entitled to go into that just as much as Mr. Weiss was entitled to do so.

This witness has testified with respect to Captain Schustman.

Mr. Weiss: That is entirely so. The difficulty is that you tendered your questions to the Board and to the witness on the expressed theory and limitation that you would confine yourself to the Allison matter. Having done so, perhaps you would like to recant that. Let us be frank.

Mr. Gates: I have no desire to repent of that.

Chairman Day: Mr. Weiss, the Board has ruled that insofar as Mr. Gates' questions concerning Captain Schustman are questions directed at the same pattern, as you discussed yesterday, they are admissible.

Mr. Gates: May I have the question, please, Mr. Reporter?

(Question read by the reporter.)

Q Will you answer the question, please?

A I don't remember direct sentences, maybe that were spoken, words, but they were telling me that in the hearing Captain Anderson had said that I had changed reports before they were sent out of the office, and I said I changed them, but not because I made the changes.

Q I am afraid you misunderstand my question.

A All right.

Q Do you or do you not recall how the subject of Captain Schustman's F-27 came into this conversation?

A I thought I was answering it correctly.

Q Excuse me, I didn't mean to interrupt you.

A I said that I had made changes on more than one F-27 and on other things too, but this particular one that the pilots asked me to present that day when the hearing was being held in Captain Anderson's office, I said that was the main thing that started all of my trouble. I said then that later on, why, I had changed something very much more serious to my thinking after that.

Q You just said, "When they called for that F-27 in Captain Anderson's office—"

A Yes sir.

Q "That started all your trouble." What do you mean by "they called?"

A Captain Anderson buzzed my desk and I walked in where they were having a private meeting.

Q When was this?

A That was just before the Saturday of the 15th; I don't know, I think it was on a Thursday, maybe, or on a Friday.

Q The preceding day or two before?

A Before the 15th.

Q And that was a meeting in Captain Anderson's office?

A Yes sir.

Q Do you recall who was present at that meeting?

A There were a group of pilots.

Q But you don't recall who they were?

A I remember a few.

Q Tell us who was there, please?

A Captain Allison was sitting opposite the desk facing Captain Anderson.

Q Right.

A And Captain Schustman was sitting next to the door, and as I walked through the door, why, he began speaking.

Q I don't want the conversation. I want to know who was there.

A Clyde McCall.

Q From down Fort Worth?

A Jim Jewell.

Q Who else?

A Calkins, I think. It has been a long time and it wasn't important to me at that time. I didn't think it was going to cause serious trouble.

Q Now, Captain Anderson asked you at that time to bring in Captain Schustman's F-27, is that right?

A Yes sir.

Q You told Mr. Schy and Captain Allison on the night of this conversation that you were having with them, that at that time you had been requested to bring in the F-27 of Captain Schustman?

A To come into his office and get it out of the file cabinet.

Q You got it out, I assume, and brought it in?

Mr. Weiss: I object to that. This is entirely new. I am entirely satisfied it should be brought out, but let us not lead the witness. Ask her what she did. Ask her did she get it.

Mr. Gates: This is cross-examination. Whoever heard of restricting cross-examination to direct questions?

Mr. Weiss: I asked that the witness not be led. This is material that was not in any sense disclosed upon her direct testimony. I have no objection to the introduction of any new evidence of this type, but, please, let the witness testify.

Mr. Gates: I will ask the Board for a ruling.

Chairman Day: Please avoid leading questions.

Mr. Gates: Mr. Chairman, how far do you go with that "avoid leading questions?"

Chairman Day: I think there are other ways to ask the witness what you are trying to find out.

Q What did you do then?

A I went into the office and opened the file cabinets and I looked in one folder that I thought it should have been in, his personnel folder.

Q "In his," whom do you mean?

A Schustman's.

Mr. Weiss: Whose office?

Mr. Gates: She said it was in Captain Anderson's office.

The Witness: It was not in the personnel folder, which I always put their hand written ones in, the personnel folders. I did that on my own accord. I had never been instructed to. I thought maybe it is in the irregularity file, and I pulled it out and stood there and looked in the irregularity file and it wasn't in it. I told Captain Anderson. The room was crowded full, of chair, standing room only, of pilots, and it made me a little bit nervous—

Q Tell me what you did and not how you felt.

A I said, "May I take this other folder out to my desk?" It was a thick folder of an accumulation of odds and ends of papers, and I said, "It might be here, if you will let me go out to my desk."

Q What folder is that you are talking about?

A It was a folder of material, for Captain Anderson's office, that I had not gotten filed in their individual folders yet, that I was going to file in the next day or two.

Q In other words, you were behind in your filing and you hadn't gotten this part done?

A I was behind, but I always managed to catch up on my own time.

Q Did you find Captain Schustman's F-27?

A In that folder out at my desk.

Q Did you bring it into Captain Anderson?

A No, to protect Captain Anderson, I walked in the other office—

Mr. Gates: Just a minute, I didn't ask you that question and I move that it be stricken.

Chairman Day: Strike it.

Mr. Gates: Captain Anderson doesn't need protection from a woman.

A I didn't carry it in.

Q What did you do with it?

A I laid it on my desk and got busy with my other work.

Q Was the F-27 brought into Captain Anderson's office at all that afternoon?

A No, it never was.

Q You are very sure about that?

A That is right.

Q Did Captain Anderson come out and get it?

A You tell me to say yes or no, but I will tell you how he did get it.

Q Please answer my question.

A He came out and got it after the meeting was adjourned and all the pilots had left.

Q None of the pilots saw it, so far as you know?

A Several of them saw it, but it was after the meeting had adjourned and they were standing around my desk and they picked it up and several of them read it. It was the original hand written one that had had all kinds—I mean several, crossed-out lines.

Q You are, of course, very familiar with the looks of that F-27, this particular one of Captain Schustman's?

A Yes sir, I gave it to Captain Anderson at that time.

Q Can you tell me from your recollection how much of that F-27, which was in Captain Schustman's handwriting, was crossed out?

A There were as many, I believe, as three or four lines, on the back, that had a line clear through to not typed.

Mr. Gates: May I have Exhibit No. 2 for the purpose of illustration?

Q Miss Seamore, I will show you Amalgamated's Exhibit No. 3 in this proceeding. Now, this is just to help you in my next question. There is a section entitled: "Reasons for Deviation and Action Taken." Now, from your recollection in the F-27 filed by Captain Schustman in his own handwriting, was there anything written in that section?

A In this section here?

Q That is right.

A Yes sir.

Q Now, the next section—

A   May I continue with that "yes sir?"

Mr. Weiss: Her answer is not complete. I submit to the Board she should be allowed to finish her answer.

Chairman Day: She has answered.

Q   The next is in part: "did system operate after occurrence, and if it did not, were emergency systems used to complete flight and make landing." And there is some space for some comment. From your recollection again, was there any comment in that section?

A   I don't remember.

Q   In addition to the handwriting on Captain Schustman's F-27, which you have described, which appeared on the face, I take it from what you have just testified that there was handwriting on the reverse side as well?

A   Yes sir.

Q   About how many lines on the reverse side, if you recall?

A   There were as many lines as there are in this right here, to my knowledge, to my remembrance.

Q   That is all you can testify to?

A   Let me tell you this.

Q   Just a minute, I want to make the record clear.

Mr. Gates: The witness in her last testimony was referring to the section "Reasons for deviation and action taken," illustrating about five lines of handwriting.

A   I am going to say this regardless, it might have been in this section instead of that because I don't know enough about these things. There was that much writing on the back.

Mr. Gates: Let me explain for the record what Miss Seamore had just said: That she is not clear that whether the handwriting appeared on the face was under the first of the two sections in which comments are called for by the form.

Mr. Drummond: I believe the Board is capable of reading that in there.

Mr. Gates: You understand what she meant?

Mr. Drummond: Yes. What are we sitting here for if we cannot listen to it?

The Witness: That has been about five months ago for me too, and it is hard to remember definitely which section those hand written lines were in.

Q Was any of the handwriting on the front or the face of Captain Schustman's F-27, if you recall, stricken or changed by Captain Anderson?

A I believe yes, but I wouldn't say definitely; but I believe, yes.

Q How about the handwriting which appeared on the reverse side?

Mr. Weiss: What is the question.

A He means was it changed.

Q That is what I do mean, Miss Seamore. Was it stricken, any of it?

A On the reverse, yes.

Q How much of it was stricken?

A I think as much as three lines, if not more.

Q That were stricken?

A Yes sir.

Q I show you here, Miss Seamore, what purports to be an F-27 dated August 3, 1951, signed by Captain Schustman.

A This isn't the one I was talking about. That is not the one.

Q Just a minute; wait until I ask you. I am going to ask you if this is the F-27 to which you have been making reference to in your testimony?

A That isn't the one I remember.

Q That isn't what I asked you. Is this the F-27 to which you have been making reference to in your testimony?

A Let me look at it.

Q Please do look at it.

A I typed dozens of these and they don't mean much to me.

Q Just a minute. I asked you a question which you can answer either way that seems appropriate to you.

A I don't think this is the one that the fuss was about.

Q You don't think that the F-27, which I have identified, is the one that you are talking about?

A It doesn't seem to me like that is the one that I was talking about when I discussed it with them.

Q Do you recall what the F-27 was that you discussed with these pilots or that the pilots were discussing on the afternoon of September 13th or 14th?

A What was that, please?

Q I say, do you recall the subject of the F-27?

A No, I don't remember any of the subject matter in these things because all I did was just transcribe them.

Q You have answered the question. Did you testify yesterday, Miss Seamore, and again this morning, that you had made many changes on many F-27's at the direction of Captain Anderson?

A I don't believe I used the word "many." I said on several occasions, and that is the way I do mean it.

Q On how many occasions during the period of three years and ten months that you were employed by Captain Anderson, or working as his secretary did you change F-27's at his direction?

A I don't know the number, but quite often.

Q Would it be as many as ten?

A More.

Q As many as twenty?

A Yes.

Q As many at thirty?

A I wouldn't go farther.

Q What do you mean, it wouldn't be as many as thirty?

A I wouldn't say that many because that is a large number.

Q But you think it was about thirty?

A No, not thirty.

Q How high would you go, somewhere between twenty and thirty?

A I would say at least as often as ten or fifteen times or more, real often when the F-27's were handed to me, maybe it would be one word, maybe it would be one symbol, maybe it would be a whole sentence or a whole paragraph.

Q Can you tell us, other than the Captain Schustman case that we have been talking about, any other single case out of this ten or fifteen, I believe you last said in which a change was made?

A I don't remember any specific F-27; I couldn't recall any certain flight or any captain's signature.

Q You cannot—.

A I wouldn't have read that one except for all the trouble that it caused; I mean, definitely who the captain was.

Q Now, can you tell us what kind of changes were made?

A You mean on one or all?

Q On any one?

A Sometimes one word.

Q What kind of a word?

A I don't remember.

Q You don't remember?

A Because the substance of those paragraphs—

Q You answer my question, please.

A I don't remember particular words, no.

Q Do you remember whether it was the change, I think I asked you yesterday, of the tense of a verb?

A No, that wouldn't make any difference if it was "was" or "were." He don't do things like that.

Q Were there cases such as the misnumbering of a trip?

A I don't think so. Oh, sometimes—whether the man had said it or maybe I had already typed it on the the heading in their mailbox when they come in off their trip, I mean just that much would be ready for them.

Q I am asking you about the changes, Miss Seamore.

A No, the trip numbers Captain Anderson didn't change. This is what I am trying to explain now, maybe they would say flight 48, maybe it originated in San Francisco a few minutes before the day— like we say, flight 48 of the 10th. Well, it originated in San Francisco a few minutes before the 11th, and we would say, through Tulsa on the 11th, and we had added that when maybe the man didn't.

Q Is that the kind of change you are talking about?

A No, that is not what the trouble is.

Q I am trying to find out what kind of changes you are talking about?

Mr. Weiss: I object to the question solely for this reason: That the Board recalls, at least I believe it is so, that she fully answered that on Yesterday's cross-examination.

Chairman Day: I cannot agree with you on this. This witness has said that changes were made on these F-27's, and it becomes a very important question of fact before this Board as to what type of changes were made. The Board wants to know.

Mr. Weiss: Let me refresh your mind. The witness said that since she was not familiar with technical matters involved that she was not prepared to state what either the significance was, either for better or worse, and that there might have been a word, a sentence or two sentences.

Chairman Day: If it can be brought out by questioning as to what some of these changes were, then the Board will know whether the changes were substantive or merely editive.

Mr. Weiss: I simply felt that the thing had been probed quite throughly. I thought we had exhausted the witness's ability to answer that.

Mr. Gates: What was the last question, please, Mr. reporter?

(Question read by the reporter.)

Q What kind of changes are you talking about, then please, Miss Seamore?

A Changes in those two blank spaces that you just now asked me about.

Q On the form F-27?

A On the form F-27, and one time—

Q Just a minute, please.

Mr. Weiss: Let her finish her answer.

A One time he had crossed out several sentences and wrote the paragraph over, and handed it to me to type it in on these blank forms. He made the statement, and that is the reason I got the idea from then on that the Federal Aviation Authority was the reason that they were being changed. (Reorganized from the Civil Aeronautics Authority.)

He said: "If they want to make a complaint like this, let them come in here and write me a letter and I will take it up. The FAA is breathing down our neck and we have to be careful on what goes on these forms. We are not writing this on this form."

Now then, if you ask me what captain, or what trip, I don't remember. But right then I got the idea—

Q How do you remember all the details except the incidents?

A Because it just struck me—along then is when I started putting all the original F-27's in the pilots' personnel files.

Q Can you tell us about when that was that you began putting the original F-27's in the pilot's personnel file?

A At least two years before I was away from the company.

Q That would be, then, September of 1949?

A Something like that, and I was told then to not ask—FAA men to the pilots' meeting.

Mr. Gates: Just a minute. I am going to ask you Miss Seamore, not to go off on these wild meanderings unless you have a question before you. We will be here for a week.

Chairman Day: Strike that.

Mr. Gates: I am going to ask that that testimony be stricken from the record.

Chairman Day: Sustained.

The Witness: But that is what I said. He asked me why—

Q Just a minute, you have no question before you and I didn't ask you why.

A That is why I was answering you; you said why did I remember it?

Q I think you are right; I beg your pardon.

A You asked me why do I remember it?

Q Is it not a fact that Captain Anderson never changed the content of one of these F-27's, to your knowledge?

A Sir?

Mr. Gates: Will you repeat the question.

(Question read by the reporter.)

A If I understand it, that is just back to all what we have been talking about for the last half hour.

Chairman Day: I assume you mean, did he change the meaning?

Mr. Gates: That is right.

A What I told you, I don't know whether the meaning was changed or not. I don't understand these things. All I did was transcribe.

Q Is it not a fact that to your knowledge Captain Anderson never changed the meaning of a single one of the F-27's?

Mr. Weiss: Just a moment Miss Seamore. I object to the form of that question. Moreover, the witness has answered that she did not comprehend the meaning. She knows that the bodies of the F-27's were changed. What the consequences of that was, or the interpretation of the F-27's meaning, she has testified to that. The question is very unfair in form.

Mr. Gates: I am asking her, to her knowledge, the meaning of any one of these F-27's that were changed, and I think the witness should be required to answer.

Chairman Day: Mr. Gates, the witness has testified she did not understand the meaning of the text of these F-27's.

Q Again, because I want the record to be very clear, you cannot give us by name a single example of where this changing took place except in the case of Captain Schustman?

A There were too many of them and it has been too far back, and at that time I didn't know there ever would be—I wasn't certain there would ever be trouble coming up and you have to make notes on that to say "yes" or "no." I didn't take notes or anything like that. I wasn't in that frame of mind about the job.

Q Did you ever remove any papers belonging to the company from the offices of Amalgamated Airlines in Tulsa?

Mr. Weiss: I object to that. There is no foundation for such a question in the direct testimony. It is not proper cross-examination. We are not here inquiring as to whether Miss Seamore did or did not properly or improperly discharge her duties to the company. Miss Seamore is not on trial here.

Chairman Day: What is your purpose in that question?

Mr. Gates: I will make her my witness for my question, if it is necessary.

Mr. Weiss: I don't care whose witness you make her. It is not a part of this inquiry.

Chairman Day: What is your purpose?

Mr. Gates: I propose to show why the woman was discharged, because it certainly goes to the credibility. I think the reasons why she was discharged are pretty important.

The Witness: I am willing to answer it.

Mr. Weiss: Just a moment. You may be, and I don't say there is anything to hide, but I am just not going to get into anything like that. Mr. Day, may I state this: I have turned over in my mind that if I could have any assurance that this inquiry made to Miss Seamore will not then lead to other inquiries as to her relationship to the company and the matter of her discharge, all things which are extraneous to this hearing, I frankly would be inclined to withdraw my objection for one reason: I don't want Miss Seamore to be under the cloud of any unanswered question of that type.

Chairman Day: I think that insofar as the questions are confined to a test of her credibility they probably are legitimate questions. I agree with you, I have no interest in why she was discharged.

Mr. Gates: I think the Board will have.

Chairman Day: Unless and if that is a reflection on her credibility.

Mr. Weiss: I can't agree with your last comment, Mr. Day. Let me say this: For the purpose of this particular question, I will withdraw my objection and reserve my right to object to any other questions along that line. I withdraw my objection to that particular question.

Chairman Day: Go ahead Mr. Gates.

Q Will you answer the question?

Chairman Day: Read the question.

(Question read by the reporter.)

A He asked me, did I ever remove any papers out of the files; is that what you want me to answer?

Q Yes, you can answer that yes or no.

A I want to make a comment on it.

Chairman Day: You can answer the question.

A The answer is no. I mean not for bad purposes. I removed things that Captain Anderson had me bring over to his desk, but not to remove and destroy on my own accord.

Q Did you ever take any of the papers from any of the files of Amalgamated Airlines to your home?

A Oh, no.

Q Did you ever give any copies or originals of any of the papers of Amalgamated Airlines—

A This is where I want to make a comment.

Q Just a minute, let me finish my question.

A The answer is no.

Q You don't know what the question is.

A You are saying did I ever give any of the original papers or copies to the pilots.

Q No, I didn't ask you that question. I was going to ask you—

A Yes, I understand.

Q Did you ever give the originals or copies of any of the papers in the files of Amalgamated Airlines to anyone whom you considered unauthorized to receive them?

A I did not.

Mr. Weiss: Just a moment, Miss Seamore. We are getting into the question of who is authorized or not. We are into pretty deep water here. If counsel wishes to ask a direct question, did she deliver papers from Amalgamated Airlines files without authorization to the pilots, I will have no objection.

Chairman Day: Do you care to rephrase your question that way?

Mr. Gates: I will ask that question.

Q Did you ever give the originals or copies of any of the papers in the files of Amalgamated Airlines to any of the pilots?

A I did not.

Mr. Weiss: What was the answer, please?

(Answer read by the reporter.)

Mr. Weiss: May I assume, Mr. Gates, that implied in that question, notwithstanding her answer of no, is: "without authorization of the company?"

Mr. Gates: Oh, of course.

Mr. Weiss: All right.

Q Why were you discharged?

Mr. Weiss: I object to that question. It has no bearing upon the matters in this hearing.

Mr. Gates: All right, I will rephrase the question.

Q Is it not a fact, Miss Seamore, that one of the reasons you were discharged was because you had made misrepresentations concerning your mileage allowance?

Mr. Weiss: I object to that question. It is entirely new, and I say this moreover to the Board, that I am under the impression that this company gave Miss Seamore in writing the reasons for her discharge. If this company desires to bring that out and we will then test the question whether it is relevant or material, then let them produce the best evidence of the company's reasons for her discharge.

The Witness: I would like to make a comment on that question.

Mr. Weiss: I know you would, but I am not going to get into the matters of your relation with the company. It is not fair to this hearing.

Chairman Day: Unless this question has a very direct basis on Miss Seamore's credibility as a witness, the objection is sustained.

Mr. Gates: I am prepared to prove by documentary evidence, if necessary, that one of the factors which led to her discharge or termination was misrepresentation with respect to her mileage allowance. If one is dishonest in one thing presumably one can be dishonest in something else.

The Witness: That is the reason I want to make a comment on what you have asked.

Mr. Gates: Again I will have to ask you to let this argument go on between the lawyers, Miss Seamore.

Chairman Day: It is the feeling of the Board, Mr. Gates, that if you wish to establish that, and you have the documentary evidence, you should present it.

Mr. Gates: I certainly have a right to ask her if it is a fact that that was one of the factors.

A Mr. Williams wrote a letter that I had done that.

Mr. Weiss: Miss Seamore, I am going to have to ask you not to discuss that.

Q Miss Seamore, I show you a copy of a letter addressed to you—

A Signed by Williams.

Q Let me finish, please. Under date of January 4, 1951.

A I remember it.

Q Signed by Mr. I.A. Williams, entitled: "Use of mileage allowance." I ask if you ever received that letter?

A I did.

Mr. Weiss: Wait a minute. I object to any questioning along those lines. The record indicates that this lady continued in the employment of the company for some time after that, and do we have to go back now and plow all that ground of the relationship of this lady to this company? I think it is completely extraneous to what we are talking about.

I suggest that even though I think it has no bearing upon this hearing at all that if this counsel wants to establish the basis of discharge, the only proper way to do it and to do it in any sense of brevity, if there was a letter of discharge to produce it, and if that is material, produce it in evidence. We are not going back some nine months before her actual discharge.

The Witness: Since he said though that I was dishonest—

Mr. Weiss: Miss Seamore, please; I know you feel you are in personal scrutiny, but I can't help it.

Chairman Day: Mr. Gates made it very clear as to what he is attempting to establish. What he is attempting to establish is certainly pertinent to this hearing; that is the credibility of the witness. I don't think it makes any difference so far as the credibility of the witness is concerned as to whether it happened yesterday or last week or last year.

Mr. Weiss: Mr. Day, I don't know what is in that memorandum Mr. Gates has.

Chairman Day: I don't either.

Mr. Weiss: But I will assume from the nature of the approach to the problem that perchance it says something about an overcharge on mileage, or whatever it may be, and written by an executive of the company to Miss Seamore. I will assume that for the moment.

Now, if that is the case, then we must necessarily go into the question, because the fact that Mr. Williams, whoever he may be, writes up a letter doesn't establish its truth at all for this Board or anyone else. We will then have to examine whether that particular claim is proper, and then we will have to examine whether any other claim or quarrel between an executive and this lady was proper and well founded, and you will inevitably get into that whole matter.

You can not open it up and then stop because I tell the Board that obviously I cannot permit it to stop at that point; and if we are going to review her relationship with this company for a period of three years, or whatever it was, then we are going to review it.

Now, on the other hand, we do know this: That no matter what is in that memo, she continued in the employ of the company for a period of some eight or nine months after that. The company having officials over twenty-one, being mature and presumably reasonable, I suppose wrote her a letter of discharge. I suppose in that letter they may have stated the reasons.

Now, they are charged with having stated them clearly and properly. Let us produce that letter. Let us see what is in that letter. If it is material, then let Mr. Gates offer it. But to go back into every little quarrel or dispute I think is beside the point entirely. It doesn't affect her credibility if Mr. Williams said she overcharged on mileage. That doesn't prove that at all. Mr. Williams may have been false. He may have been mistaken. He may have been motivated by motives we are not concerned with here.

Mr. Drummond: Could we have a five-minute recess?

Chairman Day; We will take a five-minute recess.

(Short recess taken.)

Chairman Day: We will resume the record. The Board has requested, in the light of the probable importance of this document and the length of time that would be involved to amply probe it, to request Mr. Gates to withdraw it.

Mr. Gates: Mr. Chairman, I had not yet had it marked for identification nor tendered it, so it is not necessary to withdraw it; but I will not press the point in view of your request.

Chairman Day: Thank you.

Q Is it not a fact, Miss Seamore, that you were discharged with the recommendation that you should not be reemployed by Amalgamated Airlines?

A Yes.

Mr. Weiss: I object to the question. I ask the answer be struck out.

Chairman Day: I don't think that has an apparent direct effect on her credibility and the answer should be stricken and the objection sustained.

Q Did you testify, Miss Seamore, that you had been working with F-27's ever since you were employed by Amalgamated Airlines?

A The form used to be another number. It wasn't F-27. I think it was called by another title, but it was irregularity reports to the FAA and previously the CAA. Whether we wrote those up all that three years and ten months or not, I am not sure; but if anyone wrote them up for a flight division during those three years and ten months, it was my job.

Q Is your testimony in answer to my question that you either prepared F-27's or a predecessor form from the time you came into the employ of Amalgamated Airlines?

A I did all that were prepared, the days I was present.

Q You mean by "prepared," copying what somebody else had given you?

A That is right.

Q Going back to this conversation of the first night when Mr. Schy and Captain Allison were with you, you testified that you talked about changes in F-27's, you talked about changes in George Schustman's F-27. What else, if anything, did you talk about with Captain Allison and Mr. Schy?

A The work I did on September 15th.

Q You talked about that. You started the conversation about the work on September 15, didn't you?

A Yes.

Q What did you say, if you recall?

A I don't remember words, but I know I told them that if some of the work that I did out there that day had been true and copied as true, as it had been sent to the Tulsa base, they might not have had the

subject matter to fire Wayne Allison, if he was going to be fired.
May I add a little comment?

Q I want you to state only what you said.

A Yes sir.

Q As near as you recall, is that all you said?

A Not all, but that covers it.

Q I want to know all you said.

A I couldn't remember that far back.

Q Is it your testimony that you have stated for the record all that
you recall?

A I told them the kind of work I did that afternoon, and I told
them—

Q Now, just a minute.

A You are asking me what all did I tell them.

Q You say you told them the kind of work you did—just a minute.
I want you to tell us what you told them. It is your conclusion that it
was the kind of work; just please tell us what you told them, as near
as you can recall.

A I told them the kind of work I did on that Saturday afternoon.
I said that Captain Anderson evidently had gathered it all up and put
it in his briefcase. He told me he was going to New York the next
morning, which was Sunday, on flight 48, and I thought he had gone.

So the next morning the flight 48 didn't come in to Tulsa on
account of San Francisco weather. It didn't arrive until about four
o'clock in the afternoon, and he didn't leave town that day. It was my
custom on my own time, to go to the field early on Mondays. I had
been told by Mr. Williams never to come out there and clock in early,
and I would go out there early as I couldn't do that much work in eight
hours, and I always went out an hour early. And Captain Anderson was
there.

He said the flight didn't come in until four o'clock, and he had his
briefcase and boarded the flight 48 and was gone through Thursday and
came in on flight one Thursday afternoon. So he was in his office a
few minutes, and I went in and pulled out this F-27 signed by George
Schustman and handed it to him in his hands.

I had put it secretly in a place where the other ones that had access
to the file cabinets couldn't get it. I told him, I said, "Captain
Anderson, you left this in your top drawer, and found it after you left

Saturday afternoon I hid it for you and here it is."

So he put it in his inside coat pocket. That was in his office. After he looked through his mail and sat at his desk a few minutes or so— I know, I was there one hour longer than customary, one hour overtime, I will say, that day. That was on Thursday. And he walked out to my desk and stood there a moment and said: "Margaret, all this stuff we worked on Saturday, did you give all of that to me?"

Chairman Day: Just a minute, Miss Seamore. I think the question—

The Witness: That is what I told them.

Chairman Day: That is what you told them?

The Witness: Yes.

Chairman Day: Go ahead.

A   Captain Anderson said, "Margaret, this work you did here Saturday, did you give me all that we worked on, all the copies?" because I had made several carbon copies of all of it. I said, "Yes sir."

He said: "You are sure you didn't keep any of those carbon pages out here at your desk, or carbon copies, or copies?" He might have said.

He, all that week, had been feeling bad about it, so I looked up at him and said: "Captain Anderson, I wouldn't want the responsibility of having that here at my desk." I think the only words I said was, "I wouldn't want the responsibility."

He turned around and walked out a ways, and after he was back at his desk a little bit longer, I finished writing the things he had handed me. And this is what I told Mr. Schy and Captain Allison that night.

Q   All right, that is what I am after.

A   I said I had been there, then, an hour overtime, which I had been told by Mr. Williams I would not be allowed overtime to complete the work he had assigned me. And so I went into Captain Anderson. He was very tired and had a hard week. He said he had.

I told him that I was willing to stay. I said I haven't got anything special to go home for, and I said, "I will stay."

He said: "No, I have got to get some things together here and would you..." that is as far as I think I remember.

Q   It is quite clear that you remember the rest of it and I think we ought to have the rest of it for the record, so go on. I have asked the question.

Mr. Weiss: Are you sure you want the answer?

Mr. Gates: I have asked for it.

A Mr. Gates, you said I might cause Captain Anderson's discharge. (Margaret was crying.)

Q That is exactly what I said; in view of your testimony yesterday, it might. Captain Anderson is sitting right here.

(Mr. Gates waved toward Anderson sitting some ten feet from Margaret's chair.)

A He was one of the best friends I ever had.

(Her head was down and her voice was barely audible as everyone in the silent room strained to hear her muffled admission.)

Mr. Gates: Go right ahead with your testimony. If you don't want to answer the question, I will ask another one.

Mr. Weiss: Could we have a recess?

(He too, was clearly touched by sympathy for Margaret.)

Chairman Day: (Clearing his throat.) Yes. We will take a short recess.

(A long ten minute recess was taken during which the Board held a meeting in private.)

Chairman Day: (Rapping on the table for silence.) For the benefit of closing the record, this meeting is adjourned until 9:30 Tuesday morning.

(Whereupon, the meeting was adjourned to January 29, 1952, at 9:30 o'clock a.m.)

It was a surprise move on the part of the Board Chairman, but he had evidently cleared it with the other Board Members. All could return home on company passes for the weekend.

It was quite evident that the company was devastated by Margaret Seamore's testimony, so unexpected and so condemning. The company needed time to assess its position over the weekend and to lay out a plan of action with the higher echelon. I could see that Mr. Gates and Chairman Day would be busy over the weekend.

To me, it looked like a long time with little to do. I could not afford to fly home as a revenue passenger and back again on Monday. I had been off the payroll for too long and knew I would have to reconcile myself to a quiet weekend in the Lexington. In a melancholic mood I gathered my notes and watched the turmoil as everyone seemed suddenly in a hurry to leave the hotel.

"Let's go clean up, have a couple of drinks and go out to a nice dinner." Little George spoke from behind me. "I'm staying on leave through the weekend and we's got things to do. The Shipleys had to leave for he is flying again tonight. I got big ideas for us."

Those big ideas started coming out the next morning right after breakfast. George decided that we should go sightseeing in New York City. As I have said, he was a first class tourist with an Amalgamated airplane. Now he proved himself to be one without the airplane. On our many trips to New York for hearings and my additional trips on contract negotiations, there had never been time to sightsee. It had always been a case of finishing the hearings and then rushing home to cover our scheduled flights out of Tulsa.

The company was always short of qualified pilots, at least it seemed, and insisted on us making up flying time lost on Association business. George and I both knew that the company was trying to make it as difficult as possible to serve on the pilots' System Board of Adjustment and keep up our flying schedules.

George called the desk and secured a tour guide of New York City from a bellboy. Then with that frequent little chuckle, usually followed with another prime idea, he wondered aloud if Margaret Seamore might also be alone in New York City. That took only a phone call and Margaret Seamore was eager to accompany us that Saturday morning and would meet us in the lobby in twenty minutes. George had a way of getting action along his line of thinking, but never forgave himself for trading me two for one in San Francisco. It was a sore spot with him.

To our surprise Margaret had a few suggestions of her own. She was delighted to have two escorts and quickly said so for she was too hesitant to head out on a sightseeing tour by herself and had simply planned a quiet weekend of reading with a show or two along the way. With George it was going to be different.

The first thing he had scheduled was a trip up in a high office building to see how it felt to look down a long ways without a comfortable wing in the corner of his vision. That didn't take long and we were soon on the top floor of a very tall building viewing the scenery from a corner office of a company that was working on Saturday morning, and whose employees were quite amused that a couple of airline pilots wanted to view the streets below. But they were most cordial and did have a few questions to ask a couple of airline pilots.

The viewing went well until George insisted on opening a window and leaning out to look almost directly down at the street far below— I think it was sixty some floors—which was too much for little George. He turned white and staggered back from the window. I guess you could call it a sudden case of airsickness.

"Damn," he exclaimed, looking as though he was about to lose his breakfast, "it sure is a long ways down." Then muttering to himself he headed toward a wash room. "This damned building is weaving badly and about to fall," he exclaimed again as he disappeared.

Margaret and I laughed aloud, along with the office employees. It was so amusing to see an airline pilot sick and dizzy from the altitude. The employees could not understand it, even when I explained that he was accustomed to flying at an altitude of twenty to twenty-five thousand feet, and his office was not moored in any manner. It floated.

We had to walk George around a few blocks before he was able to take a tour bus on an excursion trip. Stopping at a bar on the walk and getting him an early "picker-upper" soon had his gyroscope spinning again. We could see the color coming back into his face as the drink went down and he was soon able to be off touring.

Throughout the day, we never mentioned the hearing: we talked no business, we only chattered nonsense and new touring suggestions. It was truly a pleasant day, as always, with little George. And Margaret seemed to enjoy it greatly.

Tuesday morning the same group gathered in the same meeting room at the same hotel, the Lexington. There were approximately twenty-five pilots there at the start, seated quietly, listening and watching. They had come early, to be sure they did not miss anything. Nat Shipley had come in early by herself as Shipley was on a trip and would be in later in the day. Nat had arranged to have breakfast with George and the two were seated with the group of New York pilots. Soon the Board members came straggling in along with the attorneys.

Margaret Seamore had quietly appeared with some of the early pilots and with a few conversational exchanges with the pilots who knew her, had taken her seat in the witness chair. She had a fresh and pleasant look as she smoothed her plaid skirt, crossed her small feet back under her chair and gave the appearance of a sweet little lamb awaiting the slaughter.

I was struck by the scene and the mannerisms of those gathering. Mr. Gates was particularly striking and forceful as he neatly arranged his papers at his table and paced catlike around the room, glancing occasionally at Margaret Seamore. He was like a panther about to pounce on its prey. The prey was quite self-contained, sitting quietly and apparently totally oblivious to the frequent glances.

Gates knew he had to break Margaret's testimony and discredit her as a witness. Her testimony was too damaging to the company as well as to Anderson and others. As Nat Shipley had said, "The company was on trial."

Idly, in a detached manner, I sat and watched the members of the Board settle in their seats while my attorneys did likewise. It reminded me of two rows of Roman gladiators, lining up on opposing sides for the conflict that was to begin promptly at nine-thirty. Until then, there was friendly bantering across the neutral zone.

Then Chairman Day rapped sharply on the table and called the meeting to order with a continuation of the cross-examination by Mr. Gates. In my mind's eye I could see the gladiators sliding the swords from the sheaths. I thought, I could almost hear the blades slip free.

It was the beginning of a long day, especially for little Margaret Seamore. And the panther lost no time in pouncing. Inside I cringed, recalling how viciously he had attacked me in the first hearing. I felt a sudden wave of sympathy for Margaret and regret over having involved her in my troubles.

Then, throughout over a hundred additional pages of the record the company attorney, Gates, attacked her, sometimes slyly and gently, and sometimes savagely with almost brutal bluntness. Weiss was Margaret's shield, her protector from long, confusing questions, constantly trying to make sure she understood the question before she answered, and at the same time having to guard against constant thrusts from the chairman who insisted in helping Gates with one-sided rulings.

The chairman had a definite thirst to get into the fray in spite of the sometimes tardy objections of the pilot members of the board. They were inclined to be too lenient in questioning the chairman's rulings. But, they were new at the game.

Little Margaret Seamore knew what she was doing. She was not the least bit afraid of Gates. Neither was she bothered by his repeated insistence that she answer his questions with an affirmative or negative response. That didn't bother her. She continued to give an occasional little add-on to the yes or no that would devastate Gates by opening up a whole new subject of company guilt. It would be so damaging that he would try to clear it up, sometimes with considerable difficulty.

Quietly Margaret sat in the chair, occasionally smoothing out a wrinkle in her skirt and appearing undisturbed by Gates's pacing of the floor around her chair. She knew what she was doing to Anderson and Amalgamated. She knew what Anderson had done to me in the falsification of the F-27 and the changing of the messages which went to and from my airplane. She knew he had taken doctored records upstairs to secure approval for my discharge.

She had been a part of it. But she was not trying to be vindictive; she was just telling the truth, trying to set the record straight. She was ashamed of her participation.

Constantly, in response to Gates's questioning, her honesty and truthfulness came forth like shining lights. She would not permit Gates to confuse her and misquote her in previous testimony. Very carefully she would search her memory and make a correction on some point Gates had quoted. Once she looked up at him very directly and indignantly as she accused him of "making it sound so different than it really was."

I think that everyone in the room with the exception of the company officials were giving her mental encouragement. Frequently I would see expressions of pleased satisfaction on the pilot audience and when she accused Gates in the quotation above, it created a general chuckle. Little George repeatedly looked as though he had just landed a plane so smoothly that the passengers didn't know they were on the ground until they began to feel the swells of the runway. Nat also, with her expressive face and blue eyes, would radiate satisfaction and occasionally give me a little nod or slow wink.

Weiss too, began to realize that here was a witness that no attorney could handle, could impeach. He began to object less and less to Gates's involved questions and would let Margaret mull them over deliberately and carefully before she hammered Gates over the head with the truth.

It was very pleasant for me to see and hear her testify. In all my years of sitting on the System Adjustment Board, I had never seen a witness that could so carefully sort out the grains of truth and arrange them properly from a questioning statement that was partly true and partly false. She was like a little hen carefully picking wheat grains from sand grains.

Finally, near two in the afternoon, Gates concluded his cross-examination, more from sheer frustration than from achieving any sort of impeachment of the witness. Weiss was so pleased with Margaret's staunch testimony and conduct under cross-examination that he only asked a few superficial questions to again impress the Board of Margaret's direct testimony relative to Anderson's maintenance of a special reprimand file on Schustman and me, separate and different from that maintained on all other pilots at the Tulsa base.

This was expressly prohibited in the System Adjustment Board provisions of the pilots' labor contract which guaranteed the pilot members of the board freedom from persecution in the discharge of their duties. It thereby became a violation of the Railway Labor Act which covered air carriers as well.

With Margaret Seamore's testimony concluded, the chairman of the Board declared a recess to wait for the next witness. Mr. Weiss had stipulated to the company that he would next call Walter Braznell.

Chapter 21

The Company Witnesses

We were only a few minutes into the recess when Walter Braznell appeared and promptly took the witness chair. I had not seen him for several months. That had been when we had the stormy pilot-company controversy over the contract supplement covering the Korean operation and the flight allocation hearings. Later the Korean contract supplement had been completed with both sides satisfied, but I had not been a party to the completion. The flight allocation grievances were still unsettled during that time I had made it a point to fly westward all the time and keep my face out of New York.

I could not help but notice how completely he avoided looking in my direction as he shook hands with the attorneys, the hearing officer, and the other board members, at the same time giving friendly waves to pilots he recognized in the audience. Idly I recalled the years I had been stationed at Fort Worth as a copilot and as a junior captain before WW II, and the eagerness he had always displayed over coming to Fort Worth from Chicago, where he was a chief pilot, to go quail hunting with me behind my well-trained bird dogs.

In fact, his trips to Fort Worth in the fall of each year became so numerous that the pilots flying the runs from Chicago to Fort Worth began joking about having so many check rides they were getting sway-backed. Then Walt began sending an occasional teletype message to the chief pilot at Fort Worth requesting Allison's schedule and advising Allison that he would be in Fort Worth for two or three days.

It caused Tim Ridley, the Superintendent of Transcontinental Operation in Fort Worth, who was also a bird hunting buddy of mine, to casually join me for a cup of coffee at the airport restaurant and carelessly ask about the message. He was a good friend in spite of our different status positions with Amalgamated, and was an old Tennessee bird hunting man who had a dear love for the sport. Then, there was no such thing as status. Unlike Walter Braznell he didn't expect to be given the best shots or more shots. He was a real hunting partner.

The fact that he was in charge of all of Amalgamated's southern operations and I was a lowly copilot did not matter. That day, the dogs and the hunting was all that mattered and I never mentioned to any of the pilots that he was bird hunting frequently with me. I let Tom tell it, and Tom didn't talk much. We walked a lot behind the dogs, we shared our lunches, our hot thermos of coffee or tea, and split candy bars. And each of us remembered to save a portion of a sandwich for one of the two dogs.

Laughing at his question, I had explained the meaning of the message, that Walter Braznell wanted me to know he expected me to take him bird hunting on at least one of those days. Showing no emotion Tom had carefully stirred his coffee before remarking with that slow Tennessee Drawl.

"I never hunted with him." Then, more to himself than to me he had added, "But I never liked to do business with him. He always seemed to know too much."

That, coming from Tom Ridley, the best-liked and most respected high ranking official of Amalgamated, told me a lot. Known as the Sage of Fort Worth, the heartbeat of Amalgamated's transcontinental flights, the most uncanny weather man Amalgamated has ever known, Tom Ridley did not want to go quail hunting with Walter Braznell.

He always had something else to do when I invited him to go bird hunting along with Walter Braznell. But when I asked him to go on any day when I wasn't flying, and Walter Braznell was not in town, he always seemed to be able to go.

What did Tom see in Braznell that he disliked. What did he see in the weather maps to always be able to tell some captain of Amalgamated when there would be a tornado in a certain area along his path of flight? What did he see in the weather reports to be able to tell a pilot, within fifteen minutes, when the Nashville airport was going to fog in, simply by having an hourly report on the temperature of the Tennessee river? What did he see when he would, during the war, just happen to stay most of the night at the airport, napping on a company divan, just to tell some new and green captain to avoid a certain area where a tornado would be lurking?

Watching Braznell take the oath in the witness chair I let all those thoughts slide through my mind, knowing that I would never get the answers from Tom. He had gone on permanent sleep on that company divan during the war while I was flying overseas.

I do not think anyone in that hearing room could help but admire Braznell's slim and erect bearing, his wavy gray hair, and little gray mustache above rather thick lips that seemed to spoil the looks of his deeply dimpled chin. Nearly fifty years in age, he certainly looked the part of a very knowledgeable airline captain.

In response to Weiss's questions, Braznell disclosed that he had held his present job as Director of Flight since 1947. He admitted to having a staff job and reporting directly to the operations manager with respect to procedures, regulations, and techniques, then to the vice-president of operations, Mr. Lawrence Fritz.

Braznell disclosed that Anderson and Ogden did not report directly to him as they were line supervisors, but Ogden had called him and wanted to send Anderson to New York to apprise him of the situation in regard to my case and to check for past precedent.

Anderson, he admitted, had brought the entire file of my flight made up mostly of radio contact forms, in UARC forms, and running transcript of those messages. This was what Margaret Seamore had testified to as being changed and altered to sound so different. In addition he had brought the flight records, the flight plan and the clearance papers along with my F-27 report, the altered one.

(Questions by Mr. Weiss:)

Q Now, Mr. Braznell, was your concurrence as to the action in recommending or dismissing Captain Allison asked for by Captain Anderson that afternoon?

A Yes, in a way.

Q And did you concur with that action?

A Yes, I agreed that the action taken was justified on the basis of the evidence I had looked over.

Q And, Captain Braznell, before giving your agreement, did you in turn consult with anyone else other than Captain Anderson?

A No.

Q Did you, before giving that agreement, advise anyone else that afternoon or immediately around the time of that afternoon that you were agreeing or that an agreement had been reached on the dismissal of Captain Allison?

A No.

Q Did you, after the meeting with Captain Anderson advise—?

A Yes.

Q Now, who was it you advised?

A The Vice-President of Operations, Lawrence Fritz.

Q When was it, if you do recall, Captain Braznell?

A It was immediately following my meeting with Captain Anderson. I walked into his office, told him that Captain Anderson was there, that we had gone over the records and that he had set forth the reason for it, for the action he was about to take, and that I agreed with that action. In no way was the vice-president involved whatsoever.

Q That is to say, you didn't ask for his decision or anything?

A Not at all.

(This caused me to smile a little to myself. I could see the vice-president hot-footing it into C.R.'s office to tell him that the bounty offered for Allison's scalp had been claimed.)

Mr. Weiss then took up the subject of the flight dispatcher's duties and responsibilities. There had been complete cooperation and agreement between the dispatcher Perierra and myself in the completion of the flight 49. However, no criticism or discipline had been directed at Perierra by the company; Weiss wanted to know why.

Q Does the flight dispatcher have any responsibility with respect to the flight while it is enroute?

A Only to suggest or recommend.

This was contrary to the regulations.

Thereafter Weiss presented a number of regulations to Captain Braznell which supported the fact that the flight dispatcher had a responsibility to recommend another course of action if he did not think the one the pilot was pursuing was a safe course. He also made it clear that the pilot could not pursue a certain course of action if the flight dispatcher disapproved.

Braznell took refuge in claiming that none of those applied when the airplane was operating with an engine out. But he could not show that in the regulations. He kept insisting that the pilot was in command.

Again, under Weiss's questioning, Braznell admitted the company's printing of the Civil Air Regulations were frequently paraphrased. But the paraphrased regulations were sometimes listed as the actual Civil Air Regulations. In short, the company wanted to interpret the regulations for the pilots. It became a little sticky with Gates and Chairman Day trying hard to defend Braznell and divert the pointed questions that were being asked by Weiss. Then Weiss took up another subject.

Mr. Weiss:

Q Captain Braznell, I wish to show you—I don't know what the exhibit number is—it is a series of four letters—it is Exhibit 22; and I call your particular attention to that part of Exhibit 22 which bears the date of January 26, 1948, over the signature of W.H. Dunn, and ask you to read that.

A Shall I read this?

Q Yes, please, just read it to yourself. I want you to familiarize yourself with it.

A I have read it.

Q Now, Captain Braznell, does that part of the exhibit refer, does it not, to a policy of advancing the flight? Do you see that portion of it?

A Yes.

Q Before reading this memorandum or letter of January 26, 1948, by Mr. Dunn, were you familiar and had you heard of the policy of advancing the flight, whether it be a published or an unpublished policy of the company?

A I never heard of an unpublished policy.

Q This is the first you heard of it; is that correct?

A No sir. Mr. Gates showed that to me a few days ago and asked if I had ever seen it. Up to that time I had never seen the letter before and had never heard of it before.

(Again pilot members of the audience looked at each other with little smiles of disbelief on their faces.)

Q So that before having been shown that by Mr. Gates you had never heard of this unpublished policy of the company?

A No sir.

Q Now, Captain Braznell—

A May I enlarge upon that just a little bit?

Q I am going to ask you in a moment and you will have your chance to enlarge on it.

A All right.

Q Disregarding the statement in this letter that we cannot, however, publish this policy—putting that to one side—had you before seeing this piece of paper ever heard of this policy as being that of the company? Do you understand my question?

Mr. Gates: I would like to know what policy you are talking about?

Mr. Weiss: All right, sir. I will read it: "With reference to your letter of January 19th of the above subject, we should like to advise that the proper interpretation relative to this matter requires that aircraft land at a suitable airport. We have briefed all our dispatchers and requested that they give this a liberal interpretation, thereby permitting the captain to use discretion in the selection of a suitable airport. This interpretation means that the pilot may select an airport which will advance the flight. We cannot, however, publish this policy. Signed— W. H. Dunn."

A I cannot answer that yes or no.

(I do not think that anyone in the audience understood his reply. It caused many puzzled looks. Weiss seemed to understand and I think that he considered the reply to mean that if he said "yes" he would open up a real can of worms and probably be "fired" over it, and if he said "no" he would be lying, and actually declined to give an answer. At any rate, Weiss accepted it and continued his questioning.)

Q Captain Braznell, is there any regulation of the company pursuant to which the Superintendent of Flight or the Assistant Superintendent of Flight is empowered or required to make an alteration, change or insertion in the F-27 submitted by the pilot?

Mr. Gates: Objected to as being immaterial and irrelevant to this proceeding.

Chairman Day: There had been considerable testimony on a matter of that kind. I think it is in order the question be answered.

(I think that ruling surprised everyone, especially Mr. Braznell.)

A Well, there is nothing covered in writing on the subject. We do have facetious remarks sometimes included on those that the supervisor will check with the pilot and say, "Is it all right to delete this or that comment and merely let the fact speak for themselves?" and then changes the form that is sent in rather than have the man come out to the airport and do it himself. It is done that way.

Q I see. Other than the possible facetious remarks I think you have reference to, is the F-27—advise the Board please—essentially and solely the pilot's report of the irregularity?

A I would say so.

Q And actually, is it true that having been submitted to the company, it is then by regulation required to be sent forward to Washington.

A It goes into the First Region FAA.

Q I shouldn't say "Washington"—CAA?

A Yes.

Q Are you familiar with the form F-27?

A Yes.

Q Very much so, I assume?

A Yes.

Q Now in that connection, are you familiar with that portion of the F-27 which deals with a statement that the procedure or the incident was or was not in conformity to the Civil Air Regulations?

A Yes.

Q Are you familiar with that part?

A Yes.

Q And is it required that the pilot shall also complete that as a part of the form?

A Yes.

Q It is a fact, is it not, that the pilot's signature is below that particular statement, is it not?

A Yes.

Q Will you answer for the record?

A That is correct, yes.

Q Actually, the form of the F-27 is such that he subscribes to not only that statement but everything above it, does he not?

A Well, he signs the statement, and then there is a place for the supervisor to concur or not concur.

Q Now do you have a regulation under which the supervisor or the superintendent of flight may alter the statement or insert in the statement whether or not the procedure or the incident was in conformance to the Civil Air Regulations? Is there any such regulation of the company?

Mr. Gates: I will object to that as being immaterial and irrelevant.

Mr. O'Connell (Pilot Board Member): I think it is very important.

Chairman Day: Answer the question.

A We don't have any procedure, no; of course not.

Q I show you Amalgamated's Exhibit 3, which is simply for the purpose of bringing to your attention the form that we had under discussion, and ask you whether or not the pilot does, under such a form, place a signature below all the statements contained on that form?

A Yes.

(Mr. Weiss, in the above was nailing down the charge of falsifying a government report over a pilot's signature.)

I was sure that Dave Behncke had instructed Weiss to pursue that course of action to tie in with the flight allocation cases which had never been settled. Neither had they been dropped. Amalgamated Airlines was open to charges of violations of the Railway Labor Act as it pertained to air carriers.

The testimony of Captain Walter Braznell was concluded a short time later and he departed immediately afterwards, looking neither to the right or to the left. Chairman then announced that the meeting would adjourn for the night and reconvene the next morning, January 30, at nine-thirty in the Empire room of the Lexington Hotel.

Weiss had notified the company that he desired to question Mr. W.B. Whitacre, who had been the hearing officer on my first hearing. In turn, the company wanted to recall Captain Joe S. Anderson.

Everyone understood why Anderson was being recalled. The unassuming little secretary, Margaret Seamore, had fitted a noose quite tightly around his neck. Many of the pilots who had heard her testimony were saying that he should be fired immediately. That was going up and down the flying line as pilots who had sat in on the hearing expressed their views to others. All believed Margaret!

It seemed to me as I moodily gathered the daily notes I had made, that the hearings would last forever. I had been in New York for several days rubbing shoulders with pilots, listening to flying conversations, listening to attorneys argue, breathing the New York air, and rapidly getting sick of it. I longed to be out of there, away from New York, away from Amalgamated and, smiling in amusement at myself, I thought how much I longed to pull the nose up, up and up to get where the air was cleaner and I could think more clearly.

That night I received a call from Jean. It had been several days since I had talked with her and in all that time she had been trying to trade for a trip to New York, but to no avail. She was stuck on a little puddle jumping run to El Paso that none of the stewardesses like to fly. It was a day flight with several stops and was usually a rough flight.

It gave me quite a thrill to just talk with her and realize that she, too, was feeling quite lonely. I explained to her that the hearings would likely terminate the following day and George and I would be coming home. That seemed to make her feel better and somehow, I did also.

The next morning there were more pilots congregating in the Empire room of the Lexington along with the usual ones, the lawyers, the court reporter, the System Adjustment Board, and Anderson as well as myself. Ogden had been in and out at different times with a worried look on his face. He knew that his tail was tied rather closely to Anderson's

Nat and Ship were also there, as usual. Word had gotten out that Anderson was going to take the stand again and it had heightened interest up and down the line. Everyone had heard of Margaret Seamore's condemning testimony of Anderson's conduct and they wanted to hear this assistant superintendent of flying who had falsified my F-27 report.

Some pilots had come directly into the hearing from the flying line and early hours of flying. Some had slept a couple or three hours in the crew lounge at the field then came directly into the hearing.

William B. Whitacre made his appearance and was promptly sworn in by the Notary Public. Mr. Weiss then began the direct examination.

Whitacre disclosed that he was the director of the central division of Amalgamated Airlines with headquarters in Chicago. He admitted that he was first notified that he was to hear my case on the 18th of September by Thomas Boyson, operations manager acting for Mr. Lawrence Fritz, the vice-president of operations.

I could not help but reflect on the personal glee Tom Boyson must have felt in making that appointment. He had been one of the System Board members on the screening hearings when I had exposed him as being a signer of the directive that set up the screening program. That exposure had been made in front of Mr. Ralph Damon, then president of Amalgamated Airlines and Mr. C.R. Brown, chairman of the Board of Directors of Amalgamated Airlines, who had sat in on the briefing which drove the splitting wedge between Mr. Damon and Mr. C.R. Brown.

Vividly I recalled the way Tom Boyson had chewed on his pipe that early morning in Tulsa when I had had the two emergencies. No doubt he had been the one who had set up the little trap for me that Anderson was supposed to trigger. And C.R. had shown his disgust with the failure by giving them all a dirty look and stalking out of the room. Jimmie had picked that up for me.

Mr. Weiss questioned Whitacre relative to his experience in previous hearings and the use of a private prosecuting attorney from outside the company to prosecute my case. Normally, on other cases, the company had, in the past, used a company attorney from the Labor Relations Department. But for me, Amalgamated had hired a 'hotshot' prosecuting attorney. However Whitacre brushed that off by claiming the company attorney had too much of a work load to handle the Allison case.

Weiss then questioned Whitacre relative to his holding short discussions on the Allison case at various pilot meetings in Chicago and elsewhere before he had issued his decision. Whitacre, no doubt, was trying to prejudice the field in favor of his decision. He was given a slanted view for in none of his briefings had he mentioned the unpublished policy of advancing the flight and that it had been shown in writing at the hearing.

The Air Line Pilots' Association had received quite a few pilot complaints about Whitacre's discussions of the Allison case and Mr. Weiss took him to task about them. But Whitacre was able to defend himself quite well and in the end, I considered the exchange a draw. In fact, I had to admire the way Whitacre had conducted himself in the examination. He was real smooth.

Finally, Mr. Weiss excused him just a few minutes before noon and Chairman Day set the afternoon session to begin at two. Everyone seemed to like the idea of a long lunch break. They were anticipating Anderson's return to the witness chair.

Chairman Day, after the lunch, called the hearing to order promptly at two and Mr. Gates called Anderson to the witness chair. This was the situation Gates had hoped to avoid, I felt certain. I knew that he did not want to give Weiss a chance to cross-examine Anderson. But he had no other choice.

Margaret Seamore's testimony had been so devastating, so factual and so much in detail that he had to do something to refute Margaret's direct testimony. She had given it so sincerely and with so many minute details, such as describing the way Anderson had taken Schustman's F-27 and put it in an inside pocket after she had hidden it overnight, that no one questioned the truthfulness of her testimony. Gates knew he had been unable to discredit her as a witness in any manner.

With Anderson in the witness chair, and under direct examination Mr. Gates made an attempt to clarify the F-27 matter with Anderson claiming that an F-27 he had in hand was the one he had put in his pocket. But Weiss soon shot that down with questions relative to proving that it was as identified. But this covered several pages of questions and arguments before it was finally dropped.

Then Mr. Gates questioned Anderson about the Saturday afternoon he had Margaret Seamore prepare some data for him. I return to the certified record.

Questions by Mr. Gates: (Direct examination)

Q Captain Anderson, during the afternoon of September 15, did Miss Seamore copy or make copies of Amalgamated's Exhibit No. 21?

(This Exhibit covered the weather sequences during the period of my last flight.)

A Yes sir.

Q Now, what else did she do?

A She prepared a memorandum addressed to Captain Braznell, in which I covered the information that I had compiled as a result of this investigation.

(I leaned forward in my seat to hear Anderson better. This was the memorandum in which Margaret Seamore had testified of changes, insertions and alterations being made. It, as she had said, was the reason she was there to testify.)

Q Well now, will you please, in your own words, explain to the Board how that memorandum was prepared, what it looked like, and what its contents were?

A It was approximately—

Mr. Weiss: All right. I will ask a preliminary question. Is the memorandum in existence today?

A No sir.

Q What happened to it?

A I threw it away.

(I wasn't the only pilot in that room leaning forward and listening intently to the testimony.)

Mr. Weiss: I want to ask a preliminary question on that.

Mr. Gates: Let me ask another question.

Q By Mr. Gates: Was it ever delivered to Captain Braznell?

A No sir.

Mr. Gates: Very well. You may ask.

Mr. Weiss: Captain Anderson, when was that thrown away by you?

A It was thrown away after I returned to Tulsa.

Q Returned from where—New York City?

A From New York.

Q You took it with you to New York City?

A Yes sir.

Q Did you have it among your papers while you were discussing matters with Captain Braznell?

A Yes sir.

(All eyes were intent on Anderson as he confessed in a low voice.)

Q Was it under consideration by Captain Braznell; did you bring it to his attention?

A I don't believe Captain Braznell saw it.

Q Did you bring it to his attention?

A I read from it.

Q Did he see you read from it?

A Yes sir.

Q He saw you read from it?

A He saw me read from it.

Q Did you tell him you were reading from a memorandum addressed to him?

A No sir.

Q And then when you returned to Tulsa, you threw it away? Did you physically destroy it?

A I threw it away. I don't recall if I physically destroyed it.

Q Where were you when you threw it away—in your office?

A I was at home.

Q That is when you threw it away, when you were at home?

A Yes sir.

(It was inconceivable. A document used in securing the release of a pilot was suddenly too hot to preserve. It was thrown away. What did it contain? The confession supported Margaret Seamore's testimony that alterations and falsifications were made. Everyone in the room wondered at the same time—what did it contain?)

Mr. Weiss: (shaking his head slightly in disbelief) I have no further questions on this preliminary matter.

(The room was suddenly filled with a low level buzz of conversation.)

Chairman Day: (taking his eyes off Anderson and looking at Gates) Go ahead.

Mr. Weiss: (interrupting.) I have one further preliminary question.

Q Captain Anderson, I did not ask you, but I now ask you: How many copies of that memorandum were made?

A I believe one copy.

Q Where was the copy left, in your office, or did you take it with you?

A I had it with me.

Q And do I understand that both the original and the copy of that memorandum were kept at all times by you, in your possession?

A Yes sir.

Q And when you say you threw it away, do you mean that you threw away both the original and the copy?

A Yes sir.

Q And both the original and the copy, were they thrown away or destroyed, as the case may be, at your home in Tulsa?

A They were thrown away. I don't recall whether they were physically destroyed or not.

Q But both the original and the copy at the time?

A Yes sir.

Q And at your home in Tulsa.

(Weiss was making it quite clear that he did not believe Anderson, and knew he was lying. No official would throw away a document and its only copy as important as a very carefully prepared memorandum substantiating the firing of a pilot, that is, unless it would not stand a close inspection in the light of day.)

Mr. Weiss: All right. I have no further questions of a preliminary nature.

(It was quite obvious to all that he knew he had a weasel in the witness chair and was thoroughly disgusted with him.)

Q (By Mr. Gates:) Now, do you recall the question?

A The nature of the contents, I believe, is what you want.

Q I want you to state how it was made, what it contained, and what it looked like.

A It was approximately a two-and-a-half page memorandum in which I attempted to convey the general history of the flight from the time it left Oklahoma City until it arrived in Los Angeles. I added my observations, which were determined at the investigation for information purposes. I inserted here and there excerpts of weather and excerpts of radio contacts for clarification of my statements contained in these paragraphs.

Q Is that all?

A Yes sir.

(Thereafter Mr. Gates questioned Anderson in detail on all the papers he took to show Mr. Braznell. He tried to present it as a very factual compilation of evidence on my flight.)

Mr. Gates: All right. There has been a very considerable amount of testimony concerning Captain Allison's F-27, particularly at Tulsa, with respect to the insertion of the word "not" in the last two lines of the form F-27, which in substance provides the action of the captain was in conformity with the civil air regulations, and your insertion of the word "not," so that it read: "The action of the Captain did not conform to the Civil Air Regulations." When was the word "not" inserted by you?

A When I was in New York.

Q On September the 18th?

A Yes sir.

Q Now, excluding that F-27 which you had before you and altered on September 18th, did you make any change of any kind on any of the records in connection with this proceeding?

A No sir.

(Mr. Gates was trying to refute Margaret Seamore's testimony with Anderson's direct testimony.)

Mr. Gates: Captain Anderson, excepting the F-27 of Captain Schustman, which is in evidence in this hearing, and the F-27 of Captain Allison, which also is in evidence in this proceeding, did you ever make a change in any F-27 filed by a captain, which change was not authorized by the captain?

A Other than additions, certain amount of additions, no. The word should be "editing."

Mr. Gates: What do you mean by "editing?" I want you to tell the Board exactly what you did, as near as you can state it.

A Sometimes a captain will use bulky sentences that didn't clearly convey the meaning of his intent, and maybe by punctuation, it would clear up his meaning. That is one example.

Q Can you give an example?

A You mean the ones which I did edit?

Q Yes.

A I can't recall any right now, no.

(Mr. Gates was trying hard to whitewash Anderson.)

Q Did you ever change the substance?

A No sir.

Q Captain Anderson, did you hear Miss Seamore's testimony with respect to a conversation which she stated took place between you and her on the afternoon of Thursday, September the 20th, after you returned from New York on flight 1? Did you hear her testimony?

A Yes.

Q Did any such conversation as she recounted take place between you and her?

A No sir.

Q No what?

A It did not take place. There was no such conversation.

Chairman Day: There was no such conversation?

A That is right.

Mr. Gates: Did you have a conversation with Miss Seamore on the morning of Monday, September 17th?

A No sir.

(Anderson was completely denying any of the detailed conversations Margaret Seamore recounted in her testimony.)

Then Gates questioned Anderson relative to the separate file he had kept on me in the bottom drawer of his desk. He made it appear that it only consisted of unsettled grievances I had filed in behalf of the pilots of Tulsa.

Finally, after Mr. Gates had whitewashed it as much as possible and Anderson had contradicted Margaret Seamore's testimony repeatedly, he turned Anderson over to Weiss for cross-examination.

Cross-Examination by Mr. Weiss:

Q   Captain Anderson, did you advise Miss Seamore on Friday, September 14, that you might require her services on the following Saturday, September 15?

A   I believe that statement is correct. I am not sure that I informed her on that day.

Q   Now, to the best of your recollection, when did you tell her that—what time—what part of the day of September 14?

A   I don't recall what part of the day. It seems to me it was along toward the end of the day.

Q   And did you tell her that you would phone her the following day and give her the precise hour?

A   I don't recall doing that.

Q   Would you say that you did not or you don't—

A   I do not recall telling her that I would phone her.

Q   Would you swear that you did not so tell her or you just don't have any recollection?

A   I just don't recall.

Q   All right. Captain Anderson, when this F-27 which is Amalgamated's exhibit 24 in evidence was handed to you, were you the only one to examine it in your office or did others examine it?

A   No sir, as I recall, there were several people in the office at the time.

Q   Well, I understand, but did others than yourself examine that?

A   Yes sir.

Mr. Gates: I take it, you are referring to the afternoon of September 14, Mr. Weiss?

Mr. Weiss: That is right.

Mr. Gates: I didn't hear the question.

Q   (By Mr. Weiss):   And other than yourself, were there some pilots in the office?

A   Yes sir.

Q   In your office?

A   Yes sir.

Q   And did that include Captain Schustman?

A   Yes sir.

Q   Captain Allison?

A   I believe he was there at the time.

Q You know he was, didn't you? Wasn't this the investigation of Captain Allison's matter?

A Yes sir.

Q So there is no doubt in your mind as to his presence there?

A No, there is no doubt about it.

Q And were there still other pilots than Captain Schustman and Captain Allison there?

A Yes sir.

Q How many pilots in all would you say were there?

A I would say five or six.

Q Now, other than yourself, were there any other company officials?

A Mr. Clyde McCall.

Q And his position is what with the company, or was at that time?

A Assistant Superintendent of Flight, Fort Worth.

Q Is he an assistant to you?

A No sir.

Q Is he still Assistant Superintendent of Flight?

A Yes sir.

Q Now, was it only your judgement that this F-27, flight 24, was not the F-27 that was being discussed, or did the pilots also say that this is not the one, or in substance that this is not the one we are talking about?

Q Was it my judgement?

Mr. Weiss: I will rephrase that question. You have testified that when this was handed to you by Miss Seamore that you examined it and you just told us that other pilots also examined it. That the pilots examined it in your office; is that correct?

A I don't know in what sequences they examined it, but they looked at it.

Q I didn't ask you the sequence.

A All right.

Q You were not the only one to look at this paper?

A No sir.

Q Pilots looked at it as well in your office; is that correct?

A That is correct.

Q And after they looked at it and after you looked at, or sometime during the scrutiny of this paper, did the pilots as well as yourself say "that this in not the F-27 that we are talking about?"

A I don't recall them saying that. I didn't hear them say it.

Q Was it only you who said that?

A Yes sir.

Q Prior to this being given to you, you said that other F-27, or at least another one was given to you; is that correct?

A That is correct.

Q What did you do with the other F-27 after it was handed to you and you discovered it was not the one under discussion?

A I believe I gave them back to Miss Seamore.

Q What did you do with that after you discovered it was not the one being discussed?

A I am not sure. Captain Schustman came in possession of the papers at some time during this conversation.

Q He looked at it?

A Yes sir.

Q You have already told us that other pilots looked at it; isn't that so?

A That is right.

Q Now, did anyone other than Captain Schustman see this particular F-27, Amalgamated's Exhibit 24?

A Yes, I saw several pilots looking at it.

Q Would you tell the board how many, if you know, looked at the F-27?

A I am not referring to the time in my office. I am referring to another time now.

Q I am referring to the time in your office, Captain. You must be entirely clear about that.

A I don't know that any other pilot examined it closely in the office.

Q Any other pilot—did anyone examine it?

A Other than Captain Schustman?

Q Yes.

A No.

Q Now then, after Captain Schustman examined it, do you remember, I ask you again, what was done with this paper?

A He put it in his pocket.

Q He put it in his pocket?

A Yes sir.

Q Then what happened to it.

A I asked for it back.

Q Did he give it back to you?

A Yes sir.

Q Then what happened, what did you do with it?

A I believe I laid it on my desk and later on Captain Schustman asked that he be allowed to see it again so that some copies could be made. I gave it to Miss Seamore, and around her typewriter, that is where I saw several of the pilots looking at it and discussing the F-27 along with Captain Schustman.

Q Did you raise any objection to them looking at the F-27?

A No sir.

Q None at all?

A No sir.

Q Now, Captain Anderson, when Miss Seamore produced this F-27, did you see from what folder or file she took it?

A No sir, she was fumbling around the files, and I was at this time busy with this investigation.

Q Well, you say she was fumbling around with the files—you mean she was looking through a sheaf of papers in the file?

A Yes sir.

Q And was she by the filing cabinet or by your desk?

A Part of the time she was by the filing cabinet and part of the time she was out of the room.

Q And did she tell you she was going out of the room?

A No, she didn't tell me.

Q Do you recall her saying anything about that?

A No.

Q Now, as a matter of fact, do you have any recollection of Miss Seamore calling you and telling you that she had found an F-27?

A I don't recall that.

Q Would you swear that she did not?

A I can't swear it, because I don't recall it.

Q Captain Anderson, when the meeting was over in your office, did you then walk out into Miss Seamore's office?

A Sometime later, yes.

Q How much later?

MEN WHO FLY

A I would think it was some few minutes later.

Q And was it at that time you say you saw the pilots looking at the F-27?

A I don't believe so. I believe it was after Captain Schustman had requested that some copies be made of it. Miss Seamore's office, if I may explain a little bit, is not an office.

Q Sure.

A It is actually a hallway which I may use to go back and forth to the operations office most any time.

Q Does the Chief Stewardess's office intervene between your office and wherever Miss Seamore's desk is located?

A That is right.

Q Is there a telephone by which one can call you from the Chief Stewardess's office?

A Yes. sir.

Q Now, did Captain Schustman tell you when it was that he had made out and filed the irregularity report relating to the flight which passed over a near airport to an airport which did not have good weather?

A Did he tell me when?

Q Yes.

A No sir.

Q Did you ask him when that occurred?

A Yes sir.

Q What did he say?

A He couldn't tell me.

Q Did you ask him approximately when that occurred?

A No, I believe at that time I asked Miss Seamore to see I if she could find the F-27.

Q Since she was looking for it and apparently it had not turned up as yet, Captain Anderson, didn't you turn to Captain Schustman and ask him: "Can't you fix the time, or can't you tell us when?" Wasn't there anything like that done?

A No sir; not after the original question.

Q Sir?

A Not after the original question—did he remember the date.

Q Was Captain Schustman one of the pilots who was examining this F-27 at Miss Seamore's desk?

A Yes, he was.

Q Did he make any comment to you about it?

A At that time?

Q Yes.

A I don't recall any.

Q Now, he had actually just previously examined it in your office hadn't he?

A Yes sir.

Q But you say, nevertheless, that although he had examined that F-27, they nevertheless, examined it once more at Miss Seamore's desk?

A That is correct.

Q Are you entirely sure, Captain Anderson, that Captain Schustman was not examining a different F-27, different from Exhibit 24?

A I am positive.

Q You are positive of that?

A Yes.

Q You particularly recollect that? What jogged your memory on that score? Why do you remember this particular piece of paper?

A I can't tell you why I remember it.

Q Captain Anderson—

A That was the only one there was any discussion on that day.

Q But as things developed that wasn't in discussion at all, was it? This was not the correct paper, was it?

A That is right.

Q And there was another F-27 which also turned out to be the wrong one; isn't that true?

A That is right.

Q In fact, I think you told me there was at least—you told Mr. Gates there were more than one that was produced—this was the last one in order, isn't that right?

A That is right.

Q Now will you tell the Board what the other F-27's were about? What incidents do they relate to?

A I have no idea at this time.

Q Now after the pilots left Miss Seamore's desk, what then was done with this particular F-27?

A It was placed back in the file.

Q Along with the other F-27's?

A I don't know when Miss Seamore placed those back. I did not place them back.

Q Who placed this one back?

A I believe I did. I would not say for sure.

Q Did you mark it in any particular way?

A No sir.

Q When you placed it back, did you place it back among other papers in Captain Schustman's file?

A Yes sir.

Q Now then, I ask you again, Captain Anderson, what is it that caused you to recollect that this particular paper, this F-27's was the one that you claim was on Miss Seamore's desk?

A Because that was the only one that caused any discussion that day as far as Captain Schustman was concerned.

Q But Captain Anderson, you told us at least twice now that that was not the F-27 that Captain Schustman was talking about, isn't that true?

A I am telling you now, that was the only one there was any amount of discussion about on that day.

Q Now when you placed the paper back in Captain Schustman's file, did you make any memorandum or notation attaching it to this paper?

A No sir.

Q Captain Anderson, can you now tell the Board when it was that you in your own mind came to the conclusion that you were going to recommend or direct Captain Allison's dismissal?

A It was on Friday evening.

Q While you were at the office?

A No, while I was at home.

Q And had you taken with you Captain Allison's papers?

A Yes sir.

Q Papers concerning his file?

A Yes sir.

Q Then, do I understand you had already made arrangements to have Miss Seamore, you put her on notice you would want her the following day, isn't that so?

A That is right.

Q Now in this memorandum which you prepared and addressed to Captain Braznell, did that contain within it a recommendation concerning dismissal of Captain Allison?

A No sir.

Q Did it contain any observation by you as to what you thought the merits of the case were?

A Yes, there was a statement in there.

Q Well, Captain Anderson, if Captain Braznell had read that memorandum—he did not, isn't that true?

A That is right.

Q If he had read that memorandum, was it couched and put in language so he would get the impression that you felt that Captain Allison should be dismissed?

Mr. Gates: Just a minute, I object to the question as calling for a speculative answer, and certainly he can't tell what Captain Braznell would have thought about it. This witness is incompetent to testify to that.

Chairman Day: I think the witness can tell what he put in the memorandum. I don't think he can tell what Captain Braznell would have thought if he had done so.

Mr. Weiss: Since we don't have the memorandum, it is a little bit difficult, you know. But I will ask the question this way: Captain Anderson did you say anything which directly or indirectly indicated your determination or your feeling that Captain Allison exercised bad judgment in Flight 49?

A I believe that summary paragraph that I made a statement in it to the effect that I thought extremely bad judgment was used throughout this flight.

Q And did you in that memorandum indicate that you were recommending dismissal of Captain Allison?

A No, I did not.

Q Now, after the memorandum was prepared, did you sign it?

A Yes, I did.

Q And did you show it to Don Ogden when you saw him?

A Yes sir.

Q Did he read it?

A Yes sir.

Q And did you also take out the copy at the time you showed it to Don Ogden?

A Will you repeat that, please?

Q Let me ask you this way: You took both the original and the copy with you, didn't you?

A That is correct.

Q Now, when you went to see Don Ogden, did you take out all the papers from your folder?

A Yes sir.

Q And spread them in front of him?

A I saw that he looked at all the papers. I don't know if I spread them in front of him or not.

Q Are you entirely sure, Captain Anderson, that only one copy of an original memorandum was made?

A Yes sir.

Q Why was it that you only made one copy?

A It was all that was necessary.

Q Isn't it customary in your office to make more than one copy of an original document?

A There are times when it is.

Q Well, didn't this memorandum relate to a rather serious matter in your view?

A Yes sir.

Q And you knew when you prepared it that it might be the basis of a serious and grave recommendation with respect to Captain Allison, didn't you?

A The memorandum—

Mr. Gates: He just testified he made no recommendation, Mr. Weiss.

Mr. Weiss: I didn't say. I said it might be the basis of a serious and grave recommendation with respect to Captain Allison.

A The memorandum was not a basis of my recommendation. It was merely something to convey the results of my investigation to Captain Braznell.

Q And you say you didn't think it appropriate to make more than one copy?

A No sir.

Q Nor did you think it appropriate to leave a copy of this memorandum in your office as a part of your records?

A It didn't occur to me at that time.

Q Don't you customarily leave in your office records, copies of memoranda prepared by you?

A Not always.

Q I asked you whether you customarily do?

A The majority of the times I would say yes, but certainly by no means always.

Q In other words, there may be particular instances when you do not make such extra copies?

A There may be a lot of instances where I do not.

Q But they would be in the minority of cases, wouldn't they?

A I would say yes.

Q Now, Captain Anderson, what did you actually do with the original and the copy?

A I believe I have answered that once before.

Q No, I think you said you threw it away. Do you mean you threw it in a waste basket?

A In my wastepaper basket, yes.

Q Will you tell us again, please, when it was that you did that?

A It was after I came back from New York, I believe, on the 19th or 20th.

Q Well, now, when you returned from New York, Captain Anderson, what time was it that you arrived in Tulsa?

A 2:40 a.m.

Q And you went directly home, didn't you?

A That is right.

Q And then did you come to the office the next day?

A Yes sir.

Q Now, what time did you get to the office?

A As I recall, around noon.

Q And did you take your papers with you to the office?

A You mean the ones concerning the Allison case?

Q That is right.

A No, I didn't take them.

Q You left them at home?

A Yes sir.

Q Why did you leave them at home?

A Well, because I had prepared a letter there—I take that back—

I did bring some of the papers with me to the office.

Q Which papers did you bring to the office with you?

A The papers concerned with preparing a letter of dismissal.

Q Which papers were they?

A Papers from which I wrote the letter of dismissal.

Q Which papers were they, Captain Anderson?

A They were the radio contacts, the transcript of the radio contacts, and the messages, the weather, the clearance report, and the clearance file.

Q Now, will you tell the Board what papers you left at home?

A Well, there were, as I recall it, the letter, the memorandum which we have just been discussing, and along with some other papers that had no connection with the Allison case.

Q So that the only papers that you left at home which had any relation to the Allison case was the Braznell memorandum?

A No sir.

Q Tell us what other papers you left at home?

A A lot of other pencil copies of memoranda that I had made during the investigation.

Q And you left those at home?

A Yes sir.

Q So that all papers in connection with the Allison case that you took to New York, other than the penciled memoranda which you made in the course of investigation and other than the memorandum which you wrote and signed addressed to Captain Braznell, were taken to the office on the day after your return, or the day of your return to Tulsa; is that correct, Captain Anderson?

A Captain Allison's file was left at my home at that time.

Q His file was left at your home?

A Yes sir.

Q Now, did you eventually take back to the office all of the papers in the Allison case, which had been left in your home that day, other than this memorandum which you threw away?

A Well, I sometime later, when I had a little more time—I was pretty rushed about then—I went through everything I had and the stuff that I no longer needed, I tossed away.

Q Did you first take them to the office?

A No sir, I took—threw them away there.

Q Now when you say that you threw them away, I take it that you are referring of necessity—you have told us you threw the memorandum away—then the only thing else that remains that you threw away were the penciled notes? Is that right?

A Yes, that is right.

Q What were these penciled notes, Captain Anderson, little scraps of paper with your personal notes or comments or observations?

A I believe so, yes.

Q Is that your testimony?

A There were several sheets of penciled notes that I had taken, and they served no further purpose, and I do quite a bit of work at home, while I was working one evening, that evening I went through and tossed them out.

Q Now, they were more or less informal scraps of paper, if you will, containing your observations; is that right?

A That is right.

Q Captain Anderson, the memorandum to Captain Braznell was not an informal scrap of paper though, was it?

A It was not.

Q And having been written by you, it contained a complete summary, I suppose, of the pertinent facts in the Allison case, didn't it?

A Yes, it did.

Q And it also contained a reduction to writing of your observation and conclusion that indicated bad judgment on the part of Captain Allison?

A That contained part of it, yes sir.

Q And that was done by or dictated, you say, by you or written under your supervision in the course of your business at the Tulsa base, was it not?

A Yes sir.

Q And as such, did it not comprise a part of the records in the Allison case?

A I did not consider it so.

Q You didn't think so?

A No.

Q Now, do you remember, Captain Anderson, having inquired of Miss Seamore, whether it be on the 19th or on the 20th, or any other day, what other copies of paper were prepared that Saturday afternoon remained about?

A No sir.

Q Do you swear that you do not?

A I can swear that I did not.

(I think that most everyone in that room felt that Anderson had committed perjury.)

Q Did you make a search to see whether any other copies were about?

A No sir.

Q Why did you throw away the memorandum to Captain Braznell?

A I believe I have answered that. I thought it of no further use.

Q But Captain Anderson, you have told us just a few moments ago that you took with you the papers to your office which you wanted to use to write a letter containing our recommendations in the Allison case; isn't that right?

A That is right.

Q Now, isn't it true that the memorandum you prepared to Captain Braznell contained in chronological and succinct form all the relevant facts covering the Allison case?

A I had those facts well in mind.

Q I asked you whether that isn't true?

A Repeat your question.

Q Isn't it true that the memorandum you prepared to Captain Braznell contained in chronological and succinct form all the relevant facts bearing on the Allison case?

A Yes, it contained those facts.

Q And, in fact, that memorandum, as you have testified about it, would have served as a very convenient method of preparing a letter on the Allison case, wouldn't it?

A But I didn't need it.

Q Will you answer my question? I said it would have served as a very convenient basis on which to prepare a letter in the Allison case, would it not?

A It could have.

Q Yes, I wonder if you can explain this to the Board, Captain Anderson, since you did take a good many papers in the Allison case back to the office the day of your return to Tulsa, why did you sort out certain papers and not take those back as well?

A I took the ones that I thought were necessary for the preparation of this letter.

Q Were the other papers very bulky and difficult to carry?

A Well, not necessarily, but they were in a separate folder and I didn't see any point in taking them to the field if I no longer needed them.

Q You mean, you had this Braznell memorandum in a separate folder?

A No, it was a folder with these penciled notations.

Q Weren't the papers in the Allison case that you took with you and brought back contained in one folder, didn't you tell us that?

A In my briefcase. There were several folders of the Allison file which was that thick (indicating a couple of inches).

Q I still am not entirely clear, Captain Anderson, could you explain why it was that you did not simply take all the Allison papers back with you to the office? Wouldn't that have been the simplest thing to do?

A Not necessarily because I went over these at home before I went back to the office. I took out what I thought I needed.

Q But you did extract the bulk of the papers, didn't you?

A Yes.

Q And brought them back to the office?

A The things I did not need, I threw away. The rest of it I took to the office.

Q But you didn't throw that memorandum away at that time when you extracted the papers, did you?

A I was under the impression I did.

Q Well, didn't you tell us earlier that you threw away that memorandum in the evening?

A Well, if I did, I was mistaken. I threw it away at that time.

Q I see. So that when you went to this folder or this series of folders to extract some of the Allison papers, at that time, you threw away the Braznell memorandum; is that right?

A That is right.

Q And at that time, did you also throw away these penciled notations?

A Yes sir.

Q Didn't you just a few minutes ago tell us that you threw away those penciled notations several days later?

A No, I don't believe I did.

Q Now, I will refresh your mind, Captain Anderson, didn't you tell us just a while back that on going through your papers several days later that you then threw away those notations?

A I don't believe I said that.

Q Captain Anderson, I suggest to you, sir, that is it possible that you may be mistaken and that it was several days later that you also threw away the Braznell memorandum?

A I don't believe so.

Q Are you certain of it, though?

A Yes.

Q Do you now say that you threw away the Braznell memorandum and its copy at the same time that you threw away the penciled notations?

A Yes sir.

Q And you did that in your home in the middle of the day?

A When I awakened and felt like doing some work.

Q Well, was it in the middle of the day?

A Approximately.

Q And you now also say that you took the balance of the papers and brought them to the office?

A That is right.

Mr. Weiss: I would ask the Board for a short recess.

Chairman Day: How long, Mr. Weiss?

Mr. Weiss: Five minutes.

Chairman Day: We will take a short recess.

(A short recess was taken.)

Chairman Day: Are you ready, Mr. Weiss?

Mr. Weiss: Yes, I am.

Chairman Day: Let us go ahead.

Mr. Weiss: Captain Anderson, when did you first tell anyone that you had thrown away the original copy of the memorandum to Captain Braznell?

A I didn't think it was of any importance until this came up. I don't know whether I told anybody.

Q I ask you specifically, when did you first tell anyone that you had thrown away the original and the copy of the memorandum?

Mr. Gates: I object on the grounds it is immaterial and has no bearing on this proceeding. It is not a part of the record in this case at all. He could have prepared twenty-five memos and destroyed all of them and it wouldn't make a bit of difference.

Chairman Day: I think he answered the question. I think, he said he never told anybody.

Mr. Weiss: Is that your answer?

A   Yes.

Chairman Day: Off the record.

Mr. Weiss: I withdraw the question, and may the answer be struck?

Chairman Day: All right.

Mr. Weiss: Captain Anderson, when did you first tell anyone that you had thrown away the original and the copy of the memorandum you had prepared addressed to Braznell?

Mr. Gates: To which I object on the ground it is irrelevant and immaterial, but we are going to let him answer it. He can answer it fully.

Mr. Weiss: May I have the comment of the Board on that. I didn't hear it.

Chairman Day: I agree, it is immaterial and irrelevant, but to save time we will let him answer it anyway.

Mr. Weiss: I take exception to the observation of the Board. I think it is probably one of the most material pieces of testimony in this record.

Mr. Gates: I will instruct the witness not to answer.

Chairman Day: Off the record.

(Discussion off the record.)

Mr. Gates: I will withdraw that. Let him answer.

Chairman Day: I ruled before that I did not see wherein the question was material or relevant; but in order to save time we would let him answer it. Mr. Gates has withdrawn his objection on that basis. Let us go ahead.

Mr. Weiss: Answer.

Mr. O'Connell: What is the question?

Mr. Weiss: When, Captain Anderson, did you first tell anyone that you threw away the original and the copy of the memorandum you prepared addressed to Captain Braznell?

A   I discussed it with Mr. Gates yesterday.

Q   And is that the first time you informed anyone?

A The first time, yes.

Mr. Gates: Wait a minute.

A You asked me if I told him I threw it away; is that right?

Q That is right.

A I told him I didn't have it before then. But I didn't tell him I threw it away until yesterday.

Q I see. Then, in the light of your answer, when did you first tell anyone that you didn't have the memorandum?

A That was last week.

Q Now, Captain Anderson, so we completely understand ourselves, do you now say that last week was the first time that you ever told anyone that you either threw the memorandum away or that you did not have it?

A That is right. I didn't think it was important until it was brought up at this hearing.

Q And so that we will fix the time on that, Captain Anderson, you heard Miss Seamore testify, did you not?

A Yes sir.

Q Now, up to the time that Miss Seamore testified, is it a fact that you have never stated except to Mr. Gates that the memorandum had been thrown away or that you did not have it?

A Now—

Q Do you understand my question?

Mr. Gates: That isn't his testimony.

A I don't. I think it is in contradiction of what you previously asked me.

Q You think it is?

A It appears to me at this time.

Q Let's see if we can clarify it, Captain Anderson.

A I made the statement, I believe that the first time I mentioned to Mr. Gates concerning the memorandum was last week.

Q That is right.

A I don't think I stated it was before or after Miss Seamore's testimony. Now your question is concerning her testimony is that not right?

Q You made the statement to Mr. Gates, is that correct, last week?

A That is right; that I didn't have it.

Q I believe you said, yesterday you told him you had thrown it away?

A I told him—

Q Then you added that yesterday you told him you had thrown it away?

A That is right.

Q Other than those two statements, did you discuss your having thrown it away and not having this memorandum with anyone?

A No sir.

Q All right.

A You mean other than Mr. Gates?

Q That is correct. So that, Captain Anderson, when you heard Miss Seamore's testimony and heard her testify that you inquired of her as to whether any copies had been made and kept of any papers prepared on that Saturday afternoon, as far as you know at least, she had not been advised or told that you had thrown that memorandum away, had she?

A I don't know anything about it.

Q I say, as far as you know, you have no reason to believe that she knew you had thrown it away; is that correct?

A No reason, no.

Q Is that correct, sir?

A That is correct.

Q All right. Now, Captain Anderson, I want to refer to a question and answer—to an answer made by you to Mr. Gates' question, and ask you whether you wish to change your testimony. Do your recall having told Mr. Gates that other than the change in the F-27 of Captain Schustman and the change in the F-27 of Captain Allison, that except for editing you made no changes in any other document? Do you say that is true?

Mr. Gates: You are talking about F-27's?

Mr. Weiss: That is right, F-27's.

Mr. Gates: That wasn't his testimony. That wasn't the question I asked.

Mr. Weiss: That is my verbatim copy of what he said.

Mr. Gates: My question, I think, was important, because I asked him, "Did you make any unauthorized changes?"

Mr. Weiss: I am sorry. I will accept that. It may well be that is what it was. I will restate the question. I want to know whether you want to change your testimony to the effect that except for the change about which you have talked in Captain Schustman's F-27, and except for the change in Allison's F-27, you made no other unauthorized changes on F-27's?

A   Except for editing.

Q   Except for editing?

A   That is right.

Q   Thank you. Are you able to search your memory, Captain Anderson, and tell the Board, at least generally, what you did on the morning of September the 17th?

A   What date was that? (Witness refers to a calendar.)

Q   That was a Monday, I believe.

A   No, I don't recall exactly. I don't think I got up until pretty close to noon that morning. I was up most of the night, or up past midnight anyway.

Q   You got in at midnight; is that correct?

A   It was fairly late when I got up that morning.

Q   I think you fixed the time of your arrival at midnight?

A   About midnight.

Q   And you say you got up close to noon, is that your testimony?

A   Well, it was late in the morning, anyway.

Q   And then you saw Captain Ogden at two o'clock, did you say?

A   I don't remember the exact time. I think it was around one, between one and two.

Q   Now, the papers about which you have told the Board which you put in this separate folder, was that the folder that was kept in your desk, this separate folder?

A   Yes.

Q   And in which drawer in your desk was that kept?

A   Usually the lower right-hand drawer. It was changed around from time to time as I used it.

Q   Now I think you told Mr. Gates that those papers included, and possibly there are others, but these are what my notes show; Grievances filed: is that correct?

A   And correspondence pertaining thereto.

Q   I am going to give you a list of things, so I am not trying to be all inclusive. They include grievances filed, is that right?

A   Oh, yes.

Q And also in the event that matters came up for investigation with relation to Captain Allison they would include those papers?

A That is right.

Q And it also included correspondence concerning Flight 183, the St. Louis flight?

A Yes sir.

Q And it included correspondence concerning fueling of aircraft?

A Yes sir.

Q Now, in connection with those matters which we have just recited, were there any other papers that were included, by the way, Captain Anderson?

A Yes, there probably were.

Q Like what, would you tell us?

A I can't recall right now. The grievances, and Captain Allison's relationship between the pilot base and myself and the ALPA were the subject of a lot of them. There were some grievances filed by Captain Schustman and Captain Allison jointly; matters pertaining to that were kept there until they were settled.

Q I see. Now then, were there counterparts or duplicates of these papers also kept in the personnel file of Captain Allison?

A Not necessarily.

Q Well, whether it was necessarily so, were they kept?

A Not in all cases.

Q Were they kept in some cases?

A In some cases, yes.

Q Now, will you tell the Board in what cases you kept counterparts in the personnel file?

A Well, practically all of these papers—not all of them, but a good many of them found their way into the personnel file eventually.

Q That isn't what I asked you, was it, Captain?

A Repeat your question.

Q I asked you whether or not counterparts or duplicates of these papers in the separate folder also were contained in the personnel file?

Mr. Gates: I think he means at the same time. You certainly can answer that question.

A Certainly not at the same time. They hadn't found their way there yet.

Q Am I correct in understanding you to testify that all the papers which you kept in the separate folder, as to all those papers there were no counterparts or duplicates in the personnel file at any time?

A   No, I don't say at any time, because when Mr. Gates asked me to gather all the material, this was true up until about the 25th, I believe, of September.

Q   May I interrupt you, Captain, in order to simplify it. I will be content that you regard your answer as being made up to September 28, which I think was the date—

Mr. Gates: The date I called him was on September 24 or 25.

Mr. Weiss: Let us record the answer as being applicable up to that time.

A   Yes, up to that time. There were none that were duplicated.

Q   All right. And I think you also testified that in this separate folder you kept memoranda concerning things as to which Captain Allison was delinquent, isn't that right?

A   That is right.

Q   And as to those, specifically, were there duplicates of such memoranda in the personnel file?

A   No sir.

Q   Now, did you keep memoranda as to other pilots who were delinquent in a separate folder other than in the personnel file?

A   Yes sir, when they were delinquent over twice.

Q   So that you—

A   I kept a follow-up which included those.

Q   Well, but Captain Anderson, didn't I understand you to say that this separate folder was a folder containing the papers of Captain Allison?

A   Well now, you asked me about other pilots, did you not?

Q   Were they kept in separate folders in your desk?

A   Yes sir.

Q   I see. How many such separate folders did you keep?

A   I believe I testified last week that there were over a period of a year, there were probably some twelve or fifteen, that have been kept at the Tulsa base.

Q   And they were separate folders as to particular pilots; is that correct?

A   Yes sir, that is right.

Q   And these separate folders, did they contain material of the same character as were contained in the Allison file separate folder?

A   Yes sir.

Q   And they included follow-up memoranda, did they?

A   When they so applied.

Q   And you did not think it appropriate to keep these in the personnel file, I take it?

A   No. They were working—it was a working file at the time.

Q   Well, Captain Anderson, personnel files were very much working files, weren't they?

A   That is right, but this was a working folder of things current that needed following up on.

Q   These were special working folders; is that it?

A   Yes, that is right.

Q   And included among these special working folders was there a folder for Captain Schustman?

A   There was at one time, yes.

Mr. Weiss: I have no further questions.

Thereupon Mr. Gates entered into redirect examination of Captain Anderson, reworking old ground already worked once. Mr. Weiss also had his turn at recross-examination.

In the recross-examination Mr. Weiss only asked a few clarifying questions. I could tell that he was well satisfied, even pleased with the record. That perception made me very happy.

Mr. Weiss: (Abruptly) I have no further questions.

Chairman Day: (Turning to Mr. Gates) Have you any further questions.

Mr. Gates: No further questions.

Chairman Day: Mr. O'Connell?

Mr. O'Connell: No questions.

Chairman Day: Mr. Drummond?

Mr. Drummond: I should know, but who is the present council chairman of the Tulsa council ALPA.

The Witness: Jim Jewell.

Mr. Drummond: Do you keep and maintain a special file for him as such?

The Witness: It depends on the activity. I haven't had occasion to maintain a special file on him yet.

Mr. Drummond: That is all.

Chairman Day: I have no questions, Mr. Tiffany?

Mr. Tiffany: No.

Chairman Day: If no one has any further questions, the witness is excused. (Witness excused.)

Chairman Day: Have you any more witnesses, Mr. Weiss?

Neither Mr. Weiss or Mr. Gates had any more witnesses to appear so Chairman Day gave a short recess before the attorneys were to give their closing arguments.

Chairman Day: Mr. Weiss, whenever you are ready, we are.

Mr. Weiss: I would like the record to note that during the testimony given by Captain Anderson, Captain Ogden was present in the hearing room. May the record so note?

Chairman Day: All right.

Mr. Weiss: Now, gentlemen of the Board, by reason of the fact that the record is an extensive one, I have no intention of discussing even all of the highlights of the testimony that has been produced before you.

Actually my purpose in talking to you is simply, since I speak for the pilots, including Captain Allison, to advise this Board what we, as one of the parties to this agreement, do expect a system board to do and what function it serves in our view.

It represents to us, as I am sure it must to the company, the one basic method where we deal with each other, of settling our disputes and maintaining—because that is what we are hitting at—maintaining decent and proper labor relations, and as you gentlemen know, we treat that very, very seriously.

Now, there has been some discussion as to who shall produce the first witness and who shall bear the burden of proof. You will recall that in the interest of going forward and getting this case heard, that I agreed that we would proceed, but without prejudice one way or the other upon the issue of burden of proof. So I am back to that now because you have to decide that.

We start out basically with a contract of employment, which gives us certain rights as pilots; rights of seniority and other rights which accrue under seniority. And the company may not take those rights away from us, unless just and proper cause is established. And we as pilots, speaking for pilots, are very jealous of that particular clause in our contract.

Now, in the field of labor relations where we have contracts comparable to this, it has been decided many times that we are no longer back in the ancient days where an employer may of his own discretion fire or discharge a man or discipline him, and then throw the ball into the lap of the employee and say, 'Well, now, you prove that you are innocent.'

That is not why we have a contract.   We have a contract for precisely the opposite reason, among other things: in order to assure us of security under the seniority provisions of the contract.

I call to the Board's attention the fact that comparable provisions in system board agreements and employment contracts in the airline industry have been construed only very recently; again construed positively and beyond any doubt.   That is a case involving the discharge of a pilot, the burden of proving the justification of that discharge rests squarely upon the company, and that proof must be by a preponderance of the evidence; and I am quoting, to my knowledge at least, the most recent litigated discharge cases in the airline industry.

Now, applying that to this case, you must consider among many other questions the following: Did Captain Allison in connection with Flight 49 do anything which other pilots flying the line had done in the past, whether precisely the same or substantially the same had no particular significance?

Has Captain Allison been singled out for particular discipline for a reason having nothing to do with the particular flight in question? You must consider as well, did the company have any interest in advancing Captain Allison's flight or similar flights. You must consider also why it has not been answered in this record—what motivated Captain Allison to advance the flight. He was headed to San Francisco and diverted to where he went. Were there considerations in his mind which were attuned to the policy of the company, a policy which I think, in spite of all the back and forth testimony, is clear, was one under which the company had a definite and has a definite interest in implementing—to see that its pilots shall utilize their discretion to advance the flight.

Now, that brings us to another consideration of quite a different sort. If it appears that what Captain Allison did in connection with Flight 49, which basically I call to your attention is what we are talking about here, because that is conceded to be, shall I say, the precipitating incident which caused Captain Anderson to recommend dismissal—if what he did was in the interest of the company, then we must search and see what is this about—why has it come about—why are we here at all, gentlemen?

Captain Anderson has told us, and we know, that Captain Allison was active in association affairs, that he, among other things, had filed a grievance against Captain Anderson; that he was a member of the System Board; and I don't have to educate you gentlemen that sometimes system boards do have rather turbulent sessions.

Captain Anderson has also told us that—and I take his testimony—that a particular folder, be it fluid or constant, was kept with respect to Captain Allison. He said fourteen other pilots—he gave fifteen in all were based at Tulsa.

Captain Anderson has also told us that except for the alteration in the F-27 of Captain Schustman and Captain Allison, he made no other alterations in F-27's except for editing: and I asked him to repeat that, and he did.

Now, isn't it curious, gentlemen, that even by his own testimony, coincidentally, if you will, just the F-27's of Allison and Schustman in Anderson's career down there were the ones that were altered? Somehow or other that points to something to me.

Isn't it also coincidental that when Captain Anderson came to investigate this matter, he held the investigation on September the 14th, and mind you, this in concerning a captain who had a long career with the airline, Amalgamated Airlines. He evidently made up his mind by his own testimony that night; had already prepared the road by having Miss Seamore, on his own testimony now, be ready to come in the following day to dictate some memorandum.

Now, I say to you that that smacks of only one thing. I am just dealing with his own testimony for the moment. That smacks to me of what I would call simple a cut and dried procedure where the thing had been already decided previously.

Isn't it also curious that up until just a few days ago Captain Anderson did not disclose to anyone that he had prepared a memorandum which he threw away. I place a lot of significance upon that. Captain Anderson said he read from the memorandum to Captain Braznell. Miss Seamore testified that he prepared certain papers which included alterations; and indeed, you know that it was that which impelled her to come here to testify.

Gentlemen, let us not pretend. I have seen many witnesses, and I dislike very much leveling a charge at any individual, and I dislike it not because I hesitate to put the truth where it should lie, but I dislike it because it makes for bad relationships, and that is why I dislike it. But if ever I heard a belated explanation which explains nothing, I heard it this afternoon.

Gentlemen, you have before you a clear case of singling out a man where during the year, during eleven months, according to Captain Braznell's testimony, there were 125 precedents, not one of which did he bother to investigate to see whether it involved circumstances comparable to Captain Allison's trip, because I asked him that, and he said he didn't check. And I would have supposed that since Captain Braznell knew what this story was about and that he was coming here to testify that he would have been diligent to have checked it.

So you have a man who is singled out for one purpose, I may tell you this, without seeming presumptuous, what I am telling you now is, in fact, an open secret, there is nothing new about what I am saying; that Allison was made a goat.

Now let me point one further thing out. The best way to destroy good relationships between the pilots and the company is to permit something like this to occur. Each of us on each side of the table, I personally have been involved in proceedings involving Amalgamated Airlines where we labored for many months attempting to arrive at a solution, and then a solution was secured; and I urge you gentlemen that we on this side of the table look upon this simply as a matter of plain discrimination, and I ask you not to permit it to occur.

That is all I have to say, gentlemen.

Chairman Day: Mr. Gates.

Mr. Gates: Mr. Chairman and members of the Board; I would like to reply to some of the comments which have been made by Mr. Weiss.

This is a serious case. It is serious to Wayne Allison. It is serious to the company. And I am sure it is a serious matter as far as you gentlemen are concerned.

It is serious to Captain Allison because no man can spend fifteen or twenty years in perfecting himself in his profession and then have that threatened without it having a real effect on him.

It is serious also to the company because it is required by law to administer certain civil air regulations.

I think it is serious to this Board because it presents an opportunity for the Board to do the job which I conceive it was set up to do. Perhaps my conception is wrong.

There has been a lot of banter in this room from time to time in which I have participated, in which you have been called judges. Some people have said, well, we are the association representatives; we are the company representatives. I don't conceive of you as that at all. I think the organization of the System Board contemplates that when you get before us as a Board, you exercise completely independent judgment, untrammeled, unswayed, unaffected by your position, your connections or your employer. That goes both ways. And all I ask is that you gentlemen exercise the complete independence which you should have and which I believe that each of you does have in the performance of your function.

Now, we have a saying in the law that hard cases make bad law. And this is a tough one. If you can judge from the length of the record, I suppose it is the toughest case that has ever been presented to an Amalgamated Airlines System Board, and I suppose I will have to take my share of the blame for making it such a long record.

But boiled down, the issue is a very simple one; and that is, did Captain Allison exercise good judgment or unusually bad judgment in his conduct of the flight on September the 7th, and make an unnecessary compromise with safety.

Now, that is not a company rule alone. That is a civil air regulation. Neither you, as Board members, nor I, as a lawyer, would want to have a regulation which said in essence, when you have one engine gone out, you must land at the nearest suitable airport—because as Captain Braznell said yesterday, we feel that coerces a pilot into exercising bad judgment. The nearest suitable airport may be an airport into which the pilot has never put the airplane. It may be at night. There may be all kinds of circumstances which would really jeopardize the safety of the flight.

Now, I don't propose to get into any legal discussion with respect to the issue of burden of proof. I don't think that is important. I don't agree with Mr. Weiss's analysis of the situation. But even if I did, I submit to you gentlemen that the preponderance of the evidence in this proceeding show that Captain Allison was discharged for just cause; and that is the real issue.

Now, I do not propose to discuss in detail the evidence which has been introduced into this record. There was a lot of it at Tulsa with which you are not yet familiar, but I know each one of you plans to read the testimony which was given at Tulsa.

It was stated at Tulsa that the defense will show a discriminatory act against Captain Allison by reason of his activities and membership in the Air Line Pilots' Association.

I submit to you gentlemen that there has not been one word of testimony given in the Lexington Hotel before this Board in substantiation of that charge—not one single word.

The nearest they came to it was this afternoon when Captain Anderson talked for a few minutes in answer to some inquiries from Mr. Weiss and from me as to what he kept in those separate folders, namely, matters connected with the Air Line Pilots' Association. And after sitting as a Hearing Officer for substantially five or six full days, Mr. Whitacre came to the conclusion that there was no substantial evidence to support that kind of defense.

A second defense which has been offered in this proceeding is a suggestion that the company directed the flight to come into Los Angeles, or expressed a desire for the flight to come into Los Angeles.

Now, you gentlemen are much better qualified than I to pass judgment upon that; but I submit that any man who has had any experience in the air transportation business can't read the contacts, the radio contacts in this proceeding and come to the conclusion that Captain Allison even indirectly was told to come to Los Angeles.

And all of the testimony that went into this record with respect to past policy, with respect to advancing the flight, with respect to the convenience of the passengers and the availability of equipment avails nothing when you look at Exhibit 10 in this proceeding, which is the official Civil Aeronautics Board's interpretation of the regulation, which says in just so many words:

"Economic convenience of continuing the flight to a base where repairs or replacements can easily be made is not a factor of safety and should not be considered."

Now, one of the things that hasn't come before you gentleman in the testimony in the last five days was the testimony of Captain Allison himself; that when he made his approach, he got down to an altitude of 300 feet above sea level, which is about 200 feet above the elevation of the terrain in the vicinity of the airport, and that the visibility was roughly one-quarter of a mile.

Now I submit to you gentlemen that in considering such facts as those you can't but come to the conclusion that Captain Allison did do some things that other pilots had not done. And I ask you to bear in mind that there was not one captain who testified that Captain Allison had not done anything but which he himself had done a great many times.

You are asked also to consider whether Captain Allison has been singled out. And there I proceed to the second line of defense which has been offered; that which has been offered, shall we say, during the last five days: a discrimination on the part of Captain Anderson, alone, against Captain Allison.

If Captain Anderson were guilty of that, he was an extremely persuasive talker, because in order to have accomplished his end, he would likewise have been required to have convinced Captain Ogden, Captain McFail and Captain Braznell. And the testimony in this record—you heard Captain Braznell—but the testimony in this record will show that all three of these supervisory personnel took the position without qualification that the action which Captain Anderson proposed was justified on the basis of the facts in the record, namely, the exhibits which constitute the original documents in this proceeding.

It seems to me, therefore, that you get into a situation of how much credence you are going to give to such testimony as falsification of records. I, like Mr. Weiss, am very reticent to comment about the testimony of various witnesses. The most charitable thing that I can say for Miss Seamore's testimony is that she was confused. I think she meant to do right. But I think, also, that she did not know about which she was speaking, because she said in so many words, even though she had made the charge that the records had been changed, that she didn't understand what it was. She didn't know what it was.

Now I ask you in good conscience, if one does not know what changes have been made, I think, gentlemen, that if nothing else, you owe it to Captain Anderson to find, to make a specific finding, that there is no credible evidence of any falsification of records; and I ask you to examine all of the slips in Exhibit 5 to find any indication of anything that looks like erasures, and compare the papers in Exhibit 5 with Association's Exhibit No. 21 and Amalgamated's Exhibit No. 20, which are the summaries of the flight contact reports, and look at the weather reports.

You gentlemen know from your own experience that it is impossible to change the weather reports. They are a matter of record; and it would be so easy to apprehend anybody who endeavored to engage in that kind of activity, even if he had the desire.

Captain Allison in his justification, first, of discrimination, did not substantiate it. I ask you to bear with me only a moment while I refer to the examples he gave. He first started out by saying that he had certain controversies with the company. When he was asked about those controversies, he toned them down to say they were differences of opinion. And bear in mind he testified in this proceeding to many such controversies of differences of opinion.

But he added that all of the differences of opinion which he had were those which arose out of his representation of the pilot group, and did not relate to him personally. He said he had opposed some of Anderson's decisions, again as council chairman. He took exception to some of the decisions made by the company. There was at least an implication that he had been discriminated against because he wasn't invited to a steak dinner given by the president of Amalgamated, as I recall the testimony, and that is the testimony.

He made reference to some differences of opinion that he had with Captain Braznell, but admitted that they occurred some time ago, in contract negotiations. And then, if I may characterize it, "grasping at straws," he brought in Di Pasquale and Hamilton who were in charge of labor relations. Di Pasquale and Hamilton, by the evidence in this record, didn't have a thing to do with it. They weren't consulted one way or the other by Captain Anderson or anybody else at the time the letter of dismissal was written.

And Captain Ogden's testimony, without contradiction of any kind, is that throughout the consideration of this matter there was not even the slightest mention of Captain Allison's connection with the Air Line Pilots' Association. And I think rightly there should have been some consideration given to that, because labor unions are with us. They are a good thing, and there should be no activity of the company which is directed against a man's connection with such an organization.

I have talked a little longer than I intended, but I submit to you gentlemen that issue is a very clear-cut one. Captain Allison had a decision to make. He had that decision at 6:39 in the morning of September the 7th. He made that decision at 6:57 when he said, "I am proceeding to Los Angeles." And having made that decision, he then did proceed to Los Angeles, where the weather was below minimum—excuse me—where the weather was minimum, and there were alternate airports at which he could have landed with complete safety.

That is the issue: Did he exercise good judgment within the meaning of CAR 61.294, Company Regulation 4890; and that is the sole issue. I know you gentlemen will consider it just as seriously and as honestly as is within your power to do so.

Chairman Day: Gentlemen, unless the Board has any questions—

Mr. Tiffany: No.

Mr. Drummond: No.

Mr. O'Connell: No.

Mr. Gates: I would like to thank the Board for its indulgence and courtesy in listening to the wrangling of counsels throughout the period of five days.

Chairman Day: I am very sorry we got involved in some of the wrangling, because as you know, we are not qualified to pass on matters of legal technicalities.

I want to say in closing that I am very happy that this hearing has finally ended; that I hope we will get the transcript promptly, and the Board will be able to arrive at a decision.

With those remarks, the hearing closed.

Chapter 22

Hanging in Suspense

Schustman and I hurriedly gathered our baggage after I had said good-bye to a number of well-wishing pilots in the deserted Lexington hearing room. Ship and Nat were very optimistic about the outcome and lingered with the pilots, all voicing a belief that the company would be forced to reinstate me. It was very heartening, to say the least.

We had to rush to La Guardia field by cab to catch flight forty-nine. Because we were both traveling on revenue tickets, we were able to get by a ticket agent just before he closed the gate to the passenger concourse. Then when he recognized us we left him with a puzzled expression on his face as he surveyed our revenue tickets. Our baggage was the last that went up the tramway, and without tickets, when we threw them on the endless belt and asked the cargo handler to throw them in with the pilots' baggage. We would retrieve them at Tulsa.

"Terry and Mary are the stewardesses," George told me with a wide grin as we headed back to the passenger loading ramp, "and I don't want to hear you mention San Francisco. Dan Landall is the pilot so be sure to tighten your seat belt."

We settled in the lounge for the takeoff as we had done so many times in the past after system board hearings, rushing home to fly our schedules out of Tulsa and doubling up to make up lost time. How many times we had done that in the past five years, I wondered as I accepted a cup of coffee from red headed Mary and enjoyed her sweet affectionate smile.

George was delighted to be heading home to take flight 49 out of Tulsa the next night. He even thought to remind Terry and Mary that, due to him doubling up on the schedule, they would be flying their next trip with him to San Francisco. It was easy to see that he was eager to pull the nose up off the runway and point it toward the ridges of the Rockies.

But I had no schedule, no nose to pull up, up and up. All I had was an old drilling machine that just wanted to go down, down and down. It made me sad to think about it. Then my mind turned to Jean and suddenly I, too, was anxious to get home.

Out of Washington and enroute nonstop to Tulsa, George and I began talking over the major points in the hearing. George could do little but exult over the fact that the company attorney could not point to a single company or CAA regulation I had violated.

And too, the company had not been able to explain the policy of advancing the flight, the one that was supposed to be unpublished. No official seemed to know about it, not even Captain Braznell, who claimed to know everything that was happening up and down the line.

We were deep in our discussion of Margaret Seamore's testimony and the discrepancies in Joe Anderson's, and were on our second cup of coffee when Dan Landall came walking back. He was bulging more at the waist than he had been when I saw him a few months before.

Dan had not sat in on any of the hearings, not even those at Tulsa, but he knew all about everything. He had obtained all his knowledge from the flight dispatcher in New York, who had confidentially told him that I had feathered the engine a couple of hours before reporting it and the company had fired me for lying.

He leered at me with almost a sneer, and I knew he was trying to get a rise out of me, and find out something at the same time.

"Gosh," I exclaimed as though greatly enlightened, "was that what that hearing was all about?"

George and I looked at each other and laughed as though we had a great secret between us. Then neither of us said anything. We just let Dan talk.

Finally he decided that he had better get back up front and relieve the copilot a little, or maybe he felt the cool reception he was getting. At any rate we were soon alone again and feeling better about it.

"I think," George offered, "that Dan deserves the rank of at least a sergeant in your vulture army. He is a real pipeline from management into the pilot group and back." He laughed that little chuckle that, at times, was almost a giggle.

"The sad part about it," George continued, "is that quite a few pilots will believe what he tells them and, without questioning the source, will pass the misinformation along. Dan wanted you to say something that he could pass up or down the pipeline. Nit-picking and criticizing each other as well as having informers in our group is our greatest weakness."

He paused to hand his empty coffee cup to Terry and soon had a refill. I said nothing, remaining silent, for I enjoyed listening to the little towhead when he was in a philosophizing mood. In the past I had picked up some golden nuggets by just listening quietly.

"You know, Wayne," George explained in a confidential manner, "the Amalgamated pilots do not recognize their worst enemies and their worst faults. Everyone would prefer to be a pilot, even the dispatchers and the company officials all the way up to C.R. and he probably wanted to be one back in the days of E.L. Cord. It's professional jealousy.

"But physical failures, lack of an opportunity to learn to fly, or lack of ability thinned us out. So naturally those flight dispatchers, officials, and all who have to work forty hours each week, have a deep-seated resentment toward the pilots who they see come and go, work shorter hours, even if it is during the night, and seem to have a lot of time off."

He laughed a mirthless laugh and added, "That's why they keep finding more things for us to do on our days off, like flying the link trainer a minimum of hours each month, briefing on this and that, lectures and manual courses of instruction, anything to keep us coming to the field on our days off. They won't be satisfied until they have us working forty hours a week at something. They just don't recognize pilot fatigue and the fact that supervisors like Anderson contribute to accidents. He has been a weasel-beagle on your trail for years.

"Yes sir," George expounded: "We airline pilots are just too easy going and don't recognize our real enemies."

He studied his coffee cup, wrinkled his brow at me and I knew there was more to come. I remained silent, listening.

"Now," he explained, "take the Air Transport Association, ATA for short. It is an association of all the air carriers and that organization is our mortal enemy, but few pilots seem to recognize that fact. Right after the war, WW II, it tried to force the Air Line Pilots' Association to negotiate one contract for all companies. Dave Behncke saw through that and raised a stink in Washington about it. He created such a stink that the ATA finally backed down after he threatened a strike vote from all pilots in ALPA. Some senators and congressmen began to ask questions and that pressure helped.

"Then they tried to have one negotiator for all airlines with a committee from the ATA telling him how much he could put on the table for each airline. It was a move to keep the pay down as we went from small two engine equipment to four and doubled the size of the airplane. The fact that we had been flying four engine equipment overseas during the war for Uncle Sam on the old two engine pay scale gave them the idea that they could dish out only a slight increase for the four engines. That ATA negotiator—what was his name?"

"Hodgkins," I smiled.

"Yeah," George agreed. "He did a good job of stalling us for over two years after the war, during which time we were flying four engines commercially and taking two engine pay and the retroactivity question became greater and greater with all members of ATA insisting that it was a negotiable question. I don't think we pilots of AA would have ever received our retroactivity pay if Damon hadn't given it to us to get even with C.R. for letting him hold the bag on those Railway Labor Act violations Dave Behncke was planning to pursue."

He laughed that little gleeful laugh for which he was famous. "Dave Behncke sure set up the bowling pins when he sent the AA master executive council to New York, all twenty-eight of them, to listen in on our briefing to Ralph Damon on the 'screening cases.'"

George sipped his coffee and chuckled again before continuing. "It was sure fun to hear them fall when Ralph Damon said: 'This may be my last official act as president of AA but I have just signed an executive order directing the AA treasury to pay full retroactive pay to all pilots who have been flying four engine equipment since the war.'

"I heard," he smiled at the memory, "that the ATA was furious at AA for setting the precedent. Then Ralph Damon went over to TWA and C.R. had to come back as president of AA and explain it to the ATA as well as the failure of the 'screening' program which he had sold as an answer to the retirement problem."

He shook his head and continued: "That Air Transport Association is behind all the petitions to the CAA to increase the payloads on our transport airplanes, increase the authorized engine time on the engines, delay the installation of non-flammable interiors in the new airplanes, and do anything else that will make our flying more hazardous.

"Yes sir," he mused. "We airline pilots are just too easy going and do not recognize our real enemies."

I studied the little towhead as he leaned across the lounge table with his blue eyes intently fixed on mine while I indulged in an inward smile at the way his blond hair was arrayed in an unruly mass above his forehead, and once again I admired that sharp penetrating brain behind that tousled hair. Deep within me an uneasy feeling rose, a sense of finality to our close relationship of so many years, something that seemed to go all over me like a consuming glow of lightning igniting a dark and threatening cloud. This was to be my last flight with little George.

Two months dragged by during which time I kept busy in the drilling business. I completed a little oil well on mother's property, cased it, tubed it and set a pump jack on it. It looked good, but it was a little stripper well that would require a year to pay out. After that, it would be gravy. So I bought an adjacent lease with borrowed money and with my helper, Russ, began another one. In that time I saw as much of Jean as I could, for she was a constant companion when not out on a trip. Also, she was my mail carrier with frequent notes from pilots, optimistic messages.

It was spring in Oklahoma and a rainy one, more so than usual. That did not make the working conditions very pleasant. Russ and I struggled in the mud, moving equipment, rigging up the old machine and laying a waterline across a muddy field where each footstep sank down about six inches. Also we had to carry the two-inch pipe, a joint at a time, from the road at the edge of the field. It was heavy without the mud.

Occasionally a big plane would swing by at the minimum altitude with a big AA on its tail. Sometimes it would dip a wing a little and I would know it was a friend. Otherwise, I would suspect that it was a vulture pilot gloating and pointing me out to the copilot and engineer. But, for each one, I would give a cheerful wave and wonder if they could see how deep the mud was and how dirty and hot we were. I could not help but think about how cool and nice that cockpit would be.

Then I thought of the cockpit crud. I thought of the unsettled flight allocation cases, the unpublished policy of advancing the flight which no official seemed to know about and had disowned, the falsification of reports to the CAA by the company over pilots signatures as well as cases similar to the Jewell case in which system seniority was ignored and "fair-haired" deals made. Suddenly the mud had a nice squish to it and the air seemed to smell clean.

Once each couple of weeks I would drive to the Tulsa airport and visit the various oil companies searching for a job. I soon knew the pilots of each company by their first names. They were all quite friendly, especially Bruce Grove of Gulf. He was extremely curious about my case and wanted to know the latest development, which was nothing. The System Board had made no progress in three meetings. Wylie Drummond had faithfully reported each meeting to me by phone.

Then on my last trip to Tulsa, Bruce Grove had given me a bit of information. He had just heard that Phillips Petroleum was looking for a pilot. It was a steady job and the home office was in Bartlesville with the pilots flying out of the Bartlesville airport.

Needless to say I was in Bartlesville the next morning to see the chief pilot Billie Parker and put in an application. He was most cordial and reminded me that I had shown him and one of his pilots through a DC-6 over a year back. I had forgotten about it, but he had not.

We talked for quite a while during which I was very frank with him and explained the entire situation. He became more and more interested with each question and gave me an application blank to fill out. He suggested that I fill it out at his desk while he ran a couple of errands. Then he wanted to show me around and invited me to lunch. His three planes were out on overnight trips and he had little to do.

Billie Parker was a short stocky man near fifty with a frequent chew of tobacco in his mouth, one of which he had to discard before we entered the restaurant he chose. Then I told him about one old pilot I had flown with on AA, Stormy Mangham, in very early days in which Stormy frequently chewed tobacco and kept the window open a little in the summertime to keep the cockpit cool and at the same time take care of the amber juice. It sometime streaked the passengers windows and on one rather long flight we had landed and found the whole side of the airplane, including the windows, caked with a dried brown streak down the side and across the passenger door.

In a short time Stormy had received a letter from the chief operations official giving him one of three choices in future flights. He could wash the airplane after each flight, carry his own spittoon, or give up the habit. He had shown me the letter.

Billie Parker enjoyed that story and admitted that, in early days while flying the mail, he had also painted a few airplanes. He chuckled quite a little while over the story before asking me what choice the pilot had made. Then he really laughed when I told him that the pilot, Stormy Mangham, had begun using the rather large ash trays for emergency discharges.

Before the lunch was over Billie Parker told me that he thought I was what he wanted and to come back the following Monday to begin familiarization training. Needless to say I was there promptly, after Jean and I had spent a weekend in pleasant anticipation. But the joy was short-lived.

That Monday morning Billie Parker met me at the door of his office, and in an apologetic manner, while mouthing his morning chew of tobacco, told me that he could not use me.

"Wayne," he told me seriously, "I have just received a letter from Amalgamated Airlines telling me that they do not consider you a safe pilot. It is signed by a vice-president." He showed me the letter and let me read it with his hand over the signature.

"If I put you to work after receiving this letter, and something happened," he explained with sympathetic brown eyes probing mine, "there would go my job too. I can't take the risk." I understood, but it didn't make the drive home any more pleasant. The long finger of AA meant for me to starve.

Two months slipped by with the Oklahoma weather going into the hot summer while Russ and I drilled a dry hole. I had seen a lot of those in the past with Dad being on the receiving end while I was in the grade school and high school. It wasn't something new to me, but it hurt just the same.

There is only one sure cure to a dry hole and that is to start another exploration as quickly as possible. That way you quickly forget about the one you have just plugged and become engrossed with the new one going down, down, and down. However, it is not the same sensation as going up, up, and up. One is a lot of work with a little thrill, the other is a lot of thrill with little work.

Jean came in from a New York trip about the time Russ and I were finishing the plugging job with a metal barrel attached to the drilling line. With all the casing out of the hole we were dragging the barrel through the mud pit with the drilling machine and dumping it in the hole simply by letting the barrel lay down over a big log and the contents pour into the hole unassisted.   Then with Russ pulling the barrel back into the mud pit with the truck and a line attached to the bottom of the barrel, we were rapidly filling the hole with mud. It was simple but effective. The hole plugged much faster than it had drilled. That's the only good thing I can say about such an operation.

Russ operated the truck pulling the barrel back while I stood next to the hole and operated the drilling machine. My hard hat had about an inch layer of dried mud on it and my shirt and blue jeans had a similar layer. When Jean recognized me she ran to Mother's car for her camera, laughing and declaring that she wanted a picture of the whites of my eyes.

When the picture taking and laughing were over, she gave me a note from Wiley Drummond of Nashville. All it said that he was deadheading to Tulsa on a required route check and wanted to have a talk with me. He designated the time of his arrival and planned a return flight a couple of hours later.

I met Wiley as he came into the lobby of the Tulsa terminal and we quickly walked out to my car and were off to the truck stop on highway 66 where I had lunched with Gene Burns and Fred Mills. He was deeply disturbed about my case. Quietly he related that he and J.J. O'Connell were having a rough time with the company members of the board. After a couple of meetings the company members of the board had refused to discuss the evidence further because he and J.J. had overwhelmed them with all the evidence in my favor.

"Wayne," Wiley chuckled that quiet little chuckle, stretched his long legs under the table while I vividly recalled the way he had stretched to his full six feet and four inches when sending the message to Mr. C.R. about the aurora borealis over Nashville during the flight allocation cases, "I wish you could have heard J.J. argue your case."

He sipped his tea and continued, "J.J. had gone over the records with a fine-tooth comb and made numerous notes of reference in the page of testimony, notes of Anderson's admissions, and notes of Margaret Seamore's detailed testimony. He was great."

Wylie laughed aloud and exclaimed, "He would read a point, pop his baby blue eyes at the company members of the board and take up another point to pop his eyes all over again. He wore them out with persistent pressure."

Wylie made light of the part he had played at the system board meetings but I felt sure it was equally as effective. Finally he concluded by telling me how arrogant the company members had become, especially Carl Day, and the position they had taken as a last resort, that I was fired, period. The record didn't really matter, Day had insisted in an outburst of anger. I was fired. They wanted to deadlock the case.

"Have you talked with Sayen about this?" I questioned, thinking about the irony of having my fate in the hands of a horsetrader. If deadlocked the case would be dead after sixty days with no provision for breaking the deadlock.

"I have," Wylie responded. "He doesn't want us to deadlock but didn't offer any suggestions worthy of note."

"The thing that is really worrying me right now," Wylie offered, "is that there are a lot of stories going around about your flight that are not true, and stories about you that are not true. I have seen you work. I have seen the results of your work over a number of years, I know you are an honest man, for I have never seen you take anything that your seniority didn't deserve.

"But these stories that are going around are being fed into the pilot group, I am sure, by management, and I don't know what to do about it. I tell every pilot and any group I encounter how one-sided the hearings were, but I cannot work all pilot bases." Wylie paused and studied me silently.

I sat for several minutes reviewing in my mind all he had said. It was easy to picture what was happening. I could understand the 'weak-sisters,' the Ellis and Lindsey types, the 'vulture army' group not wanting to see the AA boat rocked further by the Allison case. They wanted to see me go quietly down the river so they could continue to suck the teat that any company official offered on Amalgamated's big sow belly. Seniority didn't matter, individual rights of pilots didn't matter. They wanted the 'fair-haired' treatment—more of that sweet teat.

"I think, Wylie," I suggested, thinking as I talked, "you should push Sayen to get out a condensed story of my flight giving the details, such as the unpublished policy which all pilots know has been in existence for over three years, a picture of my altered F-27 report to the

CAA, a summary of Margaret Seamore's testimony, in short, a synopsis. When that is sent out to individual pilots, they will read it, study it and the majority will demand that something be done. The 'vulture army' will suddenly find itself in a minority, pushed into the background and will quietly go along with the majority. I called Sayen a couple of months back and suggested it, but he claimed ALPA was all tied up in court action by Behncke. Now it is different, I understand."

Wylie nodded. "I understand that Sayen is now the undisputed president," he commented.

I recalled, "When Schustman and I were working to get a settlement of the 'screening' cases, trying to get the seven fired pilots reinstated, we had the same 'vulture army,' the company sympathizers, the same 'weak-sisters' to contend with. We kept running into all sorts of stories up and down the line."

I paused, reflecting on that hectic time over four years back then continued, "George and I wrote a report on each of the seven discharged pilots, took it to Chicago to discuss it with Dave Behncke, and asked him to get out a mailing.

"Dave did that within a week and sent a long winded letter along. In another week we could have gotten an overwhelming strike vote with little trouble. Pilots were suddenly mad as the devil at the deal." I smiled at the memory.

Wylie nodded. "I remember that, for I was a copilot then and took my copy with me on a flight to ask my captain about it. He was Ernie Dryer and we were based at Cleveland then."

Wylie laughed before continuing: "You should have heard Ernie explode with his mule skinner language about that deal."

I enjoyed a laugh too, for well I knew Ernie Dryer whose caustic sense of humor and original description, when made, would hold an audience, large or small, spellbound. He would use words not yet in the dictionary, but somehow, everyone understood him.

"That's the ticket," Wylie decided. "We must get out a letter. But who will write it?"

"Not you or J.J." I answered. That would put too much heat on you both."

An inspiration came to me.

"Maurice Schy is the one you want to write it and if Sayen does not want to send it out over his signature, I am sure Schy would do it as an association attorney."

"But Wylie," I cautioned, "don't be surprised if Sayen refuses to permit a letter to go out. A couple of months ago I called him on the phone and asked him to get the story out to the field. He took the position that it wasn't necessary. Maybe you can convince him that it is necessary."

"Don't think I won't try my best," he promised.

Another month went by during which time Russ and I were busy on another exploration. Twice I talked with Wylie on the phone and once with J.J. O'Connell. They had forced two meetings with the company members of the board, for under the Adjustment Board provisions of the agreement any two members of the Adjustment Board could call a meeting within a few days and the others were forced to attend by the provisions of the Adjustment Board section of the agreement.   So Wylie and J.J. had called the two meetings over the protests of the other two members.

The company members of the board, according to Wylie, were very resentful of the forced meetings and made it plain that Allison was a dead issue.   Again they wanted to deadlock the case.   The pilot members of the board, as Schustman and I had done many times in the past, took the position that they were going to continue to meet until the case was settled. That didn't set well with the company board members and Day again became abusive until J.J. popped his baby blue eyes and inquired innocently, "By the way, Day, while we are on the subject of the Allison case, what sort of disciplinary action has the company taken with Anderson for falsifying Allison's F-27 report to the CAA?"

It was a well known fact and commented on consistently up and down the line among the pilots that Anderson was back as Superintendent of Flying at the Tulsa base with apparently no change in status. That had created quite a bit of resentment, but what could they do other than advise ALPA headquarters and ask that some action be taken by ALPA. Enough pilots had attended at least a part of the hearings to get a good smell of the case. Their reactions had spread up and down the AA membership.

That question by J.J. set Day off in a tirade that lasted a good five minutes, during which he very pointedly informed Wylie and J.J. that ordinary pilots did not have the right to question the company management about anything. That was sacred, to hear him.

"But," J.J. had insisted tenaciously, "the Adjustment Board provisions of the agreement gives the pilots the right to grieve about anything and that word 'anything' includes the company management. So, before we get a grievance on that, what about Anderson?"

J.J.'s popping blue eyes were working overtime with that question.

"This meeting is concluded," Day had declared in an icy voice as he and Tiffany stormed out of the Lexington Hotel.

Some weeks passed during which Russ and I were busy on the drilling machine from early until late. The weather was good and we were able to get in long hours with most of them hot. I did not receive much mail during that time and sort of lost contact with what was going on up and down the flying line. Jean came and went on schedule that kept her away most of the time. However, I did manage to take Mother and Jean fishing occasionally. I don't know who enjoyed those fishing days the most.

Then one evening I received a call from George Schustman. He and Gene Burns, the chairman, wanted to see me and were driving over.

In about forty minutes they had arrived and we settled on Mother's front porch with cold drinks and an eagerness to talk. They were both quite disturbed. They did not like the way things were going.

According to Gene, he had called Sayen twice within the last couple of weeks urging him to get out a letter on my flight and update the field to put a stop to the wild stories that were being circulated, discrediting me and my compliance with regulations. Sayen had been rather evasive on the first call and expressed an opinion that such a letter was unnecessary. Gene had argued with him and finally, on the last call, had told Sayen that he was not running a boys' camp and could not run a union like one.

Gene chuckled as he related the conversation while I recalled that Gene could be real blunt, if the occasion demanded it. Normally, however, he was quiet, soft-spoken and a very polite gentleman with everyone.

But Sayen had succeeded in getting him riled. He had done more than that, he had talked to him like a professor might talk to a pupil, in a very condescending manner. That had not set well with Gene, considering the fact that Sayen had never been a captain on any airline and Gene had several years experience.

Gene related further that he had advised Sayen that he had just been in touch with Wylie Drummond and found that the system board was virtually deadlocked and in a stalemated condition. He had suggested a strike vote to impress the company. Sayen had shown no stomach for that kind of talk and scoffed at the idea.

George brought out the point that, up and down the line, the pilots were apprehensive, maybe even scared of sticking their necks out a little and being fired. By piecing the evidence together with reports of pilots who had sat through a good portion of the hearings, the rank and file membership had slowly, in spite of the company-sponsored rumors, arrived at the conclusion that I had been framed. They were uneasy and did not know what to do. But he was sure they would give an overwhelming strike vote to back me.

But David L. Behncke was gone. No one was writing a long-winded letter, a repetitious letter, alerting the field of the company's unprecedented action in my case. No one was stirring the field with an eighth grade letter that, somehow, contained all the pertinent facts, and repeated them.

During the crisis of the 'screening cases' Dave had written a six page letter that could easily have been condensed to two. It even rambled some, but the pilots had read all six pages. I know, for George and I were approached many times during the hearings at the various bases by pilots showing a desire for more detailed information than the six pages contained. But it had seemed to crystallize the thinking in the field.

The pilots had responded to those six pages by turning out en masse for each and every hearing. It had kept the pilot interest at a peak, which showed the company that it had stirred up a hornet's nest.

The Amalgamated pilots expected leadership from the Air Line Pilots' Association headquarters on my case. They expected a report after all the long hearings. But Sayen was silent.

"What about securing a neutral on your case, Wayne?" Gene asked, trying to look ahead.

George and I looked at each other and smiled. We repeatedly had challenged the company members of the board on the 'screening cases' to jointly go with us to the National Mediation Board and request a neutral to settle the cases. They had repeatedly refused.

Now, in my case, as George explained it to Gene, the old contract, which had no provision for an automatic neutral, applied, for I had been fired under the old contract. A few months later Sayen had signed a new contract with Amalgamated which provided for an automatic neutral upon the request by either side. But it did not cover me. Either the company or I could refuse to go before a neutral.

"Maybe you should go to Chicago and have a talk with Sayen," Gene suggested.

We pursued that thought for awhile. Both Gene and George favored the idea. I weighed it slowly for the next few minutes. It was a long way to Chicago by car, but a lot cheaper than by air. Also, a car would give me transportation while there.

Both George and Gene were quick to offer to help with the expense of such a trip. That, I declined, but did appreciate their concern and generosity. Finally, I agreed to make the trip and leave the following morning, a Tuesday, if Sayen would be available.

The next morning I had my traveling bag packed before calling ALPA headquarters to see if I could see Sayen on arrival. Finally I was able to talk with Miss Forrest, Akers, for short. She seemed glad to talk with me and assured me that Sayen was going to be in the office for the rest of the week. I asked her to make me an appointment for the next day, that I was enroute, and would see her the following morning.

Then I asked her if she knew anything of Behncke.

"Not a word," she declared, "since he walked out of the office a couple of months ago. He was an old tottering man then and did not seem to know what he was doing. He was in sort of a daze." I could feel the sympathy in her voice.

"But Wayne," she added, "that name is a no-no around here."

It was a long road to Chicago, especially for an airline pilot, accustomed to seeing the landscape flow under the wing. But I had much to ponder enroute and in the early hours of the morning. By then I was in the edge of Chicago and settled in a good motel for a late sleep. That part of the trip was easy to take.

It was after ten when I climbed the rickety stairs to the offices of ALPA and presented myself to Miss Forrest. But Dave's desk was missing and I felt a keen sense of sorrow at the same time enjoyed Miss Forrest's warm greeting that turned apologetic.

"Mr. Sayen is not here," she apologized. "He left here yesterday afternoon going to Washington on an unexpected trip to make an appearance before a congressional committee sometime today or tomorrow. He expects to be there several days." She rolled her expressive eyes and I wondered if she was trying to tell me something.

"When will he be back?" I suddenly felt real tired and knew I was on a wild goose chase.

"Not until this weekend." She confirmed my fear. The trip was a futile one.

"I tried to reach you as soon as I learned he was leaving." she explained, "but your mother said you had been gone for hours."

I could tell that she was genuinely sorry, knowing that I had traveled a long distance.

"Oh," she suddenly recalled, "Mr. Bennett of the legal department wants to see you."

I thanked her, told her good-bye and sought the legal department. It was a large open room with several desks and was manned by occupants of both genders. It was the same large room I had surveyed the night I had stopped by Chicago to see Dave Behncke and then gone to Dallas to find Ed Graham. The memory was quite vivid as I looked around the office.

Bennett jumped up from a prominent desk as I came through the doorway and extended his hand. He was of medium height and was an attorney I had known for several years. In fact he had presented three of four grievances to the system board while George and I were board members. Also he had presented the flight allocation cases which were still unsettled.

Now, as he shook my hand in friendly fashion, my eyes wandered over his medium build. I noticed for the first time that he had acquired a noticeable paunch. But he was the head of the ALPA legal department under Sayen which was obviously a cause of pride.

"Where's Schy?" I inquired, feeling a strong desire to see the attorney who had so ably presented, and worked with Weiss on my case, and with whom I had formed a firm friendship.

Bennett informed me that Schy had left the association several months back and was with a prestigious law firm in Chicago. It caused me to look around the office trying to find a really good looking secretary. The absence of one provoked the thought that maybe Schy had taken her with him. I smiled at the thought.

Bennett interrupted my thoughts with an invitation to sit down in the chair opposite his desk. We engaged in small talk for a little while until I asked: "You wanted to see me?"

"Yes," he replied, "I have been curious to learn why you refused to accept your job back?"

I studied him intently for a minute before inquiring, "Who told you that?"

"Sayen," he replied, showing surprise at my question. "He said he had arranged a deal with Amalgamated by which you could go back to work simply by apologizing to the company and promising to be a good boy. Of course," he added, "there would be no back pay."

"Sayen told you that?" I asked, incredulously studying him. "When did this happen?" My curiosity was quite evident.

"Yes," he insisted, "he told me that not very long ago and said that you had refused and he was washing his hands of the case."

"What was I supposed to apologize for?" I was still curious. "Was I to apologize for being framed? Was I to apologize for exposing that a company official had falsified a government form over my signature?"

There was sarcasm in my voice. "Is that what I was to apologize for?"

He studied me mutely for a good minute.

"Didn't he talk to you about it?" He was visibly ill at ease and uncertain as what to say.

"Sayen has not talked to me in months." I met his eyes in a steady gaze. "And I have not turned any deal down."

"Well," he waved a hand airily as though dismissing the matter, "maybe I misunderstood him."

"I hope so." I was emphatic on that point.

It was a long road back to Claremore, a much longer road than the one to Chicago. It was a road with many troubled and perplexed thoughts. The chief one was a question in my mind, "Was the president of the Air Line Pilots' Association a liar as well as a horse trader?" That made me think of David L. Behncke and the straightforward way he would have met the issue.

I regretted that I had been unable to see him before I had departed from Chicago. But when I drove over to his house, a short distance from ALPA headquarters, I had found it closed tight, locked, and no recent sign of occupancy. There were several newspapers on the front porch.

It was nice to get back to the quiet serenity of the oil field, to erase the memory of those miles and miles of fruitless road to Chicago. After I had called Gene Burns and given him a briefing on the trip and the conversation with Bennett, I tried to drown my thinking in my work. I left all contacts with Sayen to Gene, convinced in my own mind that Bennett had told me the truth. There seemed little doubt but that Sayen was looking for an excuse to forget Allison.

Wylie Drummond and J.J. O'Connell were my frequent contacts after each fruitless board meeting. A few scattered notes came in from the field and a couple copies of letters Shipley had written to Sayen trying to push him toward a strike vote on my behalf, were the sum total. Nat had sent these along with friendly letters in which she revealed that Shipley and Gene Burns were in close contact with other AA chairmen for support in that issue.

But there was so much going on in the company, pilots being checked out on jet equipment, interchanging equipment with the pilots of another airline, and rumors of AA soon taking delivery on new jet equipment, with no provision for adequate pay, that Allison was pushed further in the background.

The subject of adequate pay was the item most talked about up and down the line, more money. The AA fence riding vultures could smell it and they were making a lot of noise with their heads on the right side of the fence. They were almost grovelling to company officials.

Wylie Drummond called a few weeks after my Chicago trip and related with a laugh that the company was courting him and J.J. O'Connell with tempting offers of desk jobs. It amused him, for he had not forgotten that I had related to him how, when the screening cases were at a critical state, Braznell had called me to a Fort Worth meeting during which he had offered me an assistant superintendent of flying job. Such as Anderson was later given.

Ogden had been present, had said nothing, even though I was to be his assistant. With the screening cases in a critical situation, I had refused the job, but it had made me wonder. I had suspected it to be a possible bribe. Now Wylie was chuckling at having a similar offer. It amused us both.

However, he did tell me that he considered further meetings of the board to be a waste of time. The company was adamant in its position.

MEN WHO FLY

I gave him my permission to deadlock the case even though Sayen had suggested that he not do that. We both were of the opinion that Sayen as president of a union did not want to face up to a deadlock. He did not want to spoil his salesmanship image.

Two weeks later J.J. O'Connell came into Tulsa enroute home to Los Angeles from the last System Adjustment Board meeting relative to my case. It was officially deadlocked. He had all the records, a hundred pounds of them, and gave them to me, for I had obtained Dave Behncke's permission to have them before the first hearing. J.J. was very apologetic.

"I sure wish we could have done more," he told me wistfully. "There is no question but that you were 'framed' and the records prove it. Wylie and I have gone all over them and pushed the company members of the board into a corner with those records. But they know that ALPA is in a very weakened condition now and would not even discuss jointly going to a neutral, or jointly appealing to the Federal Mediation board for the appointment of a neutral to sit with the Board and decide the case.

"We have run into the same thing that you and George ran into on the screening cases. It will take a strike vote from all the AA pilots to force a neutral. Sayen has refused to consider it. You and George had Dave Behncke's backing and support. In fact he had the field ready to give that vote when you and George briefed Mr. Damon on the screening cases."

We shook hands in parting while I had the vague feeling that it would be our last meeting. In watching his airplane depart, I was quite despondent.

In a short while I was at the law offices of Disney, Hart, and Disney with all the luggage. Previously I had talked with them about the case and the possibility of having to seek relief in court, but they had nothing to go on, no records, until now. I had gone as far as I could go under the contract in effect at the time of my discharge. Now I was free to seek court action.

This wasn't the course I wanted to take. I wanted my job back. But that had been denied me, regardless of the one-sided evidence in my favor. Now, all I could do was lug the hundred or so pounds of suitcases, brief cases, and exhibits into young Disney's office and show him the sequence of the records, then give him time to research the case.

Disney had indicated in a couple of previous meetings with me that they planned to share my case with another law firm. Their leg-man, Ralph Thomas, and young Disney were going to go over the records, compile briefs of it, and would discuss it with me later.

My despondency carried over for the next few days. Jean was out of town for several days on a double-back schedule and I was alone with my gloom. I had nothing to do but visit the old drilling machine to keep the well going down. That spelled hard physical work. And it was difficult to get back to a state of constant and complete absorption in that work. The memories of the airline and the time-consuming hearings were too vivid.

Jean being away, and the destruction of the last vestige of hope for a fair resolution of my case before the system board, seemed to drain me. I found myself working silently and methodically with Russ, in a preoccupied state of mind until I noticed that I frequently had moisture in my eyes. That upset me further and I accused myself of self-pity.

Jean, I discovered, was my haven of strength. She was so cheerful, always so sweet and lovely, so sympathetic and understanding. Being with her made it easy for me to forget my problems. Until then, I had not realized how much she had grown in my thoughts, the bulwark of strength she had become.

Somehow, I struggled through the day. At home, I took my shower and scrubbed off the oil and grease of the drilling machine, more like a zombie than anything else. Mother was most considerate, realizing that I was quite despondent, she did not push needless conversation.

After dinner I settled in the front porch swing with the two bird dogs coiled at my feet while I continued my melancholic mood. I guess having all the records of my case returned to me drove home the knowledge it was all over. I was a dead issue.

Flashing car lights in the growing dusk roused me to see Jean swing into the driveway with Mother's car. I had not expected her until the following day. It was so nice to feel her arms encircle my neck. I led her to the swing. Her flashing blue eyes, so filled with affection, fanned my desire for her even without her pressing her body close. She was a truly beautiful and desirable young woman, a grown woman who knew what she wanted.

That thought struck me with great force as she settled in the swing

beside me with that musical laugh that had fascinated me on our first
meeting. We had not discussed marriage since the night she confessed
that I was the only man she had ever met that she might want to marry
someday. That someday had never been defined further.

Now, in the swing, and with my arm around her, I thought it might
be an appropriate time to return to the subject. We had become such
good friends, partners in hunting, fishing and outdoor excursions,
frequently with Mother, but always together, Jean and I. Full realization of how much I needed her had finally dawned on me. But before
I could frame my thinking into words she spoke in a low voice.

"My vacation starts Monday."

"Did you ask for it?" I was surprised.

"No, but they claim to have more surplus stewardesses and want to
wind up the vacations before we get into the fall season and holidays.
So they have just arbitrarily started assigning vacations to those who
have not taken them." She spread her hands out in a futile gesture and
a helpless look.

"Good ol' Amalgamated," I exclaimed. "That's the kind of crap I
fought for years. Have you any plans?"

"Not really." Her eyes searched my face. "I can't go home for a
visit on such short notice, for my folks are traveling in Canada and I
have no idea where to contact them."

"Well," I began to get the glimmer of an idea. "We might be able
to go hunting."

"Quail season doesn't start until next month," she reminded me
while leaning forward to pat a couple of bird dog heads. Her eyes
continued to question me while I began to see more than a glimmer of
an idea.

"We could hunt in another state," I explained. "Yesterday I
received a pamphlet from the Game and Fish Division of Colorado.
Their deer season starts next week."

I studied her face with a half-smile on mine.

"You mean—?" She was not sure she was following me.

"Why not?" I questioned. "I have several big game rifles here that
I used in Maine and Canada when I was flying out of Boston. One is
a little light weight .257 that I think would be perfect for you. We
wouldn't have to buy much hunting equipment. The licenses and
gasoline out there would be the big items; I have plenty of camping

gear. We could go back to the same place I hunted a couple of years ago, a big ranch high in the mountains out of Delta."

Her eyes were suddenly shining in the twilight as she slipped closer. "Tell me more," she murmured.

"There's one big drawback." I shook my head as I continued. "I couldn't haul you across state lines or camp out with you without a marriage certificate. I could be prosecuted under the Mann Act."

I don't know just how she managed to get closer to me but somehow she did.

"I thought you would never ask—" she repeated several times between tender kisses.

The next morning I went to the drilling machine and hung the tools on a big wrench, effectively closing the hole from any vandalism, drained the water lines against any little light freezes that might come before I returned and locked all the tool boxes. Once in my life I did not have to ask or beg for a vacation. I was just deciding to take one. Self- employment, for the first time, tasted good.

Four years slipped by as time will do. After the first year of our marriage, Jean quit her job with Amalgamated as a stewardess. She was so honest that it bothered her to conceal the fact that we were married. The company had a regulation that all stewardesses had to be single. When one married, openly, the company immediately terminated her employment.

We had concealed our marriage during that year in which she flew her regular schedule out of Tulsa in a routine manner.

I am sure the pilots recognized the fact and one would quietly, with a little half smile, ask her how I was doing, and maybe send a note. But those notes dwindled.

Jean secured a good job in Doctor Gordon's office in the town of Claremore and really settled in. She was home every night, and able to spend a lot of time with me. We bought a large trailer house and moved it in on my oil lease, near the one of Mother's, so I could conveniently look after the three little wells I had drilled on the two leases. A couple of other leases I had acquired had nothing but dry holes in that area. Now I was back drilling on the original leases.

Before the first year had ended I managed to get on with Gulf Oil on a temporary basis, flying a Lockheed Loadstar and a Lockheed twelve. Bruce Grove, as the chief pilot, had followed my case with great interest, and when the new vice-president of the Tulsa Division, which included Canada, refused to ride with any pilot that was not an airline pilot, Bruce had a perfect excuse to put me to work. That vice-president, Porterfield by name, really disliked flying.

In spite of Amalgamated's letter, which he admitted he received, Bruce hired me on a temporary basis. With three pilots who each had twenty years of service, he had to do something. So he took them all, including me, into his confidence. It would only be temporary. As long as the vice-president had to ride with an airline pilot, I would be that pilot.

That flying lasted for several months until the vice-president retired and the new vice-president located in Calgary, Canada, to be closer to the hub of his division. Thereafter the flying available to me was a little vacation relief flying each year.

Jean and I fished a lot in those four years, and hunted quail from one end of the season to the other. In addition she worked in the doctor's office and I ran the old drilling machine. Also, we managed to go to Colorado each fall for the big game hunting season when Jean would take her vacation.

That was a must, for on each trip to Colorado we brought home a carload of deer and elk, enough to fill a deep freezer.

After about a year and a half of that four I began to wind down and realized how tightly I had been wound while flying the airline. Maybe walking a tight rope for so long with Amalgamated and hearing the frequent baying of a beagle had been responsible. But I had noticed that other airline pilots were the same way, even without beagles.

Too many CAA regulations, ambiguously written, and too many company regulations paraphrasing the CAA regulations but twisting them a little here and there, together with an occasionally unpublished policy, orally given, were no doubt responsible. They must contribute to accidents. You can't shoot at a coyote three times before sunrise without making him awfully nervous for the rest of the day.

Then one weekend when we were at Mother's house, a group of four pilots from Amalgamated came to see me. They represented the Master Executive council of Amalgamated Airlines and were each chairman of a council together with the Master Chairman, Gene Sea.

I had not seen any Amalgamated pilots for quite some time and had completely lost contact with the AA pilot group, except for George

Schustman, Gene Burns, and Freddy Mills whom I talked with on the phone infrequently. These contacts had been widely scattered over a period of weeks. So I sat on the big front porch and visited, while wondering what had prompted them to come to see me, a fired pilot for over four years.

Two of the group were relatively new as chairmen as was the Master Chairman, Gene Seal, but they seemed to know me quite well. Each had a recollection of something I had done for them or members of their council. Pat Patterson, the only white head in the group was considerably senior to me and was the chairman of the large Los Angeles Council. I had known him and worked with him a number of years in the past.

Gene Seal was a large man, probably six or seven years junior to me and with large hands and feet which he kept shuffling around. I had the impression that he was quite nervous and wondered if he was that nervous in the cockpit. It caused me to recall the years I had been a copilot and how a nervous captain had always made me a little nervous. I had a fleeting memory of Johnny Pricer, whom nothing seemed to bother.

"Wayne," Gene Seal came to the point rather quickly, "we have recently held a Master Council meeting in preparation for the next ALPA convention in Chicago, which is two weeks away. The entire AA field is still upset over your case and wants something done. Sayen has repeatedly refused to petition for a neutral in your case."

"Gene," I spoke slowly and quietly, "I am a dead duck. My case was thrown out of federal court by U.S. Judge W.R. Wallace without a hearing or consideration of any evidence. He gave the company a summary judgement after asking for my case and professing an interest in aviation cases. Originally the case was on Judge Savage's docket but he turned it over to Judge Wallace when Wallace asked for it. Then Judge Wallace very promptly signed the summary judgement for Amalgamated. The law firm representing me said it was a real raw deal but they could do nothing to reverse a U.S. judge."

"We know that," Seal acknowledged. "I have even talked with your law firm. We can back up and go to a neutral with a strike vote. That will force a neutral on your case."

"But it would require a strike vote from all AA pilots," I offered hesitantly.

"We have a pledge from all the AA councils to give that vote," Seal spoke firmly. "They want a decision on your case and have pledged that vote."

I was rather stunned at this turn of events. It was something I had not expected. A pledged strike vote from all the councils was an unheard of thing. I felt Jean's hand slip into mine from her seat on the divan beside me, a seat she had taken after serving drinks.

Seal continued, "According to ALPA bylaws, before we can take that vote we have to have it authorized by either the president of the association or the convention. Will you attend that convention in Chicago in a couple of weeks?"

After a little thought I asked, "How?"

"The Master Executive Council of AA can take you as an official observer." Seal had it all thought out. "We are paying your expenses, including those of your wife. We want you there and want to get you on the floor to tell the convention some of the things you have done for ALPA. We feel sure the convention would authorize that vote."

I studied Seal's face at the conclusion of his talk. Then I laughed a little.

"You boys are most flattering," I conceded. "I greatly appreciate the efforts you have made in my behalf. I have nothing to lose. Of course we'll go."

I shook hands with all shortly thereafter and thanked them again for their support. It was a very complimentary thing to have them take the trouble they were taking. Of course I wanted my job back and all knew that. They wanted to help me.

Some time after the group had departed I sat with Jean on the front porch and occasionally patted a bird dog's head while Jean took good care of the other one.

"Little gal," I spoke affectionately to Jean, "don't get your hopes up on this. These boys mean well, but Gene Seal is a young master chairman and has the pilots' interest at heart.

"Clarence Sayen is a trader and I suspect will trade with the enemy if the price is right. Somehow I have had the feeling for a long time that he had traded my case off to the Air Transport Association which, of course, represents Amalgamated Airlines."

Jean and I checked in at the Sheridan Hotel where the convention was convening the following day. It was late in the evening and we had had a full day. We had worked in the early morning at the drilling machine cleaning the well hole of a little water which I did not want to build up in the hole and start it caving. Then we had driven to the Tulsa airport and taken a Braniff plane to Chicago. Jean wanted to see how the Braniff girls worked. The next morning we had a leisurely breakfast in the coffee shop and then gravitated, near nine, toward the convention hall officially set to open at ten. We picked up observer badges from the ALPA secretary, Miss Forrest, who greeted me quite warmly. Jean had heard me speak of her at different times and they chatted for quite a little while as Miss Forrest dispensed badges. Jean promptly offered to help as soon as the business picked up, but there wasn't that much work for Miss Forrest to need assistance.

I stood around near the main door to the convention hall to see if I could recognize any old pilots, but failed to see any familiar faces other than the Amalgamated group. They all looked so young and inexperienced as they wandered in small groups looking the convention hall over and wandering out again. I could not distinguish the captains from the copilots, as all were in civilian clothes. But occasionally I would see an older man I was sure was a captain.

Then stepping into the convention hall with Jean beside me to give her a good view of the hall and the speaker's rostrum, I was surprised to see that all sections of seats were labeled for the seating. United had a labeled section, TWA had another and every group of pilots from each airline had private seating together as a group. There was no mixing of airline pilots.

Dave Behncke had always insisted on the pilot representatives choosing their own seats. He encouraged mixing so that a United pilot could sit with a TWA group if he desired or a mixed group could sit together. He had always insisted that our problems were all basically the same, namely: (1) Schedule with safety, and (2) Security of employment.

I pointed out the seating arrangement to Jean as a few pilots wandered around. I told her about Dave and the fair and open way he had always chaired each convention. She was most interested and seemed fascinated with the little stories I told of David L. Behncke.

I told her the story of how Dave had ordered the same thing that the rest of us had when he found the negotiating committee in a bar after walking out over a Sayen proposal. He had drunk it too, in spite of being a teetotaler. But, I explained, I didn't think Dave really knew what an intoxicating drink tasted like.

Jean particularly enjoyed the watermelon story while we looked for the AA pilots' seats. I was very interested in their location.

The watermelon incident had occurred in 1949 when I was chairman of Tulsa, on the negotiating committee and also the system adjustment board. It was shortly after the successful conclusion of the screening cases and during the time in which I had become intimately acquainted with David L. Behncke. Somehow, along the way, I had learned that he loved watermelons and I had heard him complain that it was impossible to get really good watermelons in Chicago.

A short time later I was out on my farm between Tulsa and Claremore where I had a large watermelon patch hidden in a corn field. On recalling Dave's complaint I loaded my station wagon with some forty and fifty pound melons, all I could get in the car, and drove over to the Amalgamated Airlines freight section at the airport. It was a small building separated from the main terminal and staffed with a couple of AA cargo handlers.

I explained my mission, gave each a big melon to take home plus a little coffee money, then with their help unloaded all the melons in a secluded corner, after scratching "Behncke" on each melon. Thereafter those diligent cargo handlers loaded a big melon on each AA plane heading to Chicago, loading it in with the pilots' baggage and asking them to see that the melon reached Dave. They even recruited a couple of Braniff schedules.

Naturally it gave each pilot an excuse to get personally acquainted with the ol'man or renew a previous meeting. I don't think a single melon went astray.

Two days later I took over another load. It went out the same way. Then another load was being considered when the ol'man called me one night when he was working late at the office.

"Wayne," he had pleaded, "my danged office is half full of watermelons and all the help is sick of eating them. Would you feed the rest to the hogs?"

The story made the rounds, not only on Amalgamated and Braniff, but the others as well. It was too good to keep, especially with two or three pranksters mailing packages of watermelon seeds to Dave with detailed instructions on how to grow his own.

We finally found the seating for the AA pilots just as I concluded the watermelon story. It was always nice to hear Jean laugh.

"Why," she exclaimed as we surveyed the AA seating, "they're in the orchestra pit."

Indeed they were. I stood and studied the seats. They were on the front row of the auditorium right under the speaker's stand. I decided that the speaker's feet would be about on a level with the group's heads.

We wandered back to the coffee shop for a cup of coffee while I kept thinking about the seating of the AA pilots. I didn't think much of the situation, for in past conventions I had attended it had always been advantageous to sit back about two-thirds of the distance from the speaker's stand to the rear of the auditorium. That way the acoustics of a big auditorium seemed to be better. At least it was a better position from which to observe the various speakers in the big auditorium as they spoke from the floor. Also, it was a better position from which to exit the hall or return to a seat without unduly interrupting the speeches.

Pat Patterson, the chairman of the Los Angeles council and an old friend, was just finishing his breakfast and motioned for us to come over.

"I'm sure glad to see you here, Wayne," he commented. "Gene Seal was asking if any of us had seen you. He wanted to make sure you are here and available when we get the floor for new business."

"Did you see where you are sitting?" I asked, uneasy with the situation.

Pat shrugged his shoulders and sipped his coffee. "Sayen made the assignments, I understand, and refused to make any changes. Gene Seal thinks it's okay, thinks it will insure our getting the floor when we want it."

"You know," he continued, "there's been quite a lot of feuding during the last couple of years between Seal and Sayen. Gene has been putting the heat on Sayen to get something going on your case. He wants the right to get a strike vote to force a neutral. So far Sayen has refused. That's why Gene wants the whole convention to hear some of the things you have done for ALPA."

I nodded, thinking of Sayen and his trading tendencies.

"Also," Pat added, "Gene has been giving Sayen a rough time over the way he is trying to turn the association into a boys' club, a social thing. It seems that Sayen is partying a good deal with United and Eastern chairmen and everything being done now by the association is for United and Eastern while AA keeps paying almost a third of the total dues collected by ALPA."

Pat Patterson was among the top ten on Amalgamated's seniority list of pilots. He was white-headed with a ruddy and young looking face. But he was facing retirement at sixty in a couple more years.

As one of the original organizers of ALPA Pat Patterson had always been a staunch Behncke supporter. He himself had been a victim of an irresponsible firing by an irate company official along with quite a few other pilots in the turbulent days of the organization of ALPA. They had learned the importance of job security. Naturally Pat was most supportive of my case. Also I knew he was concerned about the course the association was taking with Sayen at the helm, especially with the way he had kept ignoring my case. Under Behncke a fired pilot was given top listing on convention business and welcomed to the convention floor.

Jean and I were in the back of the auditorium for the beginning of the convention. The large auditorium was almost full with over three hundred delegates. Sayen was the lead off speaker, giving a report on the past two years of ALPA activity.

He was a confident and polished speaker and had been in office well over four years after Behncke's final ouster. He had the same self-assured and smiling approach he had exhibited in presenting the IMI formula in the drive for a mileage limitation. His speech lasted about two hours, during which Jean and I slipped out for a cup of coffee.

After Sayen's speech various officers of the association gave reports, such as the secretary and treasurer, the accident investigation committee chairman, and the head of the legal department. Each made a short speech as well as the first vice-president of the association who, I believe, was a prominent Eastern pilot and a close friend of Sayen. Jean and I had more coffee.

After a one hour lunch between one and two in the afternoon, the convention recessed to give the chairmen of the various committees and their members time to work on proposed legislation that had come in from the field. Sayen had selected the chairmen of those committees, who, in turn had selected their members from the delegates. The time from two to seven was allocated to committee work.

Jean and I had nothing to do but relax in our room, take a walk, see a movie, and write some letters. Wintertime in Chicago is not a good time for taking walks, but we did try and ended with a cab to a good movie we both wanted to see.

At seven the convention assembled in the auditorium while each committee chairman had some completed work to present to the floor with the committee's recommendations to its disposal. Each proposal brought out considerable debate with many members simply practicing their oratory ability; many proposals were returned to committees for further study.

In the middle of the next afternoon it was obvious that all the proposals would not see convention action and by that time the delegates were getting tired and beginning to vote with the recommendations of the various committee chairmen. They began passing some pretty rough legislation. Many problems, as had been done in the years of Behncke, were simply passed along to the president for him to solve with the convention's approval. Now they were being given to Sayen in almost the same manner.

The convention was scheduled to end in two days and pilots were getting anxious to catch a plane back to their home bases and get back on schedule. They simply did not like tedious work with a pencil, preferring instead a large airplane.

Sayen had the Amalgamated Airlines group in the orchestra pit directly under his feet so he could conveniently look over them and recognize some speaker further back in the audience when the floor was opened, at limited times, for new business.

When a subject was being debated, Sayen was quick to recognize an AA pilot. However, he never gave the AA group an opportunity to bring up my case on the floor for convention action. He kept them well throttled.

Gene Seal was furious that night when the convention ended. Sayen had smoothly out-maneuvered him and kept an undesirable subject from seeing convention action. In fact all the AA delegates were upset. They wanted so badly to get my case to a final conclusion, which meant to a neutral judge.

I could not help but recall the fair and open way Behncke had always chaired each convention which I had attended. To Dave, a

454 MEN WHO FLY

discharged pilot would be given preference on the floor. To Sayen he was something to be suppressed, to be treated as an item in the trading stock bag.

It was late that night when Jean and I caught a southbound Braniff plane to Tulsa after I had thanked all the AA master council members for their interest and support. I was a dead duck, and had known it for a long time, ever since U.S. Judge W.R. Wallace had thrown my case out and given AA a summary judgment without looking at the evidence. I could not help but wonder how many free passes to Washington had been credited to Wallace for that summary judgment.

Regardless Judge Wallace never was able to use them for a short time later he was killed in a car accident on the Tulsa-Oklahoma City turnpike. It made me sad to read about it.

How I wished that Judge Savage had kept my case. His reputation as a federal judge was incomparable in the Middle West. In contrast Judge Wallace, who had been a corporate attorney for many years before being appointed a federal judge, had the reputation of favoring corporations.

Somehow, I felt relieved. The long battle was over. I was defeated, even with all the evidence that I had been framed. A wave from C.R.'s crooked finger had prevailed. In a small way, I think I understood how General Lee must have felt at Appomattox.

Jean snuggled close on that Braniff airplane. We avoided an AA plane some thirty minutes ahead of the Braniff one. Jean knew. She understood what I had been through in the last few years. She had been out at the machine many times when a low flying AA plane swung by and maybe dropped a wing momentarily. She had watched the expressions on my face and seemed to understand how it was tearing my heart out.

She understood my love for that flying, my love for hauling that precious ore from coast to coast. She really understood, for she had been a part of it. Somehow, it seems to get in to your blood regardless of whether you sit up front or serve meals and occasionally change a diaper in the cabin.

Now we snuggled and talked about the well we expected to drill into the pay zone within the next couple of days. It looked really promising, especially with three small stripper wells already drilled and pumping on a good-sized lease.

Chapter 23

The Golden Glow

It was a nice day when we motored the short half mile from our trailer house to the machine. The day before we had cleaned out the little water in the hole from the Tucker sand, some two hundred feet up the hole from the target zone, the Burgess. We had also drilled a little and found oil staining in the last few inches of a sample, together with a little gas rolling the drilling water at the bottom of the hole. That gas had sounded good, for it wasn't a bubbling sound. It was more like a lion growling deep in his throat in short intervals. We could feel the power of it. Somehow it caused the hair on our necks to have an odd feeling for it really sounded like a lion's growl from a deep cavern.

I had a two hundred barrel oil tank which I had bought at a recent sale. It was sitting about a hundred yards from the present location, so it wasn't too hard to lay a two-inch line from the tank to the present well location. Russ had been sick and unable to work, so Jean had donned blue jeans, a rough hunting shirt, and hiking boots to assist. We couldn't wait until I could get other help.

The pipeline warmed us up and consumed about two hours of the morning in neither warm nor cold weather, just good bird-hunting weather. But we were not thinking of birds. Next we swung the chain hoist and picked up a big control head on the edge of the derrick floor. Swinging it over the open casing in the hole, we screwed it into the well casing firmly. That put us in good shape for a wild well, even though it seemed like a lot of unnecessary precautions. But if you didn't have the gate shut when the lion sprang, it would be too late.

It was noon when we tightened the control head on the casing. So we stopped for a little rest and to eat a sandwich and drink a little coffee. Then we were ready to go back to drilling. Jean was nervous from anticipation and I paused to comfort her.

"Little gal," I insisted, "we'll get along even if it is another dry one." I took the time to give her a long hug. That hug made me realize that she was shaking in nervous anticipation.

I had heard my Dad tell stories of things that men did in the period of anticipation in drilling in a big well. Numerous times he had seen men put the wrong end of a cigarette in their mouths, have spells of vomiting, and even wet their trousers. The growl of a lion affects everyone, in various ways.

Shortly we had the tools in the bottom of the hole and were back to drilling. But things were not right in some way. The tools drilled a little, maybe six inches or a foot, then they acted crazy, like I had lost a drill bit. Quickly I pulled out of the hole to find that the last two hundred feet of line going on the spooling drum were dripping oil.

The oil almost beat the tools out of the hole and I barely had time to close the control valve before the flow line to the tank began dancing across the field. Grabbing Jean's hand, I rushed her to the tank and helped her up the ladder so that we were both standing on the top of that tank.

Pulling the nose up and up does not have a thrill that compares to feeling a big tank trying to walk around under you as a solid two inch stream of oil, under three or four hundred pounds of pressure, pours into the tank. I could scarcely believe it. It seemed so unreal, for I had never experienced it before, only heard my Dad tell of the feeling. It was so exciting!

Jean's eyes were almost as big as hen eggs and the blue in them was shining like I had never seen except in the aurora borealis of the Arctic.

"That's oil!" she cried excitedly to me above the rumble of the tank.

We stood on that tank with our arms entwined, feeling the rumble of the tank and listening to the discharge of the flow line. Through an open louvre we could see the heavy oil foam rising in the bottom of the tank with a beautiful golden glow of foam on the top.

In a few minutes it stopped flowing oil and gassed heavily for a minute or two and then went back to flowing a solid flow of bluish-green oil that became a foamy gold in the tank. A heavy vapor of gas with fine beads of oil enveloped the top of the tank as it escaped through the open louvre.

Then back on the derrick floor we went to stand and watch Mother Earth shake that string of casing with its three hundred pound control head until it rattled against the surface casing like a dog shaking a rattlesnake in a tub. It was truly an awesome sight.

I never knew who the pilot was that swung so low in an airplane with a large AA on the tail; and he didn't dip a wing, but it caused me to look up, wave, and put my arm around Jean's waist.

"Honey," I observed looking at the planes, "I have never seen a business that looked so clean and was so dirty."

I looked down at her smiling upturned face, noting the scattered beads of oil on her cheeks and nose, the oil stains on her blue jeans, the oil-spotted derrick floor and added, "And never have I seen a business that looked so dirty and was so clean!"

So we went to the corner drug store for coffee, oil spots and all. It was a truck stop on a U.S. highway where you could get a motel room, a Band-Aid, a cup of coffee, a good steak and a not-so-good girl—all at one order.

There while we coffee breaked and basked in the knowledge of our discovery, I called an oil hauling company to rush a tank truck that afternoon and ordered a new oil tank from Nowata, about twenty miles to the north.

It didn't take long for the news of a natural flowing well to get around. Maybe the coffee conversation did it, maybe my calls did it. Anyway, by evening sightseers, ranchers, and oil men began flocking to see a natural flowing well that revealed a new, untapped oil lens. All began to speculate on where such a lens might extend.

Things changed in the corner drug store area quite suddenly. Instead of being a drilled up country of dry holes and scattered pumping wells, stripper wells that delivered a few barrels of oil each day individually, it took on a smell of new oil, a whole new oil field, a nagging mystery to everyone.

Oil men came from miles around. They came from other old oil fields that had been virtually drilled-out, with old wells, on time clocks, sleepily pumping those two or three hours each day with a listless, ho-hum delivery.

They came from Tulsa. They came with money to invest, to buy leases, a part of a lease, a corner, or a partnership. If they did not have that in mind, they only had to stand on or near that oil tank, the one Jean and I had stood on that memorable day, and listen to that well gag and flow, continue to gag and flow, and they quickly developed a whole new line of thought. They were oil men, or all of a sudden they wanted to be oil men.

I began to receive propositions to buy a half, a quarter or a small interest in the leases I had coupled with Mother's acreage and its one producing well. It all made a nice attractive tract to potential investors, especially when they stood where they could hear that well talking, talking and talking. They understood what it was saying. It was telling that it was coming from a field with virgin pressure.

That coupled with the information that I had only drilled six inches or a foot into the pay zone convinced all that a pay zone, that much drilling had proven to be pinched out miles to the southwest, had taken a rebirth to the northeast.

The excitement, the sudden interest in oil leases didn't seem to bother Jean or me. We were oil people, business people with a love for hunting quail in Oklahoma, deer and elk in Colorado and maybe, maybe a little more oil in the Caney river bottom. I forgot about the airline, until some low flying plane would remind me. Then, painfully I would recall the agony I had been through.

Two months slipped by with the well continuing to flow with only a little drop-off. It was proving that it was a virgin well and coming from a sizeable reservoir. My stack of oil delivery tickets kept stacking up, as I awaited a report from the refinery's attorneys regarding proper payments of mineral rights. Initial production on any new lease always required a long delay before the oil payments were released by the attorneys, and they dared not make a mistake.

A few months later Jean quit her job at the doctor's office at my insistence and stayed close to me. Then when I sent her into the bank at Claremore to deposit the first oil check received after the long abstract examination by the oil refinery's attorneys, she came out laughing.

"You should have seen the face of that teller," she laughed.

"He looked at the check like it was a forgery, carried it around to the president's desk and showed it to him."

Again she laughed and fixed those glowing blue eyes on me before adding, "The president opened the door for me as I went out."

We laughed together as I drove out to Mother's home where we were planning dinner that night. The oil check was for more than an airline pilot's yearly salary.

It had us cloud walking for there was a wonderful bond between us. We were happy together. But George Schustman's car in Mother's driveway brought us back to reality. I had not seen him since before the convention in Chicago and had only talked with him briefly on the telephone shortly after the convention.

In fact I had not had contact with any of the Tulsa-based pilots of Amalgamated for several months and preferred it that way. Seeing one or more of them only brought back some painful memories, and if the Tulsa pilot was a friend or a good ALPA member, I thought I could detect pain in his eyes as well. All knew that I had been framed and they were powerless to help me. Sayen had taken care of that.

George's expression was glum and dejected as we seated ourselves on Mother's front porch, and I could not help but note how much his face had aged in the last couple of years. Jean brought cold drinks and left us to talk after George had declined to stay for dinner.

Abruptly George exclaimed, "The AA boys are talking about pulling out of the union."

I studied the way he had come out with that remark, but before I could react to that declaration he explained. "You've always been a strong ALPA member and have worked real hard for the pilots. At the hearings you proved that you were framed and most of the pilots know that. Now the company is just sitting back and saying, 'We fired him, so what. And if we can fire Allison on trumped up charges we can do it again to anyone. So you boys had better comb your hair right and show a little respect for officials. Otherwise it could happen to you.'

"Everyone is asking, what good is the damned union? Why are we paying dues to Sayen's outfit? It was a real union under Behncke, but under Sayen it's a boys' club, Sayen's social club."

"He refused to permit us to give you a strike vote and thereby helped keep you fired. He's working, everyone is now thinking, for AA."

His words came in almost a torrent. "They're wanting to pull out of ALPA and organize their own union," he added.

"Oh no!" I exclaimed.

George nodded and stared bleakly at me before continuing, "Gene

Seal is so incensed at Sayen that he is openly discussing it up and down the line and at council meetings. Already he has had a couple of meetings with Whitacre."

"Whitacre?" I didn't think I was hearing right. "He's a company official. What's he got to do with the pilots' union?"

"Well," George was a little uncertain, "it seems that he got wind of the pilots' dissatisfaction with ALPA and somehow he and Seal got to talking about the company problems. Then Whitacre made it quite clear that AA also was dissatisfied with ALPA and would like to see an organization that was more cognizant of the company's problems."

"Oh, brother!" I exclaimed more to myself than George. "That has the smell of a company union."

George nodded, and added: "There's a lot of us who are against any consideration of such a thing. But there are quite a few pro-company men who are bitching against ALPA and they're using your case as an example, along with the high dues assessed for the strike benefits of other airlines with nothing being done for the AA pilots. Then, of course, there are the 'vultures' or 'fence-riders' as you call them. They now think they can get a little more gravy by reversing their position on the fence. So now, they are talking about what a good union it was under Behncke, but with him gone it has no strength. So they also think we should get out and maybe organize our own union."

I sat for several minutes without saying anything as I turned the situation over and over in my mind. Then Jean came to us with the announcement that dinner was on the table and we were having elk steaks. She insisted that the steaks were from her elk, as mine was the tougher of the two, and she had cooked a steak for George. It didn't take much persuasion to convince him that he should have dinner with us, especially when he admitted he had never eaten elk.

After dinner, George and I sat a while longer on the front porch while he told me that Gene Seal had insisted that he had a good understanding of the company's problems, and AA felt that an independent union not associated with ALPA would be beneficial to the company as well as the pilots. Whitacre had hinted that, to see one established, the company would sign a very liberal contract with the pilot group.

It was quite evident to me that the so-called independent union meant a 'company union' and the new contract would be a 'sweetheart' contract, very sweet at first with generous hourly pay increases and a cut back in flying hours—no mileage limitation—but a good cut back in hours.

"George," I offered, "I think I can throw a little light on the pilots' problems different from Seal's explanations. In 1938 I was flying with Tom Hardin out of Forth Worth to Nashville and had been his copilot for almost two years.

"Tom Hardin was a strong ALPA man and was the first vice-president, that is, he was Dave Behncke's immediate successor, his right hand man and the chairman of the AA negotiating committee, negotiating the first labor contract with any airline. It was to be ALPA's first.

"The pilots of Amalgamated were nearly one hundred per cent ALPA. Dave Behncke and others, including Tom Hardin, had selected Amalgamated to break the ice with the airlines. It was a history making event.

"David Behncke, in person, represented ALPA as the union negotiator while C.R. Brown, in person, was the Amalgamated representative with Ralph Damon assisting as well as a couple of other officials. The negotiation had produced considerable fireworks. But the ALPA group had a ninety-nine per cent pledge of support from each council with signatures of all members. It wasn't exactly a strike vote. It just guaranteed a strike vote if one was needed.

"C.R. knew about it too. He really wanted the publicity of being the first airline president to recognize the pilots' union. But he didn't like putting it in writing with his signature at the bottom.

"The System Adjustment Board provisions really upset him. However, in the end, he signed the historic document and took all the publicity it drew. According to Tom Hardin there were times of intense fireworks between C.R. and Dave Behncke. He related that in one of those hot exchanges, C.R. had solemnly promised Dave Behncke that he would some day break the pilots' union."

"I remember something about signing the pledge of support," George recalled, "but I didn't know Tom Hardin."

"He was quite a man, a really dynamic figure.

"Dave Behncke, Tom Hardin and a few pilot representatives of other airlines successfully lobbied Congress into passing the Civil Aeronautics Act that created the Civil Aeronautics Board and the

Independent Air Safety Board. Tom Hardin became the only pilot on the Air Safety Board and he did a lot of good for the pilots and passengers in promoting air safety. In fact, when WW II came, the safety requirements on the airlines were so strict that President Roosevelt promised to abolish the Air Safety Board as a price for securing the airlines' cooperation in the war. Air safety then went backward."

"Then you think C.R. is behind persuading the AA pilots to pull out of ALPA?" George asked.

"I feel sure of it. Such a split would greatly weaken ALPA." I explained. "And at the same time C.R. would have his precious pilots sacked in a company union sack that he could shake any time. He would have almost complete control of them."

When he departed Jean took his chair.

"Did you tell him about what I put in the bank today?" she asked and at my shake of the the head she continued, "Let's keep that a family secret, you, me, and your mother."

I nodded, then added: "You know that elk season will open soon in Colorado. Maybe we could afford a vacation."

She laughed that musical laugh and whispered, "Why do you think we've had elk so often recently? I'm creating a real good reason for a trip to Colorado."

"Let's just move out there." I came to a sudden decision.

She stared at me in the light of the street light which did a pretty good job of illuminating Mother's front porch.

"I'd love it," she whispered softly, "but how?"

"Today an oil man made me a really attractive offer for our wells and leases. I have a sudden desire to get away from here—from all AA pilots and Amalgamated—and go where I'll never see an airplane with that big AA on the tail."

I felt her hand slip into mine. "I understand," she whispered, "for a long time I have seen the look in your eyes when a plane flies low over the machine. I know how it haunts you."

"How does Gunnison, Colorado suit you?" I asked with a smile. "We've been hunting out of there for several years now. I have had a good chance to geologize that area. There should be some new oil there just waiting to be discovered. And," I added, "Amalgamated never heard of Gunnison."

"Give me fifteen minutes and I'll be packed," she laughed.

The next day I closed a deal to sell our oil and gas leases. By haggling a little with the oil man making the offer I was able to sack a few more thousand. He really wanted that talking well.

A few days later we were headed for Colorado with all our hunting gear and a desire to relocate. The hunting fever was in our blood. In addition a touch of the pioneer was stirring in us as we discussed finding a new home in the western Rockies far from that haunting AA and the familiar faces of pilots I had known for many years. We were comforted in the venture with the reassuring thought of that folding green Jean had put in the bank, plus the additional that was following.

We were happy and we were together, firm in our determination to make Colorado our home. There we took another look at Delta, at Montrose and again were attracted to Gunnison. Maybe it was the proximity of the elk, and the fact that we had previously hunted in Gunnison County during which time I had observed the surface geology while hunting. It stirred my wildcatting blood, not just for a new well, but for a new field. I could smell it!

Soon we were camping out high on the western slope of the continental divide in an old log cabin with a corral and rented horses. A licensed guide came by regularly every three or four days to bring in hay and groceries and occasionally take an animal to the locker plant. Each of us could shoot two deer and one elk at the time. We had very good luck on both.

We returned to Oklahoma to quietly close out everything there, arrange for a trailer mover to take our trailer house out, two other truckers to load and haul the drilling machine and all my equipment, practically on my shirt tail, for it was all in Gunnison within two days after our arrival. It was good that we had made advance arrangements.

Then the years began slipping by, happy years. Years of hard work wildcatting for that elusive oil, years during which I bought a water well machine and did contract drilling for both water and oil as well as doing my own explorations with two to four employees, my big son among them.

It was a nice business, a clean business and I wasn't having to look out a windshield from a cockpit spattered with crud. I was enjoying the sunrises and sunsets, working early and late. It was healthy work, wrestling with heavy tools, wrenches, drill stems, and red hot bits dressed out to gauge with sledge hammers, as well as climbing derricks with the agility of a squirrel. The years settled lightly on both Jean and me.

Then one summer day I received a phone call from an AA pilot by the name of Malone. I don't know how he managed to locate me and I didn't remember him, but he and another AA pilot, with their wives, wanted to take Jean and me to dinner. They were out here for a week for a little fishing and cooling off from that hot Texas weather.

Reluctantly we accepted and went to dinner with them in Crested Butte. They kept talking about the union and repeatedly mentioned APA. Both pilots were chairmen and Malone, the chairman of the large Dallas-Fort Worth council, took the trouble to tell me how he never opened a council meeting without reminding the pilots and copilots present of the name Allison and some of the things he had done for the AA pilots.

It was flattering, but I didn't want to discuss it until he again mentioned APA, and I asked if he didn't mean ALPA.

"No," he had responded. "We pulled out of ALPA in 1963 and organized APA, the Allied Pilots Association." That was the year Jean and I had suddenly migrated from Oklahoma.

It developed that the union was a company blessed union, a company union whose blessings grew less and less after they had cut the cord with ALPA. That so upset me that I, in a nice way, requested that he not again mention the name of Allison at a company union meeting. He was most apologetic and wondered until I simply told him it didn't belong at such a meeting. I am not sure he understood the difference.

Also, I requested that he not disclose my address or phone number to other pilots. Reluctantly, he agreed after I had explained that I wanted to remain in seclusion, that I had always felt that the AA pilots should have done more than they did to get me reinstated.

By their passive acceptance of the company's attempt to frame me, the company's attempt to influence the CAA to pull my license by falsifying my F-27 report, then discharging me without being able to show even one company or CAA regulation that I had violated, I had the feeling that I had been sacrificed. They had allowed me to float down the river to pacify the AA management. That feeling was, in a sense, substantiated with the continued acceptance of Ogden and Anderson as supervisory personnel.

To me, they should have castrated them. But, instead, the AA pilots had gone for a company union with very sweet additional pay, liberalized working conditions, and crawled into C.R.'s zipper bag, captives of their own greed, dragging all those who followed them on AA into the same pit.

Under such conditions, how could a pilot, strong as he might be, stand up against maintenance and flying violations that jeopardize air safety without danger of being shuttled down Allison's trail? And how could paying passengers settle into their luxury seats with a sense of security and safety knowing that their pilot is trying to give them a safe flight with a cockpit filled with AA crud? He cannot object or protest; the company zipper bag is too tight around his neck.

In the fall of 1972 my drilling business was thriving and Jean and I bought a large three bedroom log house on the east side of Gunnison facing the city park with unobstructed views of the mountains to the northeast. It was a choice location with an unobstructed view of the east end of the east-west airport runway. Somehow I like to occasionally watch a pilot float an airplane in for a west landing and assist with a little mental telepathy. It seemed to improve their landing! It also helped some groan them off the runway on an east takeoff.

With time the runway was extended in sections, the airport enlarged and a large terminal built. Somehow the county commissioners found the money to meet federal requirements and attract federal aid for the numerous airport improvements. Two of three county commissioners, being pilots, made it easy for them to justify the expenditures even though they permitted roads in sections of the county to deteriorate. They were dedicated pilots.

The size of the airplanes coming in and going out of Gunnison grew and air travel came to the mountains. That attracted some skiers, a trickle at first, to the ski runs at Crested Butte tucked into higher mountains, some twenty-seven miles to the north. It soon became big business.

My drilling business continued to thrive and somehow I found more time to assist pilots through the six foot corner windows to the east and south. Some needed help, for they arrived apprehensive over their first experience in the mountains.

Then one wintery December day I began helping the pilot of a large three engine jet, a 727, arrive. A large AA decorated the tail of the jet and so upset me that I almost spoiled the landing.

It discharged some one hundred and fifty skiers bound for Crested Butte, and was soon enroute back to Atlanta, Georgia. But I did not sleep well that night. Some memories became more vivid and were enhanced with time even though I tried to suppress them.

In three to four years the skiing business became big business each winter for a period of three to four months, depending on the length of the heavy snow season. Several planes arrived each day, discharged near a hundred and fifty eager skiers, each on a package deal of a week of skiing, packed up near a hundred and fifty skiers in each airplane, who had finished their package, and within an hour and a half each airplane would be homeward bound with its load of burned faces and exhausted bodies.

I met several of the AA pilots. Some knew of my old copilots who had retired only a few years back but they had never heard the name of Allison. None had heard of a mileage limitation and were still flying practically the eighty-five hours established in 1938. I was amazed to find how much the working conditions had been compromised, with no mileage limitation after thirty-eight years. They had doubled and tripled the monthly mileage and received pay by the hour while their airline continued to collect by the miles flown.

There is small wonder that there are accidents that seemingly occur with no logical explanation. But they don't call it pilot fatigue, mileage fatigue, or anything like that. They prefer the age old criticism of pilot error. It should rightly be called mileage fatigue.

The east-west runway had been extended to ten thousand feet, but even with that, the seven twenty-seven, at nearly eight thousand feet altitude, would moan and groan and have to be rotated off the runway with very little remaining to crash land on in the event of an engine failure. AA was still running true to past practices and its officials followed C.R.'s training in constantly petitioning the government regulatory body for more gross load on takeoff, more engine time, and more airplane time between aircraft overhauls.

In the beginning it was the old political Department of Commerce before the Civil Aeronautics Act of 1938. Then it became the CAA. But AA and the other airlines could not stand the strict requirements of the Independent Air Safety Board created in the Civil Aeronautics Act of 1938, which had a very impressive safety record. I understand that

FDR traded it off to the airlines for their cooperation in WW II.

Somehow, the pilots never got it back and the CAA followed the old DOC (Department of Commerce) in going political. The FAA (Federal Aviation Authority) modified that somewhat, but the political influence remained and Congress seemed to prefer to keep it political.

I read about the Denver accident of Continental Airlines, and I followed all the news casts and T.V. accounts of the accident. It caused me to marvel at the small amount of time required of the pilot and copilot to be qualified to take nearly two hundred precious lives from city A to city B.

Then I thought back to the year of 1939 when we had the Independent Air Safety Board and recalled checking out as an airline captain and having to fly nearly fifty hours with an old chief pilot as my copilot before he would turn me loose and permit me to take a passenger flight. Then I was given an old copilot, just a dozen numbers below me in seniority, to make sure we stayed out of trouble. And that was with a simple airplane of two engines and fourteen passengers. It didn't begin to require the knowledge that Continental airplane required.

Yet the FAA and the company don't explain the small amount of time on the airplane required of both the copilot and the captain. It reads like collusion, collusion between an airline and a government agency. Or maybe we are talking about several airlines under the title of Air Transport Association. That is the combined political force of all the airlines. Congress, in the past, has been greatly influenced by that political force.

I was spellbound in front of the TV watching the explosion of the Challenger enroute into space, and closely followed the investigations, confessions, and subsequent findings. Everything was examined minutely, even the nuts and bolts were reexamined and rechecked for unauthorized ones. That was done with only eight or nine lives aboard.

What happens when an airliner goes in with a hundred or two hundred precious lives aboard? It makes headlines for a few days and the FAA puts on a big investigation, interviews a good number of people—several desk-pilots but darned few line pilots—and months later, months later, I repeat, comes out with a possible finding. The insurance company pays off, the airline buys another airplane and all is soon forgotten.

It seems to me that the paying passengers, the traveling public is being short-changed. If the government can spend so much money investigating the Challenger accident and determining the causes when only eight or nine lives are involved, why cannot a much more thorough investigation be undertaken into the airlines' operations, training programs and the apparent lack of stiff requirements by the government regulatory body the FAA?

After all, those airline passengers are paying passengers. They can be killed just as dead between city A and city B as in outer space.

Is the government regulatory body in collusion with the airlines, especially one engaged in strike breaking? A real fact-finding committee, similar to that convened in 1933, might come up with some equally astounding facts.

David L. Behncke, with a number of airline pilots lobbied Congress for the Civil Aeronautics Act of 1938 that set up the Independent Air Safety Board which did so much to improve airline safety. We should demand another Independent Air Safety Board. It was doing a great job when FDR supposedly traded it off. If we can do so much to improve safety for the few lives of the shuttle crews, then why can we not shake the airlines from stem to stern and chop a few heads so that an airline can't just forget about losing a hundred or so passengers? A fact finding committee is much needed.

I am not advocating just a degree of safety, like a new tire along with an old badly worn one. I am advocating absolute safety, or as absolute as two new tires will make a flight. At the present time, all we have is marginal safety. Airplanes are permitted to fly with many deficiencies on the pilots' squawk sheets. It is the Air Transport Association pushing for more airplane time with less maintenance time.

We had that problem in 1938 before the legislation was passed that created the Independent Air Safety Board and reorganized the old Department of Commerce into the Civil Aeronautics Authority and the Independent Air Safety Board. After the creation of that board it was amazing to me, in its short life, how quickly those persistent squawk sheets of numerous items on individual airplanes disappeared. The Independent Air Safety Board made safety recommendations and the CAA was afraid not to implement them. It was a good system of checks and balances and it cleaned up the air safety problem.

Today we need to clean it up again. The FAA, like many

government agencies, is too complacent. The Air Transport Association should not be permitted to get in bed with the FAA and influence its thinking, rape it. We need to again create a bundling board in the form of another Independent Air Safety Board. I am sure it would soon clean the crud out of the airline cockpits.

Airline passengers deserve a lot more safety than they are getting today. Too many airline executives are trying to imitate C.R.'s example and get into the business of union busting.

Look what happened on Continental. The president broke the pilots' strike and many of his pilots moved on to other new companies being formed. Suddenly his pilot force was stretched pretty thin. Those two pilots involved in the Denver crash were, no doubt, the result. You can't grow an experienced airline pilot overnight.

The working conditions of flight crews, turn arounds, layovers and any fatigue-causing feature, such as more and more miles with new and faster equipment plus more passengers, should be minutely investigated and concrete recommendations forthcoming.

Also, there is something wrong with the design of an airplane or its permitted gross load when, after running down two miles of a hard topped runway, it has to be rotated off to hang suspended for a few breathless seconds between a successful takeoff and a sure crash-landing, all depending on the continued uninterrupted operations of those engines. That is marginal safety. I suspect that there have been far too many approved applications for increased loads for takeoff and too many requests for more engine time between engine overhauls.

Recently I read about a Hawaiian airliner blowing its roof completely off at only twenty-four thousand feet altitude and sucking a stewardess out with it. Poor girl, with over two horrible minutes to walk on air. It's a pity that some of the maintenance officials of the company, who were responsible for the periodic airplane inspections, could not have been with her. It is impossible for me to believe that good inspections had been performed on that airplane.

Why didn't they immediately ground all those 727's until they shook the fleet down from stem to stern? Such an inspection should also extend to all airlines with similar equipment. A nuts and bolts inspection could have been in order. Why wasn't it? If millions can be spent to protect a few lives on the space shuttle, why cannot thousands of paying passengers be given the same protection?

A short time ago I acquired a copy of the Allied Pilots' Association's labor contract for perusal. When I was on the System Board the ALPA contract covered twenty-eight pages in a little four by five and one-half inch booklet. In contrast, the contract signed and dated in August of 1985 covers three hundred and sixty-six pages. It measures eight and one-half by five and one-half inches. There are supplemental agreements and letters of understanding covering pages and pages. They are very restrictive to the pilots.

It was with a pang of remorse that I studied the predicament the copilots of my old copilots are facing today, tightly zipped up in C.R.'s zipper bag, a company union from beginning to end. Under such a handicap how could any pilot protest very strongly against management's policies, regardless of how dangerous. How many altered F-27 reports were submitted to the FAA, or how many unpublished policies the C.R. trained officials might establish.

The System Adjustment Board provisions were especially interesting to me. Throughout the years I had been on contract negotiations and on the System Board of Adjustment, I had steadfastly refused to consider any changes that would, in any way, restrict the power of the Board. Dave Behncke had supported that stand, and company contract proposals for any changes had always fallen on deaf ears with each negotiating committee keeping those provisions untouched by any editing pencil. So they had remained year after year as originally signed by David L. Behncke and C.R. Brown until the AA pilots withdrew from ALPA.

Then, in the contract with APA, a sharp company attorney had wielded the surgeon's scalpel very efficiently while the pilot representatives were busy calculating the liberal pay provisions they would enjoy in a company-blessed union. I read the following in a contract current at the time of this writing:

"In all cases submitted to the System Board of Adjustment, the representatives designated by the parties shall, upon request of either representative, exchange all documents they intend to enter in support of their respective positions and make available, in writing, the names of all witnesses they intend to summon whom they deem necessary to the dispute, fourteen (14) days prior to the date set for the hearing."

Gone are any surprise witnesses, such as Margaret Seamore. Gone is all written or oral evidence of unpublished policies that might contradict FAA regulations. Also, the company has ample time to pressure an employee-witness so that his memory or recollection of an event becomes more hazy or confused. Winning a case under such conditions seems impossible.

A company union is, indisputably, all for the company.

Airline pilots are not peons, stupid workers shuffling boxes and crates, who can easily be replaced. The majority are artists in their work, the best and most highly trained in the world. Their brush is that long fuselage with its load of precious passengers. Their easel is the sky, sometimes a black midnight sky of changing hues with its year around weather mixing the air traffic patterns as vari-colored paints. There and then, an airline pilot occasionally earns his year's pay before the dawn.

But, like all very gifted people, they have their flat-spots, their moments of indecision and poor judgment, rarely in regard to flying, but more in the everyday life of a normal person. I think that is due to their most obvious tendency to give their own snap judgment of non-flying matters the same important consideration they give flying problems.

Most airline pilots have a consuming love for flying, a sense of happiness in feeling a big plane lift off gently, or tilt ever so smoothly into another direction. They love to make an airplane sink gradually on to a runway, the squeal of the tires on the pavement being the most noticeable thing to the passengers until they feel the swells of the runway. That is artistic work.

Then too, there is that love of climbing and lifting those passengers up out of the smog and contaminated air into a clean ozone where the sky is limitless and the view extends almost from coast to coast. There, time seems to hang still while the ability to think clearly is greatly accelerated.

Like other artists, an airline pilot is sensitive and his work is greatly affected by the moods of management. A management that resents pilots, considers them stupid peons, and even indulges in labor baiting tactics, such as I have revealed in this true account, only reduces the safety margin for the precious cargo. Both the pilots and the cargo truly need the protection of an Independent Air Safety Board.

Now, at eighty, forty years after being framed and discharged, I must confess that I sometimes hear the faint baying of that beagle, and wish sincerely that I had shot the little bastard when he first opened his mouth—then carried that smoking gun into a high office on Park Avenue—to smoke some more. Such managements need that medication!